Cartel Protector

The Cartel Brotherhood

Sabine Barclay

*"Maybe our relationship isn't as crazy as it seems.
Maybe that's what happens when a tornado meets a
volcano.
All I know is I love you too much to walk away though."*
~ Eminem

Find me writing Historical Romance as Celeste Barclay.

Happy reading,
Sabine

Subscribe to Sabine's Newsletter

Subscribe to Sabine's bimonthly newsletter to receive exclusive insider perks.

Have you read *The Syndicate Wars*? This FREE origin story novella is available to all new subscribers to Sabine's monthly newsletter. Subscribe on her website.
www.sabinebarclay.com

Sabine also writes Historical Romance as
Celeste Barclay.
Discover her Highlander, Regency, Viking, and Pirate Romances.
www.celestebarclay.com

The Cartel Brotherhood

Cartel King

Cartel Viper

Cartel Prince

Cartel Rose

Cartel Protector

Cartel Devil (Coming 2026)

Contents

Chapter One

Alejandro

The things we do for friends.

Especially the ones we've known since we were three and making mud pies together in preschool. This just isn't my jam. Those four women in dental floss bikinis dancing in front of us are undeniably attractive. Hell, one's the most gorgeous woman I've ever seen, and she's definitely got my dick's attention. But strippers don't interest me. They never really have.

"Is she your type?" My friend Julián's voice is so low, I barely hear him over the music and the other guys cheering the women on.

"Somewhere—anywhere—else, maybe."

Maybe it's because my family owns several strip clubs, and I associate them with work. Maybe it's because I just don't like that much glitter. The one who keeps catching my attention seems different from the other three.

I'm in Chicago attending Julián's bachelor party. Everyone in Chicago believes it'll be a quiet destination wedding for him and his bride. That's because they don't know how deep undercover he is. It'll be a large Colombian Cartel one in Queens.

"Come on, baby, shake those tits around. Yeah, right here in my face. I got a hundred dollars right here if you let me motorboat those big old titties."

I look over to the guy on my left. What a total douche caboose. He looks like he's ready to jack off right here in front of all of us. Nobody needs to see his *pequeña polla*—little dick—trying to stand at attention.

I shift my gaze back to the woman in front of me. She doesn't have to try to get my attention. She certainly has it—even if I can think of a million other places I'd rather be. The three women working with her look like your typical Midwestern all-American girls. This woman is different. Mediterranean—Spanish, Greek, but most likely Italian. Like real Italian, straight from the motherland. There's nothing about her that screams affiliated—like Chicago Mafia Italian—either.

That's who I'm here with. Julián—these guys know him as Vinny—may be a second-generation American by way of Colombia, but he's definitely not Italian—though these fuckers don't know that. They believe he's one of them—Mafia. He comes from a long line of members from various cartels, but the guy does impersonations like nobody else I know. He can adopt any accent out there. So, he's been the perfect plant in Chicago for a couple of years.

His fiancée's a New Yorker too. Her family's Cartel—as in *the Cartel*—the Diaz Cartel—my family's Cartel—just like Julián is now. She plays the part as well as he does, having ingratiated themselves into the Rizzo Mafia—the Chicago *Cosa Nostra* branch.

"What does a good old Southern boy like you want tonight?" The brunette leans forward to line my gaze up with her magnificent tits.

"I don't know, baby, whatcha got to offer?"

I've disguised my New York Spanish accent with one from the South. I only allow a little of the Spanish part to flavor my words. The guys on this private yacht with us think I'm from Texas, where Julián supposedly grew up. They think I'm Mexican, which I sure as shit am not. I'm Colombian through and through—as in, my parents were fresh off the plane when they had me here in the States.

These fucknuts look like they just left the Jersey Shore, even though they're from Chicago. A couple used some colorful terms for Mexicans they thought I couldn't hear. One of them cracked a joke about me being in a Mexican cartel. Pride made me want to respond, but years of training taught me to suppress those reactions to insults. They definitely were misplaced. There's an unofficial social hierarchy in Latin America. And I can promise you, Colombians are above most other countries, including the U.S.'s neighbor to the south.

"I can offer you a whole lot. Just tell me what you want, and I'll tell you how much it is."

And there's why I'm just not into strippers. I'm just not into paying for my pleasures like that. Sure, I'll pay my membership to my BDSM club, but I'm not paying a woman directly to gyrate on my lap.

"Give me a little preview, and I'll tell you what I want, *Mami*."

She keeps running her hands up and down her body. The longer I watch her, the more my intuition screams something's wrong. I've learned to listen to it. It's kept me alive into my mid-thirties. I've had way too many close calls where the hair rising on the back of my neck is the only warning I get before a bullet sails past me, sometimes even into me. I don't know what it is about this woman, but it's off.

"Mmm. Let me see what I can *come* up with."

Even if I want to fuck her, I don't want to pay for that or a lap dance. And something about her makes me think she's here for more than just tips. Her tits sway in my face as she runs her hands up my thighs, then tries to step around them to give me a lap dance.

I know she's seen my dick's reaction to her. There's no way she couldn't in my suit trousers, even if my boxer briefs are snug. I'm not worried that she knows she got me hard. I'd be more worried how she'd respond if she hadn't. I'll play along for now, even though I know something's not quite right.

"Come here, *Mamí*. Sit on *Papí's* lap. You wanna go for a ride on this crotch rocket?"

I can barely take myself seriously, and I'm certain Julián just chuckled. He was even less thrilled to see strippers aboard the private yacht than I was. He knows if he goes home with another woman's perfume on him, his fiancée'll castrate him. He made it very clear when the women appeared and the music started that his friends—including me—could enjoy. However, he wouldn't take part. He's barely looked in the women's direction, preferring to watch the skyline as we sail on Lake Michigan.

"I hope that crotch rocket doesn't go too fast, *Papí*."

When Julián and I realized his friends got these women on board without Julián or my knowing, we both wondered what else they might've smuggled aboard. If you can even call them friends. I suppose colleagues would be a better term, since they have no idea who Julián really is and never will. We'd exchanged a look I'm sure no one else noticed.

It's the same one we've shared since we were five and got in trouble together for the first time. It was the "I'll cover for you no matter what, and how can we blame this on somebody else while we're at it" look.

Conspiratorial is what my mother has always called it. I don't know too many other five-year-olds who knew what that word meant, but Julián and I soon learned it. Right around the same time we learned how to weed a garden. I'm not like my cousin Jorge who enjoys gardening. My mother knew making me work outside but not allowing me on our swing set was the worst form of torture.

"Don't you worry about that. I can take you for a long ride."

The brunette presses her tits together practically under my nose. I'm certain I smell sugar on them. It's a serious temptation to lick her since she's offering. My dick's egging me on. But I stopped listening to my smaller head a long time ago.

"Shake 'em for me just like you shook that fine ass of yours."

I sound nearly as bad as the guy to my left. The woman grins and obliges, so maybe I don't sound as cheesy to her as I do to myself. Or she's so used to dumbasses acting like this that all she sees are dollar signs for the tip. I glance around the room at the other men. One's getting a lap dance, and the others are watching two women dance around each other. They're not touching, but they look like they're ready to fuck each other. I can definitely be down for that type of porn. I've seen women fuck plenty of times at my club, but it does nothing for me here. Only the brunette has my cock begging to come out.

"You like 'em?"

"You already know I do."

I glance over at Julián, and he cocks an eyebrow. I know he's wondering if I'll take the woman up on her offer for more than just the dance. As much as one part of me begs, the other part refuses to indulge. It would be a loss of self-control, and that I can't allow. It's a great way to lower your inhibitions and get distracted from the mission.

"How about you, Mr. Bachelor? Wanna take me for a ride?"

Sure, tonight is about Julián having a good time—not that he looks like he is. However, it's also an opportunity for me to hear anything these *cabróns*—assholes—might share, thinking I don't understand what they're talking about. I'm here tonight to do the same job Julián does every day.

"I think you'll enjoy my friend far more." Julián tilts his head toward me.

He worked his way up in the Rizzo organization. He may only be mid-level, but he's earned his way to being a bodyguard for Don Edoardo Rizzo's son. It means he hears things, but he's also invisible. We created an entire phony persona for him. When the Rizzos inevitably did a background check for him, he came up as an unaffiliated guy.

"I'm definitely enjoying the show. You should have a bachelor party more often."

I waggle my eyebrows at the dancer even though I'm speaking to Julián, and it keeps her distracted as I sink back into my thoughts. We staged a minor attack on Edoardo's son and made sure Julián was in the right place at the right time to defend the guy. It earned Edoardo's gratitude and opened the door for Julián to get a low-level job as a courier. It didn't take long for him to keep earning Edoardo's trust to where he became a bodyguard.

All of this subterfuge means he knows how to ensure he's not being tracked. I'm certain there's nothing on his phone that could lead somebody here, but I'm suspicious about the yacht. Part of the reason Julián dropped hints to the other guys about coming out here for the bachelor party was that it would make it harder for someone to corner him. These guys are all still low-level. A few are almost equal to Julián. That's why we didn't worry they'd recognize me as Alejandro Diaz, nephew to the *jefe de jefes*—the boss of bosses, Enrique Diaz—the most powerful man in all of Latin America.

Hell, pretty much the most powerful man in the Western or Southern Hemisphere.

Fuck any president with nuclear codes. My *tío* could detonate a nation's economy with one text message.

"What else you got, *Mamí*?"

The brunette brings my mind back to the present when she tugs the strings to her flossy bikini top. She reveals glitter and bedazzled pasties that look like they belong on a Vegas showgirl. The woman gyrating above my dick rolls her belly and hips, and the tiny piece of floss she's wearing as a G-string leaves nothing to the imagination.

Along with her perfume, I catch the faint scent of her arousal. God, what I wouldn't give to run my fingers between her pussy lips and discover how wet she is. I can see a gleam on her thighs that I don't think is Vaseline or anything else like that. I think I might affect her just as much as her lap dance affects my dick. I planned to cut this short before it goes too far, but now I definitely need to.

"Oh, shit!"

I suddenly puff out my cheeks and look away. The boat just hit a wave, and it's perfect timing. I shake my head and press on her shoulder, telling her to back away. I stand and pivot, bolting toward the stairs leading below deck. I hear Julián's voice right behind me.

"I better check on him."

Since I'm perfectly fine, I'm not headed to a bathroom. When my friend meets me at the bottom of the ladder well, we survey the area below deck. I keep my voice low as we strategize.

"There are three guest cabins, two for the crew, and one for the captain. I'll take the captain and crew. You take the guest ones."

This is an entry-level superyacht. It's not as large as an ocean-going one, but it's certainly large. Both of us carry a small device much like a flip phone in our pockets. We unfold them and turn them on. Julián grins, and I can only imagine what he'll say.

"I remind myself of those guys with metal detectors at the beach. I just need an umbrella hat and white crew socks with sandals."

Except we're scanning for radio frequencies or anything giving off Wi-Fi.

"You can look for quarters in the couches. I want to know if someone bugged this boat or if there're any trackers on here."

"Spoilsport." He shoots me that same conspiratorial grin we've shared for nearly thirty years.

Since we're not staying here overnight, there's very little to check in any of the cabins. But we couldn't ignore them. You know what happens when you assume—you make an ass out of you and me.

We're cautious as we slip past the galley. Only the chef's in there. We had dinner aboard the boat. The rest of the crew is on deck to serve drinks and indulge whatever whims those *cabróns* come up with. When we get to the stairs at the opposite end from which we came down, we listen intently and can hear the captain and first mate talking.

I inch up the stairs so I can peer into the bridge—the area where the captain controls and steers the boat. We have our devices on silent, so they'll only flash if they detect something. Of course, they're going off now, but I expect that. I'm not concerned. There's a difference between the Coast Guard tracking the boat and the Rizzos doing it because they found out about me.

"*Nada*." Nothing.

I whisper to Julián when I return to him. We check out the engine room, but there's nothing of interest there either.

"We gotta get back up there before anyone wonders why we're both down here so long. Try to look like you just puked."

My friend elbows me in the gut before I turn away. We head back up on deck to find my Mediterranean beauty completely naked now, grinding on another guy's lap. My stab of jealousy is completely irrational and inappropriate. It doesn't stop my mind from screaming *MINE*. When I step forward, my movement catches her attention, shifting her focus to me. I'm certain that's a moment of guilt I see on her face, but it's gone so quickly, I wonder if it's contrived.

Like maybe she's trying to tempt me even more, perhaps hoping that if I'm jealous, I'll pay her for a real lap dance. As she finishes the guy's dance and backs away, he grabs his crotch as though he's going to jerk off through his pants. But when his other hand reaches for his belt and pulls it open, that's when I've had enough. I'm back at my chair with a few long strides.

"They're dancers, not hookers. Keep it in your pants."

"Oh, come on, man. You know she wants it."

"Don't be disgusting. They're dancers, not sex workers."

"Are you sure? They're only like one step apart. They came here to dance for a private show. It's not like they're at some club on a stage with a pole." The *pedazo de mierda*—piece of shit—looks away from me and back at the brunette beauty. "Hey, sweetheart. I bet for the right amount, you've done more than just twerk. It's her choice, and that's why we rented the boat anyway. What happens out here is our business and nobody else's."

I just might vomit after all. "Do you know how bad that sounds? Are you some kind of fucking predator? Did you bring these ladies out here to trap them?"

"Wait, what? No, that's not what I meant."

"Well, that's what the fuck it sounds like."

I straighten to my full height and push back my shoulders. It's not like I slouch or anything. It's difficult to miss that I'm bigger than the average guy. But when I lift my chin, push back my shoulders, and inhale, it surprises everyone—except for Julián—to see I'm practically the fucking Hulk.

"Petey, shut up before you ruin the night." Julián barely saves the asshat.

All the men in my family are big guys, taller than what most people would assume for Latinos. We work out twice a day because our jobs can get very physical. It's also time we spend together as family. We enjoy each other's company even when we don't have to be together. But I'm the largest of all the guys by half an inch in height and two inches across the back and chest.

Sometimes, we need to swap clothes. It's not like I Hulk out in theirs because they're too small or the other guys look like they're little kids playing dress-up in mine. I'm just a big dude.

The brunette says something to the douchebag that makes him calm down—he was ready to stand up and face off against me. She comes over to me, and I adjust my chair to angle it away from the douche.

"Thank you for that. I can deal with men who get a little too handsy, but it doesn't mean I enjoy it."

She glances in the other guy's direction as I sit. I let her shake her ass at me before she straddles my lap. If we were fucking, it would be reverse cowgirl. I behave myself like you're supposed to when you get a lap dance at a club. I keep my hands down at my side when I'd love nothing more than to pull her down and have her grind on my dick, which still hasn't gone down. It was at half-mast while I snooped. That's because I kept thinking of her. I told myself I was hurrying to avoid getting caught, not because I wanted to get back up here to see her.

"Part of why he got so pissed is that he noticed I was wet. He thought it was because of him."

The woman's speaking softly. The only person we're facing

right now is Julián. I'm certain he heard her, but he's pretending to be on his phone.

"You flatter me, *chiquita*."

She just hums her response as she finally lowers her ass to my lap, pressing backward. There's no way she can't tell how hard I am now. I don't know that I've ever faced a greater temptation than I am in this moment. But that exchange she had with the guy feels off even more than earlier.

"It's not flattery when it's the truth. Holy fuck."

I saw the flash of fear on the other women's faces when the organizer of this three-hour tour explained why he chose this outing. The hell he did. It was Julián's request. It was just the excuse Petey needed to be a perve.

"Thank you."

What else do I say that won't make me the perve?

I've been around strippers since I was eighteen and started working as a stock boy in our clubs the summer after I graduated high school.

Sure, I'd been curious at first. There was more than one night I went home and locked myself in my room and jacked off to the memory of the women on the stages. However, I've worked with them far too long for any of the dancers or what happens at clubs to faze me.

Movement to the left has me looking around and spotting the shore. We've already turned around, and we're nearly to the docks. The women finished their last dance and are now mingling with us, trying to drum up future work.

"Will any of you need us again for future occasions? Perhaps another private event, maybe something a little more intimate than a crowd."

My mysterious beauty asks the group, and there's that coyness I expected. She's looking straight at me as she speaks. I feel like she's propositioning me rather than just trying to sell a dance by tossing in a little dirty talk. I won't assume she's offering more than the dances, or that if she did, it would be of her own free will and off the clock.

"We'll definitely keep you in mind. I have a birthday coming up next month. I think you ladies would be gifts I'd love to unwrap."

I look at the guy who sounds like a kid in a candy store. I think his name is Mike, but I don't remember since he's just been drooling all night. Not exactly a conversationalist. I glance over at Julián, and he rolls his eyes. The brunette isn't looking at me, so I inch closer to my friend.

"There's something not quite right about her."

"What do you mean?" His lips barely move as he speaks.

"Her aura—it's too strong. Earlier, when that *gilipollas* made it sound like this was some rape cruise, it wasn't defiance or arrogance because she's gorgeous. I don't know how to articulate it, but where the other women appeared scared for that moment, she was the opposite. She wasn't even offended. And I don't mean she just has a thick skin. It didn't faze her at all. Like she could handle it if he got aggressive." Asshole.

"I noticed it too. There was a 'you-can-try' challenge about her. Maybe it was a touch of defiance. But that seems out of place for someone whose tips depend upon being coy. They're part actress as much as dancer. They pretend to be interested in customers they probably wish they'd never met. She didn't hide her annoyance."

Julián gets it. I knew he would.

"I wonder if she's law enforcement trying to bust us for prostitution."

That should make my arousal fizzle, and it does a bit, but she still tempts me. I'm not opposed to one-night stands. I don't have them anymore, but I have in the past. The memory of her grinding on another guy when I came back on deck flashes before my eyes. It reminds me all over again that it's a performance, and she's not into me. But it would be easy to forget as her gaze sweeps over me as she saunters to stand in front of me. Guess my conversation with Julián is over.

"What about you? Any birthdays or special events coming up?"

"No, but thanks for the offer."

I'm trying not to be judgmental about her job, but it's a definite turnoff to think I'm sharing her. That's only cool when it's consensual roleplaying at a BDSM club.

"For you, any time."

Her tone is extra sultry. I know the moment she realizes she can't convince me otherwise. The expression she shoots me is one of hurt and disappointment. I test the waters a little now that I wonder if she could be local police or a fed.

"It was nice meeting you, but I don't pay for my pleasures."

I shoot her a wicked grin I've perfected over the years. It gets me just about anything I want with women and even men. It doesn't work with anyone in my family, so I don't bother.

"I bet you don't have to."

She shoots me a look that masquerades as hurt. It doesn't match the attitude she had. It comes across as fake. Insulted would've been the more appropriate response. Picking the wrong fake reaction finally dampens any interest I had in her sexually. Now I'm merely curious about how she plans to fuck me over.

Chapter Two

Vita

Fucking hell.

I may have blown my cover. Alejandro is by far the most gorgeous man I have ever seen.

Fuck movie stars.

Fuck models.

Fuck all of them.

No one compares to Alejandro Diaz. I could almost forget why I'm working this party tonight.

I actually want him.

This isn't playing pretend because I have to. I would've gladly fucked him after feeling his cock. Generously endowed would be a vast understatement. But I still have a job to do. I just wish I could have a little fun while I'm at it. However, I can tell he reads me too well. He's probably had a lifetime of training to do it so subtly.

"I didn't even get to ask you your name. I'm Tiffani with an i."

That sounds so incredibly lame to my own ears. But I've used that line many times in the past in different situations when I'm trying to seduce a guy. I definitely don't need anyone here knowing my real name is Vittoria Trevisan.

"I'm Berto."

We stare at each other. My fear that he's made me ratchets up about another ten levels. I'm certain he knows that's not my real name just like I know that isn't his. Considering this job, it would make sense that I wouldn't use my real one. But maybe I should've picked something more like Candy. Hell, even Peppermint.

"It's nice to meet you, Berto."

"You sure were sweet, sugar." His pretend accent is as good as my fake one.

I put sugar on my breasts and around the pasties in case a guy gets a little too frisky and licks me. This isn't my first time impersonating a stripper. I definitely felt more comfortable tonight than I did back then. If anybody were going to lick my tits, I wish it were Alejandro. I'd hoped to score a private lap dance with him in a cabin.

I would've fucked him. I'm sure of it. I've never crossed that line during a job before. I've kissed people and let them grope me, but that's as far as it's ever gone.

Tonight...

Tonight, I would've let it go that far for my own personal reasons. It certainly wouldn't have hurt my mission. I could've gotten off while also distracting him long enough to drug him. I would've grabbed a sequined shawl I tie around my waist at the beginning of a private dance. The shawl gives the illusion of stripping when I'm already naked.

It would've given me a chance to grab the tiny syringe. It would be a tiny pinch I could play off as my nails grazing the back of his neck. The medicine is slow-acting, so the effects wouldn't have kicked in until the end of the cruise. But I missed my opportunity. We're back at the dock now.

"It's not every night there's a guy who stands up for us. I appreciate you stepping in earlier."

"It was the right thing to do. Nobody wants to see his micropenis. I was happy to help."

I'm certain he searched the cabins downstairs since I don't believe for a moment he was even a touch seasick. I found nothing during my search when I came aboard. If he'd rummaged through my purse, he would've found single-use needles labeled as insulin. But no diabetic would take what's in there. The sedative combined with nerve blockers could incapacitate an elephant once they fully kick in.

If only we'd been in a car or hotel room in private.

I know he's watching me even though he's pretending to appear a little seasick again when the boat nudges against the dock. He hangs back while some of the other guys get off. All but the guest of honor and Alejandro are drunk. There's a guy handing out cash to all the women.

It's the asshole from earlier. The one who arranged this charter and the show. When Petey comes to stand in front of me, he smirks, fans out money in his hand, then turns away from me.

"You can be an asshole all night long, but don't be a cheap one."

Guess I didn't want a tip after all. My mouth runs away from me, and I almost forget I'm standing with Alejandro and the guy who definitely isn't "Vinny." Julián suits the guest of honor far better.

"You can be a whore who doesn't get paid."

Now he's really pissed me off. I sense Alejandro tense, but he's letting me handle this.

"You don't think we know who all of you guys are? You don't think we do a little research before we accept these jobs?"

"You *think* you know who we work for? Then you're not very bright if you're talking about it."

"And you're not very bright to have come here without your wedding ring."

He flinches. I don't relent.

"Oh yeah, I saw your shadow of shame. You might've taken it off, but your suntan line screams married from a mile away. The skin on that part of your finger is so white it glows. Pay me my fair share, or I'll hop on social media and let your wife know what you've been up to. Or better yet, maybe I'll tell your boss. We know who you work for since none of us are stupid."

As the women I'm with say goodbye to the other guys, I grab my bag that was stowed out of the way. I take the money he offers and drop it in there. I slip into my slinky cocktail dress before pulling a card from the bag and palming it. I walk back over to Alejandro. I know I look desperate as fuck, and I'm towing a very fine line. But I give it one more shot.

As I press my body against him, I wish I were still naked. This dress is so short and tight that I may as well be. I have a coat in my bag I'll put on top of it before walking around in public.

"Last chance for a private dance."

He appears tempted for a moment, then regretful. It's an act; I can tell. It still stings a bit.

"I gotta get my friend home. His fiancée'll kill him if he's too late getting home."

Fucking hell.

I'm not as adept as I thought I could be. As I try to slip my business card into his trouser pocket, he grabs my wrist and pulls it away.

"You're nearly sly enough to be a Venetian pickpocket."

I force myself not to react, shocked he guessed I'm truly Italian. I'm not from Venice, but I am from that region. I know he didn't pick that city at random from the way he stares at me. I'm positive it's not my accent that gave me away. I can hide it entirely and sound like English is my first and only language. Tonight's accent isn't a Chicagoan one; it's a mild Midwestern one. Neutral to keep it easy.

He stares at the card for a moment, then hands it back. I wonder if he was going to memorize the number, but he doesn't look long enough.

"I'm heading back home in the morning, darling. I've got an early flight, but thank you for the dances tonight."

I know he's lying. I'm certain of it. Whatever he's doing in Chicago isn't just about this bachelor party. I strain to reach his neck, even in my high heels. I brush a kiss against it, ensuring I smudge lipstick on the collar of his shirt. It's utterly cliché, but it's a reminder of me.

Some of it's personal, but some of it's hoping I've created enough curiosity in him to inquire about me. It's a mighty big hope, but I won't rule it out as a possibility. And it certainly would make my life easier if he showed interest on his own.

We're positioned near a wall where the others can't see us. Not that it matters because most of the men are already on the outside deck. His hand glides over my waist and hip, down to my ass. He squeezes it mercilessly hard to where I struggle not to yelp. He tweaks my nipple through my dress, twisting and tugging.

"*Chiquita*, you're asking for a spanking if you keep being naughty."

Fucking hell.

That's at least the third time I've thought that in five minutes.

I'd lay myself across his lap right now if he told me to. My cunt aches for a good fuck. It's as though he reads my mind the next time he speaks.

"You know you got me hard, but you also admitted I got you wet. How empty does that pretty little pussy feel right now, wishing I was fucking you?"

"How much does your cock wish it were inside my cunt? We'd both enjoy it."

He stares down at me and shakes his head. "I've had enough one-night stands in my life. I don't need to have any more. Besides, I have a couple of standing arrangements for when I want to fuck."

That didn't sting or anything.

"Besides, little girl, my proclivities would surely shock you. I doubt you could handle the things I'm into."

"Try me."

It's a challenge, an invitation, and on the verge of begging. Since we're standing where others can't see us easily, and his back is to the gangway, no one can tell when he rubs my clit under my dress. I press myself harder against him as he rubs slow circles. I feel his cock twitch. I want to grind on his thigh, but I'd leave a wet mark on his pants. He pinches my clit like he did my nipple a moment ago.

Then he pulls away and walks off without saying goodbye or even a backward glance.

Challenge accepted.

I'll find a way to see him again.

Chapter Three

Alejandro

"What the hell was that, Alejandro? You've never been into strippers, and you've certainly never hired a hooker before."

"You might not have paid attention, but she's gorgeous."

"I may not have eyes for anyone but Liliana, but I'm not blind. Of course, I could see she was attractive."

"We were on that boat for three hours of pure temptation, so I indulged a little. Yeah, I toyed with her at the end. But I'm telling you, there's still something off, Julián. I don't know what it is about her. You saw her reaction when that *carechimba* insulted her." Face of a vagina.

"I noticed she barely reacted the first time. She definitely had plenty to say when he tried to stiff her."

"Did you see her reaction when I told her I don't pay for my pleasure?"

"Yeah. You'd expect her to look insulted, not hurt."

"Exactly. I don't know if she's Chicago PD or a fed, but it's like she was trying to get me to proposition her."

"But you weren't the one who announced he'd pay for sex."

"It's not like she was wearing a wire anywhere."

At least I don't think she was, since she was naked. Short of having it up her cunt or ass, there was nowhere else for her to put it.

"Alejandro, if she'd been there to bust us for prostitution, it should've been when that *pedazo de mierda* ran his mouth. But she didn't." Piece of shit.

"I know, and I'm positive the women with her had no idea she had some ulterior motive. So maybe she isn't law enforcement, but she's something besides an exotic dancer."

"Do you think she'll give up?"

I look over at Julián, who's staring at me as we ride in the back of the town car together. As is a requirement in my family, the privacy glass is up by default.

"We'll see. If she's a fed and not local PD, then she was there for me, not any of you guys."

"What? We're too low on the food chain? She wanted to bag a shark and not a minnow?"

Julián laughs, and I chuckle along with him because he's not wrong. Sure, feds might scoop up low to mid-level guys, hoping they'll flip on senior leaders in an organized crime family. But if they can nab someone as high up as I am, then they would.

"Do you think she'll go all single white female on you and stalk you? I saw her try to slip you that card. Did you look at it long enough to memorize the number?"

"Yeah."

I've always had a thing for numbers and patterns. It's not that I'm a mathematical savant, but something about numbers just makes sense to me.

"So, what next, *parce?*"

Parce or *parcero* because Colombians can't just say a simple *amigo* for our friends.

"I don't think I've deterred her. It won't be tonight, but it wouldn't surprise me in the next day or two if she showed up somewhere. She might work for someone."

"Do you think it's the Rizzos? Did they find out you're here?"

"I'm not sure. Maybe. What do you think? Could they have made you because they saw us together this week?"

If I blew his cover—which we know is a possibility, but I came anyway—then we need to extract him now. He'll be dead otherwise.

"I don't think so. I mean, I've earned Edoardo's trust over the last five years. I don't think he questions me. I know he hasn't had me followed in ages. Not since I became his son's personal bodyguard. He trusts me to be the only one guarding Elio. Especially after all the shit that went down with Lorenzo and Marco a few years ago, he takes his kids' protection pretty fucking seriously. If he's confident I can be alone with his heir, then I feel as safe as I can in this life."

Marco and Lorenzo Mancinelli. Don Salvatore's nephews. Lorenzo's an accountant, so he's equivalent to my cousin Jorge. Marco, his next older brother, is third in command. The *capo dei capi*. The captain of captains. He's one step below the underboss, who's Salvatore's heir. That's Luca—Marco and Lorenzo's older brother.

A few years ago, when Marco and Lorenzo—the youngest Mancinelli brother—were dating their wives who're also sisters, they waged an attack to remind Chicago that their glory days ended with Al Capone's death. It made Edoardo especially cautious about his children's protection details. It was perfect timing for Julián to step up.

"Do you think it could be the Oskolkis?" Julián knows they're why I'm here.

"It's certainly possible. Maybe they got wind I arrived. Perhaps they sent her as a honey trap to lure me away before they can face the repercussions for their fucked-up attempt to do that deal with *los Iglesias*. If they want to do deals with the Mexicans in Boston, they can. But they know who they pay for that privilege. Both families do, and neither did."

The Oskolkis way overreached, and now there's a lesson to teach them. The Russian bratva here in Chicago isn't anywhere near as strong as the Ivankov branch in New York. They've fucked up royally, and now they're going to pay the price for it.

"I can't believe Maks has stayed silent on this. I guess he doesn't give a shit what you do on behalf of *el jefe*."

The New York bratva's *pakhan*—Maksim Kutsenko—hasn't done shit even though he said he would.

The Kutsenkos are *the* Russians—*the* bratva. The Mancinellis are *the* Italians—*the* Mafia, the O'Rourkes are *the* Irish—*the* mob. And my family, *los Diaz* are *the* Colombians—*the* Cartel.

"He's fuming silently. We made sure of that. The Oskolkis not only overstepped by doing a secret deal with a cartel, they also overstepped doing any deal without Maks's consent."

Lots of people believe that since Pablo Escobar no longer runs the Colombian drug trade, our country is no longer the narco capital of Latin America. Of course, people in the States can't look farther south than Mexico, so they assume the cartels there dominate now.

Let them.

It just means my family operates low profile outside of New York. We don't need that many people knowing our business. *Tío* Enrique doesn't live in the lap of luxury like Escobar did, but he's more than just comfortable. He's just discreet. I've never been to a house larger than *Tío* Enrique's. Granted, that's only because I've never been invited inside Salvatore's.

Tío does a lot for charities to remain in plenty of people's good graces. And he, along with the rest of us, have plenty of legal business endeavors to keep us looking legit. We pay our taxes since we're not going down for something as stupid as evasion.

"You know if I hear anything among the Rizzos, you'll be the first to know. How'd Ireland go? You never did get a chance to tell me how things went over there."

The O'Rourkes fucked around and found out—again—not to get too close to my family. Jorge's fiancée, Anneliese, got trapped in the middle of a proxy war that's been going on for a few months between the O'Rourkes and the Kutsenkos. All of that played out in Frankfurt where Anneliese is from, but the obvious combatants were four syndicate families in Italy.

"Pretty well. When you have a hundred-forty proof whiskey

spilled all over the place, it's easy to light a distillery on fire and watch it go boom."

We struck back hard against the O'Rourkes for what they did. The Kutsenkos didn't get off mildly either.

"I bet Maks isn't just fuming about the Oskolkis. What did you do to them?"

"We robbed them blind. We cleared out their construction site on Long Island. When I say we took everything, I mean we took everything. All the equipment and all the machinery. We also blew up two of their holdings in Frankfurt."

"I'm sure that shit went somewhere overseas, so they can't just steal it back. That's got to piss them off. Maybe that's why Maks hasn't done shit to stop the Oskolkis."

I gaze out the window before focusing back on Julián. "They could be retaliating for our retaliation. We shipped everything to Germany to give to Anneliese's brother-in-law. His family's putting it all to good use."

"Do you ever just get tired of the tit-for-tat? I mean, I know it's the only way for us to survive, but the machismo—it's exhausting at times. Don't you wish someone could just get to the top and then it could all be done with? That we could do it? That your *tío* could?"

That's a question I've asked myself plenty of times, but it surprises me when Julián does.

"Do you want to retire? Do you and Liliana want to come back to New York, start a family there near yours? Would you prefer to go somewhere else?"

"Where could we go, Alejandro? Liliana does a great impersonation of a Chicago accent, and I do a great Texan one, so we don't mind it. It's become second nature to us, but anywhere else we move, we'd have to do the same thing all over again. Where could we go if we used our natural accents? It'll give away that we're New Yorkers. The tinge of Spanish in it will scream Latin American even if no one in the U.S. knows we're Colombian instead of Mexican. So, where does that leave us? We can't go anywhere in Latin America. Spain? You want us to learn that colonizer Spanish?"

He grins at me, and we both roll our eyes. We went all the way through twelfth grade together. Our parents insisted we take Spanish in middle school because it was Castilian, not Latin American. Even though we were fluent readers, writers, and speakers, they wanted to ensure we learned Castilian too. Just in case we should ever need to disguise our Spanish.

It was smart of our parents to do that. When cartel life is the only life you've known, you come into parenthood with certain wisdom most people don't.

"Do you want somewhere quiet here in the U.S.?"

He practically snorts. "Have you met Liliana? She is not a small-town girl. I think she'll do the burbs here, but she's not moving to the middle-of-nowhere America."

"Fair enough."

"I worry about having a family when we're all the way out here and so far from ours. But we've talked about it, and we're still going to live our lives like we would if we were back home. Until your *tío* or Pablo calls us back, we'll keep on keeping on."

"Do you want me to put a word in with either of them?"

"No. Liliana and I don't want kids right away, even though we've been together for seven years. We're not in a rush yet."

"Why have you waited so long? Seven years is a long time to be together before getting married."

"It is, and it's not like we wanted to see if we'd get the seven-year itch. I was establishing myself with our *jefe* and then I was establishing myself here. I didn't want to make Liliana a widow too young if something went wrong."

"And she agreed with that?"

He snorts a second time. "Again. Have you met her? Of course she didn't agree with me. But she knows her safety is more important to me than anything. Yes, I'll always obey your *tío* because he's my *jefe*. The same as I would any other person in your family, especially your *mamá* and *tías* because they terrify me way more than *el jefe* or your *tío* Luis. But Liliana and our family will come first. I believe your *tíos* understand that."

"Yeah, well, all the women in my family terrify me far more than the men, so you're smart to know that too."

"Liliana gets where I'm coming from and has been patient. She knows it's not because I didn't love her or didn't want to commit to her. I just wanted to be sure I had enough tucked away for her and that I was in a good position before we got married. You know, just in case."

"I get this life is far too unpredictable. And on top of that, you're living a double life."

He nods. We've pulled up outside his place.

"Thanks, Alejandro, for putting up with all of this. I know it wasn't your idea of fun, even if you did have a pretty girl flirting with you. We're running a huge risk as it is being seen together in public, but it means everything to me that you came, *hermano*."

We clasp hands and lean in for a manly embrace, slapping each other on the back.

"*Hermanos para siempre*." Brothers for life.

I'm an only child, and he's the closest thing to a brother I have outside of my immediate family. Our parents raised my *primos*—cousins—and me more like brothers than *primos*. *Tres J's* could practically be triplets, so their bond differs from the one they have with me or with Pablo. But the five of us have been through so much shit together. Plus, we enjoy each other's company. Pablo had a younger brother, Juan.

That *pedazo de mierda*. If he hadn't been part of the family, Pablo probably would've beaten him to death when they were still children. None of us really liked him. He was a shit disturber and spiteful. The only person who ever got along with him and really liked him was their next-door neighbor, Laura Doyle—well, now Laura Kutsenko. They were only a few weeks apart in age. They grew up like siblings.

Pablo still sees Laura as a younger sister. And now that Javier married Laura's younger sister, Madeline, they really are family. But Juan fucked around and found out what happens when he targeted Laura. He got butthurt at her rejection when she married the New York bratva leader—the same Maks who's a pain in my ass right now. I know my cousins and I miss Juan because he was a relative, and we were used to him being around for holidays, but none of us—not even Pablo—miss spending time with him.

I don't envy my *tío* and *tía's* heartbreak over losing a child. But even they weren't surprised with what happened to their younger son, since Juan was always such a *cabroncete*—little fucker. Pablo and I grew really close when we were still young. He was like the big brother I didn't have, and I was the little brother he wanted.

I watch as Julián slips into his house. I know he's doing a full sweep of the downstairs before he'll head up to his room where Liliana probably is. I wait until the single downstairs light is off before I tap the intercom button and tell my driver to take me back to the hotel that's twenty minutes away.

It's not somewhere obvious, so I'm less likely to be noticed than in a hotel in downtown Chicago even if I found a modest one. I can't help but wonder how long it'll take Tiffani with an i to find me.

You have a sick sense of curiosity. A lap dance won't be the only thing she's offering this time around. She'll probably try to kill you.

Death by lap dance.

What a way to go.

Since my driver is one of my guys from New York, and this is a rented town car, I doze on the way to the hotel. It's one a.m. when I get to my room, which means it's three a.m. at home. It's still the middle of the night, but I'm certain Joaquin is awake. The man's practically an insomniac. He can run off of the least amount of sleep of all of us, and that's saying something since far too often we're awake thirty-six to forty-eight hours, even longer than that if we're on a mission that goes sideways. I also know he's expecting me to check in and let him know I survived. I give him a quick call before deciding on a shower.

It's not that Tiffani made me feel dirty; it was the entire experience. Plus, as I look in the mirror while I brush my teeth, not only do I see the lipstick on my neck and shirt, but I also see glitter there too. It's going to annoy my dry cleaner as much as it annoys me that she stained my custom-tailored shirt. These aren't cheap, and neither is my dry-cleaning bill. The guy doesn't ask questions and can get out anything, including blood—which he's had to do plenty of times—but only when it's mine. If it belongs to anyone else, the clothes get incinerated since we don't need to leave any evidence somewhere.

As I lather the bar of soap over my body, scrubbing my neck in particular, I can't help but think about tonight. I run through the whole thing from when we arrived at the docks until we returned. Whatever's really going on doesn't stop me from getting hard all over again as I picture my naked Italian beauty.

As I think about her, my memory flashes to her giving another man a lap dance. That irritates me, and the jealousy is there all over again. I sure as fuck am not thrilled any of those men saw her naked but the fact that another man touched her—that she touched another man—bothers me far more than it should.

I wrap my hand around my cock and stroke, picturing her sucking me off, kneeling right in front of me as the water runs over our bodies. The idea of coming down her throat or splattering my cum across her tits makes me jerk off even harder. I want her in front of me, turned around, hands pressed against the wall as I spread her ass cheeks and fuck her pretty little pink pussy, watching my cock slide in and out of her. That pushes me over the edge, and I come hard, shooting ropes of it over and over. Maybe I should've taken her card after all.

I'm so fucking relieved to finally be headed home soon. I've been in Chicago four days now, and I accomplished everything I set out to. But I didn't solve the unexpected mystery Tiffani presented.

I sweep my gaze across the airfield as I board my private jet. My family has a larger one we share for business and pleasure. But I travel a lot between Colombia and New York, especially now that my *tío abuelo*—great-uncle—is dead. My mother's uncle finally outlived the last speck of usefulness he had. He violated his nearly forty years of house arrest to come after Pablo and his wife, Florencia. Now I'm the one who oversees just about everything in Colombia.

My *tío* Luis deals with men in prison who need a reminder of just how powerful his older brother is. Pablo's father, my *tío* Luis, is *Tío* Enrique's younger brother. *Mamá* is their younger sister, and my *tía* Luciana—*mamá* to *Tres J's*—is the youngest of the four siblings. They all grew up in Colombia along with *Papá* and *Tía* Margherita, Pablo's mother and *Tío* Luis's wife.

The men are glad to be on their way home. I have a quick word with them after we take off.

"When we get back, we'll debrief the mission. After that, *jefe* will give you the next three days off." My cousins and I always use our *tío's* title when we address our men.

"Thank you." There's a round of appreciation from the guys.

"This plane is even better than your last one, Alejandro. Much roomier, much nicer." Alonso's been with my family since before I was born, so he gets away with the jab.

"Be glad you even have a seat in here. Alejandro could stick you in the hold or make you fly commercial." Carlos has no problem teasing his father.

This is my second private jet. Carmine Mancinelli, little fucknut that he is, had a tantrum and blew up my last one. He thought he got revenge for shit that happened with his then-girl-friend, now-wife. It wasn't anything personal with her, but my family comes before his.

That tit-for-tat Julián mentioned the other night is exactly what happened with Carmine. I couldn't just accept his retribution for what it was, even if I felt a little bad. I had all of his cars booted each time he parked on a public street, and I blew up several race cars he owns—Formula One and NASCAR. We've had something of a truce ever since, though that could change at any moment.

I head into the cabin and close the door behind me since I

need to call my family. The men know why I came back here, so none think twice about it. They understand it's a private conversation. It's why none took seats in the row closest to the cabin. I turn on the white noise sound machine I travel with—not to help me sleep, but for when I have calls or meetings where I don't need anyone overhearing us.

"*Hola, tío.*"

"*Hola, sobrino. ¿Cómo te va?*" Hello, nephew. How's it going?

"*Muy bien.* Happy to be on the plane. Happy to be on the way home." Very well.

We continue the conversation in Spanish.

"Do you have anything to report?"

"Yeah, our men took out all the Oskolkis' Elite Group yesterday. Left none of them. The only one alive is their *pakhan.*"

Maks should've taken care of him when he had the chance. We'll give him one more shot.

"The guy knows that if Maks doesn't kill him, we will. I told him he should call Maks and let him know I came for a visit."

"Did he shit himself?"

Javier's tone is purely mocking. He's the most misanthropic of all of us, even though we each have a touch of that, since we've seen humanity at its cruelest too many times. We've been guilty of it just as often as we've witnessed it. But none of us are as jaded as he is. He can thank watching his father get murdered when Jorge was eight, he was nearly ten, and Joaquin was nearly eleven.

"He definitely came close each time I said Maks's name. He begged me not to make him call Maks. Stupid man was more scared of a guy all the way in New York than the one in front of him. However, when I busted both of his kneecaps, I disabused him of his belief that Maks's torture would be worse than mine. He believed he was going to get off easy with me."

There's a round of chuckles on the phone since my cousins and I are all enforcers for our family. We've had plenty of training on how to ensure people understand what it means to cross *los Diaz.* We don't handle day-to-day shit. Only the people who fuck up badly. I deal with our Latin American counterparts while *Tres*

J's and Pablo handle the ones here in the States. The worst face Pablo alone. I only came to Chicago because of my connection to Julián.

"Anything interesting happen?" *Tío* Enrique is almost always straight to the point.

"The man sang like a fucking canary. Unfortunately, it was nothing new. He just confirmed the Kutsenkos and O'Rourkes are still funding the war in Italy. The Kutsenkos might not be laundering money through the Oskolkis anymore, but they're still taking sides in that battle."

"*Puta madre.*" Motherfucker.

That's Jorge. He's pissed, and rightly so after everything he just went through to protect his fiancée. He proposed just before I headed to Chicago, and I've never seen him happier.

Joaquin and I are the only single men left standing. When shit went sideways in Germany, Joaquin and I flew out there to help. It's where we learned it's two against two in an Italian turf war. Marriage connects the Sicilian *Cosa Nostra* and Venetian *Mala del Brenta*, and both are Salvatore's in-laws. They're gunning for the Camorra and '*Ndrangheta*.

"Jorge, what do you want to do with them?"

Ultimately, it's *Tío* Enrique's decision. However, he'll listen to my cousin's requests since Jorge's fiancée's family were the casualties.

"I don't know yet, but we'll see how Maks reacts to Alejandro's handiwork. Maybe for a moment he'll think it was Dillan who gave the order, but I doubt it. I want to see if he follows through on his word and does away with the Oskolkis' *pakhan* like he said he would."

"I wouldn't hold your breath that he will, Jorge."

"I know, Javier."

My cousin's sounding a little testy toward his next older brother. I wonder what I've missed, though I'm sure Jorge's still exhausted from the last month. Not only did he have to protect Anneliese, but he also had to find and rescue her father. It's taking a toll on him, even though he does his best to hide it from Anneliese.

Joaquin and I talked about it more than once while we were over there. Joaquin was definitely worried about his baby brother, and I was right there alongside him.

"There was another development while I was with Julián at his bachelor party." I get us back on track.

"Oh?"

It sounds like one deep voice that makes that single syllable, but I know there's six of them there since I can see all of them on my phone screen. *Papá* is with *Tío* Enrique and my four cousins. *Tío* Luis is in Bogotá right now.

Papá rarely attends meetings like this since he's the forward face of our biggest legal enterprises. Since this involves me, there was no way he'd miss the meeting. I might be thirty-five, but it still reassures me to see *Papá's* face and hear his voice.

I look so much like *Tío* Enrique that throughout my life, people have assumed I'm his son. That is, until they meet *Papá*. Our expressions, our tone of voice, our sense of humor, and how we walk and stand are exactly the same. Even though my looks come from the Diaz side of my family—which are certainly among the strongest genetics I've ever seen since we all look so much alike—the Dos Santos family genes had just as much say in me. They just aren't as obvious.

"There was a dancer at the bachelor party."

"You don't say."

"*Papá*, it was a bachelor party."

I may be thirty-five, but my father can still make me feel as guilty about something as I did when I was six.

"This dancer struck me as different. I don't know if she was a local cop or a fed, maybe even someone from another family, but it felt weird."

I'm doing my best to keep my tone neutral, so they don't guess how much she affected me. I keep telling myself my reaction's entirely physical. That the jealousy I felt was more about me not wanting to share her cunt than it was anything about her personality.

Pablo leans forward, so he's clear for me to see. We use a tele-conferencing system that has a three-hundred-sixty-five-degree camera. It sits in the center of the table in *Tío* Enrique's office. When we are on calls like this, we can see and hear everyone.

"Just how tempted were you?"

My cousin laughs, but I don't. Joaquin can't let it rest either, so he takes a turn as well.

"Were you distracted enough that you wouldn't have felt a needle in the neck for all your troubles?"

So much for hiding my thoughts. The problem with such a close family that has five guys all within a couple years of each other is you can't have a private thought without everybody else knowing. We were all trained by our *tíos* and fathers who're just as close as we are. There are no secrets, not even mental ones.

"Well, it doesn't matter whether I thought she was attractive because I definitely think she would've drugged me if she'd had half a chance."

Tío Enrique isn't exactly dour, but I can tell he's ready to move on now that my cousins have teased me a little.

"Is she worth investigating?"

"I'm not sure yet. Maybe."

"Keep an eye on her, Alejandro, even when you get back here."

"*Sí, tío.*"

The call ends, and I flop back on the bed, ready for a nap.

Chapter Four

Vita

It's been a shit-tastic morning with a call from my employer.

Demanding fucker that he is wants to know why he got reports that Alejandro made it onto his jet home looking just fine.

"Sir, my disguise was as a stripper. Where exactly was I going to hide the needle while I was naked?" He doesn't need to know I had a plan.

"I hired you for your beauty and for your many talents. You should've gotten Alejandro alone."

I don't need him to spell out what he means by talents. I would've fucked Alejandro because I wanted him that much, not because of my job. My talents aren't being a good lay, even if my asshole employer makes it sound like they are. I may not have many limits, but I'm not a prostitute for anyone.

I've played the part of a stripper before. I've had to get naked in front of informants and targets as well, and it took me a while to get over how embarrassing and intimidating it was to be that vulnerable. But work is work, and sometimes you just gotta get on with it.

That said, I've always drawn a line. I might let someone kiss me or get a little handsy like the douche on the boat the other night, but I've never had sex with someone I'm dealing with for work. I haven't given any blowjobs or been eaten out by informants or targets either. That's why it shocks the shit out of me that I would've been willing to violate my cardinal rule for Alejandro.

"Yes, sir." There's nothing to gain if I say anything else.

The next threat is inevitable. "I won't pay you if you don't accomplish the job. I'll out you to the Diazes."

"I understand."

I hear my temporary boss's voice drone on, but his inflection tells me he just asked a question. I need to pay closer attention to the conversation. I try to think what he just said. He wants to know what I'm going to do next since I missed my chance.

"I'm headed to New York. I'll come up with another identity or persona to justify being near Alejandro. I'll change up my accent, wear a different wig, and be a different character."

That's what it feels like in this life I didn't exactly choose but wound up in. It's like being an actress. I play a different character depending on the assignment. I have a wig collection that's worth a fortune since it's made from all real hair. They're fitted to me perfectly, so it's impossible to tell they aren't my actual hair.

"You're going to have to get close to him again. You know that, right?"

"I do. You know I've dealt with worse and gotten the job done."

However, I can't let him see me until the moment I strike. It's the only way I can drug him. It's not like I can throw a dart at him.

"Yeah, but you haven't dealt with a man like Alejandro Diaz before. You know women and children are usually off limits, but he'll defend himself to your death before he gives in."

"You pay me good money because of what I can do. Have I ever failed you before, or have I killed every man you've hired me to?"

This guy's a broker—a matchmaker. If you want someone killed, you go to him. He hires the mercenary and passes along the money after he takes his cut.

"True, true, true, and yes, some jobs have taken longer than others. I'll be patient for right now, Vittoria, but not much longer."

I grit my teeth. Much longer, asshole? I only got the job five days before I met Alejandro. It barely gave me time to get to the U.S. and find and get the job as a stripper, which was no easy feat.

The man who hired me discovered Alejandro was headed to Chicago because of some shit that happened with some Boston cartel. I don't know the details behind it. Once I knew who I was hired to target, I started digging around to see if I could guess where he'd be. It wasn't me who discovered Alejandro's plans. It was my employer's chief intel gatherer who did.

The Mafioso who hired the dancers was the douchey one who also chartered the yacht and wanted to show me his micropenis. Then from there, I checked out blabbermouth's social media. He posted about it. I hacked his email and phone to figure out what entertainment he hired, since I could tell he was definitely the type who'd want strippers at a bachelor party.

Once I was in Chicago, I made a beeline for the company and got myself hired on. I told a sob story about how I needed the money because my dad got into some trouble with the Rizzos, and I wanted to give my portion of the pay directly to them that night. The guy who manages the stripper company bought it and gave me the job.

"I'll keep you posted and let you know when I've accomplished the mission, sir. You can wire me the rest of the money." He can be rude, but I'll remind him he's paying me for it.

"All right. Don't forget you don't have much longer. If you don't complete the assignment, it's not like you just get fired."

"Yes, sir, I know. I know Alejandro'll find me and torture me before he kills me."

"Right."

There's more he leaves unsaid. My employer will kill me rather than risk I'll run to the Diazes and tell them what he hired me for. He hangs up without another word. That's fine because I have nothing else to say, and he has nothing else I want to hear.

I may not have flown on a private jet to New York five days ago, but at least it was still first class. I'm paid well for travel expenses on top of money for my work. I watched a movie on the way to the city but spent half of it praying no one in the *Cosa Nostra* discovers I'm in New York. That would be a fucking disaster and a half. There's no way I'd fucking survive that.

I'm not working entirely alone in New York. I have a couple of informants my employer connected me to, and they've given me a heads-up on where Alejandro's headed today. I've been observing him for the past four days, so I've got a feel for what I believe is his routine.

He goes to work out at his uncle's house in New Jersey every morning. All the men gather there. Yesterday morning, I had to duck low in my seat as Enrique's wife, Elodie, pulled out of the gated neighborhood.

The last fucking thing I need is for her to spot me. I won't live to take my next breath if she recognizes me. That woman's got a colorful past.

Right now, I'm following five car lengths behind his motor-cycle as we head toward Jackson Heights. It's a Colombian neigh-borhood in Queens, and the Diazes' unofficial New York headquarters. They conduct most of their business there.

I make sure I stay far enough behind that Alejandro won't notice me following him. The upside of letting him get ahead of me is that there's enough room for me to see which turns he takes without missing my opportunity to take them too. Once we're in the Heights, I struggle to find a parking spot even though I'm in a compact car.

I can't circle the block a bunch of times without men spotting me. I'm sure they're his guards. I end up pulling into a lot and paying. Fucking prices aren't cheap here, that's for sure. But it means I haven't lost sight of him. As I get out of the car, I look around.

Fuck my motherfucking life.

The Diazes own this parking lot.

Of course, they fucking do.

They own half the fucking shit around here. The other half pays them protection money.

A truck passes in front of me as I wait to cross the street. By the time it drives past, Alejandro's disappeared.

Fuck.

I glance around to make sure no one's paying attention to me. Many people from northern Italy have lighter coloring than many would expect of people from a Mediterranean country. While I'm not naturally as dark as people from the southern regions, I tan really well. That means between what's natural and what the sun does, I can pass for many ethnicities. I can pull off most hair colors without looking fake.

Right now, I'm sporting a wig with long, black, wavy hair. It's much darker than my natural color and much thicker than the one I wore on the cruise. Since I have a tan from my last job in Greece, I can blend in as a Latina here. Maybe not Colombian, but I'm passable. I speak fluent Spanish, so I'm not scared I'll be a deer in the headlights if someone speaks to me in the language.

I notice men in suits standing outside a bodega, so he must be there. I'm unprepared for him to walk out so soon and hand an envelope to one guy. I duck into a store before he can look in my direction. I don't notice what the place sells until the door closes behind me.

Thank God it's not a butcher or a baker.

Instead, it's a cell phone store. I pretend to look around, making a beeline for a particular brand of phone. I keep my back mostly to the door and windows and bend over a display, but from the corner of my eye, I watch him walk past. Thankfully, the advertisement plastered to the window makes it difficult to see in or out clearly. I feel him looking at me. If he can even see me, I'm certain it's just my outline, so it's not obvious I'm looking at him too.

A sales associate greets me, but I'm quick to let him know I don't see what I wanted. I try for a brief thank you, no thank you, but he starts his sales pitch. I cut him off—I know I'm rude—but I don't have time to waste in here. I slip out the door and pretend to be rummaging in my purse for something as I check the sidewalk in both directions.

I put on sunglasses and follow Alejandro, who's a block ahead of me. He leads me toward the parking lot, so I head to the car rather than follow him. Once I'm inside, I lock the doors and pretend to scroll on my phone. With the sunglasses on and my chin tucked, I'm still able to see what's going on around me. I'll wait for him to make his next move, then follow him without him noticing.

He's working as a bouncer at the club his cousin owns. I blend into the crowd, lingering with groups of women, just close enough to appear like I'm the quiet friend without appearing obtrusive to any of them. I sip my drinks in between dances.

I'm on my third bay breeze when I spot Alejandro scanning the crowd.

Did he notice me earlier?

Did someone notice my behavior and report it to him?

Did they think I was suspicious?

While I keep my gaze sweeping the dance floor and the part of the bar I can see, I force my expression to remain neutral, like I'm just people watching. When the fourth group of women I'm near head to the dance floor, so do I. It's not long before a guy maneuvers himself toward me. Other men have danced with me tonight which has kept me from standing out. But this one gets handsy. I attempt to step away, but his arm snakes around my waist and pulls me toward him. When I don't budge, he yanks harder.

"Don't."

"Come on. Shaking your ass like that tells me you're looking for someone to pay attention."

I love to dance—not like at the bachelor party. Despite being here to watch Alejandro, I was making the most of this and enjoying myself.

But this douchebag...

"I dance because I like it not because it's an invitation. Don't."

His hand slides down to my ass and grabs it. This time I let him pull me closer. Then I knee him.

"Bitch!"

"Asshole."

He may have yelled his expletive, but I muttered mine.

"He is an asshole, and he's leaving. *Now*."

I turn my head to find Alejandro standing behind me. He steps closer, not just crowding me but the *stronzo*—asshole—who hasn't let go yet. When he leans forward, his chest brushes the back of my shoulder. It's like leaning against a brick wall. I feel the menace rolling off him as though it were a cloud engulfing me. The guy lets go and takes a step back, his hand over his crotch, but he doubles down.

"The bitch kneed me in the balls."

"I'm surprised she could find your *huevos*. She told you not to touch. Now you're leaving."

"Who the fuck are you? You're not a bouncer here."

"Are you sure?"

Alejandro kept up the conversation as he slips between the *pezzo di merda*—piece of shit—and me. His size looms over the guy, and he forces him to back away from me even farther. He's not wearing the black t-shirt with the club logo on it and cargo pants the other bouncers wear. He's in a button-down shirt and slacks. He rolled his shirt sleeves back, and his tattoos peek from beneath the material.

He doesn't look like a bouncer. He looks like he owns the place. He moves with authority that doesn't encourage anyone to argue with him.

I stay where I am as more space grows between the men and me. Alejandro gestures at someone, and two men who're clearly bouncers approach.

"*Échale a patadas y asegúrate de que sepa que está prohibido.*"
Toss his ass out and make sure he knows he's banned.

The bouncers crowd the guy, and one of them shoulder checks him as he turns to face the *pezzo di merda* who now regrets most of his life choices.

"What the fuck, man? I was just dancing with her. She went all psycho on me. She could have told me she didn't want to dance with me."

"She did. Twice."

How the hell did Alejandro know that? I didn't see him get close enough to hear me. Maybe he's guessing from my expression or body language. Maybe he's guessing I told him once, then shoved my knee into his balls after the second time.

"Don't fucking touch me. Let go. I'll leave on my own. This is a shitty club anyway."

Besides the shoulder check, neither bouncer touches him. They don't have to. He's just whining like a *piccolo cagna*—little bitch. Neither Alejandro nor the bouncers say anything. The enormous enforcers hover, intimidating him into retreating. Rather than shut up and take the smart way out, the douche doubles down. Hell, at this point, he's—like—quadrupling down.

"Do you know who I am?"

Alejandro laughs at the *cazzo*—dick—and it sends a chill down my spine. It must do the same to the man because he finally realizes he's pushed too far.

"I don't give a fuck who you are. Do you know who I am?"

He pauses for effect, his voice dropping an octave.

"I'm Alejandro Diaz."

The color drains from the man's face, and he stumbles. I swallow my smirk and my laugh. My unwanted dance partner might pass out from how quickly he's breathing. Alejandro takes a threatening step forward, his shoulders pressed back. I shift to watch him from the side. His shirt strains across his chest, and his sleeves are already tight around his bulging—yes, definitely bulging—biceps.

"My cousin manages this place. My family owns it. You look

like you know who I am, so do you want to leave on your own or find out what it means when I throw you out?"

"I—I—I'll go."

"Consider yourself banned from any establishment my family owns. I wouldn't go to any places the Kutsenkos, O'Rourkes, or Mancinellis own either. Smile for the security cameras. I'll send your photo to them."

The guy spins on his heel and practically sprints to the door. He barrels through the crowd; whereas the bouncers part the sea of people like they're both Moses. Alejandro looks toward me. His gaze slides down then up until our gazes meet. My heart pounds, worried he recognizes me. I'm a redhead tonight with blue contacts to disguise my gray eyes. I had brown contacts in on the yacht.

"Are you all right, ma'am?"

Ma'am?

How the fuck old does he think I am?

"I'm fine. Thanks for that. He wouldn't let go when I told him I didn't want to dance with him."

"I could tell."

His expression is speculative, and my worry turns to fear. If he hasn't recognized me yet, he will if I don't get away from him soon.

"I should find my—"

"Will you let me buy you a drink? It's the least the house can do."

I want to decline, but it's a club. Practically everyone's drinking, and so have I. However, I'm clearly sober, so I can't say I'm cutting myself off because I've had too much. I accept, telling myself it's an opportunity to get in some up-close reconnaissance.

"Thank you."

We walk to the bar together. As we do, I consider how he dropped his name so easily. It's not like I think he lurks in the shadows. Obviously, he has no qualms about being out in public. But I wonder how he knew his name would register with the guy. It's not a stretch that it intimidated the man once he knew who

Alejandro was. His size wasn't enough, but those two words turned everything around.

"What would you like?"

"A bay breeze neat, please."

I hate ice in my drinks. I may sound American tonight, but I'm Italian through and through. He orders, and I keep my gaze locked on the bartender. It's habit. I don't believe Alejandro'll have his employee drug me, but I'm always cautious. Considering I want nothing more than the chance to drug him, I see the hypocrisy for what it is.

"Have you been here before?"

"A couple times." That's a lie.

"You weren't dancing with that last group of women you hung out nearby. You stuck closer to the other ones."

Fuck!

"I'm in town to visit my grandmother. She goes to bed at eight, so I decided to go out. I don't mind doing things on my own, but I know to stick close to other women. Men usually don't harass me when I do."

"You don't know anyone in the city?"

We're in Manhattan, and I know that's what he means by "the city."

"Not really. I know the night life is better here, so I came over from Brooklyn."

I didn't.

"I hope you were having a good time before this."

"I was. I am."

I shoot him a flirtatious glance before staring into my glass. I angle my body, so I rest one elbow on the bar, and the other arm presses against my left breast as I sip my drink. The pressure lifts it until it's practically spilling over the top of my halter dress. His gaze doesn't falter, but I'm certain he notices.

"Where are you from?"

"Originally? Near New Brunswick. But I live in Boulder now."

"Escaped the polluted armpit of America for the wide-open space and mountains."

"Not a fan of Jersey?"

"Is anyone?"

He grins, and his teeth sparkle.

Motherfucking sparkle!

They don't look like veneers or like he whitens them. He was just blessed with great teeth. He was blessed with great everything. The dim light on the yacht—mood lighting—kept me from seeing how bright they are. I also thought he had brown eyes, but he actually has hazel-brown. They have slivers of green and gold in them. They pin me in place, and I could easily forget my mission. I could believe he's genuinely flirting with me.

I chuckle at his nonchalant yet snide comment about New York's least favorite neighbor. At my lighthearted reaction, his grin turns into a full smile. His eyes crinkle, and a dimple appears in his left cheek.

No man should be this attractive.

Ever.

I bet he was a cherubic child.

He's the devil now.

Fuck. It's my turn to say something, but I'm too awestruck. I sip my drink again. Blessedly, he fills the silence.

"Since your dance got interrupted, would you like to try again?"

I didn't expect that. I shift my attention to the dance floor. Is he blowing me off now? Does he think I'm bored because I didn't respond.

"It's gotten even more crowded out there."

"People tend to make room for me."

Oh. He wants to dance with me.

I place my now empty glass on the bar and shift away from it. I take a step, and he moves to walk with me. His hand hovers near my lower back. He doesn't touch me, but I sense it there. Much like it did for the bouncers, the crowd opens for him. He guides me to a spot that's not too close to the speakers but isn't in some corner that would make a normal woman nervous.

We sway to the music, and it surprises me he has such a strong sense of rhythm. He moves like sex on a stick. If this is what he's like standing up, I can only imagine what he's like lying down. I bet he fucks like a god.

We dance through three songs before we gravitate closer together. During the fifth song, his arm slides around my waist as my hand rests on his chest and the other is high on his bicep. When the sixth song starts, we're pressed together. His leg slides between mine, and I grind against him.

"We move well together, *chiquita*."

Little girl. He called me that on the yacht. Does he call all women that?

That dampens my mood. I don't know why I wanted that to be special. It's stupid for myriad reasons, but it's especially stupid since he's my mark.

"Mmm. We fit together."

"Should we see if we can fit together better?"

Chapter Five

Alejandro

"What did you have in mind?"

My lips brush against her neck as she answers my question with a question. They travel from her shoulder to behind her ear before I respond.

"This is a good start. What do you want?"

I knew someone's been following me the last couple of days. Not only did I sense it, but my guards warned me. The dark tint on her car windows prevented them from seeing who was inside. However, I had my suspicions, which proved correct.

Today, she felt even closer than before, so it was no surprise when I spotted her. She's definitely good at hiding in plain sight. She reminds me of me since I've been known to vanish right before somebody's eyes.

If *Tío* Luis's moniker wasn't *El Espíritu Santo*—the Holy Spirit—then my nickname probably would've been *El Espectro*—the Ghost. Definitely not *fantasma*—sounds too close to *fantástico*, and no one would say there's anything fantastic about me beyond my looks and how I fuck or kill.

Instead, I'm known as *El Caballero*—the knight. I ride in—fly in—to vanquish our enemies in Latin America on my shiny steed —my private jet.

I used to terrify the fuck out of my parents since I'd be there one moment and gone the next. I wasn't exactly getting in trouble, but I was a very inquisitive child. I may be the biggest in our family, but I'm the lightest on my feet.

Right now, I'm observing "Tiffani with an i" as she weighs her options. Even knowing she's there to spy on me, I'd still fuck her given half a chance. I wouldn't do it to learn more about her mission. I wouldn't do it to capture and manipulate her into telling me who sent her.

"You could kiss me for real."

I'd fuck her because I'm fucking hard as a fucking tent pole, and I want to know what it feels like to be inside her.

I want to taste her.

Taste her mouth.

Taste her tits.

Taste her cunt.

Taste everything in between.

"I could kiss both lips."

Her breath hitches at my offer, understanding I want to eat her out. She doesn't pull away. She doesn't knee me either. Instead, her pussy slides higher on my leg. She rubs it harder, and her hip brushes against my hard-on. She arches her back, her tits pressing into my chest as our gazes meet. She licks her lips, knowing how enticing that is.

I'll fuck her knowing she doesn't give a shit about me beyond likely trying to kill me.

What a way to go.

Dancing with her gave me the chance to be sure she isn't carrying a weapon. I've run my hands over her hips and upper thighs. My hand hovered at her lower back as we joined the other dancers, making sure she didn't have a knife she could plunge into me while no one noticed in the near dark. She doesn't have a barrette or hair clip that could really be a stiletto.

"You can't do that here."

"I can start."

I nudge her chin, turning her head to bring our mouths closer. As our lips press together, I feather my fingertips down her throat. They glide around to her neck until my palm rests heavily just above the dip between her collarbones. I don't squeeze. I don't want her to think I'm onto her and threatening her. No. It's erotically possessive—or so I've been told from women I've scened with at my BDSM club.

She attempts to take the lead, swiping the tip of her tongue across the seam of my lips. I open to her, but before she can press forward, I thrust my tongue into her mouth. Not enough to choke her or repulse her. But I lead, and she follows. I feel her gasp before she gives herself over to it. Her arms wrap around my neck as my free hand grips her ass. I squeeze, and her hips jerk closer to my dick. She grinds harder.

She likes it.

I increase the pressure on her throat and ass. She sighs then moans. I feel her nipples through the material of her dress and my shirt. They could cut diamonds. Heat from her pussy seeps onto my thigh. I wonder if I'll have a mark since she's definitely wet for me. Just like on the yacht.

I like it. A fucking lot.

She might want me physically, but I can't delude myself that it's anything more. I can't let it become more on my end. She intrigues me though. She's brave, intelligent, resourceful, and even charismatic. If I'm not careful, I might declare my devotion—at least to her body. She's sexual and intellectual puzzles I want to put together. Shift the pieces to make her come. Shift the pieces to discover what she's hiding.

Why the fuck did people give board games to an only child? Every fucking birthday, at least one classmate—or their mom—got me a board game. I've always enjoyed puzzles even with a herd of cousins. I would put them together then take them apart just to do them over again with a different strategy. I'd do the same to Tiffani just to make her come over and over.

"Mmmm."

She moans into my mouth, and I fight not to respond with a less than manly moan of my own.

"What next, little one?"

My hand glides down her chest, along the side of her breast, and settles at her waist. My other hand skims the back of her thigh where her miniskirt ends. My thumb slips under the hem. Her fingers weave through my hair as she arches her back again in the pretense of moving to see my face better.

"That was one set of lips." She cocks an eyebrow.

I'm not dragging her out to my car like some horny teenager with an eleven o'clock curfew. I'm definitely not taking her back to my place, and I'm too tight fisted to get a hotel room just for her to try to kill me. The club has a private room no one's renting tonight. There are sofas along three walls.

I withdraw my leg from between hers and take her hand. I lead her down the hallway and up the stairs to the mezzanine level. The fourth wall of the room is a one-way window. People can see out, but no one can see in. The room's position relative to the stairs makes it impossible to tell that the window doesn't work both ways. It just looks like a glare from the overhead lights makes it hard to see in. Let's see if she enjoys the risk of voyeurism.

I stand close to the door as I punch in the code, making the pocket door slide open. It won't lock from the inside without a different code, which I enter. I don't want anyone actually watching us. I know Joaquin spotted me heading up here because I already heard him tell the men through the earpieces we're wearing not to bother checking up here while they make their rounds. Unless any of them spotted me bringing Tiffani up here, they'll assume one of my cousins or I have a private meeting—a legit meeting not a fuck fest—up here.

"It's crowded tonight."

Tiffani stands beside the window and looks out on the moving throng of dancers. I rest my hands on her hips as my lips graze her shoulder and up her neck. I lift her hair and drape it over her opposite shoulder before my fingers lift the strings that keep her dress in place. I don't miss even a millimeter of her skin. Tonight, she smells like jasmine. I don't tug the straps, giving her a chance to refuse me. When she lifts her chin and tilts her head away from me, encouraging me to kiss her again, I take it as silence is consent.

I untie the bow and let the material drop down her chest. My fingertips descend from her shoulders to her elbows before my hands cover her tits. I knead them, then tweak her nipples. She arches her back, trapping my hands between her and the glass, forcing me to hold onto her.

"Are you hoping someone will look up here? See me enjoying your tits. See me fucking you."

"I wouldn't say no if they could actually see us."

She knows about the glass. It doesn't surprise me.

"Do you want an audience, *chiquita*? Is that your thing?"

"Not always. But I wouldn't be pissed if everyone knew the hottest man here is fucking me."

"Mmm. You want to make them jealous?"

"I would be if you were with someone else."

"Is that so, little one?"

I let go of her right breast to grasp her chin, my other hand pulling her body back against mine. I turn her head, so we can look at each other again. I ease my hold on her chin to let her respond.

"Who wouldn't want to be in my shoes right now?"

I chuckle. "I can think of four women."

Her brow furrows.

"My cousins' wives and fiancée. None of them have ever looked twice in my direction."

"Devoted to their husbands?"

"Just like their husbands are devoted to them. No one else exists to each couple."

"That's sweet."

I brush my lips against hers. "Mmm. You're sweet too."

I let go of her waist as my thigh nudges her legs apart, widening both of our stances. My free hand dips beneath the hem of her skirt before I grip the front of her left thigh. I pull it until it's over mine, her toes grazing the floor. With firm pressure, my hand creeps up to her cunt.

No panties.

Good little girl.

My middle and ring fingers feather along her pussy lips while my index finger and pinky press outward, a soft reminder to keep her legs open. My second and third fingers dip into her, and my cock pulses at how smooth and wet she is. She grabs for my wrist when I withdraw my hand, but I ignore her silent command. Instead, I bring those fingers to my mouth. She watches our reflection as I suck them into my mouth.

"Even sweeter than I hoped, *chiquita.*"

"Why do you call me that?"

I wrap my arms around her waist, one hand pressing against her belly as the other hikes up her skirt.

"Aren't you a lot smaller than me?"

"Yes."

I cup her pussy. "And you're a girl."

I press both hands hard against her, pinning her to me. My teeth nip her right earlobe since my lips were there as I whispered to her. She shivers once, and I watch over her shoulder as her nipples tighten. My hold on her dominates her. It's purely possessive, and we both know it. She doesn't tense, so I'm confident she knows I'll stop if she tells me to. I'm not that *caremonda*—face of a penis—from earlier.

Instead, her head lolls back on my shoulder as her hips undulate, tempting my fingers into her cunt. I don't give in. I bite and tug her earlobe instead. She shudders, and I love it. It was involuntary. I'm certain of it because there's a moment after when she tenses before she remembers this is supposed to be a role she's playing. I can practically hear her thoughts. I'm positive they're the same ones I would have if I were in her position. Both physically and metaphorically in this cat and mouse relationship we're developing.

You're no better than she is. You'd love for this to be real instead of a fucked-up, real life chess match.

How she feels is fucking real, that's for damn sure. How hard my dick is, is just as real.

Neither of us can admit it, but we both want to enjoy ourselves while we work. If we can get off without dying, then that's a good night's work.

I'm slow as I finish pulling her dress up to her waist, enjoying each inch revealed to me. In the better lighting than on the boat, I can see her ass isn't what most would consider perfection. The skin is smooth as silk, but there are soft ripples. It's perfect for me.

People say I'm the pretty one in the family, and it pisses me off. I'm more than just my good lucks. Yeah, I won the fucking genetic mega lottery. Yeah, it lets me get away with shit and opens doors that would remain shut for plenty of people.

But the same comments I've heard for the past twenty years are getting old. I'd rather people see me as imperfect than the living, breathing Latino Ken doll. That's why I like Tiffani's ass. She's gorgeous, but she isn't perfect. People know she's more than just her good looks.

If anyone in this club is jealous, it's me. I wish people would see me how they probably see her.

Buck up, buttercup. Pity party's over.

I snap myself out of my wandering insecurities and back to the temptation in front of me as my hands once again squeeze her ass, lifting and separating her cheeks. The things I want to do to her...

I kiss down her back as I pull her hips toward me. My eyes are on what's happening outside the window and our reflection. That's fucking erotic as fuck. I crouch and blow cool air against the inside of her thigh. She shifts restlessly. I won't kneel because: A. I kneel for no one, and B. if I need to stand in a hurry, I'm not shuffling around to get to my feet even if I can rock back onto my heels and rise in one movement.

I flick my tongue against her clit, then drag it along her seam, slipping it into her pussy. My fingers bite into her ass, surely leaving marks, and she pushes back into my hold.

Then my phone buzzes in my pocket.

And I grin while she can't see me.

I rise and pull it out as her head whips around to watch me.

"*Hola, primo.*"

"Is my timing perfect as usual, cousin?"

"*Sí.*"

I told Joaquin that if he saw me bringing her up here tonight, he was to call me twenty minutes later. Sure, part of it is to make sure I'm still alive. But largely it's to leave her hanging.

Sexual frustration is the worst kind of frustration, isn't it?

My guess is she speaks Spanish, and that's part of why she was hired to target me. I know she can't hear Joaquin, and I don't need to say more than yes. Even if I did, I wouldn't unless it was to mislead her. I end the call and shoot her a regretful frown.

"I have to go, *chiquita*. Something came up."

She glances down at my crotch, where my trousers don't disguise my hard-on. Her eyes appear sad, but the quirk of her lips tells me she knows I'm just as uncomfortable as she is. But I can survive not getting my rocks off.

"Pity." She shrugs before retying her straps and pushing down her skirt.

"I'll walk you downstairs."

Our gazes lock for a moment before she looks away. There was that air of confidence that she had on the yacht. A touch of defiance, arrogance, and understanding. She knows there's not a chance I'll leave her up here alone. She knows I know she knows.

I entwine my fingers with hers and walk down the stairs. They're steep, and this part of the club isn't well lit on purpose. I genuinely don't want her to tumble down the stairs in the four-inch heels she's wearing.

"Thank you."

We turn to look at each other when we reach the ground floor.

"You're welcome. Can I get you another drink?"

"No. I'm going to head out. Thank you for a—unexpected night."

I lean forward and whisper to her before grazing my bottom teeth against the skin behind her ear. "Unexpected and enchanting."

I watch her eyes widen as I straighten. I doubt she expected such an old-fashioned word.

Keep her guessing, mi amigo.

I flash her a grin before we continue to the door. I step out with her and watch her hail a cab.

"Goodnight, Alejandro."

Fucking hell!

I just realized I never got her name because I kept thinking of her as Tiffani.

"You never told me your name."

"I know."

She hurries to the corner and pulls open the car door. She looks over her shoulder and wags her fingers in a wave. My lips pucker as my jaw shifts. I struggle to repress the smile that wants to break free.

You may have put me in check, but this match isn't over until I say checkmate.

Chapter Six

Vita

What the ever-loving motherfucking fuck did I do?

That thought's been swirling around my mind on replay for the last three days.

That's how long ago I saw Alejandro. I've tried to track him, but he's been MIA. I don't know if he slipped out of town or he's at his family's "place." They all have a "place." It's where syndicates go to deal with the most unsavory parts of their job. The place where they have absolute control to deal with and dispose of people who make shit choices.

That time spent on the dance floor, then in the private party room were the most arousing minutes of my life. I've *never* been that turned on before, and I've had some pretty fantastic sex. My entire body ached for more, and my pussy was a scorching burn with need for his cock. It took every ounce of self-control not to beg him for more, not to cry when he ended things.

The fuck he had something to do. That was a power play.

How do I know?

Because I've done that shit plenty of times. Usually, it's

coupled with revulsion and a complete *lack* of arousal. Unless he slipped a little blue pill before he approached me, his hard-on was very real. My dripping cunt wasn't something I could fake either.

"Shall we take our seats?"

I nod to Patrick's question. He's my fake date for an O'Rourke charity gala. He's a guy I've worked with before and knows who I am because he's the same—a mercenary. This event isn't like the club where I could easily blend in alone. I need to look like I belong, so I'm in a designer gown with real jewels. He's handsome in his tux and real gold cufflinks.

"Yes. Our table is in a better position than I expected."

I bought our tickets to the event rather than attending as an invited guest. I figured we'd be relegated to seats in the back of the room. I guess "nobody puts Baby in the corner" is working for me tonight.

We're seated near the bratva tables. From here, I can observe the Kutsenkos, the Russian ruling family in NYC—hell, not just the Eastern Seaboard but the entire country. They, along with the O'Rourkes and Mancinellis, are the Diazes' strongest rivals.

In the most fucked-up politics I've seen, these families invite one another to high-society events. Wedding and baptism receptions—never the service—charity galas, and Easter brunches. You'd think they'd only gladly show up to one another's funerals, but instead, they make nice and rub elbows with the country's elites. The people who want to do legit business with the families and don't mind others seeing them curry favor with the families who run NYC's underworld. The deals no one wants seen are negotiated in places like nightclubs and strip clubs.

"We might not be close to the Diazes, but we can definitely watch the Kutsenkos' reactions." Patrick whispers to me as I slip between my chair and the table.

"That could be as informative as listening to the Diazes themselves."

Patrick slides my chair under me before taking his place beside me. We're a loving couple tonight, and we look good together. He's got sun-bleached blond hair and cornflower blue eyes with a body made for modeling.

I have a thatch-blonde wig and green eyes tonight. A little temp color lightened my eyebrows. He had his arm around me earlier, and now he takes my hand as we rest them on the tabletop. We look natural leaning in to whisper.

"We have a pretty clear line of sight for the Mancinellis too. I just wish the Diazes weren't across the room from us."

"Liz, what we can't see of them, you know the other families can. We just watch them and listen as best we can to what people say when they come over to the bratva."

Liz Cullens is who I am tonight. I would've been Giselle Harting if Alejandro'd asked at the club.

"Hopefully, someone gets drunk enough to approach the Kutsenkos or their Andreyev cousins. That family won't volunteer a damn word, but someone else might drink enough to loosen their tongue."

At least one person always does at events like this. They'll approach a syndicate's leading family with too much confidence only to meet an untimely accident within the next month. Discretion is everything to these families, even if they do throw lavish parties for the press to snap photos.

Patrick and I watch as Dillan O'Rourke picks up a mic to welcome everyone to the event. He introduces the CEO of the charity, who gives a little song and dance to ask for healthy donations by the end of the night. Then the meal begins. The hum of voices once again fills the room. During college, I took a lip-reading course as part of a specialized training. I can't hear what's happening at any other table, but I can read what is.

"Looks like Katerina Andreyev, Misha's wife, is pregnant. The rest are sipping champagne, but that's definitely ginger ale. Misha just asked how she's doing with all the different scents in here."

"I think Sinead Mancinelli is in the same boat. She's looking a bit green, and Gabriele looks like he's about to pass out while he hovers."

There's derision in Patrick's voice. The perpetual bachelor, and not just because of our occupation. He's the living, breathing embodiment of "if one vine breaks, swing from another" or "the best way to get over someone is to get under someone else." He's commitment phobic. The fuck if he doesn't have an anaphylactic allergy to it. It makes him the perfect partner. We've fucked a few times, but I know he'll never ask for more, so it's never weird in the morning.

I follow his gaze to the Mancinellis and watch Salvatore whispering to Luca, his oldest nephew and heir. Salvatore's been the don for over thirty years. The man's nickname is *Pantera*—Panther. If he doesn't have nine lives, then I don't know what the fuck he does have. Luca's been his underboss for nearly a decade. The man's jagged scar from his cheekbone to below his collar appears as menacing as his personality actually is. I have an obstructed line of sight of their bodies, but I can see their lips.

"Can you get what they're saying?"

I'm not surprised Patrick doesn't understand. They're speaking Sicilian. They really don't want anyone to understand. In most cases, Italian suffices for them, but when they truly want to keep something private, they use Sicilian. Just like the other families, all the members learn their mother country's language before or simultaneously as they learn English. They're all fluent readers, speakers, and writers of the language from their family's country of origin. It grounds them in tradition and keeps them tied to their homeland's—economies, shall we say.

"Luca overheard some Polish guy speaking to Bogdan about a construction deal. The Kutsenkos are pissing off the Polish workers because they only want to pay union wages. They want more under the table. Salvatore just laughed and said the man will wish he'd kept his mouth shut when they all lose their jobs in the morning. Christina—Bogdan's wife and head of their construction company—will fire them because the guy's like a burning hemorrhoid. Constantly up their asses. Luca told him it's the perfect time for them to swoop in and delay the project further to get the clients to cancel the contracts for failure to complete the job on time."

"Would this client be dumb enough to dump the Kutsenkos?"

"Mmm. Hang on. I can't see Salvatore's mouth. Though, they'd be stupid to risk it."

The man's hair remains nearly entirely jet black with just a little gray woven through it and at the temples. He's still a silver fox at nearly sixty. Fucking fine as red wine. But I can't see his face while he reaches for and takes a sip of his wine.

When he turns back, I glance away. I swear these families have a sixth, seventh, and eighth sense for being watched. I focus on Patrick and brush a kiss against his cheek before returning my attention to Salvatore and Luca. If Salvatore noticed me, then hopefully, that peck convinced him I'm no threat.

"Salvatore's telling Luca to complicate things by delaying the lumber shipment. He's to take the wood to Gabriele's hardware store. Gabriele's to cut it down to smaller pieces and sell it as fast as he can. Luca's agreeing and said he'll make it look like the Diazes did it."

"That'll go over well."

We watch as Luca calls over Gabriele. The man's a giant oak tree. He's the largest in their family. Technically, he's more of an adopted nephew since he's not related by blood. His family's been working for the Mancinellis for generations. His father is Salvatore's best friend, but his mother and father returned to Sicily a few years ago. Gabriele's best friends with one of Salvatore's actual nephews, Carmine. I've known him since I was a kid, so I doubly can't risk being recognized.

"Gabriele's agreeing. Apparently, it's the least they can do for the Diazes since the Colombians blew up some Amazonian lab the Mancinellis built in Colombia. I heard about that. The Diazes allow the other families three labs each as a goodwill offering. The Mancinellis tried to sneak in a fourth, and the Diazes found out. Enrique had Alejandro set it ablaze the last time he was down there."

The Mancinellis were definitely in the wrong, and they know it. But machismo requires they retaliate for the retaliation that was likely retaliation for some other retaliation. It's the circle of life for these families.

"What do you think the Diazes will do when they find out the Mancinellis made them their patsy?"

Patrick keeps his voice low as though he's whispering sweet nothings, and I have a loving expression plastered across my face. Sometimes I wish I had someone I could genuinely direct affection toward. Then I wake up hot and horny.

"Destroy something else of the Mancinellis' then destroy something of the bratva's for not being smart enough to see through the ploy."

I swear these men handle their squabbles like King Kong meets Godzilla meets the Hulk meets Megalodon. It's a clash of the Titans on the daily. They're like toddlers past their naptime going on a rampage through their stacked building blocks. Smash! Smash!

Patrick brushes his lips against my temple for good measure before speaking again. "Who'll decide on the plan?"

"I don't know. Alejandro's their chief strategist, but *Tres J's* are their general enforcers. Enrique owns the family's construction and real estate development company. Joaquin's taken on most of the day-to-day stuff over the past couple years. If they go tit-for-tat with building equipment and supplies, then I guess Joaquin. If they want something more subtle, then Alejandro'll probably come up with it."

If I could discover whether Alejandro's the mastermind, then I might find a way to get closer to him. I don't know what that would look like, but I'm keeping it as an open opportunity in the back of my mind. *Tres J's* are his cousins through his mother. Joaquin, Javier, and Jorge—The Three Colombian Musketeers. All for one, one for all.

"You better get close to your mark because the clock's ticking. Your boss won't remain patient. Can you work this to your advantage?"

"I don't know about the construction, but I know I have little time left."

Left to finish this job or to live if I fail.

Dinner is uneventful as the families chat amongst themselves, talking about vacations and children. All four are pictures of domesticity once the women join the conversations. The syndicate world is supposed to be the men's domain. Women are supposed to be untouchable. If you don't see that the women at those family tables are the deadliest here, you don't grasp what it means to be a wife and mother.

I'll keep a wide berth from Catalina De Santos Diaz. She won't think twice about skinning me alive and feeding me my skin if she knows I've had even one thought about harming her son. Alejandro's her only child, so her attention's undivided.

This might appear like a charity event with the richest of the rich here, but it's also a room filled with the most infamous men in NYC. It makes the mothers extra protective of their young and the women extra territorial of their husbands. It's a den filled with she-wolves and lionesses waiting to gut you with a smile.

"Worried about Catalina?"

"I'd be a fool not to. His aunts aren't any less ferocious. You know who Elodie is. You know she's the deadliest person here."

Enrique Diaz, the *jefe de jefes*, married a woman the underworld believed disappeared. Oh, no. The woman's a psychological thriller author now. She was an accountant for years. But those aren't her only sets of skills. She makes me look like I'm still riding with training wheels on.

"You really think she's worse than her husband, the most notorious narco in the world?"

"You haven't seen her work—or the remains."

"I wouldn't underestimate his other aunts. Margherita and Luciana have their own earned reputations."

"Believe me, I know."

I shift my gaze from the Diaz family before any of them sense I'm watching them. I look at the women from the other families.

"How much do you know about the families?" I whisper this

because we're risking a ton having this conversation where someone could overhear.

"You know I keep my work mostly overseas these days. I prefer Switzerland to America. I'll take fresh snow over New York's stench."

I force myself not to roll my eyes. Patrick's cultivated his playboy image, and he has the money to maintain it.

"The three O'Rourkes sisters who married three brothers are a force no one wants to reckon with. They've been a mob boss's daughter and sister. They're mob wives and mothers now. One's the current boss's mother, and the other two are his aunts. They once put a hit out on a guy, and he's been a vegetable since. They did it just to remind their brother—the then-boss—that he might've been the head of the family, but they were the hands that turned it. The women who married into the O'Rourke family are no shrinking violets either. Some people might be foolish enough to believe they're trophy wives because they're all stunning. But they can all wield a knife and a gun with precision."

I scan our surroundings, knowing what I risk gossiping. But if shit goes sideways tonight, which it easily could, I need Patrick to know it's the women who'll shoot and stab first and fastest. With diamond rings the Space Station could see, he could easily underestimate these women. I'm not looking to die tonight or drag his ass out by the collar.

"And the other two families? Just as bad?"

"As bad or worse. The women who married into the Kutsenkos-Andreyev family are no milder. The three older bratva wives—" I nudge my chin toward the most stunning woman most people have ever seen—Galina Kutsenko—and the bratva leaders' mother. "—survived growing up in Moscow with husbands who were in the KGB and old school Moscow bratva. Galina and Svetlana are sisters, and Alina's Galina's best friend. The younger wives all have complicated family histories with syndicates that have forced them to defend themselves."

"From what I've heard, the Mancinelli women—well, shit—they're no better."

Did Patrick just shiver mentioning them? I swallow my chuckle.

"The older generation of women are daughters, sisters, and wives of Mafia dons and lifelong Mafiosos. Maria Mancinelli is the most untouchable woman in NYC. She's the don's niece, the *consigliere's* daughter, the underboss's and the *capo dei capis'* sister, and the wife, sister, and cousin of senior *capos*. She's also a new mother. Sylvia's the don's wife and the daughter of a Palermo dons. Serafina, Carmine's wife, is the daughter of the Venetian *Mala del Brenta* don. Her mother is Sylvia's sister. She's Mafia three times over. Salvatore and Sylvia are her aunt and uncle through blood and marriage."

"Fucking complicated."

"Seriously. You should see the family tree I tried to make once. When you try to connect sisters who married brothers who're linked to other syndicates or are best friends with their husband's rival's wife—fucking hell. Just don't bother."

I want to rub my forehead just thinking about it. God help the mercenaries of the world if the newest generation intermarries among the syndicates. Crime and punishment, and war and peace will have new meanings.

"You—"

I duck my head before I continue because Alejandro's headed in our direction. I believe my disguise is good enough to keep him fooled, but the third time might not be the charm. Patrick rests his bent forefinger under my chin and presses a soft kiss to my lips. Nothing inappropriate for the event, but it's enough to shield my face. I turn my head away, and Patrick brushes a kiss on my temple.

"Sweetheart, would you like to dance?"

The servers are clearing away the dessert plates, and couples are moving to the dance floor. Patrick's offer will steer us in the opposite direction from Alejandro but put us closer to the Diazes. My date is a smooth dancer, but he's nothing like Alejandro was at the club. Patrick's competent and waltzes well, but he lacks the natural grace Alejandro has with every movement.

As we shift with the dancers, Patrick squeezes my waist. "Heads up. One of Enrique's *toros* is headed his way. He just came in through the east doors. He's making a beeline to *el jefe*."

A *toro*—bull—is an official soldier in a cartel, but not one high enough that he'd attend a gathering like this. Patrick leads me through a turn so I can see the guy. He appears casual as he winds his way through the room, but it's clear he's on a mission to reach Enrique. From where Enrique's standing with his oldest nephew, Pablo, both Patrick and I can read their lips. We waltz into a spot where two couples keep us from being obvious.

Since both Patrick and I speak Spanish, neither of us interprets. We read lips as though we're listening to the voices.

"*Jefe, Patrón*, the ATF raided the brownstone in Park Slope."

Patrón is one of several titles Pablo holds. He's a *jefe* in his own right since he runs NYC specifically. But with his uncle next to him, he receives the lower form of address.

"How much damage did they do just to find nothing?" Enrique's expression is somewhere between annoyed and amused.

"Tore the place apart, *jefe*. Even put sledgehammers through the walls and tore up flooring."

Pablo flashes a—from what I've heard—uncharacteristic grin before he responds. The man is *dark*. Like his soul left the building years ago.

"A day late, and a dollar short. How pissed were they?"

"Nowhere near as pissed as Louisa made it seem. The woman should win an Oscar. Every stereotype of a Latina's temper—*dios mío*. She had their *huevos* in a vice. When she arrived at her supposed home being ransacked, she let loose Spanglish that would make you both blush."

Huevos—such a better term than balls or nuts. They are fragile like eggs.

"She chase them out of there with her *chancla*?" When Enrique grins, panties drop.

A *chancla* is a sandal, but in this case, it's a wooden-sole slipper Latin *abuelas*—grandmothers—wield to scare children into behaving. They're deadly in the hands of an old woman. The threat is effective.

"No, but she did reach up to take her earrings out. A Mexican-American agent told them they needed to hurry and leave."

All three men belly laugh, and it draws some looks. Colombian or Mexican—some stereotypes have their advantages. The men sober, and Pablo continues the conversation.

"They didn't arrest her, did they? Threatening a federal agent and all."

"Fuck no. They listened to that agent and tucked tail, then ran like little bitches. Jesus and I watched it all and couldn't stop laughing in the van. Jesus started coughing he was laughing so hard. The feed in the basement showed them getting close to the stash, but they never found the mechanism on the baseboard to release the latch. You really can't tell there are any seams in the concrete around the hatch. You did good work on that, *jefe*."

There must be a hidey-hole in the foundation. There's probably a sensor or button hidden behind a baseboard that, when pressed, releases the locking mechanism to the trapdoor. It's probably a shoestring thin wire under the concrete. The *toro* makes it sound like Enrique laid the concrete and cut the hatch himself. He's a true silver fox and jack of all trades. Unlike most, he's a master of all.

Patrick presses me a little closer, so his lips are beside my ear. "Drugs, guns, or cash?"

"Any. All the above. I don't know. It could be their granny's jewels for all I know. I was unaware they used a townhome as their stash spot. Park Slope's one of the best neighborhoods in Brooklyn."

"Sounds like the woman was a *zorro*."

"Probably."

A fox—a woman who spies for the cartel. Some even get embedded in rival ones and do *whatever* they have to blend in. I'm certain the Diaz Cartel has several on NYPD and as feds but expect none of the women to trade sex for info. All the syndicates have women who spy for them because women and children are supposed to be untouchable. Of course, unless they're like me and killers for hire. The unwritten law makes for the best cover, though, it's gotten a bit flimsy in the last seven years. Not so much the children, but the women have been targets.

When the soldier leaves, Enrique and Pablo switch to a language neither Patrick nor I understand. It's most likely *Macaguán*, a Colombian indigenous language that's practically extinct. A few hundred people speak it, and among those are the Diaz family. They may as well speak in code for all anyone else understands.

We watch Alejandro join them, which signals *Tres J's* to join their uncle and cousins. I know we won't get anything else out of the men tonight now that they aren't speaking English or Spanish. I'm about to switch our attention to the Mancinellis again when Enrique separates from the men and reaches out his hand to his wife.

Fuck my life.

Fuckity-fuck-fuck-fuck.

The couple heads to the dance floor. I can't afford for Elodie to get too close. I don't doubt she'd recognize me in a heartbeat. It'll obliterate my cover if she does. The woman'll have me dead before I can run.

"Patrick."

"I know."

He twirls me, and we slip between the two couples behind us. He maneuvers me through the steps until we can get my back to *the Cartel's* ruling couple. There are plenty of Colombian, Mexican, Brazilian—fucking Latin America as a whole—cartels. But there is only one that warrants a capital C. Where saying *the Cartel* only means one family.

And now one of the most brilliantly deadly women in the world is being whisked around the dance floor by her husband mere feet from me.

I think I'm going to be sick.

I keep my gaze averted as the elegant pair draw people's attention. I'm certain they're doing it to rile the O'Rourkes by stealing the limelight from their hosts. But you can't deny what a perfect couple they make. Enrique's in his late fifties, and Elodie's in her late forties. You'd never guess from their agility and grace. They simply glide along the floor. It's obvious how in love they are from how they anticipate each other's next moves. It's really quite remarkable.

Until Elodie turns in my direction.

I purposely bump into the woman next to me, allowing Patrick and me to stop dancing long enough for me to apologize. The woman's gracious, but only because she's not part of a syndicate. The last thing I need is any syndicate holding a grudge against me in case I need to use this disguise again.

"I'm pretty sure she saw you, Liz."

"But did she recognize me?"

"I don't know. She lingered over watching you, but her expression told me nothing."

"*Fanculo.*" Fuck.

I mutter it under my breath not needing anyone wondering why I swear in Italian.

"Let me grab my purse and duck into the restroom for a few minutes."

"All right."

With my arm looped through his, Patrick and I make our way to our table. I pick up my purse, and we walk toward the bar. I leave Patrick there and head to the ballroom doors. I recognize Alejandro ahead of me, pushing a door open. I keep my pace natural, not wanting to catch up to him yet. The last thing I need is him holding it open for me.

I leave the ballroom and look around, spotting him walking toward the restrooms. Perfect excuse for me to head in the same direction. The hallway leads away from the well-lit mezzanine and to a more shadowy corridor. I silently snap open my purse, ready to reach in to remove my stun gun.

"Hello, beautiful."

My head jerks up as a swarthy man steps in front of me. Two more men approach. Their posture's casual, but I know they're all getting a read on me. When their gazes dart to my open purse, I pull out a tampon and cock an eyebrow.

"The ladies' room is in the opposite direction." I don't know which of *Tres J's* he is, but he's undoubtedly one.

"Oh. Thank you. I've never been here before. I assumed it was near the men's room since I can see a sign for that."

"Nope."

This second brother definitely doesn't mince words. I can't tell if I personally irritate him or he just hates people in general. I saw him with a blonde with a sunny disposition early. If ever there was a grumpy-sunshine love story, it would be them. His face would crack if he smiled.

"If you'll excuse me."

"You only looked in one direction when you left the ballroom, and you couldn't have seen the sign for any restroom from that far away. What made you turn this way?"

The third brother's quieter than the other two, but it almost makes him more menacing. Three to one in most situations isn't odds I fear. Tonight? They'll have knives pulled faster than I can drop my tampon back into my purse.

"Our *tía* Elodie said she thought she recognized you. She'd love to say hello to an old acquaintance. We didn't want you to leave without saying hi." The first brother flashes me a smile that would be sexy as sin if I didn't already know Alejandro.

"I really need to use the restroom." I hold up my hand with the tampon, which fits mostly in my palm.

"There are some notoriously unscrupulous men here tonight, and many of them have been drinking. It might be safer if we escort you."

Brother three steps closer as he speaks. He's not wearing a wedding ring. He must be Joaquin, the one who heads up the family's construction company, or Jorge, the accountant. Can I trade information for my life?

"I've been going to the restroom on my own for decades. I'll stay alert."

I'm about to be more assertive, but I can't help but see

Alejandro approaching from behind the brother who just spoke. I spin on my heels and lift my gown. I don't linger, especially not once I hear the four men's rapid Spanish. I'm certain the reaper in the form of a hot Colombian is on my heels when one of them says *pistola paralizante.*

Stun gun.

How the fuck'd any of them see that? I never opened my purse wide enough. At least, I didn't think I had. I don't recall any of them looking down, but one of them must have. I can't avoid going to the restroom if I don't want them knowing I heard them.

As the door swings closed behind me, I consider the housekeeper's uniform I stashed in here when Patrick and I arrived. I hid it beneath the bag in the trashcan. I could switch into that and take off my wig, pop out my color contacts, and scrub off my makeup. That won't be nearly enough after how closely they stood to me. I also doubt they'd believe a maid came in here without cleaning supplies when there's such a high-end event going on.

ME

Tres J's are outside the restroom. They confronted me. Rescue me.

I pray Patrick feels his phone vibrate and looks at it. It feels like forever before there's a knock on the door.

"Darling, are you all right in there?"

"Just a moment."

Meno male. Thank God.

I pull open the door, and Patrick's practically in the doorframe. He angles himself to keep me hidden from the men lurking. I don't see Alejandro, but he's probably nearby.

"Are you all right, *señora?*"

Patrick tries to answer for me. "She'll be all right. Sometimes the mo—"

"Mimosas hit me a little hard, sweetheart."

I speak over him and cut him off. I know the excuse he was about to use. It's one we've used before. But having flashed a tampon, claiming morning sickness won't work. There's nothing Patrick and I need to know from the other families, and my shoes are killing me.

"Shall we go?" Patrick wraps his arm around me.

"I was just thinking that."

Before I can turn away so we can return to the table for my wrap, I lock gazes with Alejandro.

Chapter Seven

Alejandro

My second shadow's following me again today. She has been since I returned from Belize right before the charity gala. It started right after Chicago and hasn't stopped. My men still haven't identified her, even when they've sensed her. Even when my cousins confronted her as she followed me toward the restroom, she didn't miss a beat. They warned me she had a weapon in her purse that looked an awful lot like a stun gun.

The yellow butt gave it away. It surprises me that: A. she'd have a weapon with any distinguishable color on it, and B. she thought she could follow me—even use the weapon on me—at such a large event.

She couldn't have carried my ass anywhere once I was out. She couldn't just leave my body there. And there's not a fucking chance in hell she could've interrogated me. I wouldn't have given up shit, and my family would've found me if I'd been gone another five minutes. As is, my cousins were standing guard while I received payment from a council member who needs a few permits rushed through the city planner's office.

She's still good at being a ghost.

Except today's different, chiquita.

I've known all along my shadow is the same woman I keep bumping into, but I wasn't ready to spring a trap until today. I'm in Jackson Heights, meeting with a *timador*, a *gallo*, and a *cameleo*. An extortionist, a rooster, and a camel. I don't know why extortionists don't have an animal name in cartels, but they live up to their name.

They intimidate for a living. A rooster leads a band of men who view laws as optional; they're selectively obedient to the government. A camel is an OG cartel member; one who's outlived most of their peers.

All three serve a purpose in neighborhoods like the Heights. They mean my cousins and I usually only come on Tax Day—protection money day—each month. They're our eyes, ears, and mouths the rest of the time.

"Tiffani with an i" was already at a mom-and-pop pharmacy when I arrived in the neighborhood. I need to learn how she knew I'd be here today since I only scheduled the meeting this morning. When I came out of the flower shop, she didn't expect me to turn left.

I watched a woman scurry away. I recognized her through the window of the cell phone store. It's the same place she ducked into the first time I sensed her following me in the Heights a couple weeks ago. She thought it disguised her, but it didn't. I recognized her profile and her silhouette. After all, I've been fantasizing about her for weeks now.

The hair—a wavy brown bob—is a nice touch, but I liked the wig from the yacht the best. Since I've seen her wearing ones as part of whatever disguise she's in, I assume her hair wasn't natural on the yacht, even though I would've said it was that night.

I'm tired of this cat and mouse game. It's time for Tom to catch Jerry for once. I approach the car she's in from her passenger side blind spot. She headed to it while I ducked into a bodega so I could observe her. She's scrolling on her phone as though she's looking for something or killing time. She's caught completely unprepared when she hears the car doors unlock.

Then I'm slipping into the front passenger seat with a gun pointed at her.

"I didn't take you for the stalker type, but I've been told I fuck well enough to tempt women."

I shoot her a lazy smile. It doesn't distract her from my gun. However, her bravado doesn't waver. She responds with a shrug of her right shoulder.

"I didn't know it could take so little to get your attention."

"It's either that, or someone sent you to kill me."

I'm certain she's considering whether she can survive me shooting her if she tries to make a break for it. My gun's muzzle presses against her upper ribs. She remains quiet, looking straight ahead.

"What do you want? Who sent you?"

She doesn't react to my questions, giving me the silent treatment.

"Are you wondering how I got into the car when you locked it?"

Not even a shrug this time or a frown. Her expression is impassive.

"You know, the data grabber on the yacht isn't the only tool I have at my disposal. If I got into this car that easily, then you must know what else I can do. Yet, you've underestimated me twice. Seems rather foolish. Do you think you'll live long enough to do that a third time?"

Now that I've encountered her more than once, I'm certain she knew what I was doing when I went below deck on the yacht. I don't expect her to respond, and she doesn't. I'll do the talking then, and I'm fine with that.

"So, Tiffani with an i..."

She blinks at that. Not a flinch, but it was something of a reaction. Probably my tone because it's so mocking.

"You're a mercenary, and I can think of a few people who likely hired you. You know your line of work makes you fair game. Normally, I'd never intentionally hurt a woman, but it's a gender-neutral occupation once a mercenary's caught. If I'm your mark, then you know the family I'm from. That's why you came to our club and watched us at the gala. You know our reputation is earned, not given. You know the role I play in my family and what I could do to you."

When she finally turns to look at me, it's as though she can see straight into my soul and knows I'm bluffing about this. Not that I wouldn't torture a woman, but I wouldn't torture her.

"You shouldn't assume, little one, that you know anything about me, even if you got a full dossier when you took the job. You wouldn't be the first female mercenary I've killed without remorse."

That's the truth. There's nothing I won't do to protect my family. I'll kill at any and all cost. If they're a threat, then they deserve to die. It will always be us before anyone else. That doesn't mean I'm eager to make that the truth with the woman who sits beside me.

"Tell me what's going on, and perhaps I'll spare you and make it a quick and easy death, maybe even painless."

She turns away from me and stares out the windshield again.

"You know, even POWs give their name, rank, and serial number before they give their captors the silent treatment."

Her nostrils flare, and she looks at me this time. "I didn't realize cartels complied with the Geneva Conventions."

"We don't, so I'm not worried about being charged with war crimes for what I'll do to you if you don't cooperate."

Silence yet again.

Tedious.

I sigh.

"So, it's really your choice. How difficult do you want to make this? It doesn't have to be that bad."

"You won't shoot me in here. Blood splattered across every window will be obvious to anyone looking in this direction. You won't get out of the car covered in my blood. The real question is how difficult do *you* want to make this? Call the police and get a restraining order against me for stalking. I followed you to New York because I concocted a fantasy of us being together."

"Concocted a fantasy is right. You know I won't be the one to die. You know there isn't a chance in hell I'm going to the police about anything. Though you flatter me once again to suggest you'd stalk me for my pretty face or big dick. Why would I take out a restraining order to keep you five hundred feet from me when I can keep you away permanently without a paper trail?"

I've been told I give off BDE—big dick energy. I was told I was BMOC—big man on campus during college. I didn't let my family association keep me from playing Division One sports, captaining the chess club—yes, I'm a nerdy jock—or being treasurer of my frat. I would've run for student body president or president of my frat, but that was asking for too much attention. Why anyone thought they should allow me to be in charge of the money is beyond me, but I never stole from my frat brothers. I made them a shit ton of money instead.

"You're not going to let me get out of this car, so what I want is irrelevant. I'd say I'm being pretty fucking compliant right now."

"So, you're easy?"

That makes her snarl and glower at me.

I wink.

I can see her hands, and I expect them to twitch. Either with a desire to slap me or clench them into fists to keep from doing that. She does nothing. My free hand reaches toward her hair, and she finally reacts. She grabs my wrist and digs her nails into a pressure point. It might make a weaker person stop, but I've been trained to overcome my body's natural reaction to surrender. It's not that she's weak; I'm stronger.

I grasp the wig and tug. It doesn't move.

"Ouch." It's said with no bite.

I pull harder this time, and it still doesn't budge.

"Super glue?"

"Are you seven and in a school yard? Are you pulling my hair because you like me?"

"Like you? I wouldn't go that far. Want to fuck you?"

I leave that unanswered.

We're back to an impasse as we stare at each other. I acted on impulse and got into the car. I hadn't decided what I would do to or with her. I don't have a strategy, which is beyond unusual for me. I could've observed her observing me. I could've learned more by playing dumb. I'll likely live to regret this.

"You and I are going to have a far lengthier conversation than either of us wants while sitting in a car. You're going to take me to your hotel, and we'll talk there. You do *not* want me to choose our location."

If I do, it'll be the bodega on Long Island where we handle our most unsavory work. If she goes there, she'll never leave alive. I haven't decided if I need to do anything that extreme. I'd prefer not to torture her or kill her, but I reserve the right to change my mind.

"I'm not going anywhere with you."

"You can't get out of the car faster than I can shoot you. You can't draw a gun or knife faster than I can shoot you. And you can't shove a needle in me faster than I can shoot you. Turn on the engine, put the car in drive, and go."

I reach back for my seatbelt while I speak. While I'd be more comfortable not having to hold up my arm that has the gun pressed to her ribs, I can do it for hours. Another thing I was trained to do. The men in my family have the endurance of a woman in labor for seventy hours. We're trained to stay awake for days at a time. To stand or squat for hours, holding our arms out to the side, in front of us, or overhead. Sweaty palms or not, we can hang from a beam practically by our fingertips while a weight presses on them. As *the Cartel* family for generations, we'd be an anthropologist's wet dream.

"I suppose my choices are wait it out here until sundown when your men can drag me out of the car and stuff me in the trunk of another vehicle, or let them follow us, then drag me out."

"I'd never let anyone stuff you in a trunk, *chiquita*."

Her eyes widen a fraction at my adamance. Her gaze sweeps over me before she dips her chin.

"You'd torture me and confine me in some other kind of cage, just not the trunk of a car."

"Depending on how things go from now on, you'll discover whether you're right. Drive, Tiffani with an i."

"For fuck's sake." She mutters more than speaks, and I chuckle.

"If you don't like me calling you that, give me another name. Who would you have been at the club? Who were you at the O'Rourkes' gala?"

She swallows when I mention the last place I saw her. She thought I hadn't recognized her. I knew who she was the moment my gaze landed on her table. Every syndicate man's gaze sweeps our surroundings every couple of minutes. No one lets their situational awareness dull, especially not when our women and children are around. There aren't any kids in my family—for now—but my mother, aunts, and cousins-in-law were there.

"Since I haven't pretended not to know you, I suppose there's little point in denying I was at either of those places."

"There's no point at all. So, Tiffani with an i, what would you rather I call you?"

"I was Giselle at the club and Liz at the gala."

"Mmm. Giselle is certainly more fitting. Though, wouldn't it be Gisella?"

Her left index finger curls a centimeter on her lap, but it's a tell. I've mostly ruled out her being Latina, though she could be Brazilian. My guess is Italian or French, maybe Swiss. With current syndicate geopolitics, I'm leaning heavily toward Italian. It's just a question of where. Naples? Venice? Calabria? Sicily? Apulia?

So many choices from so many people who'd love to kill me. As long of as none of them touch my pretty face.

I want to roll my eyes at myself.

Threats either taunt me about not marking my supposed best feature, or that's the first thing they promise to shred. I'm more partial to my dick working than worrying about how straight my nose is. But if Cartel life doesn't work out, there's always *GQ*.

"Call me whatever you want. Will it really matter?"

"No, not since the only name that'll be screamed is mine."

She looks at me now. "You think we're going to fuck?"

"Such a dirty mind, *chica*. Though you'll be begging for mercy."

"You going to tie me up?"

My lips twitch as I fight not to laugh. "Tsk, tsk. Still thinking about sex at a time like this. Do you have a gun fetish?"

"You're the one talking about sex, not me, Alejandro."

"Mmm. Say it again."

"Se—"

"My name." I lean over and whisper it in her ear like a puff of air.

"Fuck off."

"There you go again. Sex, sex, sex. Is that all I'm good for? Uh-uh. My eyes are up here, *chiquita*."

I flexed my pecks, and I knew she'd naturally look down at the distraction.

"Arrogant ass."

"So, you've noticed that part of me too."

"Shoot me already."

"No. Drive."

When she does nothing, I move the gun to press against her carotid artery. A shot to the ribs wouldn't automatically kill her, but a shot to this part of her neck... That would definitely be messy. Her foot moves to the brake before she turns on the car, then her hands reach for the wheel, as she looks at me from the corner of her eye. Her pupils dilate as her fight or flight instinct kicks in for real.

"I'm going to reach back for my belt."

She eases her left hand off the wheel and reaches back. When she pulls the belt across her chest, I cover her hand and guide it to the buckle. Her hand's warm but not clammy. It's neither moist nor freezing from fear. She still thinks she has control. When her left hand returns to the wheel, her right reaches for the shifter, putting the vehicle in drive.

I allow her to concentrate as she pulls out of the parking lot and merges onto the street. My gaze sweeps over her, the windshield, and the side view mirrors over and over. My arm still isn't tired from holding up the gun, but it's an awkward angle for someone whose shoulders are as broad and arms are as long as mine.

Woe is me.

I suppose it could be worse.

After all, I could be the one with the gun pointed at me.

Dios mío.

She would be staying in Bay Ridge, about as far from Jackson Heights—in Queens—as you can get in Brooklyn. At best, this is a forty-five-minute drive. Today, it's close to an hour of silence. Neither of us makes small talk, and discussing anything more important isn't wise in a moving vehicle. Hitting a nerve might mean hitting the median if I piss her off too much. She seems a bit temperamental today.

My guys follow us in cars and motorcycles, so they surround us when she pulls into a spot. I'm not worried about her taking off while I get out of the car. I don't have "go, go Gadget" arms, and I'm not Gumbi, so I can't keep the gun on her as we move in opposite directions. Ah, the classic cartoons my parents let me watch. No Pokémon for me. I was such an underprivileged child.

My men herd her around the front of the car and toward me. I holster my gun at my lower back and slide my arm around her waist. My fingers slide beneath her shirt and the top seam of her jeans. If I weren't intimidating her, I'd appreciate how smooth her skin is. But I press my fingers into the front of her waist while my thumb does the same from the back. I'm not pinching, but I am steering her.

My guys hang back, and I know they'll fan out to surround the building. A couple will say they're waiting to meet a friend in the lobby. Not entirely a lie since they'll wait for me to return. We have this protection plan well-choreographed from years of practice. The guys in the lobby will watch where the elevator stops and radio the guy in the stairwell to tell him awhere to meet us. He'll stay by the emergency exit.

One of my guards searched her purse as we walked up to the

building, so I already have her key card. When we're at her door, I step behind her, reaching past her to swipe the piece of plastic against the sensor. I nudge her, and she presses down on the handle.

"You're really going to use me as a human shield?"

"Do you fear going first?"

"Not very machismo of you."

"*Chiquita*, I may want to fuck you, but I don't love you. I'm not protecting a woman being paid to kill me."

The words tumble out of my mouth, devoid of any softer sentiment, but I don't mean them. If I believed something on the other side of the door posed a threat, I wouldn't let her go in first. But she doesn't need to know that. I might not willingly endanger any woman, but she doesn't need to know that either. She needs to believe I'm treating her like any other mercenary. I'd have killed most already.

The bathroom door and closet doors stand open; a safety measure she took to ensure she didn't enter her room to a hidden surprise. It makes it easy for me to assess the situation, seeing no threat. I reach behind me and flip the deadbolt and latch. It might keep my men from coming to my rescue, but it also means the fucker from the other night or anyone else isn't coming to her defense.

She spins around, thinking she can take me by surprise as she attempts to wrap her ankle around the back of my lower calf to knock me off balance. My arm's still around her waist, so I merely lift her off her feet. She kicks my shins, but I don't flinch. I grew up playing soccer with cleats but not always shin guards. What can I say? My cousins and I were dumbasses trying to prove our *huevos* had dropped.

I shift and lift her higher, guiding her legs around my waist. It presses her pussy against my cock. Neither of us is surprised as I harden, but it keeps her from kicking me. I consider taking her to the bed, but I don't need her to panic. Instead, I walk over to the chair she definitely moved away from the window. With its arms and back curving as one piece, it traps her legs behind me. She's not getting off unless I let her.

Double entendre intended.

"Tell me who sent you."

Silence.

"Tell me you don't want me."

Silence.

My right hand trails up her thigh and slides around her hip to grasp her ass. She doesn't react. I squeeze—hard. Her hips nudge a fraction of an inch forward before she stops herself. She plays it off as though she's tempting me. She is, but I have control.

My other hand finally has the chance to enjoy her skin that's smoother than any satin I've felt. I feather my fingertips up both sides of her spine until I reach her bra clasp. Our gazes are locked, and I know she reads the desire in my eyes as clearly as I read it in hers. I inch my fingers beneath the band, and I feel her ass tense in a way that means she must have Kegeled. My hand on her ass presses her forward and harder against my dick.

My other hand's fully beneath her bra clasp now, my palm resting heavily against her back. I tilt my hips, pushing her higher onto my dick. Her hands go out to brace herself, resting on either side of my shoulders.

"Hands behind your back, *chica*."

She obeys but not before they trail down my shoulders, over my chest to my abs. My fingers turn to claws as I dig into her ass cheek. She squeaks and hurries to follow my command.

"Good girl."

Her nostrils flare, and I know she likes this. We both know we shouldn't—like it or do it. But this has been building for weeks.

"You could've tried to kill me at least six different ways since we came in here. Why haven't you?"

"At least eight, and I'm curious." She gives me a nonchalant one shoulder shrug.

"Curious to see how many other ways you can conceive of killing me? Or curious about how soon we'll fuck?"

"Very sure of yourself."

"As easily as you can feel how hard I am, I can feel the heat from your cunt through your jeans and my trousers."

We both know I can't, but she doesn't refute it. We both know I could slide my hand down the front of her jeans and panties and find her soaked. Her nipples poke against her bra and shirt.

Definitely not padded.

Having seen all but her nipples, I already know how endowed she is. Not obscenely or artificially. I wouldn't care if they were. My mouth's practically watering to taste them since they're at eye level.

"How about we play a little game, *chiquita?*"

"A game only you can win?"

"No. You can definitely win some rounds if you play nicely."

She cocks an eyebrow.

"For each piece of information you give me, I get to take off a piece of your clothes. I'll also get you another step closer to coming. We both win when you play along."

"And if I lie just to make you make me come?"

"I'll know you're lying, and I'll punish you. Not only will I edge you until you cry, I'll spank you until your ass burns like a five-alarm fire."

"Promise?"

She licks her lips and rolls her hips. Before she can anticipate it, I release her ass and bring my hand crashing down across the center of it. She yelps and jerks forward, moaning as her clit rubs against the seam of her jeans and my dick. Her breast comes to my mouth, and I snap my teeth next to her nipple with a growl.

I sound fucking feral.

You practically are.

Her hands remain behind her back, using her core strength and thighs to hold her up as her back curls toward me. I lick her nipple through her clothes.

"You ready for the rest of the rules, little one?"

She nods.

She has no words, and I'm fighting to find mine.

"When you agree to abandon the hit and help me kill your

boss, I'll fuck your tight little cunt all afternoon and through tonight. Then my breakfast will be peaches and cream."

"*Stronzo arrogante.*" Arrogant asshole.

"So, you're Venetian. Good to know."

I unfasten her bra with one hand before trailing my fingers around to beneath her breast. I crawl them up the front until my thumb's on her tightened nipple.

"Why do you—"

"Dropped consonants and those unique vowel sounds, almost singsongy. All characteristically Venetian."

"That could be one of my many personas."

"But it's not. You muttered it too naturally. Even if Italian were your second language from childhood, it still wouldn't have sounded that natural. It's the language you think in."

"Trained linguist?"

"Close study of human nature." I shrug. "I'm observant."

"You're a native New York Spanish speaker. You grew up using English and Spanish interchangeably, but you don't have quite the same Colombian accents as your relatives who grew up there."

"Should I be jealous of how much time you've spent studying my uncles and cousins? Don't tell me you're after my *papá*."

"You look more like Enrique."

"And I'm certain you already know my *tía* Elodie. You know how unwise that mistake would be."

"Why would I know her?"

"No, no, *chica*. Not your turn to ask questions unless you're trying to get me naked too. Shirt off. Lies will get you spankings."

"I didn't answer a question for you."

"But you did. I asked if I should be jealous of my uncles and cousins. You'd prefer *Tío* Enrique, but you'll settle for me. Shirt off."

"That wasn't what I meant."

"You still answered. Shirt—off."

I won't force her. Instead, I rest both hands on her thighs, my thumbs sweeping along the inside of her legs. She studies me for more than a minute—I started counting the seconds after at least fifteen passed. Then she teases me as she unbuttons the shirt as slowly as she can. I'm the one who set myself up for a tortuously slow striptease, but I know what lies beneath her clothes. It's worth waiting until the end of time.

She lets it slide down her arms until it pools over my knees. My left hand fists the front of her jeans and yanks toward me while my right hand pushes her bra cup down. I won't take it off since I said one piece of clothing at a time, but with it unfastened, it makes it easy for me to latch on. I flick her nipple twice, then sweep my tongue around her areola before practically inhaling her breast. I torment the tight nub, and both of her hands go to my head.

Her fingers burrow into my hair, and I allow it just long enough for her to commit the sin. I pull back and slap her wet breast. She yelps.

"Alejandro—"

"Sir. You are not my friend, Gisella. I much prefer that to Tiffani or Liz. You are my captive, at my mercy for pleasure and pain. I didn't say you could touch me."

I already have a deep voice, but it drops at least an octave to what I sound like as a Dom. Her belly sucks in, pushing her chest out. She recognizes the tone.

Even better. She fucks rough and can obey.

When she wants to.

When she doesn't, she knows how to accept punishment.

Fucking perfection.

The thoughts whizz through my head, and I'll come embarrassingly fast if she touches my dick with any part of her bare skin.

"Yes, sir."

She moves her hands back to where they were, crossing them at the wrists again.

"Next question. When did you accept the job?"

I want to know how long she's had to prepare for the mission. How long she studied me before making contact in Chicago.

She hesitates to answer, so I return my lips to her nipple. I toy with it before sucking. When her back arches rather than her hands going to my head, I bite. Not hard enough to break the skin, but enough to shatter the lust haze when I do nothing to soothe her. I sit back and clasp my hands behind my head, appearing far more casual than a suspect waiting for the police to cuff them.

"Answer me, and I'll go back to the pleasure. Deny me, and I will punish you again."

That confidence I love sparks in her eyes, and I know she's weighing her options. I'm impatient though. I pinch and twist her nipple before tugging.

"Sir!"

"Want to give me that answer now?"

"Not particularly."

I push down the other cup and pinch both nipples before tugging, elongating them.

"Hmm. Have I found a new little painslut to play with?"

Her hands whip around to push against my chest, but I wrap mine around her wrists. I tug her forward then press her hands to her lower back. I hold her wrists in my left hand as my right tunnels into her hair, guiding her mouth to mine. It all happens in a matter of seconds. I don't know if her moan or my groan is louder as we dive into the kiss. It's not long before I'm unsatisfied with her not touching me. I'm gentle as I guide her hands back to my chest.

Mine are softer as they hold onto her hips, guiding her to dry hump me. The kiss draws on as we grind against each other, finally giving in to what we've wanted since we met. It would only go from good to great—hell, sublime—if I were inside her right now. We can't get enough of each other as our tongues twist and curl.

When we pull apart, my five o'clock shadow's abraded her lips and chin. If my fingers haven't marked her, then my stubble has. It feeds a possessiveness I shouldn't have.

"Good girl, *chiquita.*" I cup her cheek with a foreign surge of affection.

"Don't call me that ever again. I prefer it when—" She cuts herself off.

"I won't, little one. Are you familiar with the term though?"

"Yes. Whether I am or am not one doesn't matter to me."

"Shh, *chica*. I won't call you a slut or a whore. Cunt is a body part, not who or what you are. I'm sorry."

My apology stuns us both. It could put the power in our dynamic in her hands, but my regret takes the wind out of her sail. My thumb strokes over her cheek, and I'm tempted to end this game. I test the waters as I slip her bra down her arms. She doesn't fight me.

"Thank you for answering my question."

She swallows, and goosebumps form on her arms. It's not cold in here.

Is she nervous about the next item to come off?

Is she embarrassed to be half naked when it isn't dark in here?

Is she regretting this?

Does she fear what'll come next?

I don't know the answer to any of those.

"Do you want to stop, *chica*?"

"No, sir."

"Will you let me make you come?"

"I need you to."

"That doesn't tell me if you will."

She reaches back and unzips her left ankle boot and pulls it off, along with her sock, letting them drop to the floor. She does the same to the right shoe and sock. I'd asked two questions. Adding to her pile of discarded clothes is her answer.

"Will you set aside your mission and help me kill your boss?"

It's a big ask, so I waited for a big piece of clothing. If she answers, her jeans will come off next.

"You might fuck me all night and into tomorrow, but that won't save my life when I leave a failure. Orgasms don't pay rent. At least, not when I'm receiving rather than giving."

I grit my teeth. I hate the idea of her giving anyone other than me an orgasm. I hate the idea of her paying for anything through sex.

Yes, I see my hypocrisy. I don't need anyone to point it out.

I'm forcing her to buy her freedom by obliging my freaky-deaky game. I'm a sick fuck. I guide her to stand up and unfasten her jeans. She pushes them down on her own. I might come just looking at her. I catch a whiff of her arousal along with her floral perfume. It's a heady combination. I want my head between her thighs.

She remains standing.

"Will you let me save you?"

Chapter Eight

Vita

Will I let him save me?

From him?

From my employer?

From myself?

I stare blankly. He's already a guy I can't fuck and forget about. I'd be out of my mind to trust him.

"Save me? Are you planning my death by orgasm?"

I glide my right fingers up the outside of my thigh and move them toward my pussy. He snatches them away and holds my arm out to the side.

"Uh-uh, *chica*. I didn't give you permission to touch any part of yourself. You may have answered my question with questions, but that's still an answer."

He releases my wrist to slip his fingers beneath the waistband of my thong. He fists it and pulls. When I take a step forward, his long legs cage me.

"Be a good *chiquita* and take off your panties."

I open my mouth to refuse, but his dark eyes bore into me. Staring into the pools of whiskey is intoxicating.

Does he have mind control powers?

I want to obey more than my rational mind can insist this is beyond fucked-up.

"Remember what awaits you if you play along."

I'm practically salivating at the idea that he'll make me come. I want to know how so badly that I'm biting my tongue to keep from asking. I know he won't tell me—at least, not the truth. I make the most of it and shimmy the thong down my hips, teasing him as I do it. Once it's around my ankles, I step out of it and kick it behind me. He lifts me to straddle his lap, my bent legs resting over his. My shins press into his thighs, and my ankles cross just like my wrists.

"If only you'd given me a proper answer to my last question."

His right hand lands across my ass even harder than the earlier spank.

"Ow!"

Fuck!

Fuck to the pain, and fuck to me reacting aloud.

I'm prepared for the second one, but I'm not ready when his hands work in tandem—one spanking me, and the other rubbing my clit.

"Care to give me a proper answer? Will you let me save you?"

"You can save me from death by edging."

He chuckles, and the sound makes my pussy burn with an ache that began the night we met. My vibrator hasn't done shit to help. I turned down Patrick's offer to hook up. Tempting as it was because I knew he'd get me off more than once, it didn't appeal to me. I only want Alejandro.

I must be clinically insane. Truly.

"Come on, Gisella—"

"Vittoria."

"What?"

"My name's Vittoria. It seems pointless to use an alias when you know what I am and why I'm here."

"Sharing your real name makes me think you believe you'll die today."

I bark a laugh.

"Hardly. I'll live to see another sunrise. Now that you've seen me up close and in good lighting, and you figured out my accent, you'll discover who I am. No point in keeping up pretenses."

"Then tell me who sent you. It's better if it comes from you than finding out from the dark web."

He'd stopped spanking me while we talked, but he didn't stop rubbing my clit. It's a steady circular motion that's making me so wet I fear I'm dripping on his trousers.

"I don't give information away for free."

"I didn't expect you to. I told you earlier that if you cooperate, I'll give you orgasms all night."

"That's not the only currency I accept. I prefer dollars or euros."

I try to shift off his lap, but he spanks me again. This time, it isn't my ass. It's my pussy. The slap lands, shooting a blaze of fire through my clit. The heel of his hand is firm as his fingers dip inside me to the first knuckle. I desperately want to come.

"Agree to my help, and I'll make you come. Tell me who sent you, and I'll make you come. Admit you're ready to sell your soul to feel me inside you, and I'll make you come."

Each statement has an accompanying spanking across my ass. His index and middle fingers slide into me as his thumb returns to rubbing my clit.

"Answer my questions, and I'll give you an orgasm—sir."

"I'm not worried about getting off. I will when I fuck you, and I don't have to tell you a damn thing to do it."

He lifts me high against his ribs as he stands. He's unfastening his belt and pants as his forearms support my weight. I wish he were naked, so I could see his raw strength through his rippling muscles.

"Let me go into the bathroom. I have condoms in my toiletry bag."

"No need. Since running into you at the club, then at the gala, I've started going out prepared. I knew this day would come."

"I need—"

"To find a way to drug me? How will you hide a syringe when you're naked? I won't drink anything you give me, so no powders or tablets to dissolve."

He lays me down on the bed but doesn't climb on with me. I'd wrapped my legs around him on instinct, even though I knew he wouldn't drop me. He reaches back and unhooks my ankles.

"Vita, no means no. I won't force you. If you want this to stop, it will."

Vita?

I've been called Toria before but never Vita. I loathe Vitto and Vitti. One sounds like a man's name, and the other sounds like an Italian greyhound's name.

Here, Vitti, Vitti.

Fuck off.

"I don't want this to stop. But I also don't fuck without protection. I didn't know you had any. I was being responsible."

He turns his head a fraction and looks down at me as if to admonish me with "Don't bother lying."

He leans to his left and slides his hand under the pillow. Instinct tells me to roll and reach for him, but he's larger and faster than me. He finds the knife I hid there when I arrived. I don't have housekeeping come in unless I must. I make my bed to look like they have, but I don't want strangers around my stuff.

He stretches and flips away the farther pillow. I let my eyes drift closed as I exhale. When I open them, he looks no more surprised to see the gun than he did the knife. Occupational hazards I'm certain he's used to. He loosens his tie and lifts it over his head. He moves to slide it over my eyes, but I use my heels on the edge of the mattress to push myself away.

"No."

"Fine."

He rests his fists next to my shoulders, and he climbs onto the bed, kneeling on his right leg. His left sweeps over mine, pressing against it and sandwiching it between his. I move slowly as I raise my hands to push off his suit coat. He shifts his weight from one arm to another as I help him. He tosses it on the end of the bed. His lips once more devour me as I unbutton his shirt.

It's the promised land as my fingers travel from his waist up to his shoulders and down again as he nuzzles my neck. I usually hate being licked, but it makes me purr when Alejandro trails his tongue from my jaw to my collarbone. Being naked beneath him when he's still clothed is about the hottest thing ever.

"What?!"

I'm wholly unprepared for his hands to wrap around my lower ribs and lift me to turn me on the bed, my head landing where a pillow was. He climbs fully onto the bed, his body hovering over mine. His left hand trails up my leg as his right forearm bears his weight. When he gets to my hip, he lifts the hand from his bicep and kisses my knuckles before lacing his fingers with mine.

This is like something out of a steamy romantic movie. Way hotter than some choreographed porn.

He raises my hand over my head, shifting his weight to grasp the other one. I'm punch drunk as he kisses the opposite side of my neck from before, lavishing attention everywhere.

But it all comes crashing down.

Once he has both hands above my head, he snatches his tie from where he'd conveniently left it as he settled me onto the mattress, positioned exactly where he wanted. His tie wraps around my wrists and tightens like a noose. With a tug, he rolls me onto my belly and drags me to the edge of the bed. He forces my head to hang off the edge as he uses his tie to fasten me to the drawer handle of the bedside table.

"What the fuck?!"

I'm saying it to him as much as I'm saying it to myself. How could I have lowered my guard enough to let this happen? How did I let him get the better of me so smoothly?

This was all a production to manipulate me into what he really wanted—access to my room and me out of the way. This shit is supposed to be the other way around! *I'm* the one who uses men for access and secrets.

I'm pissed at myself as much as I'm pissed at him. My only

consolation is I can see he's still sporting the hard-on he's had since he pulled me onto his lap the first time. He didn't lie when he said he'd edge me. I'm as aroused as he is, but he definitely doesn't appear to suffer the way I am. Even with this shit he just pulled, I want to fuck him into next week.

You are a sad, sick, little bitch.

So what if I am?

"Vita, tell me what I want to know, and I don't search your room. Don't tell me, and I'll tear it apart from your clothes to the fixtures. Decide."

I shoot him a mutinous glare, straining my neck to twist my head to see him. I roll my eyes and rest my head on my arm as he turns away from me. He's systematic, I'll give him that. He moves to the far corner diagonally across from me, sweeping his hands over the wall. He stands on the chair to reach the ceiling and squats to touch where the baseboards meet the carpet.

He goes around the entire room, pulling the armoire and dresser away from the wall. He practically pulls the headboard from the wall when he tries to examine the space behind it. He feels every inch of all the furniture, leaving nothing unnoticed.

He takes a risk when he slips his shoes off and shuffles over all the carpet he can reach. Who knows what I could have left to spike his foot. But I didn't booby-trap the room since I hadn't planned to let anyone else in. He lifts out my clothes one piece at a time, checking every hem and every seam, turning pockets inside out. He barely keeps from ripping the lining of my luggage.

He moves into the bathroom, and I can only hear him moving around. Undoubtedly, he's as thorough in there as he was in the main part of the hotel room. I even hear him lift the lid off the toilet bowl and unscrew the showerhead. He returns to stand beside the bed.

"The only thing left, *chiquita*, is a cavity search."

"I've never had a cavity in my life. I brush and floss." I lift my head as I speak, radiating defiance.

"You didn't mind my tongue inside your mouth, and I'm

certain you wanted my fingers deeper in your pussy. My dick in your ass is my preferred way to search you."

"You're vile."

"Says the woman here to kill me. I think I'm entitled to some shock factor when I'm facing my would-be executioner."

If he weren't saying it to intimidate me, I'd gladly accept the offer. Anal may not be my favorite, but I'm not opposed to it. I wouldn't be opposed to most things with him. No extra taboo kinks, but we both know I enjoy him spanking and edging me. At least I did until twenty minutes ago.

"You found nothing. Let me go."

"But I promised you you'd come all day and all night. I wouldn't lie to you. Scouts honor."

I snort.

"Since when is Berto short for Alejandro? And where'd your Southern accent go, sugar?"

I exaggerate the second sentence, making it sound as sweet as jasmine and mint julep on a hot summer day.

He unties me from the bedside table, but he doesn't untie my wrists. At least he lets me lower my arms after he helps me roll onto my back. He props me up against the headboard. Strands from my wig stick to my lip. He's careful as he lifts them off, then tucks hair behind my ears.

"I'll let you loose long enough to take the horrendous wig off and pop out those contacts."

"Why should I show you the real me?"

"Because I just let you see how I am."

"Strategic? Manipulative? Arrogant?"

"Vita, I could've killed you a couple dozen times over since we met. I could've beaten you senseless and dropped your body in the worst part of the Bronx. Better yet, the East River. I could've bound and gagged you the moment we walked in here."

"No. You used sex to manipulate me."

"Like you didn't do the same damn thing. You believe I found nothing in the bathroom, but I did. I found the insulin I'm certain isn't yours. No glucose monitor anywhere. It's what you wanted when you claimed you had condoms—which we know I found in one of your purses, not the bathroom. You would've told me you suddenly didn't feel well and needed to give yourself a shot. You would've banked on me checking on you or at least being close enough to surprise me. You would've stuck the needle anywhere you could reach. There are enough vials in there to put me in a coma. Once I was disoriented and dizzy enough, you would've gone back for more and shot me up until I passed out. Hell, that's assuming it's even insulin. I'm inclined to think it's some sedative and nerve blocker."

"That's a lot of speculation."

"Not when we both know I found your Taser. The one you had at the gala. The one you planned to use when you followed me out of the ballroom."

"Again, speculation. I was with Patrick, but New York is a dangerous city. As you can imagine, I have enemies. I carry it for self-defense. Shooting bullets isn't always inconspicuous."

"Bullshit."

We stare at each other as he sits beside me on the bed. I could've gotten out of the binding around my wrist while he searched my room, but the short-lived freedom would've been futile. I'm naked after all.

"I'll ask you a third time. Will you let me save you?"

Chapter Nine

Alejandro

I know the third time won't be the charm. I wish it were.

Mercy isn't an emotion I indulge in. It's pointless in my life. At least, most of the time it is. I didn't exaggerate when I said I could've killed Vita a couple dozen ways since meeting her. I could've made a show of it or done it so covertly, she wouldn't even know she was dying. But I can't bring myself to even plot a single way.

I don't want her dead.

Just the opposite. I've never wanted to ensure a mercenary remained alive. I don't know what drove her to this life. I can't think of many people who grow up wanting to be one.

A vigilante, yes.

A mercenary, no.

I want to know everything about her. The driving curiosity is as foreign as the mercy. She intrigues me in a way no one—man, woman, or child—ever has. I want to discover her past and am eager to hear and see what she'll do next.

These emotions signal imminent death. My death.

It's dangerous to entertain any of them, yet I don't stop myself.

But I'm equally disappointed that she won't accept my help, even if I'm not surprised.

Her mission'll fail. There's a good chance her employer will put a hit on her to silence her. I don't know what her success rate or body count are, but I know they must be high. She's too experienced to think otherwise. But I'm her last target unless she accepts my help.

My protection.

And that's the last thing she'll admit she needs.

"Your silence in your answer, *chiquita*. 'Pride goes before destruction, a haughty spirit before a fall.'"

"You paid attention in Sunday School."

"And Catholic elementary school. My sins started early. My first crush was on a nun."

She stares at me, uncertain whether I'm joking.

The woman was only a postulant—a nun-in-training.

"'Put not your trust in princes, nor in the son of man, in whom there is no help.' I paid attention too, Alejandro."

"You assume I'm lying. That I'll play you for a fool."

"You most likely will."

"Why bother? Like I said, you could already be dead if I wanted. Do you think I'm toying with you?"

"You said this was all a game."

"The striptease, not your life."

She shrugs a shoulder. I get nothing more. Since she's nearly in the center of the bed, I pull back the covers. She lifts her hips, staring at me in confusion. I pull them back over her, tucking them beneath her arms. Such a shame to hide such magnificent tits that tasted like the jasmine she mentioned earlier.

"You'll get cold. Since I won't untie you to put a shirt on, this is the best you're getting."

"You could let me put on a pair of pants if you're not going to make me come."

"You're just using me for my body." I waggle my eyebrows.

"Not all of it. Just your fingers and your dick." Her expression appears so innocent despite the dirty things she says.

"A mind is such a terrible thing to waste."

"We can go tit-for-tat with scripture and slogans. I'm bored. Turn on the TV."

If she genuinely meant her dismissiveness, it would hurt. I like our sparring.

"Frustrated that you're losing, *princesa?* Or should I say *principessa?*"

"Your accent's nearly passable."

I only have a smattering of Italian. Pablo's the one who speaks it. He also speaks Russian. *Tio* Enrique and Jorge have French and German covered. Javier speaks Japanese and Korean. Joaquin speaks Mandarin, Vietnamese, and Cambodian. *Tio* Luis and I speak Brazilian and European Portuguese. We have all our major trade partners and rivals covered.

The only one we haven't bothered with is Irish. Those pissant O'Rourkes aren't worth understanding. We run our own guns, and no one in my family likes whiskey. We prefer our Colombian *aguardiente*—fire water. It's a lower proof than whiskey, but at least the anise-flavor doesn't taste like ass.

As I watch Vita, I know I wouldn't mind licking hers. That's usually not my thing, but if she enjoyed it, I would.

"You're just annoyed that you aren't winning, *chiquita.* Not our war of words or the race to see me dead."

I walk around to the other side of the bed as I slip off my already unbuttoned shirt. I haven't bothered fastening my pants. Seems rather pointless since the woman I'm with is completely naked. Vita watches my every move, and she's not unaffected when she sees all of my permanently sun-kissed torso covered in tats. My physique is the result of necessity. I work out twice a day most days because I often lift heavy crates or my relatives and run for my life. It doesn't hurt when I want to get laid.

I'm not indiscriminate with my partners. Just the opposite. I don't date, and I don't do random hookups. I like my sex rough and kinky. That's not for everyone, so I satisfy myself at my BDSM club. All the men in the Four Families have the same proclivities. I suppose it allows us to exert the control we crave—

also out of necessity—while doing it constructively. Compared to our usual need for control, it's a far healthier outlet.

There's a finite number of clubs in the tri-state area, so our memberships overlap. So does our silent ownership. Now that most of my generation is married, we're far more careful about not overlapping our visits. We used to maintain neutrality and pretend like we didn't know each other when we ran into each other. For the sake of the wives, through mutual silent agreement, we do our best to uphold their privacy with preferred days of the week. Some couples have their own playrooms at their homes and don't frequent the clubs often.

"What're you doing?"

Vita's brow furrows as I recline on the bed. I glance at her before shifting to reach over her for the remote on her bedside table. She knows I could've picked it up before moving to my side of the bed. I take the opportunity to kiss her, nipping at her bottom lip as my fingers wrap around the controller. I kiss along her jaw until I reach her ear. My voice's a whisper after tugging her earlobe between my teeth.

"You wanted to watch TV."

I shift back to my side, shoving a pillow behind me. I didn't give Vita that comfort. I turn on the TV and flip through the channels unsure of what's even on these days. I settle for a *telenovela* my *abuela* would watch when she visited. I don't care if Vita understands. It's oddly comforting to me.

Vita. Life in Italian.

Why do I call her that?

Because she could hold my life in her hands?

Because thoughts of her monopolize my life now?

Because she could be the love of my life?

That last thought is disturbing enough to make me want to jump off the bed like it's ablaze.

Be real. You knew you wanted her from the night you met. You wouldn't have called her chiquita if you didn't. Your instinct could've been wrong, but you haven't stopped calling her that. You know what it means to the men in our family.

No man in my family calls a woman that unless she's "the one."

I've had weeks to consider how irrational that is. Hell. I spent the entire flight to and from Belize weighing my options. She's determined to refuse me, and I'm determined to make her mine—without keeping her tied up to do it.

Days in syndicate life are like years in a normal person's life. When you have to decide whether to live or die in a matter of seconds—when how fast you can draw a gun or knife determines the rest of your life—the luxury of days and weeks is a rare gem.

"Lost in thought?" Her voice surprises me because I was.

"No. Getting caught up on my favorite show."

She chuckles. "You are drawn to melodramatics."

I shoot her a wry smile. "Hardly."

She raises her hands and looks over at the bedside table.

"That was practicality."

"Mhmm."

I place my hands behind my head much like I did when I sat in the chair. I contract my abs as I cross one ankle over the other. I'm the picture of overindulged ennui. The playboy I'm often accused of.

"When will you let me go, Alejandro?"

"When I get bored. Shh. My show's on."

Five minutes pass before she raises her hands and points to a man on TV. "He's going to get slapped before the end of the scene."

"You understand Spanish?"

"I don't have to, to know it's nearing the end of the episode, and no one else has been."

"Ouch, *chica*. Such stereotypes."

I haven't even finished the last word when an actress hauls back and lands a ringing slap against the guy's face.

"Hmph."

It's not like it was unexpected. *Novelas* usually have at least one physical confrontation. It's also no surprise when the couple falls into each other's arms for a passionate kiss. Vita and I turn to look at each other at the same moment. Art reflects life.

When did you become a man of so many clichés?

When my life turned into one.

We watch three more shows before Vita's lids droop. I don't believe for a moment that she's sleepy. Even if she were, she wouldn't lower her guard enough to fall asleep with me here. But I'll play along. I slide down the bed when she does. I roll onto my stomach and watch her as I drape my heavy arm over her belly.

"What're you—"

"Why not take a nap? I usually don't have so much free time."

"You're not going to shackle me again?"

"And I'm the melodramatic one. Shh, *chiquita*. Rest. If you behave, I'll keep you up all night."

"I've heard that one before."

"Just because I haven't made you come yet doesn't mean I lied. We have plenty of time ahead of us."

I pull her closer and shift the pillow to share it with her. She tries to roll onto her side, but I don't let her. Being on her side would make it far easier for her to back away from me. I watch as she closes her eyes. I told her earlier to take out the contacts and take off the wig, but I didn't make her.

I wonder what her real hair looks like. I wonder about its length, its color, its texture. I wonder what color her eyes really are. They've been a different hue each time I've seen her. She might've changed the most recognizable features, but she didn't disguise her pert nose or cupid's bow lips. I'd recognize those anywhere.

I noticed the tiny dark freckle on the top and toward the end of her left shoulder the night we were on the yacht. I see it now. I'd recognize that too. I know what's beneath the covers. I've touched her and etched her into my memory. Blindfold me, and I'd still know it was her just by touch.

I close my eyes and slow my breathing. It's at least an hour before she moves more than to breathe. It's subtle, but I can tell she brings her hands up to her mouth. I'm certain she's using her teeth to release the tie. Her movements are slow so as not to disturb me. It would work if I were asleep. But I'm not. I was foolish to be so impetuous today, but I'm not foolish enough to sleep anywhere near my enemy.

It takes her several minutes, but I know when she gets loose. She remains still for at least another twenty minutes. She's patient. I'll give her that. Like a tortoise escaping a fox, she's slow but purposeful with each movement until she's free of my arm. Once I know she can't see my face, I open my eyes a crack. She's silent as she moves, but I sense where she is. She gathers her discarded clothes and rushes to put them on.

I watch as she scans the room for the things she most needs. She can't get the gun or the knife she hid beneath the pillows because they're too close to me. That wasn't an accident. She evaluates what she's willing to leave behind, knowing she must abandon this hotel. She hurries into the bathroom, and I'm certain it's to get the syringes and vials of insulin.

I didn't force her to share the room safe's code. I knew she'd open it eventually, whether I insisted or she did it while trying to escape. I close my eyes almost entirely, but I see her from beneath my lashes. I knew she'd check over her shoulder while pressing the buttons, fearing it would beep when it unlocked. I pretend not to notice. She withdraws a gun, money, and passports that she shoves in her purse. The last thing she does is grab the keycard from the top of the dresser.

I hear her swing the latch away from the door, and the bolt turns as she presses down on the handle. I know what awaits her on the other side.

"Going somewhere, *señorita?*"

My eyes snap open, and I laugh. She knew I was awake but gambled on my overconfidence, thinking I'd still get her, while she planned to reach the door before I could move. Vita stumbles backward, and Pablo follows her into the room. His gaze darts to me, and I laugh again when he rolls his eyes.

"*Vuelve a ponerte la camisa, pituso.*" Put your shirt back on, pretty boy.

I've been hearing the colloquialism since I was a tween. It's my turn to roll my eyes as I sit up. Vita whirls around as I reach for my shirt. I pull it on, then fasten my pants as I stand. I don't bother with the belt.

"What the fuck?"

"Pleased to meet you too, *señorita*."

Pablo, followed closely by Javier, is the least charming member of my family. His wife adores him and thinks his brooding is his most redeeming quality. She's the only one. *Tres J's* saw the most fucked-up shit growing up in Bogotá without a dad for several years. It scarred them and jaded them. I've done fucked-up shit working mostly alone in Latin America.

But Pablo—he was a sweet kid who had any gentleness exorcised from him as my generation's chief enforcer. He doles out the worst punishments because of his role as heir to Latin America's wealthiest and deadliest cartel. He's been building his reputation since he was a teen in preparation for when he becomes *jefe de jefes*.

Tío Enrique had to do the same thing when he was younger. Except Pablo's already in his thirties, and our mutual *tío* will likely live at least another twenty years. Our mutual *abuelo*—grandfather—died when our *tío* was in his early twenties. Our *tío's* ruled most of the Western Hemisphere's underworld for more than three decades.

Fuck Salvatore Mancinelli and his claim of dominance. They're close in age and ruled for nearly the same amount of time. I'll give Salvatore his due for controlling all the Mafia branches in the US, and his word is law in most of Sicily. But he doesn't have the clout my *tío* does. Nobody does.

"What're you doing here?" Venom drips from Vita's words, and she practically snarls when I answer for my cousin.

"I invited him. I had plenty of time while snooping through your toiletries. *Primo*, sorry for making you wait so long." Cousin.

"I heard the *novela* in here, so I watched it on my phone. I love how you can skip watching for a few years, then pick up right where you left off. Reminds you of *Abuela*, doesn't it?"

"*Sí.*"

Despite the situation, Pablo and I exchange a glance. We both miss our *abuela*. She was a wonderful woman who spoiled us as much as she threatened us. If anyone could've wielded a *chancla* like a machete, it was that woman. But she never needed to. She had *the look*. It conjured more guilt than any priest or nun could and made you obey faster than thumb screws would.

Vita's backed herself against the wall on the far side of the dresser and armoire. She can watch both Pablo and me, and neither of us can sneak up behind her. Not that it matters. I'm certain she can defend herself. She might even be a match for Pablo or me.

But the two of us?

Not a chance in hell or heaven.

"What're you going to do to me?"

Before I can answer—Pablo will defer to me, especially now that he's seen Vita and me together—the window shatters. I'm across the room and yanking Vita against me as I drop to the floor. I glance up at Pablo and see blood blossoming on his shirt as more glass breaks from at least two other shots.

"*Puta madre!* That burns like a mother no matter how many times it happens." Motherfucker!

"*Primo!*"

"I'm not dying. It's in my clavipectoral triangle."

"Okay, Dr. Science. Did it go straight through your pec groove?"

My cousin's a highly trained biologist and chemist. Like Harvard, then Cambridge, then MIT. He's into scientific accuracy.

"Yeah."

"Then grab a shirt and put pressure on it while you look for the bullet."

"Me? For fuck's sake, *Primo*. I just got shot."

I glance down at Vita, whose gaze is darting between Pablo and me. She's probably wondering what the fuck is wrong with us. Nobody likes getting shot. But you get used to it.

"El Tigre? Patrón?"

One of our guys hammers on the door, calling out to Pablo, then me. The Tiger is one of Pablo's titles. In the Cartel, the Tiger is the *jefe's* top general. Since we're not on a mission, our man doesn't call me brigadier—as in the lowest rank of a general—or the lesser rank of *capo*—captain. Since I run Bogotá, even from a distance, I've earned the title *patrón*. Because my cousins and I have so many roles, the titles can get confusing. When in doubt, the men choose the highest ranking one for the situation.

"Le dispararon al Tigre. Tenemos que irnos." The Tiger's been shot. We need to go.

I rise enough to crouch before guiding Vita toward the door. We both draw our guns. Me from my lower back holster, and her from her purse. I push her forward as I reach out for Pablo. He hunches over as he squats. I apply pressure over the shirt he found in a drawer.

"The bullet."

Vita points toward the wall behind where Pablo stood. We see an indentation, but nothing's protruding. She hurries over as she reaches inside her purse. She pulls out a cosmetic bag and unzips it. From it, she produces a pair of tweezers. Another rummage in her purse leads to a tiny bag. The kind you'd put powder or pills in. It must be clean since she drops the bullet in without touching it. She presses the bag closed and sticks out her arm, offering the evidence to me.

I grab it as I pass her. I open the door and practically shove Pablo through it before turning back to Vita. My hand clasps her wrist as I nearly drag her from the room. I want them both safe before I consider what to do next. Once I know they'll both live, I'll light this motherfucking city up to find out who shot at my *primo* and my *chiquita*.

Chapter Ten

Vita

Being shot at through a fifth-floor window wasn't on my bingo card for today.

What the ever-loving fuck?

That shocked me.

I was doubly shocked at how fast Alejandro dove toward me and shielded me.

I was triply shocked that he teased his cousin, who was practically spurting blood from his chest. Neither man was alarmed by the injury.

What kinda pincushions have they been? It didn't faze either of them.

Or they're that well trained they can't show fear or pain.

That's monumentally fucked-up either way.

I've been shot twice, and I definitely wasn't feeling chatty either time. I barely kept from passing out, which would've been worse than the bullet. My pursuers definitely would've caught and killed me. Pablo's weaving a little, but he's upright and walking on his own.

"Jaime, get him to Madeline. She doesn't have a shift, but I don't know if she's home. Call Javier and *Tío* Luis. Do *not* call *Tía* Margherita yet. I'll take the blame."

"Definitely don't tell *Mamá* yet. She'll skin me alive for getting hurt."

"I'm taking Vita to the safehouse in Greenwich."

Pablo looks over his shoulder at Alejandro now that he's upright and can staunch the bleeding himself. He observes how Alejandro's arm's wrapped around my shoulders. Alejandro whispers to me what'll happen.

"Madeline's my cousin Javier's wife. She's a midwife, but she's removed plenty of bullets before. We trust our men to get him to my cousin's house safely. When we reach the lobby, our men will be waiting outside the elevator. The men who waited in the hallway with Pablo already radioed the rest of them."

No one speaks in the elevator. We step off, and the Cartel men surround Pablo, Alejandro, and me. While Pablo and Alejandro are taller than some of the men, I veritably disappear among the huddle. When we reach the first SUV, Alejandro gives Pablo the bullet I collected.

"He'd normally be the one to collect fingerprints and DNA, but considering he's about to go into surgery or at least get patched up, one of *Tres J's* will do it—while Pablo bitches that they're doing it wrong."

The four men who must've come with Pablo climb into the SUV with him. The men who came with Alejandro continue to encircle him and me. There's a second SUV waiting. My guess is it's what Alejandro rode in to get to Jackson Heights. There's a vehicle leading and one following. They'll ensure no other cars get too close until Pablo goes in one direction toward Queens, and Alejandro and I go in another toward Connecticut.

Once we're inside the vehicle with the doors shut, Alejandro reaches across me for my seatbelt. It's not that I can't do it myself, but it feels like his protectiveness is on high alert. Once again, he whispers to me, his mouth so close to my ear that the warm breath makes me want to shiver. He doesn't want anyone overhearing him.

"I downplayed my fear for Pablo just like he downplayed his own. Neither of us wanted to alarm the others nor give away how dire it might be. The physical and mental fortitude it takes is beyond a normal person's capacity. I won't take any chances with you, *chiquita*. I won't hide that. I need to personally ensure you're safely fastened in, or my adrenaline'll only keep surging."

I watch him, then capture his hands as he pulls away. I keep my voice as low as his, not wanting the men to hear me.

"Alejandro, I'm all right. Been here, done this before. Nothing happened to me."

"It could've. It's my fau—"

"You don't know that. You know what I am. There's no more speculation. This could've been entirely about me. It could be a reminder to hurry up or a punishment for not completing the job. It could be retribution for any number of crimes I've committed. It was my hotel room they targeted."

"With Pablo and me in it."

"That could've been a coincidence."

"Or motive."

"Neither of us has an answer to that. Why do you and Pablo fear his mother so much?"

He knows I'm changing the subject to keep us from a pointless argument neither of us can win. He indulges me as he shares a story that makes the hair on my arms stand up.

"Pablo's father will hover worse than a brooding hen, but his mother will wage a one-woman war until she finds who hurt her son. Pablo's younger brother, Juan, died for his sins against the bratva. It surprised none of us, even if we still grieve the loss of a family member. Only my *tío* and *tía* miss him. The rest of us sometimes miss the boy he once was but never the man he became. But with only one son left, my *tío* and *tía* won't survive losing Pablo too."

Alejandro looks beyond me and out the window for a moment, lost to some memory. Maybe he's fighting to keep his composure in front of his men and me. He's not whispering as quietly as before, and there's deep sadness in his tone.

"*Tía* Margherita's a legend in Colombia. When her sons were little, she was part of a convoy to our family's summer home—winter in the Northern Hemisphere—when it was ambushed. The lead and last vehicles blew up, but the reinforced SUV smuggled in from here protected my *tía* and cousins. She had Pablo huddle on the floor of the SUV with baby Juan next to him. She grabbed a rifle from the back and shot several of the men in the rival cartel."

He pauses and shakes his head. I know he was too young to remember any of this, but he's clearly heard the story enough times to recount it as though he were an eyewitness.

"When she ran out of ammunition, she got out of the vehicle, supposedly surrendering to protect her children. When the leader approached, assuming she capitulated, she threw down the rifle and pulled a knife. It was in the man's aorta and sliding across his throat before anyone knew what was happening. The guy never even felt his death."

I get one of his wry smiles that makes me melt. He even looks a little sheepish as he continues.

"So, needless to say, I'm not eager for *Tía* Margherita to hear about this until we know what's going on. *Tío* Luis, along with my *papá* and *Tío* Enrique, hovers and whittles when any of us get hurt. *Mamá* and my *tías* have to send them away. They complain the men get underfoot and don't let any of us sleep because they fear we won't wake."

He'd moved one of his hands to fasten his seatbelt when he began the story. He left his other hand on his lap with mine covering it. He turns it over and laces our fingers together. Unlike the ploy it was earlier to bind my wrists, he's sincere now. His thumb brushes over the back of my hand.

"Bravado is worth nothing when you fear for a family member's life. No man in mine—in any of the Four Families—fears showing his love and devotion. It doesn't weaken us. It only shows the world our family ties can't be broken."

He expresses what anyone who's around a syndicate's leading family knows. The part about the unbreakable ties that bind. The other part is quite profound. It's not a sentiment shared by all syndicate ruling families. It's not one expressed aloud by most syndicate men.

People have long said the NYC syndicate leaders are odd. Some scoff at their open displays of affection. But those who are wise and wish to live understand these families are genetically wired differently than the rest of the world. Their devotion is a strand in their DNA. A strand that can't be extracted without the rest disintegrating.

To hear Alejandro describe it is moving. While plenty have witnessed what he's describing, hearing him share it with me is a vulnerability I doubt anyone outside his family sees. He told me earlier that he'd shown me the real him, but I'd scoffed at it. He didn't elaborate, letting me change the subject. Now I know he spoke the truth. The gravity of that keeps me silent.

I don't fight the urge to sag against him. We've been through the same traumatic event, yet his shoulders feel broad enough to carry the weight for both of us. It's a cop-out on my part after my own show of bravado ever since he climbed into my car. He stiffens for a moment as my head rests on his shoulder, then he moves to wrap his arm around mine like he did in the hallway and in the elevator. It's only when he draws me closer to his side that I feel him relax.

My willingness to let go of control and give it to him calms him as much as it does me. I'm exhausted from today's mental and emotional workout. I want to close my eyes and let someone else—only Alejandro—take over. Releasing the weight of it all leaves me feeling depleted but safe. I realize taking on the burden of protecting both of us—me not fighting him anymore and allowing him to decide—makes him feel...I don't know. Safe? Needed? Respected? I don't know him well enough to tell, but he's calmer.

"Rest, *chiquita*."

How the tides have turned. When I close my eyes this time, I allow myself to drift away. My mind clears for the first time in I don't know how long. No whizzing thoughts. No suffocating worries. I don't doze, but the drive's shorter than I expected. Even with his men around us, Alejandro kisses my forehead as he brings me back to reality. I sit up and look around. We're pulling into the garage of a large yet modest home in one of the wealthiest extended suburbs of NYC.

It's not until I hear the garage door land against the ground that the driver switches off the engine. It's not because he wants to give us carbon monoxide poisoning. It's in case we need to make a hasty retreat as soon as the garage door rises again. Hell, even before the door is up. I know the protocols.

Alejandro releases my belt before undoing his own. The driver and front-seat guard both get out, opening their respective rear door. I look up at Alejandro, and he nods. I'm unaccustomed to asking permission or relying on someone else for my safety. It's a novelty I haven't had since I was a teenager.

We enter the house through the kitchen and are soon in the family room. There are books along one wall with games for all ages. A variety of toys are in stacking bins and cubbies. My brow furrows when I look up at Alejandro. He doesn't have children and neither do any of his cousins.

"This is a family safehouse for any higher-ranked men who need somewhere for their family to go. We keep it stocked not only with necessities but things that will make both the parents' and the kids' lives easier while waiting out whatever danger they're in."

"Thoughtful."

"Loyalty's rewarded."

I nod as he takes me on a tour. We head upstairs, and I spot two children's rooms and a nursery. There're a regular guest room and the main bedroom. We don't enter them, but I can easily see inside all of them.

"Choose which one you want, *chica*. We'll be here tonight and possibly tomorrow night."

"Is there one you usually prefer?"

"I've never stayed here. I've never needed to come here before. My *mamá* and one of my *tías* are in real estate. They handle almost everything to do with the family's properties, especially when it comes to preparing temporary living arrangements for families with kids."

Alejandro's mother, Catalina, and her younger sister, Luciana. Both are among the most successful real estate agents in the country. Luciana handles mostly commercial properties and escrows while Catalina focuses on residential and interior design. I learned about them from the dossier sent to me before I arrived in Chicago.

It warned they're as deadly as Margherita, but it said nothing about how they demonstrate their loyalty to the Cartel. Caring for those who rely on you is a duty and privilege for the ruling families. How well they do it speaks to their loyalty.

Discovering my stash of insulin, my attempted escape, and being shot at certainly changed the tone. While we were seducing each other, I would've said Alejandro and I would share a room. Now, I have no idea if he'll have guards posted outside my door.

"I really don't mind which room, Alejandro."

"Then we'll take the main one."

"We? Will you chain me to the bedframe to make sure I don't get away?"

"I could do that in any bedroom. No. You and I have some promises for me to fulfill."

I stare at him agog.

"Little one, I know you're here to kill me. The insulin wasn't a surprise. Of course, you were going to attempt an escape. I would've suspected you far more if you hadn't. And we agreed we don't know who the target was. Just like I could've killed you a few dozen times already, you could've done the same to me. I doubt your job was just to observe and report back on my comings and goings. I doubt your employer's patience will last much longer. Yet here I am. Alive and breathing while in arm's reach of you. I don't have any shackles or chains at the ready. I could get zip ties within seconds, but I'd never use those on you. Wild as I suspect my parents are—" He shudders. "—I don't think my mom stocked the house with fuzzy handcuffs. You'll stay in that bed because there won't be anywhere else you want to be tonight."

"You're egotistically sure of yourself."

He slides a finger through one of my jeans' beltloops and tugs. Like he did in the hotel room with just my panties, he slides his fingers beneath the two layers of fabric with his palm facing him. He fists the material and pulls me until my body collides with his. He turns his hand despite the restricted space and inches his fingers closer to my pussy.

"It's only fair I get to feel how wet you are when you can feel how hard I am."

"*Porca miseria.*" Holy shit.

He slides his middle and ring finger into me, hooking them to anchor me in place. His right hand wraps around my throat, forcing my chin up. The tip of his tongue licks my lips before he whispers beside my ear.

"The correct response is 'thank you, sir.'"

"*Grazie, signore.*" Thank you, sir.

I'm too dazed to realize I lapsed into Italian. That never happens. I think in whichever language I'm using or around. This man destroys all my defenses. For reasons I'm not ready to piece together, I allow it when I never have in the past. I've been attracted to men before. Hell, Patrick's hot as fuck and is a great fuck. But I'd never allow him control over me. Not in or out of bed.

I surrender to Alejandro.

When he leans back, I see his pulse thrumming in his neck. I keep the pressure much lighter than him when both of my hands cup his neck. His heart's racing. His calmness is a façade I cracked.

"I will fuck you all over this house by the time we leave tomorrow. I'll fuck you against this wall at least once. But our first time together won't be standing up with our clothes on."

"Yes, sir."

I grin at him, hoping for sultry. The way he playfully nips at me makes me think I succeeded. I release a quick whine as he pulls his hand free.

"If you had more clothes with you, I'd shred the ones you have on right here, right now. I'd spank you for that. Good little girls are patient until their—tell them what they can have."

What the hell was he going to say?

Dom?

Master?

He just skipped over filling the blank. I know there was something he wanted to say. He wasn't at a loss for words. He didn't want me to know what he was thinking. How does he see us?

"Do want me as your sub?"

"No."

He slides his hand into mine and leads me to the bedroom where he shuts the door behind us and locks it just like he did in the hotel.

Chapter Eleven

Alejandro

"Vittoria, you need to tell me who hired you."

She glowers at me, and I'm not completely sure why. Her expression darkened the moment I started speaking.

"I'm suddenly Vittoria." She cocks an eyebrow.

"Our game is over."

She's still glaring at me, and I'm still not sure why she's pissed after what I thought was the lead up to something passionate. I suppose I killed the mood.

"And if I'm not done playing you, Alejandro?"

She backs away from me, the dresser to her back. She remains away from the windows and nowhere near the closet where I could shove her. She won't trap herself in the bathroom either.

"If that's true, why are you backing away from me? I can dump you outside the neighborhood gates and see who comes for you if you don't want my protection."

"Or I could call a rideshare and leave you to whoever the fuck is after you today."

"And I thought you were special. The only one."

Her expression shifts as she stares at me. I've revealed too much. She knows deep down I don't mean she's the only one trying to kill me.

"Don't call me Vittoria. I don't like it."

"Okay, Tiffani."

She snarls.

"Giselle."

"Stop it."

"Liz."

"Enough!"

I prowl toward her. She doesn't slide along the dresser to get away from me. Instead, she presses back against it. I lift her to sit on it and push my way between her thighs. I rest my hand on the side of her neck, my thumb resting in the hollow at its base. We gaze into each other's eyes, and I sweep my thumb up and down. I seem to spend a lot of time whispering to her, even when no one else is around.

"*Chiquita.*"

She swallows.

"Yes."

Her voice is strained even though I keep the pressure light around her throat. I slip my hand around to rest at her nape. I draw her toward me, and she comes willingly. Our lips brush before the kiss deepens. There's something not only exciting but also reassuring about it. It feels like I should always kiss her. Never stop. Never with anyone else.

Her hands rest on my pecs, but I grasp her hips and pull her against me, making sure she feels how much I want her. She slides her hands up and wraps her arms around my neck. Her fingers graze my scalp before tangling in my hair.

"Vita, do you want this to end?"

"What?" She jerks back.

"If you don't let me help you, this will end with one of—both of us—dead. Is that what you still want?"

She's slow to respond, but she shakes her head.

"I can't tell you anything, Jandro."

We freeze, staring at each other before resting our foreheads together. She's never used any nickname for me. Her hands wrap around my neck, her thumbs sweeping over my cheeks. She tilts her head and kisses me. This one tastes like regret.

"Will you take a cyanide pill before revealing your secrets to me?"

Her smile's half-hearted at best as she shakes her head.

"*Chica*, those shots could've been aimed at Pablo because he's the heir. He's committed his sins, and there are plenty who would love retribution. The same is true for me. It could've been someone else sent by your employer. They could've been meant for you as revenge or as punishment. In comparison, the chances that they were meant for Pablo or me are slim."

"You know how this job works. It's kill or be killed. You won't let me walk away. Neither will my boss. Can't I enjoy what I have left to look forward to."

I step back and cross my arms. I observe her, fighting to rein in my temper. Of all of us, it takes me the longest to anger. Things piss me off left and right, but I refuse to lose control of my emotions enough for anger to take over. But now...

"Vita, if I wanted you dead, I would've pushed you in front of the window."

I'm seething.

"I—I—"

"You were just using me for my body." I think I'm genuinely insulted.

She wraps her legs around my hips and tries to pull me forward. We both know I'm not going anywhere I don't want to.

"You should hate me for wanting to kill you. I hate myself for knowing I should but not wanting to. I don't enjoy being conflicted and feeling weak!"

I fist her hair and pull her head back. Not enough to hurt her neck but enough to make her scalp tingle and to exert my dominance.

"Believe me, right now, you are *not* my favorite person, *chiquita*. Do you want me to hate you? Do you want me to kill you?"

"No to both!"

Her eyes grow watery. It could be from me pulling her hair. I stare into her eyes, then I'm kissing her yet again. This time, we're tearing at each other's clothes. We can't get them off fast enough. I pull my button-down over my head while she does the same with her shirt. I had to fasten my pants before leaving the hotel room. I wouldn't humiliate Vita that way in front of my men. Whatever they might guess, I won't confirm it.

I toe off my shoes and reach down for my socks as Vita kicks off hers. Then I lift her off the dresser and carry her to the bed. I put her on her feet, so we can both peel off the rest of our clothes. When we're naked, we take a moment to appreciate what we see. Even though I've seen her as close to naked as I could get, seeing her with an unobstructed view makes my *huevos* ache. I stroke myself twice before picking her up and tossing her on the bed.

I don't hesitate to crawl on and hover above her. I lower myself onto my forearms as I settle between her legs. A moment's hesitation, and I shift to place my knees outside her legs, pressing hers closed. I bring us chest-to-chest. She can't get away unless I let her. The moment she refuses, I'd move aside, but she slides her arms up between mine. She crosses her wrists as she lifts them. Our gazes lock as she arches her back.

"Tell me now, *chica*, if this is still a game."

"Was it ever really a game?"

I cup her right breast, my thumb sweeping over her nipple until it hardens. I rock back onto my right elbow and bring my mouth down. I think for a moment about toying with it. Instead, I suck it into my mouth. My teeth tug twice before I'm sucking like a starved baby. She moans and writhes. Her mound rubs my cock, and I nearly lose my mind.

I've wanted this woman for weeks.

I've craved her touch, her scent, her sound, her looks, her taste.

Every motherfucking single inch of her.

Mind, body, soul.

I might dominate her body, but she dominates my very being.

Mi vida. My life.

Mi Vita.

Mine.

My kiss is brutal and punishing. Being out of control makes my skin crawl. It makes my heart race. I want to fight the feeling until my last breath. If I let this consume me, I'll hate her for it.

I rock my hips in a rhythm that tells her what it'll be like once I'm inside her. Her moans soothe the beast within me. Each sound calms me until I feel rational again.

"Jandro, my body's on fire. You're burning me from the inside out, and I'm letting you. *Please*."

"Please what, *chiquita*? Stop and let the fire burn out? Extinguish it by making you come?"

Her eyes water once again. "I don't think there's any way to put this out. Not until there's nothing left of me. Not until you've destroyed me."

"Is that what you believe I'll do? You think my offer to protect you is a lie? That I'm offering you safety from someone else just so I can destroy you?"

"I don't think you'd do it on purpose. I think being with you will kill me one way or another. Someone will kill me for not killing you. Someone will finish the job, and I won't be able to stand knowing you're dead. Giving all of myself to you and not getting all of you back."

I roll us, making her straddle me before sitting up. The position is erotic as fuck.

"The Cartel will always own part of me. My secrets are ones I can never share with anyone who isn't a man in my immediate family. The things I do I'll never reveal to protect the ones I love and the ones who rely on me. That part of me is a monster. It's a beast no cage can contain. You will *never* get that part of me. I hate that you know enough to understand what I mean. I won't let you anywhere near it, so I'm glad I can't give you all of me. You'd never unsee who I really am."

Tears trail down her cheeks, and my own eyes sting with unshed tears. Sex is no longer currency between us. Intimacy is no longer a ploy or tool. This has gone too far too fast, and neither of us can undo what we've started. Our only choice is to walk away or let it swallow us whole.

She initiates our kiss, and I let her lead. Her cunt grinds against my cock. She rises onto her knees, and the tip slides between her pussy lips. I feel her drenching it, and the temptation to thrust and claim her is like she's possessed me.

"I'm clean, *caro*." Dear.

The sentiment sounds a lot better in Italian than English. She isn't eighty, and I didn't just shovel her driveway. No butterscotch candies from the bottom of her sensible purse.

"Me too. I test regularly, *chica*."

"I do too. I'm on birth control. I have a condom in my purse."

"I have one in my wallet."

I watch as she considers our choice before she shakes her head. My fingers dig into her waist as I push her onto my cock. She screams, and I groan as I fill her.

"You will drip with my cum. It'll slide down your thighs, and every sticky moment will remind you that you belong to me now, Vita. There's no going back. You will tell me the whole fucking truth when we're done. If you don't, I will spank you until you do."

"Will you spank me anyway?"

"*Fuck!*"

I roll us once more, pinning her torso beneath me as I hammer into her. Her hips rise and fall to meet mine. I'm practically crushing the wrists I have in each hand, pressing them into the pillow beside her head.

"Fucking mine. All mine."

Her possessiveness only drives me wilder. It makes me want to claim her too. I will when I come inside her.

"That's right, *chica*. You will get a part of me no woman ever has."

Her surprise makes me smile.

"I've always worn a condom, even when I've known my partner is clean and on birth control."

"And I'm different?"

"I can't give you all of me, but I can give you something no one else can ever have."

She lifts her head from the pillow, and I release her wrists when she strains against my hold. She brings her hands over my ears as she grasps my head. Her kiss means everything to me. It's one of genuine happiness.

"You're the only one too, Jandro."

"Fucking mine. All mine."

"*Si, tesoro.*" Yes, darling.

We kiss everywhere we can reach. Each other's faces, shoulders, and chest. Our hands skim over every inch we can touch. This is purely vanilla—a type of sex I haven't had in a decade. It's passionate, and it's rough. But it's filled with feelings I've never had before. From her expression whenever I catch a glimpse, it's the same for her.

"May I come? Please."

"Yes. You beg like such a good girl, but you don't have to ask today. Take."

"Thank you... *Dio mio!*"

It works in both languages. I'm ready to call out the same thing if I didn't fear my father's mother hearing me from her grave all the way in Colombia. She wasn't a fan of anyone taking the Lord's name in vain. She'd definitely not appreciate it while I have the best sex of my life with a woman who isn't my wife.

"*Joder, chiquita!*" Fuck, little girl!

"I'm so close... Don't stop... Please, don't stop. So close."

"I have no intention of stopping until you scream my name, and your cunt's full of my cum."

I push back to kneel, lifting her hips and lower back from the bed. I pound into her, rubbing my pubic bone against her clit. She clutches the sheets, and I see the sheen of sweat on her brow. Her body glistens, and she's breathtaking. I can't get my fill of how she glows as she comes.

"Jandro!"

"Vita!"

I thrust into her one more time before dropping onto my forearms, continuing to rock my hips as I draw out her orgasm. I want to collapse because I'm spent, but I don't want to miss the chance for her to come again if she can. I roll onto my back, letting her take control as she rides me. She rocks against me until she throws her head back, the cords in her neck straining.

"Come for me, *chica*. Come for D—"

Fucking hell. I barely stop myself. Where the ever-loving fuck did that word come from? It's *never* been my thing. Like I've called no other woman *chiquita* or *chica,* no woman's called me that disconcerting name.

Her entire body tenses, and her nails scratch my pecs as she braces herself. I watch her abs contract, and her thighs squeeze my hips as she comes.

"Daddy!"

Chapter Twelve

Vita

Oh, fuck!

Oh, shit!

Oh, fucking shit!

Why did I scream that?!

Why?!

I want to shrivel up and hide in the tiniest hole ever made. I'm unprepared for Alejandro to roll us yet again. I'm not the lightest woman in the world, but he moves me around like I weigh nothing. His entire body pins me to the bed. I fear his reaction. I want to cringe, but I refuse to show my fear. That was enough vulnerability to last me a lifetime.

"That's fucking right, *chiquita*. Who's promised to take care of you? Who's protecting you right now? Who's going to make sure no one *ever fucking touches you again?*"

By the end of that last sentence, the protectiveness in his voice demands my agreement. I've never felt so fucking cherished in all my life.

"You."

"Whose cock do you have buried inside your tight little pussy?

Whose cum is filling you right now? Who belongs to you to serve and protect?"

"You."

I can't keep my lips from twitching. I don't want to ruin the moment, but a leading Cartel man just used a police slogan. A bit ironic, don't you think?

"You looked shocked by what you called me."

I want to crawl into that hole.

I stay quiet and let him keep going.

"You did it because the answer to all those questions is the same. Me."

"Is that what you like from your subs?"

His expression darkens, and his face lowers inches from mine.

"No woman has ever called me that. I would never allow it. I'm not a Daddy Dom and never want to be. I am *not* your Dom, and you are *not* my sub. No woman but you has the right to any terms of affection. Not to me and not from me. Do not doubt that, little girl. Your cunt and your ass will regret it if you do."

"Regret it?"

"Because I'll keep them sore from fucking you until you understand."

That sounds like a solemn pledge. I believe he means it to his very marrow.

"Hmm. Maybe you don't mean—"

His hips drive him into me, and I feel him harden. I know he'd almost withdrawn, his dick done with my cunt. But now, not so much. He pinches and pulls my right nipple until I'm ready to beg him to stop. He lets go, cupping my jaw and holding it in place instead.

"Only play that game if you're prepared to lose. I don't make idle threats, and my promises are few and far between. The ones I make I never break."

Not threats and not promises.

He leaves that unsaid, but I know it.

"Yes, Daddy."

"Good girl."

He thrusts twice more before pulling out and sitting up. He swings his legs over the bed and rises. I stare with my mouth open, then I squeak when he turns around and lifts me into his arms. He carries me into the bathroom and puts me back on my feet by the shower.

"Wait."

I step around him until I can see in the mirror. I check the medicine cabinets and luckily find some rubbing alcohol swabs in a first aid kit. This is hardly going to be fast or sexy. I rub the alcohol pad along my hairline from ear to ear. Alejandro patiently watches—naked and confident because why wouldn't he when he has a body like Adonis? I move on to going over my hairline with warm soapy water and my fingers. I break the adhesive seal from the wig glue and ease it off. Then I work the same process to detach the skull cap.

He steps forward as my nearly waist-length chestnut hair tumbles down my back. It's hardly at its finest from being folded and tucked into the cap. I've considered cutting it super short to make it easier, but my hair is the one thing about my appearance that makes me feel like me when I'm not pretending to be someone else. I pop out my contacts and rinse them down the drain.

Sorry, Mother Nature, but I can't leave any evidence. I don't want anyone to have to change the trash bag for something so small. He steps forward and draws my hair over my left shoulder. He places his hands on the outside of my shoulders before kissing my right one.

"You are so fucking beautiful no matter what your hair or eye color is. But seeing you like this... You take my breath away."

We step into the shower, and he pulls the door shut. He shields me from the spray until he has the temperature right. Then he shifts and allows me to enjoy the warm water. He'll brave the cold rather than let me.

I tilt my head back to get my hair wet, and he kisses my collarbones and up my neck. He smatters kisses over my face before dropping to his knees. His lips nip then suck over my left hip bone. I look down and know he's marking me. He moves to the inside of my left thigh, leaving two love bites before repeating his actions on my right hip and thigh. He moves to the center of my mound that was waxed just two days ago. He leaves four there.

"I will never mark you where someone else could see. I won't humiliate you like that. But I will mark you any and everywhere else."

"And if I wish to do the same."

"Then the men in my family will smirk and roll their eyes."

My brow furrows as he stands.

"You know things get messy. Sometimes I work without a shirt, and sometimes I have to change my clothes. It's not like we parade around with our dicks swinging in the breeze, but neither are we so modest that we can't see each other get changed."

"I guess I'll have to stick with sucking your cock to be on the safe side."

He crowds me until I'm pressed against the shower wall. He wraps my hand around his semi-hard cock and makes me stroke. It takes little to get him ready for me to suck or for him to fuck me. He spins me around, and my right cheek presses against the tile. His body leans against mine while his hands spread my ass cheeks. His cock slips along the valley before it presses at my backdoor.

"Do you want me here?"

"I want you everywhere."

"Can you take it? Or should I train it first?"

"I'll wear a plug if you want me to, but I don't need it."

"Mmm. There's a store in Parsippany we need to visit."

"A store where?"

"New Jersey."

"Why would we go there?"

"Because I own it. I have a fantastic employee discount on anything we want to enjoy together. We're definitely getting a vibrator I can control from anywhere. Even when I'm not nearby, I will control your pussy."

The thought excites me so much I close my eyes. I picture what that would be like.

Fucking hot.

"I might text my men and tell them you weren't feeling well that morning. Ask them how you're doing."

"You wouldn't dare! You wouldn't make me come in front of them, would you?"

"How would I know what's happening without me there to see it?"

"You wouldn't."

"I told you I don't make idle threats, and my promises are few and far between."

"Is that a threat or a promise?"

"Oh, little girl. It's most definitely a promise."

He kisses between my shoulder blades before turning me to face him again. He pumps shampoo into his hand and nudges me so that my body is under the showerhead, but my head isn't.

"Let me take care of something besides making you come."

His fingers are like magic. Even better than when my stylist cuts my hair. I let my head drop to rest my forehead against his chest. It might make it awkward for him, but it's heaven for me. He takes a step forward, and I shuffle one backward until my hair's under the water. He rinses the suds clean, and I spot a face cleanser that'll wash off my makeup without leaving me like a racoon. I hurry to scrub my face then rinse it.

"That was divine."

"Happy to help, *chica*."

I pump a dollop of shampoo into my palm and point down. He grins and lowers himself to his knees. It's the only way I can easily reach all of his hair. While I return the favor, he returns to marking me along the inside of my thighs. He hooks one over his shoulder, bracing me tightly. When he's left another five or six on one leg, he switches to the other. His hair doesn't need nearly as long to wash as mine, but it takes twice the time to do it since he refuses to rush his feast.

"I'm saving the rest of you, little girl, for dessert."

"I look forward to a *cannolo* later."

"You can suck the cream out anytime."

We rub each other's bodies with shower gel and poofs I can tell have never been used before. This whole process from watching me remove my wig to washing each other is so intimate. Something a legit couple would do. We're both aroused the entire time. We both want to give and get oral as well as fuck, but we don't. We're normal for a few minutes—not a narcotrafficker or a mercenary, not predator or prey.

When there's nothing left to wash, we embrace. He felt how wet I am for him even after wiping the cum from between my legs. I see and feel how hard he is. But it's still not about sex. He's so fucking gentle with me, even when he's leaving love bites.

"Let me hold you, *chiquita.* Just a little while longer."

"Yes, please, Daddy."

I test the word I cried out as he made me come. It doesn't feel weird to say it outside sex, but I'm still unsure whether he likes it or tolerates it.

"I like that, *mi chica.*" My little girl.

The difference one word makes to an already possessive term of endearment. He's making me fall for him harder and harder. At first, it was just sex appeal. I wanted to fuck him on the yacht. I would've done it for pure enjoyment.

I could've followed him to his hotel and killed him on his way to his room. I could've been a sniper and taken him out any of the days I followed him. I could've shot him and Pablo after the window shattered and Pablo was already injured, and Alejandro was distracted.

"Don't let go."

How fucking needy can I sound?

"I won't."

I enjoyed our intellectual sparring—our verbal table tennis— too much. I respect how he treated people in the neighborhood. Yes, he was there extorting plenty of them and likely doing some shady-ass deals. But everyone greeted him with a smile. I've heard the same isn't true for Pablo or *Tres J's,* probably because all four are enforcers. Alejandro seemed like a favored visitor.

He's charming. Kids ran up to him and greeted him with fist bumps and secret handshakes. He kicked a soccer ball back to a group the first day I stalked him into Jackson Heights. He kissed old women's cheeks and heartily shook hands with the elderly men. There were plenty of adults who gave him a wide berth, clearly terrified of him. But just as many welcomed him.

"Your fingers will be raisins soon, little one."

"I don't care."

We continue to let the warm water run over us as we hug.

I witnessed him with his family at the gala. He was attentive to his mother and aunts. He laughed with his father and uncles. He and his cousins are clearly best friends, looking like a bunch of college jocks who were just as nerdy as they were athletic. Despite his power and authority, he obviously deferred to the older generation in his family.

He didn't disguise his disdain when he encountered men from the other rival families, but he was polite and respectful to the women, moving aside to let them pass, pushing chairs out of their way. He could've been a complete dick to them, but etiquette was clearly engrained in him from an early age.

"You're exhausted, Vita. I felt you twitch."

I respect—even admire—him for all of these things. From what I saw, I know how deeply his sense of duty and loyalty run. I know there's honor among thieves when he's around. All these traits attract me to him in a way that defies common sense. The way he is with me—the way he could be but isn't—makes me feel—cared about. He could've hurt me countless times, accidentally or intentionally. But he hasn't. He's been careful not to when he's within his rights since any deferential treatment to me as a woman doesn't exist in my occupation.

"Did I?"

"Yes. We still have much to discuss, *chiquita*. But let's take a nap first. Just don't kill me in my sleep, please."

I lean away from him, insulted he'd say that. I heard the jest in his voice, and there are creases at the corners of his eyes as he smiles. That's not a joke I want to hear after what we shared. I don't blame him for thinking I'll carry out my mission. I haven't told him I won't. But I thought he'd realize by now, there's no way I can.

"You must know the job is over for me."

"You want me, but do you want me more than the money?"

I nearly fall out of the shower as my back hits the glass door, and it swings open. I catch myself and step out. I grab a towel, wrapping it around me as I continue to back away from Alejandro. Normally, I'd twist my hair into a towel, and there're enough out for me to do that, but I want space from him.

I have no right to be so hurt. It's a fair question. But I thought he'd figured out enough about me not to need to ask. I reach behind me to open the bathroom door, but his arm shoots out and slams it shut. His other hand finishes tucking the towel in around his trim waist as he speaks.

"I don't know what lingers in the back of your mind. I'm sure you value your life more than mine."

The urge to slap him like the woman in the *novela* surges through me. I feel the heat rising in my cheeks, and steam's veritably shooting out of my ears.

"Are you so sure because that's what you'd do in my place?"

He crowds me. If he were anyone else, I'd plot how to escape, doing as much harm to him as I could. Instead, I'm riveted in place by his penetrating stare.

"No, little girl. I've protected you. I've shown you that I pick you despite your job. I pick you, even though I know you haven't agreed to give up the job. You've accepted my help."

"Exactly."

I say that one word as though it explains it all. I keep my palms pressed flat against the door while my chest heaves from sucking in deep breaths to calm myself. He cocks an eyebrow, waiting for me to elaborate. He won't let me get away with just implying anything.

"Accepting your help means I've crossed my employer. I'm

not a whore, Jandro. I've never had sex with a target. Hooked up and fooled around a bit, yes. I admit that. But never sex. Certainly never without a condom. I'm a killer, not a sex worker. I may not have said it, but I've sure as fuck shown you I quit that job ages ago. You know I'm no novice, yet I haven't succeeded. You know it's not lack of skill. I haven't wanted to carry it out! I can't!"

I turn my head away, unable to look at him. He nudges my chin, but I don't oblige. He grasps it, forcing me to look at him lest I hurt myself.

"I will give you my undying loyalty and protection if you're telling me the truth. I'll give you every freedom I can because of that protection. But if you're lying to me, I will lock you away in a golden cage. You will sing for your supper, and I will take you out to play whenever I want. Then I'll shut you back in until I remember you again."

There's no light in his eyes like there has been in the past when we traded barbs and threats. If I betray him—hurt him— he'll punish me tenfold. He'll neither forgive nor forget.

"Then let me tell you the truth."

Chapter Thirteen

Alejandro

I see the goosebumps rise on her arms, but once again there's that aura of self-assuredness and defiance. That's still the best way I can describe it, yet it feels insufficient for how magnetic it is. There's a healthy dose of bravado in it from how she fights not to tremble.

I back away, giving her room to turn around and open the door. I grab another bath towel from the rod as we leave. I step beside her as she looks around, unsure whether the bed is the best place for us to go. I hand her the towel, and she stares at it then me.

"Thank you."

She bends over and wraps the towel around her sopping hair. She hadn't even wrung it out before rushing out of the shower. I let my simmering anger get the better of me, and I put both physical and emotional distance between us before I even issued the threat. She walks to the dresser and gathers her clothes.

I don't follow her; instead, walking to the closet. *Mamá* and *Tía* Luciana keep a few odds and ends of clothing here in case a family left their home without packing. There are two heavy robes on hangers. I grab both. I step behind Vita and wrap the smaller one around her shoulders before pulling her back against me.

"You're freezing, little one."

She releases a shuddering breath before sagging into my arms as I wrap them around her and kiss her temple. I see her eyes are scrunched closed. I turn her before helping her slide the robe on properly. I tie the belt then put on my robe. We pull our towels loose, and I watch her for a moment before I return all three to the bathroom and hang them up. I want to give her a moment to compose her thoughts.

"Can we do this somewhere else? Somewhere without a bed?"

I offer her my hand as an answer. We walk down to the living room in silence. She releases my hand and walks to a rocker recliner. A chair that only fits one. I sit on the sofa, choosing the spot in the middle. There's room if she wants to join me without crowding her by sitting too close or shutting her out by sitting too far away.

"Jandro, I'll tell you what I know, but you have to realize it's limited. I can offer you what I've deduced and inferred. But I can't guarantee any of it will be useful."

"I understand."

"If your men cleared out my hotel room, they'll have found the dossier under the mattress. Cliché, but less obvious than the safe these days. I'll give it to you. You can see what I've been working with. Someone referred me to my employer, but I genuinely don't know who. It could be someone I've partnered with in the past, or it could—family."

I notch up my chin. "Let me guess, *Mala del Brenta*. You're Venetian after all."

"Yes. My father's the don's *consigliere*."

Holy hell!

Her father's Nicolò Trevisan!

"You were brave to be in the same room as Serafina."

Her father's the don. The women must have grown up together.

"I was more worried about Elodie."

"Fear both of them, and you might survive them."

It's no surprise she knows my *tía*. She married into the family a little over a year ago. She's *Tío* Enrique's soulmate. She's the only woman who could match such a powerful man. Her family's Boston *Cosa Nostra*, but she cut ties when she divorced her douchey ex-husband.

Her sons aren't bad, even if they are Red Sox fans. I couldn't give two shits about the Yankees, but it pisses them off when my cousins and I wear our baseball caps. Their payback is to remind us of what happened the one and only time we drank with them last New Year's Eve. I want to hurl just thinking about it.

"I'm *Mala del Brenta* by birth, but I can't say for sure that they hired me. Maybe. But it wasn't Don Piero or my father. I'm not even sure if my employer is Italian or a man, even though it's a man I've spoken to. Whoever they are, they were very specific that you are the mark. Collateral damage is fine, but you're the priority. I don't know why. That's not something I ask, and it's rarely offered."

"Do you know if they sent anyone else? Maybe today's shooter."

"I checked the dark web after I got the initial call. I didn't see anything that resembled a hit on you. The ones that alluded to a cartel weren't your family's. Mexican mostly."

We know about those. We placed them. Speaking of Boston— *los Iglesias* need a reminder that they exist because we allow it. Their fealty isn't to some rinky-dink syndicate near the border. They're too far away for the border cartels to get to them in time, so they pay for our protection. They also pay a tariff on everything they import into Boston. We make sure they're buying mostly from us. Double dipping? Fuck yeah.

"How long ago?"

"The week before Chicago. They didn't give me much lead time."

"They wanted me dead far from my family. Make it look like the Chicago *Cosa Nostra* did it. Hit my family hard without risking bringing the other New York families into it."

"Probably."

"Nothing happened to you when you didn't do the job there?"

I hate thinking there's someone out there after her, but after today, there's no way to ignore the possible threat.

"It pissed off my employer, but it wasn't my fault they left me with such a narrow window. The yacht was recon with the hope that I could get you alone to do the job."

"Why not just get it done when we both got here?"

"You're only alone at home at night. I knew I couldn't break into your condo and survive. Between the arsenal I'm certain you have and your building's security team, there was no way it was worth the risk. At first, I followed you to learn your routine and discover a time and place that would be best without a spontaneous shooting. I wanted to avoid a sniper kill. That narrows the candidates down too far now that Robert Simms and Elodie are out of the game. There aren't enough people who could take the shot from the distance I'd want between us. Those who know about me would know I did the hit."

She's not boasting. She's being straightforward, and I believe her. Robert Simms used to head up the leading mercenary ring in the world. He was a ghost and allegedly had the highest body count since the end of the Cold War. He started racking up kills while he was KGB. That came out after his death. Elodie only had one employer, but she was infamous.

"There may not be that many professionals out there with those marksman skills, but don't underestimate the women in the Four Families. Maria Mancinelli could be a fucking Olympic gold medalist. She's the best shot I've ever seen after *Tía* Elodie."

"So I've heard. Apparently, Laura Kutsenko and Katerina Andreyev are the best in their family."

If our families could make nice, Vita would probably get along really well with Laura and Katerina. But it's already complicated enough that Javier's wife, Madeline, is Laura's little sister. Needless to say, no one in the bratva, especially not Laura's husband—the *pakhan*—was thrilled to discover they're in love.

"They are, but Anastasia Kutsenko has some past no one

outside their family knows about, but it's enough to make Salvatore keep his distance by yards if not miles. I'm certain you know what Serafina can do."

"All too well. We used to compete against each other growing up. If I won, she'd bake for me. If she won, I'd do her laundry for a month. It's a miracle I didn't have cavities after all those sweets, and she had the freshest, most well-starched wardrobe of anyone I know. We went shooting together several times a week until she left for college a year before me."

That intrigues me not because I want Vita to spill family secrets about the wife of the Mancinelli's biggest shit stain. Fucking Carmine. Fuck that motherfucker.

Focus.

I want to know whether her shooting alone is what led to her current career. I want to know if she's been a gun for hire for long. But there's more she needs to know if she's going to stay anywhere near me.

"Don't underestimate any of the O'Rourke women. Allie's a doctor, so she'll only shoot if there's truly no other recourse. But don't discount the training her husband's given her. The rest of the women—they're the most like the women in my family. Before marrying into the O'Rourkes, two came from mob families, one from a Mexican cartel family, and another is a former DEA agent. Plus the moms. Saoirse, Siobhan, and Brenna are like *Mamá, Tía* Luciana, and *Tía* Margherita. They're syndicate daughters, sisters, wives, and mothers. They've known no other life. All six women have killed more times than any of us are supposed to know."

"Not too different from my family. You know Don Piero's wife, Allegra, is from one of the ninety-four families of Sicily. I know her sister too. Sylvia was deadly long before she became Salvatore's wife."

"Yes. Don't let the Torettas know you think they're anything less than number one."

"I'm aware. They were frequent visitors in Venice, and I traveled to Palermo with Serafina."

I want to ask her more because I want to learn more about her childhood, but I have to tread carefully. If it ever got back to Carmine that I asked about her trips, he'd take it as a threat to Serafina. That I was digging up information about her family. He'd lose his fucking shit.

We're all possessive men and protective by nature and nurture. Take that and add to it that Carmine's a fucking psycho, and I don't need that kind of shit in my life right now. Neither of us has time to keep blowing up each other's jets.

"Now I know who you know, and you know who to watch out for here. What else can you tell me about this job?"

"It's one of the best paying I've ever had. Twenty million just to off you. An extra five million if I get you alone and leave no trace. Ten apiece if I get anyone else in your family besides Enrique."

You have to pay for quality.

I doubt she'd find me funny.

"Were you going to try for anyone else?"

"Only if that was the only way to get out alive. Taking you on was enough of a challenge."

"How much did you get up front?"

I expect her to say fifty percent. Anything less, and I'll be insulted on her behalf. She carries all the risk.

"Half wired to an account even Jorge and Elodie won't find."

Jorge's our accountant for everything, and Elodie's a former forensic accountant the underworld knew as the "Ball Buster."

"They'll expect it back."

"I know. But they'll have to find it first. I'm not turning shit over. I have a no refund policy regardless of whether they agree with me or not. What's theirs is mine, and what's mine is my own."

"Are you an only child too?"

"Yes."

The way she said that...

"You weren't always one."

"No, I wasn't. I had an older and a younger brother. My older brother was stabbed through the neck when he was twenty-five, and my younger brother was shot through the heart when he was nineteen."

"And your parents know what you do?"

"Of course."

"And they're fine with it?"

"When my first career blew up, there weren't too many other jobs for my skill set."

"What did you do before this? Were you a spook?"

I'm joking, but she doesn't crack a smile. She stares at me.

"For which country?"

"Italy, of course." Her chin jerks back, and her nostrils flare.

"I'm Colombian. Why anyone would be proud of being anything besides that is beyond me." I give her a lazy shrug.

"Your dossier said you were born here in the States."

"By accident. There was an early snowstorm that shut down the city for like four days. *Mamá* and *Papá* planned to go back to Colombia in time for her to deliver there. Instead, *Tía* Margherita braved a blizzard to get from northern New Jersey to Queens to deliver me when *Mamá* went into labor two weeks early."

"Your aunt delivered you? At home?"

"She's a midwife like Madeline."

"Why try to leave in winter just to give birth in Colombia? You'd be Colombian through your parents, regardless."

"For starters, it was summer down there which is always preferable to winter up here. We're Latinos. We're not designed for that cold weather bullshit. All of my family was born there. Even Pablo and Juan were despite *Tía* Margherita and *Tío* Luis already living in Jersey. It's just how it is. Or at least was. I don't know whether my two cousins will want to fly to Colombia to have their babies."

"Huh? You only have male cousins."

"We don't talk about in-laws. Once you're a Diaz, you're family. It doesn't matter whether it's by blood or by marriage. So, my cousins' wives are my cousins. Period. Florencia, Pablo's wife, is Colombian, so she'll probably happily go down there since her mother still lives in Bogotá. I doubt Madeline, who's American, or

Anneliese, who's German, will want to deliver babies in a country where they don't fluently speak the language. It seems like an unnecessary complication when they'll already be in pain."

I shrug again. I hadn't really given it much consideration until now. Though, as I stare at Vita, my mind jumps ahead of what common sense says I should be thinking. Would an Italian woman married to a Colombian be willing to give birth there?

"Do you speak Spanish?"

"Yes." She's taken aback by my seemingly random question.

"Just wondering."

"Are you worried I'll understand whatever conversations you have with your family? They'll inevitably either show up here or demand to see me somewhere else."

"They won't demand, but they will expect."

"They won't demand?"

"They know better."

"What do you mean?"

I stare at her for a moment, my gaze intense as my jaw sets. Surprise registers on her face before her brow furrows.

"They know not to make demands on my woman."

"Your woman?"

She scoffs until she realizes I'm serious. Her expression sobers. I hold out my hand, which she peers at before finally standing. She takes it and lets me pull her forward. I guide her to straddle me. I untie her robe before doing the same to mine. Her gaze darts down to my hard-on. She tilts her hips, and I feel how wet she already is. I lift her and guide her onto my cock. She's ready to move, but I hold her hips, keeping her still.

Confusion flashes across her face until she relaxes. She practically flops forward as she leans into me. I slide my arms beneath her robe and wrap them around her. My right hand rests between her shoulder blades while the left glides down from her ribs to her ass then up again. I do it over and over, soothing her.

"*Chica*, we can't avoid my *tío*. It'd be better if he heard these things from you rather than second hand from me. He has to see you to believe you're no longer a threat."

"You believe I'm not."

"Yes. You could play me for a fool, but only if you're willing to die alongside me. You know you won't kill me before I can kill you too."

"Mmm." She sounds unconvinced by my assertion.

"Were you a spy for real?"

"Yes. I studied international political economy at the London School of Economics. *Agenzia Informazioni e Sicurezza Esterna,* or AISE, recruited me straight out of LSE. The External Intelligence and Security Agency is the Italian CIA."

"Oh, I know."

And I do. All too well actually. My entire family is basically on every international watchlist ever created.

"They recruited me because I already spoke Italian, Sicilian, and Spanish. I studied Russian at university."

"I'm guessing they weren't interested in you as an analyst."

"No, they were not."

"A honey trap."

She grimaces. She doesn't appreciate the term. At least I don't have to interpret for her.

"Being attractive helped, but they knew my education and intelligence counted for more."

Helped.

That's putting it mildly.

She's a fucking femme fatale.

"What did you mean by your career exploded?"

"My father pulled *a lot* of strings to keep my family connections from ruining my opportunity to get into international relations. They recruited me without realizing who I was. My father only agreed to let me go to LSE if he could wipe my student records of anything short of my real name and birthdate. He paid a shit ton of money for my anonymity and false background. It all came out during the recruitment process. My father ensured I got treated fairly, all things considered. I worked for the agency for six years, from being twenty-two to twenty-eight. I was great at my job. I was one of the better field agents because I didn't complain about any jobs. I did what I was told and had few reservations about how to complete the mission."

"What went wrong?"

"Everything. My older brother's murder made headlines across the country and half of Europe. Because he had many government contracts, Interpol and other countries' law enforcement agencies investigated his legitimate businesses for corruption. They found nothing. Our family is like yours. It knows how to keep enough companies above board to disguise the ones that aren't. But the damage had been done. Someone leaked photos of my parents and me to the press. I became too recognizable. The Agency claimed it compromised me too much to do fieldwork, which might've been true, but they didn't even want me as an analyst. I was damn good at that too, but they really wanted to distance themselves from anything to do with the Mafia. I was out on my ass."

"How long ago was that?"

"Two years."

"So, from spook to mercenary?"

"Yes. My father arranged my first job. It was supposed to be a favor. I did too good a job. After that, Don Piero suggested I make it a career. My father lost his shit. It's the only time I've ever seen him give Don Piero even a disagreeable look, let alone speak out against him. The money's amazing. It feeds the adrenaline junkie I guess I've become. And I get to keep traveling."

"Don't lie to me, Vita."

"I'm not."

"Omissions are still lies."

"You're one to talk. You'll omit plenty of shit when we talk. You'll lie to my face and behind my back."

"To keep you safe. To keep my family safe. To keep the people who work for us safe. Do you think I want to keep things from you? That any of us hide things from our women for shits and giggles? It's not like we're fucking every pussy we see. We're not lying to cover up infidelity, being an addict, or being a gambler. I will never lie about how I feel about you. I will never jeopardize your safety by omitting details that can keep you alive. But yeah, I will lie about the things I do as that monster I warned you about. You know it's not the same fucking thing. Why did you become a mercenary?"

"To fucking kill the piece of shit who killed my baby brother. I didn't think I'd ever get the chance, but I took the job when I heard about it. Someone paid me to get the revenge I'd wanted for five years. I did that for my mother and father. They deserved their son being avenged. Six months later, I killed the man who stabbed my older brother and left him to bleed. That was a year-and-a-half ago."

"Who were the men?"

She hesitates to tell me. I know she's weighing her options.

"Radek Janković, the Serbian oligarch, killed my younger brother, Beniamino."

When she pauses, I feel like she's trying to brace me for what's coming next rather than finding the nerve to tell me. I already know I won't like it.

"Filippo was murdered by Rafael De Santos Rúiz."

She leans away and watches me.

"You murdered my cousin."

Chapter Fourteen

Vita

"I killed your second cousin once removed who you met twice as a toddler."

He radiates anger, so I try to rise from his cock and his lap. His arms become a vise.

"Oh, no you don't. You don't drop that little bomb and run away from the explosion. My family knew it was a hit, but no one knew why. What did he have to do with your brother?"

"He was a fucking sore loser in Monte Carlo. He thought he was James Bond at the baccarat table. My brother laughed at someone's joke about the upcoming Grand Prix and how some driver needed to pray before hitting the Circuit de Monaco. Rafael thought Filippo was laughing at him for his loss. Apparently, my brother tried to smooth things over and even left the table. But that wasn't enough for Rafael. He followed my brother into a restroom and killed him. Your piece of shit relative fled that night and went back to Colombia to hide. Since there's no specific extradition treaty, your government wouldn't hand him over. It could've fallen under the UN Convention against Transnational

Organized Crime. Neither country wanted the attention. Turns out, neither did I."

I don't disguise the disdain I feel for Alejandro's relative. He got what he motherfucking deserved.

I sigh, waiting for Alejandro's condemnation, waiting for the thin thread of trust we created to snap. Instead, he runs one hand up and down my back while the other sweeps up and down my leg from knee to hip. He strokes over my ass, and it's insanely soothing. My anger isn't gone. It never is when I think about how I became an only child. It settles into the pit of my stomach where it can quietly fester.

"Is that why you accepted this assignment? Because I'm Raf's relative?"

"No. That was about the money and the accomplishment."

"What was I to you? Your white rhino?"

"Something like that."

"You'd never be able to claim the clout in public."

"I don't need to. Private satisfaction is stronger than public validation for me."

God, how I wanted to scream from the rooftops when I took out those two murderers.

How I wanted people to know they better stay the fuck away from my family.

The Romans invented the word vendetta.

The modern Italians perfected it.

I'm unprepared for him to lift his chin and sit forward to kiss me. It's so tender. I don't know what to do other than return the affection.

"*Chiquita*, I'm sorry someone in my family wronged you and yours. Nothing about your story surprises me. He's barely missed. *Tío* Enrique didn't even go to the funeral. Rafael was *Tío* Enrique's extended family through marriage, but he'd normally attend for *Papá's* sake. They've been friends since high school. My *tío* didn't even glance at his calendar to see if he was free before saying he was too busy."

I feel marginally better, but who knows what Alejandro's

parents will think when they find out. Maybe his father was close to his second cousin.

"Thank you for understanding."

What else do I say?

"Why did you accept this job?"

"Honestly? Besides the money and knowing I could take out a Diaz without anyone stopping me, I was curious to see you."

"See me? There are photos of me online."

"Yeah, some shitty ones from public events. You have next to no social media, and what you do have are profile shots of you at sporting events. It's just enough to make you look normal without giving away anything about your life."

"And you have an active social life online?"

"More than you. I hide in plain sight."

"What did you want to see about me?"

I suck my lips in between my teeth. My cheeks heat, and I try not to laugh as I gaze down at his uncovered abs and pecs.

"I wanted to see if you're as hot as people claim. Like untouchable hotness."

"And?"

"And what?"

We're back to tormenting each other. It lifts a crushing weight off me that's threatened to flatten me since I agreed to tell him the truth.

"We both know I'm very touchable for you. Am I hot?" He waggles his eyebrows at me.

"Egotistical."

"Because I'm hot enough to be proud of it?"

"Arrogant."

"My mother says charming."

"She does not! There is no way she finds your arrogance charming."

"Because I hide that and only show her my best manners."

I laugh hard enough to snort. He groans when my cunt contracts around him. We freeze as desire courses through us. We fight to ignore our urge to move, our need to get off.

"Seriously, *chiquita*. You said you don't know who hired you, but you have to have some hypothesis. You wouldn't take the job if it wasn't someone you could trust even a little."

"I've ruled out the families here and the *Cosa Nostra* in Chicago and Boston. But it could be anywhere with a cartel presence. Your family is *the Cartel*, so you have more enemies than most. It could be Triad or the Golden Triangle. But I suspect they're European not Asian."

He tilts his head back and exhales a heavy sigh.

"It's either your family or the Torettas."

"Why them?"

"Because they're in a feud with Jorge's fiancée's brother-in-law's family."

"What?" And this is why I gave up trying to create family trees for these fucking orchards.

"Anneliese's new brother-in-law is connected to the Camorra branch in Germany."

"And they're allied with the *'Ndrangheta*. The four Mafias are in a proxy war funded by the bratva and mob here in New York."

"Yup." His tone's sarcastic, but his expression's resigned.

"Couldn't the Kutsenkos or O'Rourkes have put the hit on you?"

"No. Definitely not. We might wind up killing each other in a fight one of these days, but no one in a leading family is putting a hit on a member of another leading family. It'd be Cold War level MAD. No family would survive that mutually assured destruction. It's in no one's best interest to spill that much blood. It's messy. It draws too much attention, and the potential power vacuum will invite pretenders to the throne. Death by accident is fine. Death by hire is not. We have lines we won't cross."

"Scrupulous syndicates. I doubt anyone would ever believe me."

"You know our ethics are situational in the outside world. In ours, they're absolute. The rest of the world believes we're—at best —morally gray. You know our morals are fucking crystal clear among us. We all take oaths that are basically the same regardless of the language or motherland. It's how we keep each other in check. The bratva and mob might not stop an outsider from killing me, but they wouldn't hire someone to do it."

"Because of all that politics or because they know your mother?"

I jest, but he looks me dead in the eye.

"*Mamá*. And she doesn't travel alone."

He warned me about the women in the Four Families, but his reaction is chilling.

What the fuck will she do to me when she finds out?

"*Chica*, I can read lips just like I suspect you can. You didn't keep that thought to yourself. She'd be more pissed than a shaken hive if she met you without me. But once she knows I've accepted you and that I won't give you up, she'll understand."

He won't give me up?

That sounds like a declaration of love from a man like Alejandro. The men in his family might have subs, but they don't keep mistresses.

He already said I won't be his sub, and I doubt he'll become the first to have a mistress.

"*Chica*."

"Hmm?"

"The gears are spinning hard enough to put out steam. Do you really think you're sitting on my dick because we're just fuck buddies for a few days?"

"Nooo."

I draw out the syllable because I know that's the expected answer, but I'm not convinced it's true.

"Vita, you might already be part of this world, but you aren't part of my family. Yet I've told you things about my family's past. I let you get close to my cousin rather than just our men. I brought you to a safehouse rather than giving you a plane ticket. I *stayed* in this safehouse knowing you might still try to kill me. You said it yourself. I'm hot. If all I wanted was pussy, I wouldn't go after the one belonging to a woman paid to kill me."

"Maybe you have a God complex. Maybe you're a narcissist or

a megalomaniac. Maybe you believe your size is enough to stop me."

I don't believe any of those things.

"That's bullshit, and you know it. You wouldn't have told me about your past or your family if I was just a guy to fuck and forget. Why do you think the sex is so good? Because we're both hot? Hardly. You know it, and I know it."

"What the hell are we supposed to know?"

"You already claimed me. You said I was all yours."

"During sex."

"Don't lie."

Do I want this?

Yes, but—

Your family will never accept this. You'd turn against them for what?

A chance at happiness.

More like a chance this'll fucking explode in your face and leave you with nothing.

"I'm not."

His hands grip my ass like steel claws. In a weaker person, it would be excruciating. He's not careless. He knows what I can manage. He brings our lips together, and I don't stop him when he practically swallows me whole.

I couldn't even if I wanted to.

He doesn't relent, not even when I give in and let him take control. With an arm around my waist, he flips us, so I'm lying on the sofa.

"If sex is all I'm good for..."

He thrusts into me over and over.

"Daddy, please!"

His smile is pure sin.

"Now you remember. You'd never call me that if this was just about getting off. You have two hands and a vibrator for that. I liked the purple."

Of course, he found that when he searched my room. I was

mortified but said nothing. There was no point. He couldn't unfind it.

He pulls the belt loose from his robe and binds my hands like he did in the hotel, except this time, he bends my arms and presses my wrists between my breasts. With my belt knotted with his, he soon has me in some makeshift Shibari-style halter. The belts loop around my breasts, accentuating them while keeping my arms locked in place.

If I told him to stop, he would. I don't doubt that for a moment. He could gag me, and if I snapped, he would end this. But I make no move to do that. My hips rise and fall to his cadence while our gazes are locked.

"Admit it, *chiquita*."

I shake my head.

"You're brave enough to fuck me and to kill me, but not to admit we have something real already. You're a coward."

My eyes widen as the air whooshes from me. Now I fight against him. Calling me a coward is tantamount to saying I have no honor. In our world, that's nearly the worst slight anyone can issue. He knows that.

"Take that fucking back, Jandro. I won't forgive you if you don't."

"You're too scared of what our families will think and say to admit you want me as much as I want you."

"We barely know each other."

"You know more about me than most people outside my family. I may not have shared every detail of my past, but I've told you some. That's more than any woman's ever gotten. Why's that? Because you fucking matter to me. It's why I haven't killed you and have offered my protection instead. You were brave enough to tell me the truth about the assignment, but now you turn into a—"

"Don't say it again. I seriously won't forgive you."

"*Cobarde*."

"To hell with you. Saying it in Spanish doesn't make it okay. Get off."

"Believe me I will. Your tight little cunt has me nearly there already."

We both know my physical struggle is half-hearted, even if I mean all the venom in my words. He lowers himself until his chest is only inches above my fists still tied to my body. He slows his strokes as he continues to thrust into me.

"*Chica*, you have a right to be afraid of what'll happen next. But you're lying about that and about what you want. You refuse to admit it out of fear. Why when I'll be beside you the entire time?"

He brushes hair back from my temple before kissing the corner of my mouth. I turn my head to capture his lips. The kiss is languid after the struggle a moment ago.

"Take it back."

"When you accept what's happening."

"What do you want from me, Daddy?"

That word. I'm still not used to hearing it, but it feels so natural to say.

"You can't tell me all your secrets just like I can't tell you all of mine. But you can be honest about your feelings. I told you I'd never lie about how I feel. Can't you do the same?"

My visceral reaction after years of training is to scream "no." That admitting anything about me is handing over the keys to the castle for someone to use me and hurt me. But my gut tells me that's the last thing Alejandro would do.

If you admit your feelings—at least the ones you think are starting, you know you'll never find a man more loyal or dedicated to you.

He trusts even less than I do, but he's taking the chance on me. He wouldn't do that if this weren't real. He'd find some other way to manipulate me. He was right that he told me things about his family he'd never tell a woman he's just banging. He wouldn't tell me to lure me in to kill me either.

I killed a member of his family—unliked or not—and he isn't treating me any differently. Just the opposite. He listened, and he consoled me.

He took your fucking side!

Alejandro remains silent, rocking his hips into me as I think. He could get himself off while my mind's a million miles away. Instead, he's letting me work through all my thoughts while bringing my body closer and closer to heaven.

"Let me go."

I try to raise my hands, but there's little room between us. He stares at me, debating whether I mean just untie me or I'm leaving. He plucks at the knot, releasing my arms. I grab the ends of the belt and pull them up to tie around my neck like a halter. It lifts my tits as I arch my back.

"Thank you, *caro*."

"*Mi chica*."

He sighs as his hands slide beneath my back and up to hook over my shoulders. I let my outside leg drop off the sofa, my foot pushing into the floor to lever my hips as he returns to pounding my pussy. I graze my teeth along his neck, wishing I could mark him like he did me. I'll find somewhere I can.

"Here."

He points to a spot on his chest that has particularly dark ink. My teeth skim along it before I pull my chin down. My lips latch onto his skin and suck as hard as I dare. When I release him, I see the faint hint of red. We'll know that mark is there.

"Here."

He points to a place on the other side of his chest near his nipple. I nip at the tight bud before trailing my tongue over it. My lips rest on the spot he showed me. I latch on, once again leaving a bite only we'll know about. I kiss a spot over his heart. A place where I think I could mark him, but he hasn't offered. I gaze up at him, and he nods. Something in his eyes tells me he loves me claiming him. I leave the third mark before resting my head back on the sofa cushion.

"Jandro, I won't be scared if you stand with me."

"Always."

We move together until we're screaming each other's names. We're breathless as we come. He pulls me up as he sits. He unties the robes' belts before helping me arrange the robes to cover us. Neither of us thinks someone will walk in, but we're both trained to expect the unexpected and not recklessly leave ourselves vulnerable.

"*Chiquita,* I don't expect you to love me yet. But I expect you to give this a genuine try. You owe it to both of us."

Yet.

What if I already do?

Chapter Fifteen

Alejandro

My stomach feels like it doesn't remember the last time I ate. I'm a big guy who works out twice a day. I'm used to eating three to four thousand calories a day. Anything else feels like I'm fasting in the desert for forty days and nights.

After running upstairs to redress, Vita and I head into the kitchen to see what's available in the house. While the fridge is virtually empty except for condiments, there're plenty of options in the pantry. I silently thank my *mamá* and *tías* for always being prepared.

I consider all the things the women in my family do to support the Cartel. They're all willing and able to defend the people they love most. All have had to do that, but the everyday running of the Cartel falls on the men's shoulders.

The women do all the things behind the scenes. They ensure families have enough food and proper roofs over their heads. They protect the women and children from men who can't separate work life from home life. They even look out for the men whose women never reconcile with the life they live and take it out on their partners.

The women in my family are the silent strength behind the men. They're the beauty and the brains that keep us going. Hell, half the time they're the brawn too.

"There's plenty of rice in here. I'm certain we can do something with that as well as this canned tuna. It may not be the most delicious meal you've ever had, but I can make something that resembles a tuna casserole."

Vita's brow furrows at my suggestion. "A casserole? How very American of you."

I chuckle. "When in Rome."

It's her turn to laugh.

"They're little more than peasants living on a hill. When they can survive living in a city that floats on water, then they can brag."

Her dismissive tone makes me grin. While the world knows of the ancient Roman Empire, there's certainly plenty the Venetians have offered through the centuries.

"There's an unofficial hierarchy of countries in Latin America. It seems like in your mind there's a hierarchy of Italian culture."

She vigorously nods her head.

"Absolutely, even if it may only be in my mind. Though, ask anyone in a Mafia family, and they'll certainly let you know where their hometown ranks."

"At the top, I assume."

"Of course, and everywhere else is a million miles below."

"So, I shouldn't buy you Neapolitan ice cream."

She rolls her eyes. "Not the American shit you people call a dessert. Find me a proper gelato, and then we can talk."

"*Cholado* is what you really need to try."

It's sort of a mix of fruit cocktail, a drink, and a frozen dessert. Delicious.

She pauses for a moment; her mouth hangs open as though she's deciding what she wants to admit.

"I've had that several times."

That grabs my attention as I set a pot of water to boil in preparation for the minute rice.

"How much work have you done in Colombia?"

"Not a ton, but a few jobs here and there for my family."

If that's the case, this is something she should've revealed to me several hours ago, certainly before having mind-blowing sex.

She shakes her head. "No, not for your family and except for your cousin, never against your family. It was when I first got started. Lesser cartels squabbling with one another. Nowadays, no one but your family could afford me in Colombia. I already told you what the bounty was on you."

"Bounty? It wasn't dead or alive."

"Semantics. You know what you're worth to my employer."

I watch her grab a can of fruit cocktail and green beans. Rice, tuna, green beans, and fruit cocktail. Definitely not the Michelin star meals I'm accustomed to, but it's certainly better than remaining hungry.

"What would you—"

Vita's question's interrupted by hammering on the door, then Joaquin's voice calling out to me.

"Alejo?"

"*Sí, estamos en la cocina.*" Yes, we're in the kitchen.

Even though I can't hear them yet, I'm sure his brothers are with him. I've just poured the rice into the water when *Tres J's* joins Vita and me in the kitchen. I study their expressions as they survey our little domesticated scene. With a synchronicity that defies even the most well-studied genetics, their left nostrils curl in disgust as they take in the cans on the kitchen island. Their gazes snap to me as they frown.

"You can talk to your *mamá* or mine about the food they stock here. Would you like to let them know you disagree with their selections?"

Three identical scowls make me chuckle. From a distance, they're difficult to tell apart for anyone outside our family. They bear a close resemblance to one another, but up close, it's easy to distinguish their differences.

Their gazes shift to Vita as they assess her. I turn my attention to her and watch her reaction to my cousins' arrival. She's standing with her hands on the kitchen island, palms against the marble. She's suggesting she isn't a threat. Her shoulders are back and chin is up. It's not defiance. It's that aura I've realized she projects when she's uncertain of a situation and is prepared to defend herself verbally or physically.

I step beside her and shoot my cousins a warning. I restrain the urge to cover one of her hands with mine. It's a sign of solidarity I'm not ready to share with my family. Not unless I have to defend her. When I return my focus to them, their expressions are bland compared to what they looked like when they assessed our meal prep. Those who don't know them would say they appear unemotional. However, we read each other so well, there are few secrets among us.

I know they're wary of her because she's an outsider. Add that to their awareness that she and I met because of the hit put on me. It surprises me they didn't come in with guns drawn ready to light her up, assuming she'll continue her attempt to kill me.

"How's Pablo doing?"

It's Javier who answers without shifting his gaze from Vita. "He's fine. Complaining that Florencia isn't sympathetic enough."

"Is she?"

"No. She told her husband he should've ducked."

My cousins and I chuckle, but I watch Vita's brow furrow.

"My cousin's wife grew up in Bogotá with a complicated family history connected to my other cousins' parents." I nudge my chin toward the men as I speak.

Once again, their expressions don't change, but there's a hardening in their gaze. It's not toward Florencia or the thought of her but toward her father's family and all that *Tres J's* and *Tía* Luciana lost because of them. If it hadn't been for Florencia's father's family, my *tío* would still be alive.

When I turn my head toward Vita, I know she's considering what she just heard. When the realization hits, she must know more about that part of my family's history than I realized. I wonder if that comes from the dossier she received for this job or perhaps information she learned during her trips to Colombia. She senses me watching her and turns to face me. Her only reaction's a nod. Javier's words turn my attention back to my cousins.

"*Primo*, we need to talk in private."

Never before have I hesitated like I do now. I don't want to be rude to Vita by leaving her alone to likely go and talk about her. There's a flash of hurt in her eyes. I suspect she believes my hesitation comes from me not trusting her to be alone in the house while my cousins and I meet behind a closed door. She doesn't understand I'm trying to consider her feelings.

The path to hell is paved with good intentions.

"*Tres J's*, I'll meet you in the living room in just a moment."

I know we won't speak Spanish while we meet, so I'm unconcerned about Vita hearing us. We'll speak *Macaguán* instead. Once my cousins file out of the kitchen, I slip my right arm around her waist and tug her toward me. She's resistant at first, but my arm's a steel band around her waist. Rather than let me knock her off balance to get what I want, she turns and steps closer.

"*Chiquita*, you can finish cooking if you want or go up to the bedroom and watch TV. There's also the den. I bet there's a TV there too."

"If you trust me to be that far out of your sight."

There's a bite to her tone. Not that I can blame her. I brush my knuckles against her cheek before bussing a kiss on her lips.

"*Chica*, this isn't about trust. My hesitation was about being rude and leaving you alone while I speak with my cousins."

She stares at me, weighing my words, unconvinced of my sincerity. If I wouldn't have had the same reaction, I'd be hurt by hers. However, I understand. It takes a moment before she nods.

"Thank you for being so considerate, Jandro. I'll see what I can manage in here and let you know when it's done."

We both look at the stove where the rice sits ready. There's a can of tuna on the counter beside it. There's very little else to prep.

"I spotted some mayonnaise and relish in the fridge. I suppose I can make something like tuna salad."

Neither of us appears excited by her suggestion, but we'll make do. I give her another quick kiss and tap her on the ass before I head to the living room. I don't bother with Spanish and speak to my cousins in *Macaguán* instead.

"The least you could've done is bring us something to eat if you're going to arrive without any warning."

"I knocked."

Javier's the brusquest in our family. He's not exactly anti-social, but he hates people. The only people he wants to people with are the people he already loves. Needless to say, with a stranger in the house, he's not at his most outgoing right now.

"You could've called or texted me."

That makes three sets of eyebrows shoot up to their hairlines. Joaquin smirks, and I know what's coming.

"So that's how it is, huh?"

I know he's referring to the married couples' households. We always had an open-door policy to each other's homes. If Pablo's parents or my parents were home, we'd give them a courtesy text or call since both couples are still as frisky—shall we say—as they were when they married. No one wants to walk in on a couple's intimate moments, so that policy now applies to *Tío* Enrique and *Tía* Elle, along with my cousins and their wives.

Javier and Madeline got married two months ago, and Pablo and Florencia got married two days before I went to Chicago. Nobody wants to walk in on either of those newlyweds. Jorge and Anneliese picked out a wedding date in two months. Nobody wants to intrude on the new couple either. *Tres J's* understand Vita and I are now like the other couples in our family.

"You've always been the biggest thrill seeker of all of us. *Tía* Catalina's always worried that one of these days your lack of fear will get you killed. Are you trying to prove her right?"

I grit my teeth as I stare at Jorge. His eyes widen as he realizes he didn't hit just a nerve but an entire bundle. I don't appreciate his implied jest that Vita might still try to kill me, and that I'm putting my life in her hands for a quick fuck. He throws his hands up and shakes his head.

"I didn't realize, *Primo*."

"Well, now you all know."

Joaquin tries to keep the peace when he leans forward. "I'm certain Pablo would've told us if Madeline hadn't knocked him out before pulling out the bullet. Then Florencia insisted we all leave him alone and let him rest."

I offer them a jerky nod. Silence hangs among us for a few seconds before Jorge launches into why they came besides to check on me. He's our accountant and best understands the programs the Four Families use for our selective bookkeeping.

"We know the Kutsenkos and O'Rourkes are funneling more money into Italy to keep this war going. They're keeping it on another continent so none of their hands get dirty and the feds don't notice how much money we're talking."

The Kutsenkos support the Camorra and '*Ndrangheta*, while the O'Rourkes support the *Mala del Brenta* and the *Cosa Nostra*. Joaquin's our head intelligence gatherer, so he'll have found the data and passed it along to Jorge to interpret.

"So far, about twenty million dollars a side."

I shoot them a lopsided grin. "That's the going rate for me, apparently."

"What?"

Javier's clearly not interested in me changing the subject. I suspect he wants to get home to Madeline, so he can have a proper dinner rather than what good manners will insist I offer them.

"That's the price on my head. Twenty-million dollars. An extra ten for collateral damage."

Joaquin shoots me an expression of pure disgust. "An extra ten-million-dollars just because you're the pretty one in the family?"

"What can I say? I'm a total package. Brains and beauty."

That earns me a snort from all three of them. We all know it's something personal with whoever took out the hit, but it's also because I'm the chief strategist in our family. Taking out Pablo, who's the heir, would cause too much of a stir. *Tres J's* are our head enforcers and all-around shit stirrers, but they each have their own roles.

In addition to Jorge being an accountant and Joaquin being our intel analyst, Javier's our attorney. Neither *Tío* Enrique nor *Tío* Luis can practice anymore. They'll help when they have time behind the scenes. They'll draft briefs and do research if Javier's particularly busy. But my cousin handles all the litigation and is the forward face for most contract negotiations.

Jorge brings us back to where we were. "The Mancinellis hit the Kutsenkos, wiping out their entire construction project, and they're trying to make it look like we did it. I'll give Gabriele and Matteo credit where credit is due. They did a pretty fucking good job fucking us over. They hired a bunch of Puerto Ricans to do the job and set them up to take the fall. The Kutsenkos got at least two of them. We know the bratva recognizes these guys are Puerto Rican, not Colombian, but we suspect the Mancinellis have these men's families. So, none of them will admit who hired them. Instead, they're claiming it's us."

I scowl. "Wonderful. Just what we need. I bet Maks is extra pissed that this is a distraction from what's happening in Italy. Any insight into their plans to hit us back?"

Joaquin shakes his head. "Not yet. It's annoyingly quiet on their end. There's no chatter going on, so they're still in the planning stage. We know that means they're only meeting in their own homes."

Despite all our wealth, no one in the Four Families keeps a staff at their home. We don't even have housekeepers. Partly, it's for privacy and security. The other part is all of us grew up with an expectation that no amount of wealth means we're entitled to be lazy. Whether it's doing dishes or scrubbing toilets, no one is above any job or chore.

The only time we might bring someone in is if a couple hosts a large family gathering. They might have help catering or cleaning up afterwards. But even then, it's not like anyone leaves a mess in someone else's home. Bachelors might have somebody come in if they've been away on an extended trip, but only when we're in the home. No one in the Four Families will trust strangers alone in their house.

"So, what do we do, Alejo?" Javier brings my attention back to the present.

"We need to call *tío* and Pablo if he's well enough."

I pull out my phone and put the call on speaker. I greet *Tío* Enrique and ask him to hold on a moment while I try to get Pablo on the line too. He sounds groggy but with it enough to join the conversation. *Tres J's* shares what we just talked about. As they fill in our relatives, I consider our best course of action.

"Pablo, reach out to the Carosis and offer the *Mala del Brenta* help. With everything that happened to Jorge and Anneliese, none of *Tres J's* can do it. With a hit on me, I can't either."

Tío Enrique's voice comes through the speaker. "Why can't you do it?"

This is the part I'm not looking forward to explaining.

"The mercenary is Vittoria Trevisan."

There's an unnerving silence that greets my declaration. Everyone recognizes the last name as the one belonging to the *Mala del Brenta consigliere.* I inhale a deep breath before continuing.

"She's his daughter, so you can see why it can't be me. She doesn't think her father knows about this job. Not who hired her nor who her current mark is."

"You truly believe that."

Tío Enrique's skepticism fills the silence. My gaze darts from one cousin to another before I look down at the phone in my hand.

"Yes. I know why Vittoria became a mercenary. I'm confident she doesn't share her employer's names with her family or who her targets are. She separates work from family just like we do. If Pablo reaches out to Piero, they're going to want to know why we're making the offer. Pablo, you can tell Piero it's our way of showing the O'Rourkes our appreciation for such a good time at the charity gala."

We all know that's a weak excuse, but it will do since Piero won't expect us to be more forthcoming. He'll probably do some research to find out why, but there are limitations to his reach.

Pablo's voice is strained when he speaks, but we can still hear him. "What do we offer the *Mala*?"

"Tell them we want to block the Kutsenkos' expansion goals into Spain. That only native Spanish speakers are welcome. Let him know Jorge already warned Maks to stay out, and now we're following through on that promise. Find out how much Pasha offered them and give them more."

Pasha Kutsenko's a cousin of the four brothers who lead the Ivankov branch. He's their family's accountant for all their questionable dealings. His wife, Sumiko, now handles all their legit accounting.

When there are big bribes to be paid, each of the Four Families relies on their accountant to make it happen. It's not like anyone isn't well versed in how much they can spend or where the money's going. But the accountants know best when to adjust offers and counteroffers.

Tío Enrique asks the next obvious question. "And when they ask what we want in return?"

"Tell them we want contact with Italy's best female mercenary. Tell them we have a job we want done against the *Sacra Corona Unita*."

United Sacred Crown—they're one of the largest organized crime groups in Italy. While the *Cosa Nostra* claim they're the only organization who deserve the name Mafia, it's not given to any Italian syndicate.

My *tío* sounds unconvinced when he responds. "The *Sacra Corona Unita* have next to nothing to do with any of us. Why would we target them?"

"Because they're not involved in this war. They think they can fly under the radar for everything, but they can't. It's time they know they're being watched just like anyone else. It'll be a good reminder for them that nobody's business is as private as they think."

Javier's skepticism comes through in his next question. "Do you really want to draw them in?"

"Not particularly. If we have to—to keep this excuse going—then we can. But it's something to tell Piero."

"All right, when do you want me to make the call?"

"Not right now, Pablo. You sound like shit. Whenever you're feeling better will be soon enough."

"Fine. Give me until tomorrow, then I'll do it. Do you want to be on the call too?"

"Possibly. We'll see what's going on."

Tío Enrique asks what I don't want to answer quite yet because I'm not ready to share how things stand.

"And what if he names Vittoria?"

Chapter Sixteen

Vita

I wish Alejandro were still in his private meeting with his relatives because we weren't arguing then.

"*Jandro.*"

I hiss his name to interrupt him, but I don't want his cousins to hear me use the nickname.

"I am *not* going to Enrique and Elodie's home. How on earth can you believe that's a good idea? Are you trying to get me chained up by my fingernails?"

"We don't do that type of stuff at home."

I practically snarl at him. "That's not reassuring."

We're in the dining room now while his cousins remain in the living room. We abandoned the food since none of us could stomach it. Alejandro introduced the idea of us going over to Enrique and Elodie's home by suggesting we could have a proper meal there.

I was tempted to listen at the door while Alejandro met with his cousins since I'm certain they included Enrique and Pablo in the conversation, if not Alejandro's father and other uncle. But I knew they were likely using the Amerindian indigenous language his family speaks. There's no way I would've understood, so there was no point in attempting to eavesdrop.

"Going to my *tío* and *tía's* house is the best option for you. It'll keep you safe."

I shake my head hard enough to make my hair swish across my back. "No. Stick me in a hotel somewhere. Out of sight, out of mind."

"That didn't exactly work the last time."

"Yeah, because I wasn't alone."

"*Chiquita*, you have to face *Tía* Elle at some point. It's better she be on your side than not. Let me introduce you to her as someone other than a rival mercenary."

I clench my jaw.

"Jandro, this is not a good idea. In fact, it's probably one of the worst ideas you could ever have."

"*Chiquita*, you're going to be around them at some point. May as well get the introductions over with now."

He makes it sound as though we have a future. If we hadn't met under the circumstances we did, I might believe that. Reality's setting in. I can't picture any of his family welcoming me. And I certainly can't picture Enrique sanctioning our relationship. He may have found out about his wife's past, but she never worked against the Diazes.

"*Chiquita*—"

"Will anybody else be there?" I cut him off before he can try placating me again.

"Probably."

I cock an eyebrow, and he has the decency to look down before meeting my gaze again.

"Yes, there's a good chance my parents will be there too."

"Because they heard about me, and your mom wants to skin me alive, and your father's sharpening her knife."

"No, not entirely."

His casual tone grates on my nerves. I try to turn away, but he shifts to block my way as he speaks.

"*Chica,* people will be at the house because we always gather for Sunday dinner. They'd be there anyway."

"Marvelous. You want to introduce me to your entire family during a time that's set aside for just the family."

I'm rigid when he hugs me. I can feel an invisible noose tightening around my neck. Today is surely the day I will finally die. He strokes the hair down my back and kisses my temple. My forehead falls to his chest. This is yet another time where his touch is soothing. However, the circumstances keep it from calming me the way it has in the past.

"Do you fear *Tía* Elle more than you do meeting my parents?"

"No, I dread them equally. How could I not? I told you your mom is probably waiting to kill me, and your father will hand her the weapon. How could I not fear meeting them? Pablo's probably told them all about me already."

"I told them about you."

"What?"

I jerk away from him, or at least I try. He loosens his hold enough for his hands to rest on my waist.

"I sent a text to my cousins and *tíos* when I was in the bathroom in your hotel room. I asked Pablo to come with extra guards and wait outside the room. Right after that, I sent a message through our family group chat saying I'd be introducing them to someone soon and that they'd better not pass judgment until I explain the situation. That—as usual—there's more to this than the obvious."

"I can't believe you did that, Alejandro. What the hell? You didn't even know I wouldn't still try to kill you, and you told them you'd bring a girl home to meet your parents? Great. Not only are they going to dislike me because of my job and how we met, but they'll dislike me in general because I'm some stranger to them who they think is after their son. I can't believe this is happening. This is truly one of the shittiest days I've ever had."

I stare at Alejandro as though he sprouted a second head. When he opens his mouth, I glower at him.

"Don't you dare tell me to calm down."

"I wouldn't dream of it. The last thing you do is tell an irate woman to calm down."

"You are not funny."

I curl my hands into fists to keep from jabbing him in the chest with my index finger.

"You're assuming the worst before anything even happens, *chica*."

"They've had hours to plot my demise, and you're just springing this on me now, telling me that we're leaving in ten minutes? I don't appreciate this, Jandro."

"Well, I don't appreciate you trying to kill me, but I'm not holding that against you, am I?"

Now I try to pull away in earnest. "That's a seriously fucked-up thing to say."

"But am I wrong? I think if I can get over you stalking me, intending to put a bullet through my brain or heart, then you can get over the surprise of Sunday dinner with people you're going to get to know pretty damn well."

"Why? Why would I get to know them well?"

He stares at me as though I'm the one who sprouted a second head.

"Do I really have to spell this out for you, Vita?"

"Clearly you do because I'm missing something."

"We talked about this already."

"Maybe in your head, but definitely not out loud. What are you talking about, Alejandro?"

"Well, Vittoria—" The sarcasm in his voice makes me want to throat punch him.

"Don't do that. You've called me Vita since you learned that's my name. I called you Alejandro for a lot longer. It's not the same."

"Yes, it is. You stopped using my full name when you started calling me Jandro. So, if you don't want me to scold you, then don't you do the same to me."

We glare at each other. Our tempers flare to boiling.

"You know damn well that neither of us would've shared

anything about our real life if this thing between us was going nowhere, *chiquita*. You also know two hot people who like to fuck isn't a guarantee the sex will be as good as what we have. You know it's because there's more between us than just physical attraction. Don't pretend there isn't. I've told you before, don't lie to me about your feelings. I get you may not be able to tell me the truth about everything. But if I can tell you the truth of my feelings, then you can give me the same courtesy."

"How we feel about each other isn't what will keep me alive."

"Vita, it's about the only thing that'll keep you alive."

He practically snaps at me. It's his turn to take a calming breath.

"Look, we can go around and around, *chica*. Or you can admit what we both know. If there was nothing between us, one of us would be dead by now. And it's no guarantee it would've been me. You know I see a future for us, and that's why I'm taking you to my family."

"There might be a future between us, but we barely know each other. Neither of us can say something with such certainty."

I can tell I'm sorely testing his patience as he takes another deep breath before responding.

"If you deny you've imagined what things could be like between us, then you're only fooling yourself. I know I've been thinking about it nonstop since Chicago. That means we've both had far longer to consider our choices than we normally would for most things. You and I both make life-changing decisions in the blink of an eye. As often as we might plan our course of action and do our best to create scenarios we control, we both know that's not always possible. Our minutes are like days for most people. Hours are weeks. Days are months. None of us think years in advance. Will you deny considering what a future would look like with me?"

I don't want to lie to him. It would be pointless to try. I bring my palms up to rest on his chest.

"Yes, I've imagined that. But all it was, was imagining. It's not real."

"Only because you say it's not. Only because you won't let it be real. It could be if you wanted it."

He's so insistent that I could almost believe him.

"In what world does this work out?"

He stares at me as though I'm stupid, and I feel my temper flare all over again. He must read it in my expression even though I didn't think it changed.

"*Chiquita*, the very couple I want us to go to are the ones who prove it's possible."

"That's different, and you know it. This lifestyle never consumed Elodie like it has me. She left it behind."

"No, she didn't. She could've killed me, and she chose not to."

The words tumble out of his mouth. My eyes widen to where they hurt.

"Vita, she did a job where I was the only one who walked away. If I didn't look just like *Tío* Enrique, I'd probably be dead too. She took out all the men around me and left me alive."

It couldn't have been that long ago. I know Elodie and Enrique have been together for less than two years.

"I thought she retired years ago."

"She thought she had too. But there was a job she couldn't avoid. If *Tío* Enrique—or more importantly my parents—could overlook the danger I was in, then they can accept you."

"But you were never her primary target. Just the opposite. That you weren't her target at all is why you survived. They're going to see things with me differently."

"Can you please just trust me to know my family better than you do? If I bring you home with me, they know it's because we're together."

"For now, until we resolve all of this."

I fight against the possibility of a future with Alejandro because I don't want to be disappointed when it inevitably doesn't happen. If I don't open my heart, then it can't be slammed shut when this fails.

"No, not just for now. There's no 'just for now' with couples in my family. Either we're all in or not in at all."

I stare at him. That's a lot to take in. It's not a declaration of love, but it could be a life sentence.

"Look, Jandro, I'm not ready for this yet. It would be better if I went to a hotel rather than stay with your family. That's assuming my waiting for you to return is the best option. I know you're not just going to your family's for dinner. Wherever you're going afterward, I should be there too. If somebody else took on this job, then I'm the best person you can have with you to protect you."

"Absolutely not. I'm not making you a secondary target."

"But would you recognize all the mercenaries out there? You didn't even recognize Patrick, and he's worked for you before. If somebody's around that's there to kill you, I'm far more likely to recognize them than you are."

"You don't even have a change of clothes, let alone any of your disguises."

"I don't need my disguises to be able to point out who's there to kill you. I have better tracking skills than anyone else in your family purely because of my job. If my tracking skills were such shit, I wouldn't have found you."

He has the audacity to laugh.

"*Chiquita*, it's not like it was hard to figure out who I am. It's no secret I'd be in Jackson Heights. I was the richest man there each day you visited. It's not like I tried to blend in. It was obvious who I am. You've met *Tres J's*. They practically look like triplets. And everybody knows I'm a younger version of *Tío* Enrique, and Pablo's a younger version of *Tío* Luis. There's no way anybody could've confused me for any of my cousins. Plus, I'm sure you had photos of me in your dossier, and we met in Chicago and the club. It's not exactly like you had to be Sherlock Holmes to find me."

He word vomits, and it does nothing to endear him to me. He may not be wrong, but his tone certainly has the opposite effect on me from making me want to comply.

"Jandro, that's not the point."

"Of course, it's the point. Hell, I caught you. That's why we're together right now."

"Don't you think if I wanted to hide, I would've tried a little harder? Maybe I didn't mind getting caught."

Now it's my turn to vomit my thoughts. His hands cup my jaw as he swoops in for one of those kisses that leaves me drunk. I fist his shirt and tug him closer. I know *Tres J's* can hear our argument, and they probably think we're fucking or killing each other right now. But this is what we both need. When we pull apart, we rest our foreheads together.

"Fine. Come to the house with me, and you can be part of the conversation."

While that's what I wanted, I know that means Elodie will be part of it too.

Chapter Seventeen

Alejandro

Tía Elle stands in the doorway like she's guarding a castle. Her expression is unflinching, and she could be carved out of stone. She stares at Vita, and it makes me regret bringing the woman I've fallen for straight into the lion's—lioness's—den.

"I'll let you enter my home, Vittoria, but it doesn't mean I'll let you leave."

Well, that's not at all ominous.

I definitely regret my decision now. Has my *tía* just put a bullseye on my maybe-girlfriend?

Tía Elle backs away and makes room for us to pass. She stares at me and my arm wrapped around Vita's waist. She's laser focused, and it feels like her gaze could burn straight through. She closes the door behind us and follows us into the living room. As though she's not enough to take on, *Mamá*, *Tía* Margarita, and *Tía* Luciana are there with *Tío* Enrique and *Papá*.

Tío Luis is traveling right now. He's dealing with some forgetful men in Bogotá. Their memories need refreshing. They owe us money if they want to avoid a rival gang going after them in prison.

I guide Vita over to one of the love seats. The living room in this house is massive with two sofas, three love seats, and four armchairs.

Mamá and *Papá* sit in the love seat next to ours. Everyone's gaze is riveted on how I hold Vita's hand between us. I want to draw them onto my leg to reassure her, but that would do the exact opposite for her.

Tía Elle and *Tío* Enrique sit on a sofa, his arm draped around her shoulders. My parents sit the same way. *Tres J's* each take an armchair, and my other two *tías* share the last love seat.

"Thank you for having me here."

Vita sounds unsure of herself, and her tone is so contrary to what I know that I give her hand a squeeze.

Tía Elle's hand rests on my *tío's* thigh. When he opens his mouth, I suspect she applies a little pressure because she's the one to speak next.

"It's been a long time, Vittoria. You're looking better than you did the last time we saw each other."

That comment sucks the air from the room. My gaze darts to my parents, and *Mamá's* eyes narrow. She's forgiven *Tía* Elle for the danger I was in because *Tía* Elle spared my life. But now *Mamá's* questioning my good sense, bringing a woman into our family who clearly has a past with a fellow mercenary.

"Elodie, I'd say we both came out no worse for wear."

I've never seen that expression on my *tía's* face before. It could freeze lava.

"I see your arm works just fine."

I shift my gaze to Vita for her reaction.

"I see your breathing's not so labored anymore."

There's color rising in *Tío* Enrique's neck and up into his ears. It's hard to tell with his perpetual tan, but I know him better than most. I recognize it better than anyone because the same thing happens to me when my temper is about to combust.

"Ellie, what are you two talking about?"

His tone could cut diamonds. My *tía* cocks an eyebrow as she stares at Vita, daring her to explain.

"Your wife shot me, Enrique."

I don't notice how tightly I'm squeezing her hand until she flexes her fingers. I glance down at them and realize she's probably lost feeling in most of her hand by now.

"Well, you did break my ribs and left me to find my own way to the hospital in Budapest."

Oh, fuck.

Oh, fuck.

Oh, fuck.

Tío Enrique is going to lose his ever-loving mind. None of us carry guns in each other's homes, but we all still have knives in our pockets. He may kill Vita here on the spot. My heart's racing as I wait to see what'll happen next.

I'm ready to throw my body in front of hers. Realizing I'd protect her means I'd choose her over my family. It might make my heart stop. It's the first time I've ever wanted to choose someone who doesn't share my DNA.

Vita's chin comes up, and her gaze doesn't soften as she shifts it from *Tía* Elle to *Tío* Enrique.

"We both lived to tell the tale, and if anything, Enrique, I think that proves you couldn't find a better woman than Elodie."

Once my heart beats again, I know I've found the perfect woman for me. Assuming we both make it out alive, that is. I want to cut in, but *Tío* Enrique's stare makes me snap my mouth shut. There's no changing the subject yet.

"Ellie, explain."

He doesn't exactly bark an order at his wife, but we all know this is the *jefe de jefes* speaking.

"Kiko, it was a long time ago."

How long ago could it have been if Vita's only been in this job for two years? Perhaps it was while she was a spy.

As though she can read my thoughts, Vita looks up at me.

"It was while I was with AISE. Our paths crossed."

"You worked for Italian Foreign Intelligence?"

I think there's a smidge of respect in my *tío's* tone that wasn't there a moment ago.

"Yes, for six years."

"What made you leave?"

I'm unprepared for *Tía* Elle to come to Vita's rescue. "Kiko, that's a story for another day."

Only my *tía* calls him that. No one else would dare. Sometimes, *Mamá*, *Papá*, and my other *tío* and *tías* call him Rique, but never the other diminutive.

My gaze meets *Tía* Elle's, and I realize she knows more about Vita than I guessed. She must be aware of what happened to Vita's brothers and what happened to Rafael. She's protecting Vita in front of my father. I dip my chin, hoping it's an unnoticeable movement to anyone but her. However, both of my parents and *Tío* Enrique's eyebrows shoot straight up.

For fuck's sake, can no one in this family have a private thought or moment?

It's *Mamá* who jumps in. "What isn't Elle telling us?"

Tía Elle shoots Vita a questioning expression, but instead of watching her, Vita looks up at me. I release her hand, and there's a flash of fear in her eyes that I hate. It's not what I intended, so I'm quick to wrap my arm around her shoulders and nudge her closer to me.

"Do you want me to explain?"

She shakes her head. "I wish you could, but it'd be better if I did."

She swallows before turning to look at my parents.

"I had two brothers, an older one and a younger one. They were both murdered. My older brother died in Monte Carlo."

She pauses to see whether my parents can infer what she's talking about. I see recognition in both of their gazes, but they give nothing else away. I'm not sure if they're giving her enough rope to hang herself with, or whether they wish to hear things from her perspective.

"Rafael De Santos Rúiz murdered my brother."

The declaration's met with silence, which I suppose is better than yelling and knives drawn. She must agree because she continues.

"I grew up *Mala del Brenta*. Rafael grew up cartel. He knew who my brother was, but he did it anyway."

My gaze locks on my father while I hold my breath. This can only go one of two ways.

"I'm surprised that little shit lived as long as he did."

I wait for my father to say more, but that's it. I rub small circles over the back of Vita's shoulder, trying to calm her, since I can tell she's still unsure of how things stand with my family.

I can guess her thoughts. She's probably wondering if my father's trying to fool her into believing he's fine with what happened, but all the while plotting her death.

I shoot my father a look he understands. While I bear the closest physical resemblance to *Tío* Enrique, my mannerisms, expressions, and speech mirror my father. It's the same expression he's always given me, and it means "make this right."

"Vittoria, Rafael was more trouble than he was worth for most of his life. It surprised no one when he died. It had only been a matter of when and how, not if. Even if no one in my family knew the mercenary who did it, it was obviously a hit. You did a clean job, but you sent the message."

My brow furrows since I knew about Rafael's death, but not all the details.

"What do you mean?"

"It was obviously a professional job, but she also made it obvious that it was only about him, not about our family. We all thought whoever commissioned it had a personal grudge with Rafael and that it had nothing to do with business. Rafael made a lot of stupid choices in a short time. There were too many people to count who'd likely want to off him, so nobody dug that deep to find out who orchestrated it."

"I worked alone. Even my parents don't know for sure that it was me. They heard he died, but no one came out and said it was me. It would be speculation anyway, since before admitting this to Alejandro, the only person who knew was Rafael himself. My parents wondered if someone had done them a favor, but when no request for reciprocation came, they figured he'd angered someone else. It was just a pleasant surprise for them."

When *Tío* Enrique nods, it catches my attention. "Is there anything else we should know?"

I glance over at Vita, and I can tell she's flashing through her memories, considering whether there's anything else that concerns my family.

"I can't say that there isn't, but nothing comes to mind. There might be something that involved your family that I didn't know connected you to me. If anything comes out later, it wasn't because I intentionally hid it."

"That's fair."

Vita looks at my parents. "We all know why I met Alejandro. I can't change who I've been any more than any of you can, but this job ended well before today. I've had assignments that have taken me weeks to accomplish because of the amount of surveillance I've needed to do and evidence I've had to gather. Ones that were far more logistically complicated than this one. I didn't want to admit it to myself and certainly not to anyone else, but the job was over when I met Alejandro. I've never hesitated before."

She speaks clearly and without reservation. I know my parents won't entirely believe her yet, but I can tell they recognize her sincerity. If I attempt to vouch for her, they'll accuse me of being biased, which I am. My gaze locks with *Tía* Elle, and it's her turn to dip her chin.

She's far more inconspicuous than I am, but I know it means she'll vouch for Vita. Considering how confrontational they were when we arrived, I'd say we've moved forward by leaps and bounds.

"Elodie—"

"It's Elle."

My *tía* interrupts her with what is such a benign comment in most situations, but in this one, she's proven Vita is someone she trusts. The only people I've heard her introduce herself to like that are my cousins' wives.

"Thank you."

Vita's voice is softer than it has been since we arrived. I don't think she feels on the defensive as much as before.

"Elle, perhaps I can help you make a list of the most likely hitmen. We could narrow down who would take a job with your nephews or me as targets."

Over the next fifteen minutes, the two of them list nearly four dozen people. The rest of my family sits in some state of awe as the two women go back and forth, not only naming men and women, but assessing their skills and likelihood to take on a job where they targeted my family or a fellow mercenary. It's a conversation I'm certain no one in my family ever expected to hear.

When they've exhausted the possibilities, Vita inhales and looks at *Tío* Enrique.

"I should call my father."

The statement hangs in the air as everyone stares at her.

"My parents know what I am, but they've never asked, and I've never offered information about my work. I've asked about jobs I've heard about that could affect me, so it wouldn't be unprecedented for me to be curious about a hit on someone like Alejandro. That's one that would've caused a commotion if I'd gone through with it. There's always the chance my father could find out if there's a hit on the mercenary who's failed. He could find out whether there's one specifically on me. He and I have worked with people who would tell my father, some out of respect and others with glee. I don't have to come right out and say what I'm asking for and why. I can allude to it."

I've sat quietly through most of this conversation, but now I speak up.

"You're not taking that call alone. I won't say anything, but I will be there for it."

Vita's head slowly turns toward me, her expression shifting from incredulous to stubborn.

"I will speak to my father *whenever* I want, and I don't need *your* permission to do that. Do you not trust me again?"

I'm kicking myself for speaking up in front of my family. I'm not an impetuous man by nature, but there's something about this woman who makes me act before I think. The entire room stares at us. My gaze darts to my cousins who are laughing like hyenas. *Tía* Luciana shoots them a silencing glare which only makes them sound like balloons withering.

This isn't the best place to have a whispered conversation, especially since it'll be about my family, but I got myself into this shit. I lean over to bring my lips as close to her ear as I can.

"I trust you, Vita, and right now so does my family. Given who your father is and the situation we're in now, my family'll be far more trusting if I hear the conversation. No matter what's said, I'll remain silent."

I sense she's just as uncomfortable as I am about whispering in front of everybody. I can also tell she resents the situation I put her in, but she goes along with it as she whispers her reply to me.

"Are you always going to listen in on all my conversations?"

"No. I offered to before anyone could insist my *tío* or cousins be there too. I'm offering you as much privacy as I can."

She huffs, clearly not in agreement.

"*Chiquita*, I'm doing this to protect you. I know you rarely agree with, want, or appreciate my type of protection, but I still give it freely."

She turns her head, and our noses practically brush together. She narrows her eyes and glares at me before continuing to whisper.

"I may not want or agree with your type of protection, but I've never been unappreciative of it. I can dislike it while still being grateful for it. If I've come across as unappreciative, then I'm sorry."

We both calm down, and our expressions relax. There's something deep and even tender that passes between us as our gazes lock for a moment. Her temper looked like it was ready to combust, but she reined it in. I realize a simple explanation rather than insisting went a long way. I know that's common sense to most people, and it would be to me in most situations, but my protectiveness ran away with my mouth.

I remind myself she survived six years as a spy and two years as a mercenary before we met. She's obviously capable of taking care of herself, but now that she doesn't have to do it alone, I want to share that burden with her. Instead of communicating that, I was simply overbearing. I sweep my thumb over her knuckles.

We whisper "thank you" at the same time.

"Jandro, I know you're just trying to help."

"If you know my intentions are sincere, why must you insist upon rejecting my help?"

"Because I'm used to doing everything on my own."

"You're not alone anymore, *chiquita*. Take my help with the sincerity it's offered. If you keep rejecting it, I'll spank you."

Heat flares in her eyes when she nods. I can tell she takes my comment as a challenge rather than a warning. I speak without shifting my attention away from her.

"*Tío* Enrique, may we use your office for that call?"

"*Sí, sobrino.*"

We rise and walk down the hallway to my *tío's* study. Vita pulls her phone from her pocket and unlocks it. We sit on a sofa together as she hits her father's contact. It rings twice.

Nicolò sounds groggy. "Toria?"

"*Sì, papà.*"

I have a moment's fear that their entire conversation will be in Italian. However, she eases that worry.

"I'm somewhere where I need to speak English. Otherwise, it'll draw too much attention if anybody catches a word here or there."

"Are you not somewhere you can speak in private?"

"I am, but I just don't want to run the risk of anyone hearing Italian."

"All right. It's the middle of the night here. Are you sure everything's okay?"

"Yes, this is just my only opportunity to check in with you. I'm hearing things about you and the Torettas. It doesn't sound good."

"What do you mean by that, Toria?"

"I don't know. It doesn't make sense to me. We've been allied with them for decades, but I couldn't tell from what I overheard whether that's still the case. I caught something about our family clashing with another. Then I heard the Torettas' name."

There's a long pause before her father responds. I didn't think she'd begin the conversation about something unrelated to me, but maybe she's warming him up.

"Did you hear this in passing or because of whatever your current assignment is?"

"My current assignment led me somewhere that caused me to hear this. It's why English is better."

She hasn't lied to her father, but the way she's phrased things suggests she's in Italy, and that's why she can't have anyone over-hearing her speak the language. It shows she has just as flexible a relationship with the truth as I do.

"The Carosis and Torettas are fine. It's the 'Ndrangheta and the Camorra that we have problems with."

"Don't we always have problems with 'Ndrangheta? What do the Camorra have to do with this?"

There's another long pause before he responds. "The power struggle is a little worse than it usually is because each alliance has some outside help."

"Outside help, *Papà*?"

"Foreign syndicates based in New York."

"Do you think anyone in the Camorra or 'Ndrangheta knows who I am?"

"You know that's a possibility, *tesoro*." Treasure.

That's what she is to both her father and me. I'll remember not to use that endearment and leave that as something special with her father.

"Why are you asking? Did something happen?"

"There was an incident today."

"What do you mean incident?" His tone went from a concerned father to vengeful Mafioso in a heartbeat.

"I'm not sure if my job's gone sideways, and I just got caught in the middle of somebody else going after my target, or whether my employer is dissatisfied with my work. I was wondering if someone made me and targeted me because I'm your daughter."

"Are you hurt, Toria? Did they shoot you? Stab you?"

"*Papà, Papà,* calm down. I was near my target when somebody shot in our direction."

"Come home, Toria. With this war going on and the New York bratva and mob sticking their hands into it, it would be better if you laid low here for a while."

We've been looking at the phone in her hand, but now she watches me while responding.

"I can't, *Papà.* The job isn't done."

"I'll send men for you. They'll escort you home."

"If this was about me, then that's far too conspicuous."

"Toria, you need to come home."

"*Papà,* if you push this, then I'll disappear. You know I can. I'll come home when things are settled here."

"Can you at least tell me which country you're in?"

"I'm in the Western Hemisphere, *Papà.*"

"Northern or Southern?"

Vita doesn't answer.

"Fine, Toria, but you know if you can't go home, you go to Serafina."

"I know, *Papà.*"

"She won't ask questions, and she can get you back here."

"I know. She knows as much about what I do as you and *Mamà.* I know I don't have to explain anything to her. She'll help if I ask for it."

"Toria, I'm serious. If I suspect there's something wrong, I won't give you a choice. I'll call Serafina and tell her to expect you. I'll tell Carmine to find you."

"Yes, *Papà.*"

That hits me between the eyes. I deduced from what she said earlier about them being shooting buddies that they were close, but I didn't realize they were still close enough for Serafina to know what's likely one of the most guarded secrets her *Mala del Brenta* family has.

"I'll let you know if I need anything, *Papà*, or if anything comes up."

"*Ti voglio bene, tesoro.*" I love you, treasure.

"I love you too, *Papà*."

She ends the call as I try to gather my thoughts, that are now racing a million miles a minute. I hate the idea of her turning to the Mafia for help. I understand it, but I hate it.

"Would you really go to Serafina?"

Vita's reluctant to answer, so she slowly nods.

"Only if I absolutely had to. Now that I know your family, and we're—well, whatever we are—I would come here first. If I had no other option, then I would go to Sera and Carmine."

"If Serafina knows who you are and what you are, would she admit if her family was involved in the hit against me?"

"Even if she knew, she wouldn't tell me. Just like I wouldn't tell her."

"What if I went with you, and she saw we're involved?"

"That would give away far too much since she'd never keep that from Carmine."

"We could pretend I don't know what you are, but we're involved." I don't believe it as the words come out.

"They'd never believe you haven't dug into my background or that if you had, you found nothing."

"Then we say we're together, and I know your father is *Mala del Brenta*, and that's how you know Serafina. That would explain why I wouldn't let you go to Carmine's house without me. We could say that without giving away that I know you've been a gun for hire."

She stares at me incredulously. "You cannot believe Carmine would think you're dating a woman without knowing her entire background. Do you think he thinks you're that big a fool?"

"No. But he'll understand you're important to me. And if his family's in this up to their eyeballs and you're near me, it'll make them think twice about their involvement."

"Are you sure about that?"

"Positive. The Mancinellis know their involvement in

anything that could risk you getting hurt will cause World War III."

"Because he knows your temper?"

My gaze hardens to the one I use to intimidate people. Not because that's what I want to do to her, but so she understands how far I will go to deal with someone else.

"He'll understand what the fuck's going on when I show up with my woman."

"Your woman?"

"Vita, you're the only woman I've dated in more than fifteen years. You're certainly the only one I've ever brought home. You're the only one I'd risk showing up to a rival's home with. There's no misunderstanding what that means when all the men in the Four Families are the exact same about the women they date, then marry."

She must be coming around to the idea because she barely bats an eyelash at my proclamation.

"Then is it worth letting him know the real reason we're there?"

Chapter Eighteen

Vita

Alejandro considers my question while I work through his pronouncement that we're getting married. It's hardly a proposal, but he states it like a foregone conclusion. In the back of my head, I already know it is. We aren't in love yet—at least not all the way in love—maybe halfway to being in love—but I don't doubt we'll get there. Something just clicked when I met him.

I know I wouldn't have gotten so aroused on the yacht if I hadn't felt safe with him. It had me questioning my sanity once I got back to the hotel and all the way to NYC. It wasn't me creating a false sense of security for my mark so I could lure him into my crosshairs. The way he defended me wasn't about me personally. I recognized he'd do that for any woman, but that alone made me admire him. It wasn't self-serving to get me to fuck him. It was genuine and altruistic. Those aren't qualities often found in the men I'm around.

I haven't known him long, but he was right about how time is measured differently in our world. I feel like I've known him for years. Today's been eventful—perhaps the understatement of the year. But it's given me a chance to see him in several situations.

He could've killed me in the car or the hotel room, but he didn't. He could've gagged me rather than let me explain; instead, he listened. He could've let me get shot, but instead, he dove on top of me to shield me. He could've saved himself and Pablo and left me in the room for whoever the fuck shot at us.

The sex—the sex was unlike anything I've experienced before. It was like an existential experience. It has me questioning everything I know about life and myself. It was more than just special. It was life altering. I don't know that I could go back to meaningless orgasms. I don't bang every guy I'm attracted to who looks my way. I'm selective with my partners and return to the same ones, but I feel nothing but lust when I'm with them.

There's affection between Alejandro and me. I haven't had that since university. I'd told myself that I didn't have time to miss it. For the most part, I hadn't. But now that I have it, I don't want it to go away. I want to hold onto it and cherish it. There was a closeness I've *never* felt before when I sat on his cock to talk to him. A type of intimacy that made me feel like I could share everything under the sun with him despite my hesitance and even resistance.

"Vita, if we go to them, then we control the narrative. It'd be better than them finding out, and Serafina confronting you."

"What do we tell them?"

"We met while we were traveling and bumped into each other at one of my family's nightclubs. We've been hanging out, and now we're dating. None of that is a lie, just the convenient parts of the truth."

"We have to stick to that. If we make up anything or even for a second look like we're withholding anything that isn't private between a couple, Sera will know I'm lying."

"Besides giving her a heads up, what do you want to get out of the meeting, *chiquita*?"

"What do you think Carmine will share if you're there? If he knows or can find out who put the hit on me, would he even tell you?"

"Only because we're in a relationship."

"Are we going to define that relationship?"

"You're my girlfriend—for now."

The way he says it doesn't sound like he thinks we'll break up. Just the opposite. It's a precursor to fiancée, then wife, and that's an irrefutable fact.

I like it.

I like it a lot.

"I should call Sera to make sure she's home and not at one of her bakeries. Do I give her a heads up that I'm coming with my boyfriend? She'll demand to know who it is before she lets him in her house. Do I admit it's you?"

"Tell her you want to bring someone with you, but you can't tell her over the phone on an unsecure line. She'll understand that. She's smart enough to guess it'll be Joaquin or me."

"How?"

"We're the only two left standing. If it were someone outside the Four Families, you'd at least hint at it. All the rest of the men in the families are already married."

"She'll tell Carmine the moment we hang up."

"I know."

I stare at my phone and almost want to toss it away from me like a scalding stone. Instead, I take a breath and pull my big girl panties on. I unlock the screen and pull up Serafina's contact. It rings twice on speakerphone before she answers.

"Toria?"

"Hi, Sera."

"Is everything okay?"

"I'm in town. I hoped to see you."

"You didn't answer my question. What do you need?"

It could sound accusatory, like she expects I'll demand her help or money or something. But she's offering protection or a way to escape.

"To see you. Some stuff's come up that I think you and Carmine should know about."

"Car!"

Good thing the phone isn't by my ear even though I know she held hers away from her. She's always had a voice that carries.

"Fina, what's wrong?"

I hear running footsteps approaching, and I can only imagine the panic the man's in. He's completely besotted with Sera even after a few years. There's nothing he wouldn't do for her.

"Do you remember my friend Vittoria? She's in town, and she'd like to come over. She said she has something to talk to us about."

"Hello, Vittoria."

"Hi, Carmine."

"Are you safe?"

That's not the first question normal people ask each other, but it's pretty fucking standard in syndicate life. I don't know if Sera's told him what I do now, but he knows my family because he knows Sera's.

"Yes. I'd like to come over with someone because I need to tell you something."

"Someone?"

Carmine and Sera speak at the same time.

"Yes. My boyfriend. But I shouldn't say anything more over the phone."

"Fuck you, Alejandro."

I jerk back, not expecting that at all.

"Charming as always, Carmine."

I shift my attention from my phone to Alejandro. He's grinning and rolls his eyes.

"How'd—Never mind. May we come over?"

"Yes." It's Sera who answers.

"Carmine, you know I won't wait in the car. I will leave my gun there. I'll drive us, so no guards."

"Why would you bother when you've got a dozen on each side of me?"

My brow furrows as I continue to look at Alejandro.

"Pablo and Florencia live to the right, and Madeline and

Javier live to the left. They fell in love with their houses. It's not their fault there's an eyesore between them."

"Fuck you, Alejandro."

"Broken record, Carmine. You sound like Niko's fucking parrot."

I'm completely lost, so Alejandro explains.

"Niko Kutsenko, the third oldest brother, has a swearing African parrot. The animal's cool as shit even if his owner's a piece of shit."

I don't know a ton about the Kutsenkos beyond there are four brothers who make up the Elite Group—Maksim, Alexei, Nikolai, and Bogdan. Their cousins on their father's side are Anton and Pasha, and their cousins on their mother's side are Sergei and Misha Andreyev. The four cousins are the next most senior members of their branch. With the shit we might be in the middle of, I suppose I'll learn more about them soon. I sure as fuck will if —when—I marry Alejandro.

That last thought doesn't feel as scary as I assumed it would.

"We're home, Toria. Come over when you're ready."

"Thanks, Sera."

"My men will search you, Alejandro."

"As long as they don't like it too much."

"*Vaffanculo, bel ragazzo.*" Fuck off, pretty boy.

"*Come una polla, Carmine.*" Eat a dick, Carmine.

Sera and Alejandro chuckle, and Carmine mutters something. I'm clearly missing something *again*. Alejandro leans over to whisper to me.

"Apparently, while they were dating, Carmine pissed her off. She sent a penis cake to Salvatore's house that had that written in English in raspberry glaze. There were photos Joaquin came across when he hacked Gabriele's phone a couple years ago. We shared it with the bratva and mob. He's never lived it down."

"Shared?"

"Being nice to those twats was worth it at Carmine's expense."

"It's getting close to your bedtime, Alejandro. Hurry up."

"You're the one who needs to catch up on his beauty sleep."

"Boys." Sera's voice interrupts, and I giggle.

"We're coming from New Jersey, Sera. We'll be there soon."

I don't know how long it'll take to get from northern New Jersey to Queens. I'm guessing half an hour at least. We hang up the call and join the others in the living room.

"We didn't learn much from my dad, but I'm confident he'll dig now that he knows I might be in danger. He'll check in with me soon if for no other reason than to make sure I'm still breathing."

"We're headed to Serafina and Carmine's."

Alejandro's announcement puts scowls on everyone's faces. I feel like I should speak up, explain that Sera and I grew up together. I fear that'll only make it worse though. Enrique assesses me before he speaks. It doesn't help that I already feel like I'm standing before a firing squad.

"How well do you know Serafina?"

"She's my best friend."

I want to wince since I didn't explicitly tell Alejandro that. I probably should have. His arm's around my waist, with his thumb against my back. He rubs it up and down to reassure me. I suppose it wasn't hard for him to figure that out from what I already told him and from how Sera and I sounded on the phone.

"She won't tell you anything about her father or your father's dealings if she knows anything."

"I wouldn't tell her either. We've never talked about it. I don't expect her to tell me how the Mancinellis are involved—if they even are. But she'll tell me if the Mancinellis know whether I'm the new target. Carmine knows what we mean to each other. He wouldn't keep that from her, even if I am Alejandro's—"

Fuck!

"Girlfriend."

He fills in the blank, and I breathe easier. I didn't know what to label myself as, and I didn't want to presume what he'd tell his family. There are knowing looks on the older generation's faces, and *Tres J's* appear bored. I do *not* need Catalina and Matáis thinking I'm sleeping with their son as mere fuck buddies. I mean, I'm certain they've guessed what we've gotten up to, but ugh!

I'm not a prude but having them know I'm intimately involved with their son just feels icky. Not just because of how we got together but in general as his parents. Their expressions tell me they know what Alejandro's already told me—I'll be his wife sooner rather than later.

Frankly, if I weren't in this for good, I wouldn't be standing here. My silence on the matter has been consent. If I didn't want this, I wouldn't have come here. I would've dug my heels in or escaped—at least tried to. My resistance comes from what I've felt like I should think and say.

As I gaze up at Alejandro, I know my resistance is futile. I don't want to fight this. When he stares down at me, the rest of the world slips away.

I'm yours.

It's as though I can read his mind, and he can read mine. Some energy passes through us, and I'm positive we're thinking the same thing. When we look at everyone else, I lean my head against his chest. I don't realize it until Alejandro tightens his hold on me. When I attempt to lift my head, embarrassed by the slip, he squeezes my waist.

"We need to get going. Sorry we delayed dinner, but we're going to skip it."

Alejandro makes our excuses. I didn't even think about keeping the family from their meal.

"Let me fix you both something to take with you."

Catalina rises from the sofa and looks at me. She tilts her head toward the kitchen. She speaks as though this is her home rather than her brother and sister-in-law's. I leave Alejandro's side and follow his mother into the kitchen. She immediately pulls plates from the cabinet, and it takes no time for me to realize she's as comfortable here as she would be her own home. I stay out of the way.

"Keep my son alive, and I'll learn to love you like you've

always been my daughter. Endanger him, and you'll wish you'd never been born."

She speaks while piling food onto two plates. She covers them in cling wrap and hands them to me with a smile like she's giving me brownies at a bake sale not a death threat.

I respect and admire her while being terrified.

"Mrs. De Santos, I—"

"Catalina."

Progress?

Elodie lets me use a nickname, and Alejandro's mother's letting me use her first name. Maybe I'll still be breathing tomorrow.

"I hope I can earn your trust. None of this is happening the way I thought it would. I don't know how I got so fortunate, considering the sins I've committed."

"Repentance and forgiveness are what we tell ourselves to get by."

What the fuck does that mean?

"Yyyes."

I draw out the word because what the hell else do I say?

"We live the life we were given by birth and make the most of it. We can repent for our sins we don't plan to commit again and ask for forgiveness when we can earn it. You've done that today. But even God can't turn a blind eye to the ones we do over and over. You've admitted to why you met my son, and I see what you're like together. You can't fake what you two share. I can forgive a great deal, Vittoria. This life has forced me to, but it's also given me a long memory."

I'm a C and E—Christmas and Easter—Catholic because I share the same sentiment—God can't ignore the sins I willingly commit over and over. It feels too hypocritical to keep confessing and hoping for reconciliation when I leave church and pick up the gun I put down right before Mass. While it's a blessing that Catalina understands, she's given me a healthy dose of Catholic mother's guilt.

God help me when she meets my mother.

Never mind God, the two of them might smite me where I stand.

"I understand."

"I know you do, *gordita.*"

Context is everything. I'm pretty sure she means sweetie or honey and not the literal chubby little girl. I prefer to take it as a compliment.

I glance down at the food before looking toward the living room. After that little warning, I'm glad I watched her prepare the plates. Otherwise, I'd fear her poisoning me.

"Alejandro and I really should get going."

We join the others, and Alejandro takes the food from me. He looks at Catalina, then me, and his brow creases. I'm certain he's wondering what his mother said to me. I fear I'm either white as a ghost or red as a firetruck. Either way, he's watching me like he fears I'll pass out.

"*Chiquita?*"

Chapter Nineteen

Alejandro

I can imagine what my mother said to my girlfriend in the kitchen. *Mamá's* an avenging angel if you get too close to her family and look at us the wrong way. She'll perceive Vita as a threat until she doesn't—Lord only knows when she'll change her mind. From her expression, I think it'll be soon. I pray it's soon. As best I can tell, *Mamá* likes and approves of Vita as much as she could anyone who's an outsider.

I'm an only child, so my parents can be a wee overprotective. I was a mini-Houdini as a toddler. I could escape anywhere. I was climbing out of my crib at one and figuring out childproof locks by the time I was three. I'd disappear practically before their eyes. Usually, it was because I was hungry or wanted to play on our swing set.

Apparently, when I was four, I decided I wanted to play with Pablo. I found a pair of my dad's shoes and made it to the end of the driveway before a guard spotted me and carried me back inside. If I hadn't grown up on a gated property, I would've been halfway to Jersey before they realized I was gone.

I wasn't a disobedient child; I just took their warning to stay in one place as an instruction meant in the here and the now. It wasn't applicable to the future until they specifically said so. Situational ethics through the lens of a preschooler.

"I'm ready to go, but what're we going to do with all of this food if you're driving?"

"We'll take a town car with a driver that way we can eat. We'll park at Javier and Madeline's and walk next door."

We say our goodbyes and head to the car. The privacy glass is always up unless the occupant puts it down. After giving the driver instructions, I climb in beside Vita. The moment the door shuts, I'm on her like she's an oasis after my forty days and nights in the desert. We nearly crush the plates between us.

"Eat so we don't make a mess, *chica*. Then we have some unfinished business."

We both eat with gusto since it's been so long since breakfast, neither of us having had time for lunch. We abandoned the tuna and rice. She compliments the food, which *Papá* and *Tío* Enrique cooked.

It's a family requirement that everyone learns how to. We take turns hosting Sunday dinner, and we're naturally frugal in our everyday lives. We all like nice things and own plenty of extravagant luxuries. But we can do that because we don't piss away our money. We eat at our homes most of the time, and none of us appear to be starving.

When we're finished, I set the plates beside my feet. I twist to release Vita's belt before lifting her onto my lap. I unfasten mine and pull her close. I cup her cheek as she leans in for my kiss.

I can't get enough.

Our tongues tangle as our hands roam over each other. She shifts and slides her hand down my trousers as best she can. I might come just from her fingers brushing the tip. I force her to release me when I lift her shirt. I immediately unclasp her bra, tossing that aside too. She fumbles with my belt, button, and zipper. Thanks to all that's holy because my cock's ready to burst within the confines of my trousers. I lay her on the seat before stripping her of her pants and panties, holding up the latter.

"Don't wear these again, *chiquita*. Your pussy is mine. I decide when you come. That means when I want it, I'll have it. No unnecessary layers between me and the promised land."

"Promised land?" She chuckles before moaning as I suck her left breast.

"Yes. I promise to pleasure you daily."

The confines of the backseat make it difficult for me to do everything I want. Next time, we're definitely taking a limo. I hurry to move the plates to her side and kneel as best I can. I lift her right leg over my shoulder before lowering my head to her cunt. The first taste of her is the nectar of the gods. She slaps her hand over her mouth to keep from screaming.

It's soundproof glass that separates us from the driver, but she doesn't want to risk him hearing her. Knowing the couples in this family, he wouldn't think twice about what's happening back here. At least one of us was probably conceived in the back of a chauffeured car.

My tongue flicks her clit over and over until she's writhing on the seat. Her left hand clutches the headrest as she tries to lift her hips to meet my questing tongue that now slides into her. I press my hand on her belly to hold her in place.

"I told you I decide."

"Daddy, please."

She's already practically insensate with need. My heart races knowing I can drive her to this point so easily. I remove my hand from her belly to pull down my boxer briefs before they cut off my cock's circulation. I stroke myself as I slide three fingers into her cunt. She's so wet, and she's taken me before. I know she can handle it.

"What do you want, little one?"

"You. More of you, please."

"You beg so nicely. Let me hear more of it."

"Daddy, please give me your cock. I want to taste you too. I've never given road head before, but I want to right now."

"I'm not the one driving."

"We're on the road, and I want to taste you."

"Next time. I'm having dessert. You must earn yours."

I return to licking her clit before sucking on it. I continue to stroke myself to ease the ache. I watch as her free hand reaches for my head, but she catches herself. Instead, she lifts her arm overhead and grasps the door. I watch her belly contract and release as she pants. I ignore my dick's protests when I let go in favor of massaging her tits and toying with her nipples.

She releases a long moan, and I know she's coming. Color rises from her chest up her neck. Her nipples tighten even more, tempting me away from her pussy. But there's a more immediate need.

I pull away from her and flip her over as she tries to catch her breath. I maneuver her until her legs are bent and beneath her. Then I land my hand across her ass. She jerks forward, but my hands are already around her waist to keep her from slamming her head into the door. When she settles back, I spank her three more times in rapid succession.

"Alejandro! Fuck! That hurts."

"I know it does. You came without permission."

"You told me earlier that I could come without asking."

"That was then. This is now. I explicitly said I control your pleasure. You didn't ask."

I spank her twice more, enjoying how her ass is turning rosy. I spread her ass cheeks and slide my tongue along her slit once more. She shies away, but I keep her in place.

"I'm sorry."

"I'm sorry what?"

She hesitates. Her private term of affection slipped out twice earlier, but now she's considering what she's doing.

"Say it, *chiquita*. You know who I am. Say it."

"I'm sorry, Daddy."

I climb on the seat behind her then plunge into her.

"Was that so hard to say, *chica*?"

"No, Daddy."

She hesitates before looking over her shoulder at me. Then she's rocking her hips to accept each thrust. Her left hand rises to press against the window, bracing herself better since I'm not gentle. I lean forward, my chest resting against her back as I reach around to play with her nipple. I nip at her left shoulder.

"Do you have an idea what it does to me whenever you call me that? It's never been my thing before, but—fuck—it drives me crazy. It's because it's you."

"I'd never call another man that. Only you've protected me, and only you've promised to take care of me."

"Because you're mine."

"Yes!"

"And I'm yours, little one."

"Fuck!"

That promise makes her move faster, pushing her cunt against my dick harder. I let her control our pace for a moment before I pull out.

"What?!"

I thrust my fingers into her again, my thumb rubbing her clit. I was getting too close. I needed to slow down. We haven't even crossed the river yet, and I was ready to blow my load. I want to make this last. It's close to an hour from Short Hills in Jersey to Forest Hills in Queens. I won't be a two-pump chump.

I glance down at my glistening cock, and I nearly abandon my resolve. I once again spread her ass cheeks before running my tongue from her clit to her rosebud. I flick that before pressing my thumb against the opening. The very tip of it slips in.

"This belongs to me too. I'll fuck your ass whenever your cunt's too sore to take me again."

"Yes, Daddy!"

Her ragged tone tells me the idea excites her. She wiggles her hips, and I pinch her ass cheek. My fingers work her G-spot, her moans telling me she enjoys my ministrations. I slide my fingers farther along the wall, searching for the true Holy Grail.

"Oh, fuck, Jandro! That's it... Fuck... Yes!... Oh, God. It's different... I—"

I find her A-spot—careful not to press against her cervix—and stroke her. When I realized how into kink I am and that BDSM feeds a deep need I have to be in control while pleasuring someone else, I studied the female anatomy. I've always been an excellent student and an overachiever.

"Please... So intense... Going to come. *Please!*"

"Come for me, *chiquita.*"

I wish I could see her face while we share something I've attempted but never succeeded. Uncertainty fills her gaze as she looks over her shoulder at me. My silent wish is granted as her expression morphs into surprise. Her back bows as her body contracts.

"Jandro."

It's a ragged whisper as our gazes lock. I hear her suck in lungfuls of air as she goes still. She turns around, and I sit. She climbs onto me, straddling my hips as I slide into her again. Her head drops against my shoulder as she rides me.

"*Chiquita?*"

"Shh, Daddy. Let me enjoy all of this. I can't think."

We start slowly as she rocks her hips before rising and falling. I keep my hold on her light but guiding her motions. When her urgency increases, I know I won't last much longer. I thrust upward as she grinds her clit against my pubic bone.

"Please may I come, Daddy?"

"Yes, baby girl. I'm close too."

I tilt my head back as my cum surges from my cock. I pulse over and over as though I have an endless stream of cum. The primal need to breed her, so she can't leave me just about knocks me sideways. Pregnancy is the one thing I've avoided like the plague. I've practically double bagged it even when I know my partner's on birth control. Previously, the thought of kids was such a repellant that my dick wanted to hide inside me. With Vita—the idea fills my chest to bursting.

What the fuck is wrong with you?

No!

Yes!

Maybe?

No!

Just not yet.

I feel lightheaded from my whirling thoughts and from my labored breathing. I close my eyes as I attempt to compose myself. Vita still has her head resting against my shoulder, so I take my time to come back down to Earth.

When she finally leans back, and I can see her expression once again, there's wonder that turns mischievous as she speaks.

"Jandro, that was a kind of orgasm I've never had before. It came from so deep within me. Instead of a kinda tingly sensation, it was like a deep warmth. You rarely hear about the A-spot and cervical orgasms. They should definitely be talked about far more. I highly recommend."

We sit connected until my body no longer cooperates. Even after I withdraw, we sit with Vita curled around me. She smatters kisses along my neck as I trail my thumbnail along her spine while my other hand cups her ass.

"*Chica*, we'll be there in five minutes."

"Huh?"

Her kisses slowed about ten minutes ago, and I think she was nearly asleep. I nudge her until she sits up and looks around. I reach for her clothes and help her dress. She's lethargic until she fully comes around and realizes we're nearly at my cousin's house. We'll see her friend in a few minutes. She rushes to finish as I straighten my shirt and tuck it in.

We're about to get off the Union Turnpike—I purposely asked the driver to keep us away from Jackson Heights and take the less predictable route—when a barrage of pings hits both sides of the vehicle. Like in the hotel room, I push Vita to the floor and cover her body with mine.

"Jandro?"

"I don't know what's happening. Hold on."

I move to sit up, but she reaches behind me and fists my shirt, pushing me down.

"The car's completely bulletproof. Let me see."

It was instinct that had me shielding her, but I don't fear getting shot if I look out the windows. I ease away from her until I can see more clearly. There are SUVs on both sides of us. Our windows are tinted to a hair's breadth from illegal. I know whoever's beside us can't see me. I look out the rear window as another SUV speeds toward us. I slam my finger onto the button to lower the privacy glass.

"*Ellos van a embestirnos.*" They're going to ram us.

"*Lo se patrón.*" I know, boss.

"Who?"

I glance down at Vita before reaching for the compartment beneath the bench seat. I press, and a drawer springs open. I pull the gun out that I placed there on the way to my *tío's* house. Vita reaches for hers, which we stored beside mine.

"I don't know yet. We're safe in here but stay down. I won't take any chances."

I look out the rear window again, and the vehicle's within a few feet of us. I pull Vita onto the seat, and we both rush to get our seatbelts back on. We sense when the impact's coming, so we bend over and cover our heads. A force harder than you would expect plows into the back of us. My driver speeds up, but it's not enough before the SUV slams into us again. This time it's hard enough to make the ass end of our car swerve.

"Watch your elbow."

I warn Vita as I lower the center armrest then pull a latch that allows me to reach into the trunk. Through it, I ease a rifle. It's not easy to maneuver it to keep it pointing toward the ceiling and away from Vita until I can point it between my feet.

I know it's loaded and ready to go, but gun safety's been drilled into me since the first time I saw a firearm. I was four and got away from my mom, who was trying to convince me to take a nap. I wandered into my dad's study, hoping he'd take me to the park. He was cleaning one of his handguns.

After his initial shock that I made it into his study wore off, he carried me to the sofa, keeping our distance from his desk where the gun lay. I got a stern lesson about entering rooms uninvited, then he explained how dangerous guns are. I heard the same warning until I left for college—two years after I went on my first mission.

"Watch out!"

Vita's warning comes a moment before the SUV on her side swerves to strike our passenger side front quarter panel. A moment later, there's a corresponding impact on my side. I hurry to grab a second rifle and pass it to her.

"Aren't they worried someone's going to call the police?"

"No. Someone paid for a traffic break. Look."

I point out the back window, and she strains to see. In the distance, there's a faint view of a police car weaving across lanes to keep vehicles from passing it. It's allowing us to move without any traffic congestion. There aren't too many people with the power and influence to do that. It makes me wonder if this is a government agency rather than a private citizen who's paid hitmen.

"*Patrón*, they got the driver's side tire."

Unlike our SUVs that are veritable tanks, the town cars and limos have their limitations. The SUVs have special tires that will continue to roll even if they've been punctured. The town cars only have regular commercial tires. We're forced to stop.

I grasp Vita's hand and give it a squeeze before she and I both lower our windows enough to get the muzzle of our rifles out. Neither of us opens an indiscriminate spray of bullets, but we are shooting wide, hoping to take out our attackers as well as their vehicles much like they did ours.

However, our attempts cease when the three of us watch in horror as a man with a gasoline can comes and pours it along the cracks in the hood. While the car might be bulletproof, it's not fireproof. A moment later, he drops a lighter onto the car, and the hood ignites.

"Vita, come out after me on my side."

"The hell I am. I'm not using you as a shield. We have people on either side of us. You take care of yours, and I'll take care of mine."

Arguing with her is futile. Smoke's already filling the car. We have no choice but to get out or be cremated. We tuck our handguns into our waists at our lower backs and ready our rifles. Ronaldo, our driver, already has a rifle propped in the front seat. It's standard protocol for all our drivers ever since someone attacked *Tía* Elle and Madeline.

We each open our door a sliver, continuing to fire before stumbling out of the vehicle. Despite the men's bodies I see littered on my side and the ones I'm certain are on Vita's, we're still overpowered. All three vehicles were filled to the brim, each seating seven. It's nearly two dozen to three.

"Vita!"

I bellow her name after I hear fist hitting skin. I can't tell who struck who.

"I'm all right, Jandro, but somebody didn't like having his *huevos* shoved up his ass."

I take a fist to the sternum as two men grab my arms and pin them against me. I rage, headbutting the guy who punched me, doing my best to elbow the guys at my side. I rock to my left, driving my shoulder into the fucker. I rock back toward my right, and I know the man braces himself for me to use my shoulder against him. Instead, I stomp on his foot and grind my heel into his toes. I struggle with all my strength, wanting to get to Vita.

"Vita, talk to me. Are you okay?"

Before she can respond, the sound of a gun being discharged fills the air. From the corner of my eye, I see Ronaldo drop to the ground, a bullet between his eyes. I have to live through this if for no other reason than to do the honorable thing and be the one to inform his parents of what happened and attend his funeral to pay my respects.

"Ah!" It's a male voice in pain.

"You shouldn't have put your hand so close to my face. I thought it was an invitation."

I hear Vita make the exaggerated sound of gnawing on something.

"Don't worry, I won't bite you again. You're a bit bland for my taste."

She says it with such a benign tone that if I didn't know her, I would wonder about her psychopathy. I laugh and spit straight in the eye of the shitbag in front of me. Vita's not the only one who can rely on children's tactics when you're fighting for your life.

I take an uppercut that snaps my head back. Luckily, I'm tall enough that my head doesn't hit the vehicle. Otherwise, the force from both sides would've knocked me out. I settle down enough that both men eased their hold on me without realizing it.

I seize the opportunity to thrash, throwing my fist sideways as best I can until my left hand breaks free and I can reach back for my handgun. I get off a round to the head of the man in front of me. But three more men rush forward, one with an iron pipe. A moment before everything goes dark, I hear Vita call out to me. Then there's the sound of her surely dropping to the ground.

My head's pounding as I come around.

I've had more concussions than anyone should. I've also been drugged before. I can tell from the way my arms and legs feel. It's as though they're no longer attached to me except by a few sinews. My head pounds like one of the fucking O'Rourkes is dancing a jig inside it. It makes me wonder how long I've been out and just how far they took us.

I open my eyes a sliver and look around until I spot Vita to my right. I observe her and can tell when she wakes, even though she keeps her eyes closed. It's the most subtle shift in her breathing for a moment. Then she becomes aware enough to return her breathing to a slow, even pattern like it was while she was unconscious. I continue to watch her until her eyes slide open just a fraction. It's enough for our gazes to meet, but not enough to convey our thoughts.

"*Chiquita?*" I say the word more as an exhalation than anything else.

"Daddy." It's garbled, almost like a grunt.

We're both careful in case the room is bugged. I'm fairly certain it is.

Where the hell are we?

Chapter Twenty

Vita

This isn't the worst I've ever felt, but death would be mercy. I feel as though I'm a disembodied soul with the worst migraine ever known to man. Whatever they drugged me with is giving me an out-of-body experience. But before they drugged me, one of the biggest guys I've ever seen took a crowbar to the side of my head. Fortunately, he didn't use the end with the hook, or he probably would've gouged a chunk of my brain out. He also didn't apply the full force he could've. There's no way I would've survived it.

As I come around, I do my best not to give away that I'm awake. It's the most reassuring feeling I've ever had when I spot Alejandro to my left. He looks like absolute shit. It makes me reconsider how badly off I must be. It's clear somebody went to town on him. There's blood on his shirt and collar from a gash on his right cheek. It looks like bruises already cover his face, and it looks like his shoulder isn't sitting in place. I pray it's just the angle they tied him, and that it's not dislocated.

I evaluate my body in more detail, beginning with wiggling my toes inside my shoes. I'm working my way up by flexing my calves and thighs, my glutes. I hardly think this is the time and the place to test a Kegel, so I skip that. I bend my fingers and contract my arms. When I'm confident everything is still in one piece—albeit painfully—I respond to Alejandro's concerned voice.

"*Chiquita?*"

"Daddy."

It's more of a grunt than a word because my throat is so sore from earlier, when one of our attackers wrapped his hand around it and squeezed until I thought my head would explode. I do my best to keep my lips from moving as I speak barely louder than a whisper since I'm certain this room is bugged.

"Where are we?"

Hopefully, Alejandro has a clue, since I don't know how long we've been out and how far we traveled. I'm not that knowledge-able of New York and New Jersey. I mostly know Manhattan and a few spots in the outer boroughs like Jackson Heights.

"I don't know, *chica*."

I allow my eyes to open a little wider, enough for me to sweep my gaze over our surroundings. It's difficult to tell whether we're in a warehouse or a basement. It's just concrete walls and floor. There are no windows, no storage shelves or equipment. It's an entirely wide-open space that's disconcerting as fuck. The only objects—besides us—are the two chairs we're sitting on. There's truly no way to know what time it is or even what part of the day or night we're in.

It's essentially sensory deprivation, since it's all so silent in here except for when Alejandro and I whisper. There's no hint of a scent, not even mustiness. I strain to hear anything that might be in the distance. It's as though we're in a complete void.

"How long do you think we were out?"

We continue to whisper so softly that I have to guess at some of Alejandro's words.

"My best guess is a few hours. I wouldn't feel this shitty if it were less than two. Soreness has set in. What hurts the most, *chica?*"

"My head. It's as though my arms and legs are numb, yet I can feel how stiff they are when I try to move them."

"Same."

"Your shoulder? It looks dislocated?"

"No. It's just the way they tied me."

"What do you think they used?"

I dread his answer since it could be any number of narcotics or poisons.

"I have no idea, but we have a doctor on staff for anything that exceeds Madeline or *Tía* Margherita's abilities. They can both do far more than a midwife should. They can deliver babies and perform emergency medicine, but they have limitations."

We fall quiet for a few minutes as we both consider our surroundings.

"Do you see the camera?"

Alejandro lets his head loll to the right as though he passed out again. I do the same, except my head lolls to the left. We're not sitting close enough to touch, but it shrinks the distance between us, even if it's only psychological.

"What do we do, Alejandro?"

We've spotted the cameras that confirmed the suspicions we both naturally have. At this point, pretending to remain unconscious is pointless. If we formulate a plan before our kidnappers return, then all the better. I'm certain they won't leave us alone for much longer now that we're awake.

"We wait for now, *chica*."

"Do you have any idea who it was?"

"No. Did you recognize anyone?"

"No, not at all. But I saw the hint of a tattoo."

When I saw the ink protruding from one guy's shirt, it made my blood run cold. As I look over at Alejandro, I can't help but wonder if this is about me, and they beat the shit out of him as leverage against me. But then again, this could be entirely about him, and I'm collateral damage.

"What was it?"

"A finger over a pair of lips."

"The *omertà*?"

It doesn't surprise me that Alejandro knows the symbol for the highly guarded oath men take when they're being made. Plenty of movies have speculated about the promises sworn and sealed in blood. Some have gotten pretty damn close. Others are ridiculous. The oath varies a little from syndicate to syndicate, but it's pretty universal for all Mafias.

"Do you think it was Camorra or *'Ndrangheta?*"

I inhale deeply before I admit my suspicions. "No. My guess is *Mala del Brenta.*"

"Your own family? Don Piero? Your father?"

"I really don't know. I can't imagine it's my father. I just can't. He's devoted to Piero and our branch. He'd give his life for our don without a second thought, but I'm confident the only way he'd disobey Piero is if it was my or my mother's life over anyone else."

"Could he have made that argument to end the assignment you're on, and Piero's punishing him for that?"

"That's not entirely impossible, but it's unlikely."

"Why else would it be a *Mala del Brenta?* It's not like they have a presence here in the U.S."

"I know. It's almost strictly Venetian, and there're few branches, even if there're several influential families. Do you think anyone knows what happened yet?"

I change the subject because I'm struggling to wrap my head around recognizing the symbol designed the way *Mala del Brenta* men get it. I need to think about it more, but I can't do it out loud. I'll grow too emotional if I do.

"They absolutely know something's gone wrong. We told all of them where we were going. If nothing else, Serafina will try to call you, and when she doesn't get through, she'll have Carmine call me. When I don't answer, Salvatore will call *Tío* Enrique. But before that could even happen, several alarms will have gone off. I activated the tracker on my watch. The moment there was more than just a door dinging the body of our vehicle, an alert went to the guy who heads up our fleet of cars. There's always a vehicle tracker running too. At the very least, they'll have our last known location. I can't tell if there's any signal in this building for my watch to transmit."

"Do you think they left anything at the scene? I'd imagine they have cleaners to get rid of the vehicle and your driver."

"They likely do, but there's always a chance they left something behind. These men were professionals, but their work was still sloppy. They took too long to knock us out and left blood behind. And then, one of them was careless enough for you to see a tattoo."

"I'm sure they assume we'll be dead before we can tell anyone our suspicions." If I were running this mission, that's what I would do.

"I'm sure that's what they think too, but that's an arrogance that'll get them killed. You know better than most that you always assume something could go wrong, that your mark could get away, so you leave no distinguishable traces."

"True. If it's been a few hours, do you think we're approaching dawn yet?"

"It's possible. If only I could see my wrist. It surprises me that they left me with my watch and my belt. They must know one of those accessories is a tracker. They must be confident it isn't working. I doubt they even bothered to look where it was located."

"I can tell they took my gun. I assume they took yours. Can you still feel your knives?"

I know he carries one in each pocket. Every syndicate man carries at least one, but most carry two or more. Getting your first knife around fourteen is a rite of passage—your first step into full initiation. Guns are easier to take, but men aren't thrilled at digging into another guy's front pockets.

"Yeah. I have both. Dumbasses. They assume I can't get to them. When they come in, I'll start working the knots while they're distracted talking to or beating me. I don't want them to notice me fidgeting on camera."

I run my hands over what I can of the ropes binding my wrists. Fucking idiots to not use zip ties. Is this the nineteenth century? Handcuffs, then zip ties have been standard for like a hundred and fifty years.

"This was a planned job, so they shouldn't be improvising. Do you think the rope is a setup to get us to try to free ourselves?"

"I assume so, but they were still foolish enough to use it. Do you think you can work yours loose?"

"Yeah. From what I can feel, I recognize the knot."

It might be an old-fashioned method to restrain a hostage, but I was still trained to escape various types of knots. Plus, I like shit kinky and have been bound several different ways.

"Ransom or live stream?"

Do they want our families to pay for our freedom, or will they torture our families by forcing them to watch our torture and death? Either is a strong likelihood. I wish I knew more about our captors because even a slight hint of who they work for can help me narrow down whether this is sanctioned or rogue. Either's possible.

"*Chiquita*, we're going on a luxury vacation the moment we're free of this shit. Do you want beach, lake, mountains, or desert?"

He's thinking about romantic getaways?

Not a bad distraction.

"You'd think growing up in a floating city would make me tired of being on and around the water, but I'll always choose that over any other destination. Beach is preferable, but I wouldn't turn down a trip to Banff or Lake Como. I'll even take the Alps as long as it's not winter. I don't do snow. What do you like?"

"I prefer the beach. I will never choose the snow. I'm genetically disinclined to cold weather."

I hear the humor in his tone, and it lightens the mood for a moment.

"Islands?"

"Sure. The Azores, Seychelles, South Pacific. Any of those works for me."

"Mmm. I've never been to the Seychelles. I prefer warm water."

Despite all the water around Venice, I wouldn't get into any of it. It's freezing and disgusting.

"Me too. Is a month too short?"

"A month?"

I barely get more than a few days' vacation each year since I'm always on call. The idea of an entire month of lazing on a beach with my gorgeous boyfriend is enough to make me want to work out the knots immediately.

"*Chica,* are you picturing sex on the beach?"

"I wasn't, but I am now."

"I'm definitely picturing you at least topless."

"Are you a sex addict? Do you think about anything else?"

"Now that I know you, yes. Yes, I am. It's entirely your fault for being so hot."

His tone is dead serious now. He means what he's saying. He looks at me like the most gorgeous woman in the world—when he isn't—wasn't—thinking about how I'm—I was—trying to kill him. I much prefer that to his suspicion.

"Jandro, you know this isn't a setup, right? Like, I didn't arrange this to trap you."

"I never thought you had. We've moved past that."

"Thank you, Daddy."

We're still keeping our voices low, but I whisper that word extra softly. I know he heard me though because I see the corner of his mouth turn up. We fall silent while we're both lost in thought. At least, I am. Perhaps he's resting, but I doubt it. He's never struck me as a man whose mind is at rest. To keep my mind from spiraling, I consider counting the minutes, but that'll only drive me nuts.

At least another hour passes before we hear a door opening in the distance behind us. Neither of us has turned our heads to look around that much. High heels clack against the concrete floor followed by a man's heavier tread. My mind races to what woman would target me. Who knows what previous sexual partners Alejandro has who'd go all *Single White Female* or *Fatal Attraction* on him.

I wait with bated breath.

If I weren't bound to the chair, I'd fall off my seat.

"*Zia* Cosima?"

Alejandro's head whips around to stare at me for a moment before shifting his focus back to the stunning woman before us. I've seen her baby photos. She came out gorgeous, so her name—beauty—has always fit. She's my mother's sister. I cannot for the life of me fathom why she'd be involved in this.

I mean, she's cold-blooded as the day is long, but we've always been super close. I don't know why she'd target Alejandro, but if she has, and she hired someone to kill him, I wouldn't put it past her to punish failure. However, I can't imagine her choosing torture or murder over me. I can think of other ways to handle me for not completing the job.

"*Caio, Vittoria. Hai un aspetto di merda.*" Hello, Vittoria. You look like shit.

"*Anche a me fa piacere vederti, zia.*" Pleasure to see you too, Aunt.

I only look like shit because your goons attacked me.

That might be a bit confrontational.

I watch her wander over to Alejandro as though she hasn't a care in the world. My claws are ready to unsheathe when she grips his chin and tries to turn his head from side to side.

Don't motherfucking touch my man.

Years of training kick in as I control my reaction. I keep my heart rate from spiking, breathing even, and temper in check. I know she's antagonizing me as much as she's insulting Alejandro. I won't take the bait—at least, I won't let her see me take it.

Don't lose your shit.

There must be a reason—even if it's shitty—for what's happening.

"You had a simple job to do, Vittoria."

I guess we switched to English, so Alejandro can understand —more likely to taunt him.

"You hired me?"

"I'm aware of who hired you."

"*Papà?*"

"No."

"Don Piero?"

"No."

Are we going to go through the list of *Mala del Brenta* men? This will take a while. Then again, it could've been anyone who hired me, but my *zia* brought *Mala* men. Her husband is a senior *capo*, but he's the definition of pussy whipped.

When my *zia* says jump, he apologizes for not already hopping like a fucking bunny. So, if she wanted to bring some of his men, he couldn't stop her. I doubt he'd even put up much of a fight. He has far more of a backbone dealing with his don and *consigliere*. My father doesn't respect him, and neither do I. But I love my *zia*—or I did.

"Did Alejandro wrong a Mancinelli, so the Torettas told Don Piero, and you took it upon yourself to help the Mancinellis?"

"No, but good guess."

"Did Alejandro do something to our family?" She knows I include the Carosis in that.

"Not directly."

"*Zia*, are we going to go around and around?"

"Think a little harder, *Nipote*." Niece.

My head still hurts to think much more than I already am. It's ringing like *Campanile di San Marco*—the most famous bell tower in Venice.

"*Zia*, you know I feel like death warmed over right now. Your men drugged me and knocked me around."

"You were never a biter as a child. You shouldn't have started now."

"You shouldn't have kidnapped me. What is going on?"

There's not an ounce of remorse or regret in her expression. It's not precisely glee, but she appears pleased that she's making me jump through hoops. I'm not her husband; I won't play her games. If Alejandro wants to question her, he can. I opt for silence again as I feel around for any part of the rope and begin plucking. I look straight ahead, but I still observe Alejandro from the corner of my eye.

He doesn't appear perturbed in the least. Just the opposite. It's like he's watching family sitting around on Christmas morning.

His shoulders are down, and his head's slightly tilted to the left. He's amused.

If I weren't sure it was a ploy, I'd be annoyed.

"You know me, but I have no idea who you are beyond being Vittoria's aunt."

Not quite dismissive, but unimpressed. He's striking at her vanity. He'd better watch out before she strikes out in irritation. She's the one with claws. Her perfectly manicured nails could gouge a chunk of skin. I've seen how she peels oranges.

"Cosima Contarini."

"It's certainly a displeasure to meet you."

I want to cringe, but my *zia* chuckles—like a James Bond villain. Who the fuck is this woman? I don't recognize her. She's a grade school teacher for fuck's sake. She teaches the equivalent of American third grade. Kids are the only people she likes and the only ones who seem to like her. Is she some secret operative more undercover than me? Or is this something deeply personal that she's taken upon herself? I just can't wrap my head around any of this.

"You're nearly as charming as your uncle."

"Which one? I've been told they're both silver foxes."

This time, her laugh is less sinister. Not what I'm used to, but it's not freezing the blood in my veins.

"Either. Both."

"Are you waiting for one of them to show up?"

"Hardly. They don't know where you are."

"Is this about me or your niece?"

His tone hardens when he mentions me. He can tolerate the threat to himself, but he won't put up with anyone—let alone family—targeting me. It nearly makes me laugh to consider how protective he is of me considering I have a body count higher than most war veteran snipers.

It's sweet.

"Both."

"Because Vittoria hasn't killed me or because we're involved."

"Fucking. That certainly hasn't endeared her to her employer since she's never crossed that line before. Her employer's generally patient, but that ended."

Alejandro probably has far more to say, but like me, he seems disinclined to play twenty questions. He turns his head just enough to look past her. I'm accustomed to long hours of silence as I scout and stake out my targets. His dossier told me he often does the same on missions in Latin America.

He's his uncle's fixer. Luis visits the prisons and handles the cartel and gang members who step out of line in their prison industry. Alejandro handles the more refined negotiations, but he rolls up his sleeves whenever needed.

My *zia* steps in front of me, attempting to force me to look at her. I may as well have x-ray vision because I look nowhere but at her midsection. She tsks as though I'm an obstinate child—which I absolutely was. Drove my parents crazy. She was one of the few people who could negotiate me into compromises. It won't work today.

"Vittoria, finish the job right now. I have a jet waiting to take us home."

If she gives me a weapon, I'll kill her before I do Alejandro.

That's an unsettling realization, but it's true. I'll pick him before my family. I never imagined this scenario. Not just having a family member hold me captive but choosing someone who isn't blood or our *Mala del Brenta* branch. But I don't have to think twice about where my loyalty lies now. I shouldn't feel this devoted to Alejandro so soon, but I do.

He's become a part of me.

I need him like my next breath.

How the fuck did that happen?

It happened because you've never felt more comfortable with a man than you do with him. You've never felt so intuitively understood as you do when you're with him.

He calls you Vita for the same reason. He said as much.

"Vittoria, your stubbornness will get you in as much trouble now as it did when you were a child."

"Except I won't concede anything. Let Alejandro go, and we stand a chance of not being enemies."

"You'd pick this *cazzo d'Orro* over family?"

Golden prick. Basically, a man who marries a wealthy woman because he's a good fuck.

"Family? That word means nothing since you did this to me. Betrayal works both ways. What do you think *Mamà* will say when she learns of this?"

"You assume she doesn't know."

"My mother sanctioned you having men accost me, assault me, drug me, and tie me up? Bullshit."

"Do not swear at me." *Young lady*.

I can practically hear what she doesn't say.

"*Fanculo*." Fuck off.

Alejandro chuckles. He may not speak Italian, but it doesn't surprise me he can swear in the language. I'm certain he heard plenty of curses from the Mancinellis since he grew up in the same neighborhood as them. It's the same one his cousins bought homes in. His dossier included places I'd most likely find him. A map showed me his parents' home is only a few blocks from his cousins'.

The man I heard walking in with my *zia* finally steps into view. I wondered who loitered behind us, but I didn't want to look away from her long enough to find out. At this point, I don't trust her not to stab me the moment I shift my attention from her.

Holy motherfucker.

"Zorzi?" The Venetian form of Giorgio.

And my ex-boyfriend.

We dated from our last year of secondary school through most of college. I broke up with him when the AISE came calling. I couldn't see how I'd maintain a romantic relationship with someone when I couldn't tell anyone what my job truly entailed. I wasn't the analyst I claimed to most people.

"Hello, Toria. Long time no see."

Not fucking long enough.

"Why?"

"Why not?"

"Hiding from me and now hiding behind my *zia*. Your cock's as small as I remember."

"*Cagna*." Bitch.

I shrug as best I can. He's always been easy to antagonize. At least with me he was. He's *Mala del Brenta* too, so he's patient with his prey. But I could wind him up when I wanted. Our arguments were epic, but so was our making up. At least, it seemed like it since I had no one to compare back then. It was adolescent fumbling when I consider how things are with Alejandro.

"What do you want, Zorzi?"

"To kill you."

Chapter Twenty-One

Alejandro

Hearing any man—especially one Vita clearly has a past with—threaten her makes me want to bay at the moon. My best guess is that he was a serious boyfriend for a long time. The way he looks at her is part longing and part resentment. He's not over her. She's the one who got away. From her tone and how we've fucked, she doesn't feel the same way about him.

If only I could make his death slow, but I won't have that luxury.

Whoever tied my ropes wasn't meant for the navy. I've been slow with each step to ensure my shoulders don't move. I've already untied one knot, and the rope's loosened significantly. I don't know if Vita's been buying us time by dragging out the conversation or she knows these two won't be more forthcoming. Either way, I'm making progress. I wish I could look over to see if she is too.

"Zorzi, did you put the hit on me? Or did you find out Vittoria moved on with me, got pissed, then stuck your nose in this?"

"He couldn't afford the hit." Vita's comment is nothing less than snide.

I still can't reason through who wants to kill me enough that they're taking on my entire family. There's no way they wouldn't avenge me. When my great-uncle murdered his own brother—*Mamá's papá*—my *tíos* went on a rampage through Bogotá. There're places that are still in rubble thirty-odd years later. They destroyed everything in their path—buildings, careers, lives, government offices. They punished anyone who'd ever looked upon *Tío* Humberto with a moment's approval.

They ensured no one doubted *los Diaz* rule Colombia.

What we giveth, we taketh.

When *Tío* Humberto helped pay for a rival to murder *Tío* Esteban right in front *Tres J's, Tía* Luciana made my *tíos'* brutality look like child's play. She caught the men, beheaded them, and threw their heads into busy streets in the most dangerous part of Bogotá to be knocked around like soccer balls. Then she had the men's bodies strung upside down from the busiest bridge in the city. She hacked off a *huevo* from the man who orchestrated the hit and sent it gift wrapped to the man's wife. She included a note that said if she couldn't have her man, then the woman wouldn't have hers either. She ensured *everyone* understood that the Diaz women don't play when it comes to family.

Needless to say, this incident won't go over well with them. *Tía* Luciana's the most easygoing in the family even if *Mamá* and *Papá* are more outgoing. If my *tía's* reaction to her husband's death was anything to go by, I can't even conceive of what my death would do to my mother. And I say this as a man with no limits. *Papá* won't stop her either. He'll guard her back.

I consider what Vita just said about this Zorzi fuck not affording the hit.

"You have *Mala del Brenta* men, but I suspect you're working independently. Who did I piss off enough to convince you to go against your don and agree with an unsanctioned hit?"

"Who said it's unsanctioned?"

I laugh.

"What's so funny?"

Zorzi sounds like an irritated toddler who had his favorite toy taken away. Before I can answer, Vita speaks up.

"You're holding the nephew of the most powerful man in the Western Hemisphere."

"Bullshit. Enrique Diaz has an overinflated opinion of himself, and his family spouts that shit, hoping to intimidate people into obedience. He's nothing but a *vu cump*—"

"Don't you dare finish that, you *pezzo di merda!*"

Vita sounds like she's about to come unglued. Whatever Zorzi was about to say was enough for Vita to go on the attack. I finally fully look over at her, and she's beyond livid. She glances at me.

"He was about to use an extremely derogatory term for immigrants."

"Immigrant? I was born here."

I don't know how that phrase could be that bad, but it struck a nerve with her. Maybe she's just as over the top protective as I am. It's an odd realization since she's not part of my immediate family. Nothing in the world comes above family, and from that, loyalty, honor, and duty are ingrained into our core. I expect that kind of defensiveness from someone I share DNA with. I'm unused to it from an outsider. Maybe it's a sign she's accepted what I already know—we're soulmates.

I feel the rope loosen enough to pull it over the heel of my hand. I strain to sense anyone else who might lurk far behind me but could assist Zorzi and Cosima. Unless the person has a high-powered rifle, I doubt they could hit me faster than I can get my knife out and kill both Zorzi and Cosima.

I've carried the knife that's in my left pocket since I was twelve. The rivalries in NYC are so heated that boys carry knives much younger than in other syndicates. My generation might not have gone on missions until we were sixteen, but we got into bloody fights while in middle school. The closest we've come to an outright street war was high school when a melee broke out at a party the Four Families all accidentally showed up to. We had different friend groups, so we never socialized together.

That night, no one got the memo.

Maria Mancinelli's Spanish wasn't as good as it is now. She misheard Javier and thought he called her a flat chested bitch when he was warning Joaquin, who was a senior, to stay away from Maria's friend, who had a crush on him. Maria lost her shit and called out to Carmine, who had Gabriele next to him—of course, because they share a set of *huevos*.

The Kutsenkos heard *Tres J's* insulted a girl, so they had to jump on their white horses and storm in like knights to the rescue. And the O'Rourkes—those asshats—egged on the rest of us until they got drawn into the fight too.

It was Maria who saved all our asses. She recognized a police officer whose father was *Cosa Nostra* and convinced her to have the cops leave. Everyone fled in different directions when we heard the sirens. Afterward, our respective leaders were so irate, we all thought we were safer with the knives and guns at the party. Punishment was swift and merciless for all of us. *Tío* Enrique hated it, but he had to make an example of all of us. He couldn't appear soft toward us if we were one day to stand beside him as leaders of the Cartel.

Since then, there's been an unspoken rule that if someone's injured or killed in a mission that goes sideways, then so be it. But the Four Families don't target each other. That's why I can't imagine it's the Mancinellis, Kutsenkos, or O'Rourkes.

Even if the Kutsenkos think we're bogarting their deal to fund the *Mala del Brenta* and *Cosa Nostra*, they wouldn't do this. The O'Rourkes might be pissed that we're tipping the scales away from their side, but they wouldn't do this. The Mancinellis might hate that any outsiders have influence in Italy, but they wouldn't do this.

"Alejandro."

"Huh? Sorry. Spaced out. Got bored."

Cosima snapped at me. I have no idea what she or Zorzi said when I was strolling down memory lane.

"You pissed off the Galicians."

What the fuck?

If anyone should be pissed off, it's me.

Those motherfuckers fucked me out of over three million dollars in imports.

Spain is a major European hub for importing Colombia's most notorious semi-organic product. The Mafia there was supposed to run a shipment through Galicia and distribute it to Madrid and Barcelona. Instead, the *caremondas*—faces of a penis—let it get seized. They took the fall since they were the ones in possession, but it cost us all the trade.

"Oh, really?"

"Yeah. You reneged on your end of the deal."

"The hell I did. It wasn't my fault they didn't take care of the port properly. If this were true, what does it have to do with you?"

Cosima glances at Vita, and there's a flash of regret before she smirks at me yet again.

"Your expansion into Spain won't happen."

"Into? We're already there. We *deserve* more."

Entitled much?

You better fucking believe it.

My family's earned it, so we deserve every motherfucking thing we want. We've invested in communities, putting new roofs on churches and six figures into the coffers for orphanages. We've supported political campaigns to ensure the least corrupt people get into office. That we remind them to say thank you—frequently —is neither here nor there.

But if Spain is the issue, then it's the bratva that has an issue with us. We cut off their trade expansion into Spain and Portugal for not truly retaliating when this proxy war sucked in Anneliese and Jorge. They're feeling the squeeze because the O'Rourkes have made serious inroads in Eastern Europe, which used to be a given for the bratva. Mother Russia hasn't been anyone's favorite since the Eastern Bloc fell, so the people there welcome the Irish American backing.

"If you weren't such self-involved pricks, maybe no one would want to kill you."

"I don't believe for a single moment Maksim sanctioned me as a mark. The man's not the smartest potato in the field, but he's not entirely stupid. He isn't going after someone like me to teach my *tío* anything. This is your family trying to stick your noses so far up his ass that you can smell the vodka on his breath. All that'll happen is he takes a massive shit on you."

"That's a lot of speculation."

"You're not denying it, *Señora*."

"It doesn't merit recognition."

"Sure."

I'm dismissive as I get the last of the rope off my wrists. I catch it, so it can't fall to the floor. I can't look over at Vita without giving away where my attention shifts. I don't want Cosima or Zorzi wondering why I'm checking on her. They obviously know we're involved, but I won't give away just how much she means to me. I don't think that'll save her or me, but I don't need to fuel our tormentors.

"Bastardo arrogante."

Not exactly difficult to guess what Zorzi calls me. I pretend to pout as I mock him. He clenches his fists.

How the fuck did Vita ever date this hijueputa? Son of a bitch.

I suppose there's a reason they broke up, and I suspect she dumped his sorry ass. If it were just the two of us, I'd say something obscene about having more money, a bigger dick, and fucking his woman. Instead, I switch to the most patronizing smile I can muster. It pisses off most men and makes women think I'm aloof—and worth the chase.

Vita clears her throat softly. Zorzi and Cosima look in her direction. I know it's her signal to gain my attention. I drop the rope and launch myself out of my seat as my hands slide into my pockets. I whip out both knives, my muscle memory placing my index fingers over the triggers to release the blades. I slash Zorzi's throat before anyone realizes my intentions.

Hope Vita doesn't mind.

I have Cosima in a chokehold with one blade at the back of her neck ready to hack my way to her spine, and the other gripped and positioned to drive it into her sternum.

Vita reaches out for a handful of her *tía's* hair and yanks the woman's head sideways, giving me room to move the blade to her jugular. The sound of Vita's hand meeting Cosima's cheek rings throughout the cavernous space.

Fuck!

She slapped the woman *hard* for it to be so loud in such an enormous area. Sensing my curiosity, Vita pulls Cosima's hair even harder, making it possible for me to see the scarlet handprint on the older woman's cheek. My woman isn't playing.

"I don't give a shit whether my parents ever forgive you for this. I don't give a shit if they even sanctioned this. I will kill you for endangering my man."

Her bone chilling tone warms my shriveled heart.

She cares about me. She really, really cares about me.

I'm having my Wednesday Addams's goth girl moment.

My lips twitch, then purse as though I'm blowing Vita kiss. Her eyes widen for a moment before she laughs.

"Mwah."

She makes a smacking kiss sound. I'm certain Cosima believes we're equally psychotic or just hamming it up. I think Vita and I are a match made in heaven.

"What do you want me to do, *chiquita*?"

"Hold her."

My arm tightens around her neck, shifting the blade away from her, favoring making her pass out rather than bleed out if she fights me. I move the knife from her sternum and wrap my long arm around her torso, pinning her arms to her sides. She isn't moving unless I allow it. Vita releases Cosima's hair and steps in front of her. She reaches out her hand, palm up. I hand her the knife that's near Cosima's neck.

My heart lurches as I watch Vita spin the knife in the air, catching it by the tip. The blade is wickedly sharp. It's part of my morning routine to clean both knives and run them across a whetstone if I used them the previous day. She flicks it again, catching it by the handle. She pretends to balance it on her palm, as though finding the right place to grip it. Then she turns her hand sideways and places the tip of the blade under her *tía's* nose.

"It sure would be a shame to mark up your pretty face, *Zia*."

"It would be a shame for you to be dead, *Nipote*."

"I want her phone."

I loosen my hold since I know the demand is perfunctory. Vita snatches it from Cosima's front pocket. She holds it up, prying her *tía's* eye open wider for the retina scan. She taps the screen before putting the phone to her ear. I wonder why she doesn't want me to hear whatever the other person says. I assume I won't understand her since the call's likely to be in Italian. People say Italian and Spanish are close, but not close enough for me to understand a conversation well enough to keep up.

"*Mamà*, what the hell is going on?"

I guess she's going with English as a favor to me. But I still don't know what her mother's saying. Maybe she doesn't want Cosima to hear, so she can't interject. I hate being left out, though.

My mother's still trying to teach me that, as an only child, not everything is all about me all the time. Doubt I'll ever learn that lesson.

"Do you know where *Zia* Cosima is right now?"

I don't know what her mother said as an answer to the first question, but I have the answer to the second a moment later.

"She's holding my boyfriend and me captive. She had us attacked, beaten, drugged, then tied up."

It's muffled, but I hear a string of what must be Italian curses because Vita holds the phone away from her ear. She taps the screen, and I see the call switch to video. She flips the camera and pans around what we can now see is an empty warehouse. It looks more like a fucking bunker. She walks over to the chairs and tilts the phone to show the ropes on the ground.

Then she returns to Cosima and me. She holds up the camera, and I turn my head from side to side before she flips the camera back around to face her. She does the same thing so her mother can see the bruise over Vita's left cheekbone. I will cut off each finger of the hand that touched her, then I'll disembowel the fucker.

"Toria, are you injured more than I can see?"

"No, *Mamà*. But I have no idea how long Alejandro and I were unconscious. We don't know where we are either. Who did this? *Zia* won't say. We wasted enough time that Alejandro and I got free, but we're no closer to understanding what's happening than when the attack started."

She flips the camera yet again, so the sisters stare at each other.

"I don't know, but you can be sure I'll find out. Cosima, you hurt my daughter. If there were any chance you'd survive this, I'd kill you myself. You will not take my last child from me."

I'd forgotten Vita lost her two brothers. I know how *Tío* Luis and *Tía* Margherita still silently grieve Juan, both his death and the man he could've been. That was one child. To have lost two and have a third in an occupation where she could die at any time? What a fucked-up world we live in.

"Orsa, you've gotten too soft on your daughter."

"Our parents may have named you for beauty, but I'm named for a bear. You've come after my child. You will learn what kind of *mamà* I am. I'm having lunch with Aurelia and Iseppo today. Take one from me, and I'll take both from you."

I assume those are Cosima's daughter and son. I can't see her reaction, but I can see the pure hatred on Vita's mother's face. It's the expression only a mother could master when her child's in danger. I've seen my father and *tío* when my cousins and I have been in danger. They're fierce as fuck. They're both big guys who intimidate most people just by walking by.

My *mamá* and *tías* are tiny compared to the men in our family, but even their sweetest smiles can be terrifying. If this woman's going to be my mother-in-law, I'll remember what it means to run afoul of her.

"You wouldn't." Cosima couldn't convince a nun to say a prayer.

"Wouldn't I?"

The sisters glower at each other for a protracted moment before Vita steps in again.

"*Mamà*, get her to tell you who's behind this."

"Cosima."

When the woman says nothing, I steer her to the chairs and force her to sit. I'm quick to secure her to one. My bindings aren't coming undone unless I do them. I doubt even Vita could figure out how to release these knots.

I pull the second chair over and place it facing Cosima. I figure since we're going to be here a while, at least Vita should be comfortable. I usher her to the seat, and she holds out the phone so her mother can see all of us. I notice Orsa's gaze darts to me over Vita's shoulder. She shoots me an appreciative smile, and I see approval.

"There's nothing any of you can do. Things are too far gone."

As though on cue, an explosion rattles the entire building. Heat rushes forward as doors at the far end blow open.

Well, shit.

"Vita, what do you want me to do?"

With my knives, I can get Cosima loose in time, but I need to know right now.

"*Zia*, choose. Tell me what the fuck I need to know, or *Mamà* will plan your memorial."

The woman shoots her niece a defiant glare, and I see the family resemblance. Except Vita's expression won't get her killed.

"*Mamà?*"

I hear the doubt in Vita's voice as she asks her mother whether she should save the woman's sister.

"Alejandro, save my daughter."

Her daughter's just as likely to save me as I am her, but this isn't the time for semantics. Vita and I back away from a screaming Cosima as we both search our surroundings. There aren't any doors besides the ones we can see through. Flames block the view of anything beyond them.

"Stay here, *chiquita*."

"What? No!"

"I can promise you I'm faster."

I don't wait for my Vita—*mi vida*—to argue. My life is nothing if I lose her. I've saved my *papá's*, *tíos'*, and *primos'* lives more times than I ever should have needed to. I would run into that fire for them without reservation. But the drive to keep Vita alive and unharmed is like I've been possessed.

I sprint to the doorway, pulling my shirt untucked to cover my mouth and nose. I wish I hadn't left my suit coat at my *tío's* house. I get to the doors, and ash already billows in the air. Between that and the heat, my eyes sting like someone poured bleach into them.

I focus on the colors of the flames and which ways they move. I'm no pyro, but fire fascinates me. It's a living, breathing thing with a mind of its own. But if you watch closely, it'll tell you what it's thinking.

There's no way Vita and I will escape unscathed, but I see a path. We just have to take it now. There's no chance to free Cosima.

"Vita! Come!"

She's been watching me. She doesn't shift her focus, not even for a moment. She doesn't give her *tía* a second glance. She bolts to me, the phone still in her hand. I hear her mother's screams as she approaches.

"End the call, *chica*."

"No!"

Both women scream at me, but I ignore them. I pluck the phone from her hand and end the call. The betrayal on Vita's face breaks my heart.

"Do you want your mother to watch?"

Vita inhales a shuddering breath as she shakes her head. She knows I mean if we get trapped in this furnace and die where we fall.

"Tuck your hair into your shirt and pull up as much as you can to cover your face without exposing all of your torso."

Once she's done that, I wrap my arm around her shoulders and press down until we're as close to the floor as we can get without waddling. I scan the area, knowing our path has already changed in just the couple moments it took Vita to get to me. I guide her, and she never hesitates, switching course when we have to. I slide my arm down to her waist, covering the exposed skin at her lower back as best I can. I slap at embers that keep attaching to my trousers.

"Jandro!"

She grabs my shirt in the front and back, tugging me as hard as she can. I barely avoid the chunk of ceiling that lands where I was standing only a second ago. It catches my right trouser leg on fire. I smack at flames, but I only burn my hand. There's not enough room for me to stop, drop, and roll. My leg hurts, but we have no choice. We have to press on.

"Alej—"

Vita splutters too much to speak. I pull her along with me as I hobble. Fortunately, the rest of me doesn't catch on fire. Small moth-bite-like holes form in the material, and the heat singes some hair on my leg, but it doesn't travel higher.

Welp. There goes my perfection.

I'll definitely have scars that won't add to my manly intrigue. These random and ridiculous thoughts sustain me. I can't lose my shit. I don't have that luxury if I want Vita and me to survive. I pull her in front of me and shield her with my body when the path gets too narrow for us to walk side by side.

"Daddy!"

"Keep going, *chica*."

The pain's making me lightheaded, and dark spots dance around the edges of my vision. My lungs feel like they're burning as badly as my legs. My shirt's doing nothing to protect me from the soot. I stumble, and fortunately, Vita keeps me upright. With each step, I'm leaning on her more until I fear my weight will knock her to the floor and crush her.

"Stay with me, Daddy. We're almost there. Come on."

A jagged piece of metal catches my cheek, nearly slicing and burning it. I push my left arm up and knock it away, singeing that arm while I'm at it. Everywhere hurts. My body screams for me to stop, to rest, to just let go. But then I feel Vita moving in front of me. If I give up and give in, then there's no one to protect her. I swore I would. I'll protect her from the grave if I have to.

We make it outside, and she practically drags me away from

the building. We're coughing as we sink to our knees. When she looks at me, I can tell it's tears filling her eyes, not just them watering from the heat and polluted air. She dives at me and pushes me onto my stomach, whooshing the little air in my lungs out through my mouth. She lifts my shirt, and the cooler night air only makes it worse.

"Fuck, Jandro. I need to get you to a hospital now."

"Just home. Our doc can—"

"No! You need a burn unit."

I don't have it in me to argue with her since she's right. We avoid hospitals like the plague. Too many questions, but I know my limitations.

"*Chica*, O positive, December seventeenth, tonsillectomy when I was twelve, and appendectomy when I was nineteen."

I rattle off my social security number, not that I believe she'll remember. I convey the vital information she'll need and tell her she'll find my insurance card in my wallet.

She pulls the phone from where I tucked it down the front of her pants. I rattle off my father's number as she dials.

"Matáis? Oh, thank God. Alejandro's hurt. He needs a hospital, but I don't know where we are. Can you ping his tracker?"

She has the phone on speaker, and it's a good thing, or my father's voice would've burst her eardrum.

"Alejo! Alejo!"

"*Sí, papá.*"

"*Háblame. ¿Qué pasó?*" Talk to me. What happened?

"*Fuego.*" Fire.

"*¿Qué tan gravemente herido estás?*" How badly are you hurt?

I look up at Vita as she pulls a knife from my pocket and cuts away at my shirt. I don't remember when I put them away, but I did. They're such a part of me—like a limb or an organ—that I only notice when I don't have them—which is pretty much only when I'm in the shower or in bed. Then they're on the bedside table.

"*Yo—*"

I cough too hard to continue; I'm not sure what I was going to say. Fortunately, Vita speaks Spanish, so she continues in that. I know she understands that in this crisis, both *Papá* and I reverted to the language we're most comfortable in. I grew up speaking English and Spanish equally, not realizing they were different languages until I reached preschool. But *Papá's* first language was Spanish.

"We have to get Jandro to a hospital. He needs a burn unit. Can I call an ambulance?"

"If you believe it's that bad, then yes. Alejo?"

"Yes, *Papá*."

"Your tracker just came back up. We lost you five hours ago. You're just outside Yonkers."

I can only imagine the panic my family's been in.

"*Mamá?*"

"I hear her. She's coming."

Just as my father finishes speaking, it's my mom's turn to practically burst an eardrum.

"*Frijolito!*"

Little bean. Apparently, she's been calling me that since her first ultrasound because I looked like a tiny bean in the grainy image.

"*Sí, Mamá.*"

Just like with my papá, her first language was Spanish. They both grew up in Colombia and didn't move to the States until college. We continue in that, and I don't have to think as hard.

"What hurts, little bean?"

"Everything."

"Catalina, I need to get off the phone to call the ambulance. As soon as they're here, and I know where they're taking us, I'll call back. I'm sorry, but we have to hang up."

"We understand. We'll meet you wherever you go. The SUVs are waiting."

They'll need at least four seven-seater SUVs to get them all here along with the guards they'll bring. If they flew from the regional airport in Queens to Yonkers, it'd be about ten minutes. However, the time it would take to get the plane ready would be a waste. Plus, they'd need mine to accommodate everyone when they add Vita and me.

I can't believe I'm thinking straight enough to consider any of this or to have followed along with the conversation. But the distraction's the only thing that's keeping me from howling in pain. Nothing has ever hurt as badly as it does now. I've had broken ribs, punctured lungs, bruised kidneys, bone bruises, stab wounds, and bullet holes. This shit right now is for the fucking birds.

Now that I'm not trying to downplay things for my parents, my mind's growing fuzzy. I'm so exhausted that all I want to do is close my eyes and nap. Vita's squeezing my hand, telling me to stay awake as she dials 911. I don't have it in me anymore. I hear her speaking to the dispatcher, but it's like she's miles away.

"Hello? I need an ambulance. My husband's been badly burned in an explosion... I'm not from here. I don't know where we are."

Husband? When'd I get promoted?

Chapter Twenty-Two

Vita

Husband.

The word tumbled out of my mouth as though I've said it a thousand times.

I wish.

Today's been a startling day of revelations, and realizing I want Alejandro to be my husband is utterly reassuring compared to everything else.

I said it because I know that's the only way I'll have a say in what happens while he's in the hospital. I'll step back when his parents arrive, but for now, he needs someone who can decide and give consent. He's barely conscious, and as the pain sets in further, I doubt he'll remain that way.

"I wonder if my scar will make me as menacing as Luca."

"Huh?"

Alejandro's babbling more than anything, so I'm not following his train of thought.

"What scar?"

He brings his fingers toward his right cheek and points.

"The cut. It'll scar. I wonder if it'll make me appear more

menacing like Luca Mancinelli. I'm tired of people assuming God gave me looks but no brains. A scar would be manly."

I nearly choke as I struggle to swallow my laugh. Alejandro's the manliest man I've ever met. Yes, he's fucking genetic perfection and gorgeous beyond measure. But he's everything I could want: intelligent, funny, strong, caring, protective, determined. My list can keep going, but I need to pay attention to the dispatcher.

"Stay on the line with me, ma'am. We have an ambulance on its way. Is your husband still responsive?"

"Barely."

"What parts of his body suffered burns?"

"His right leg and arm, and there are wounds on his back too. He cut his cheek on some metal. Plus, the smoke inhalation."

"Ma'am, are you suffering from that too? You sound out of breath and raspy."

"Yes. But it's my husband who needs more attention."

"I can send two ambulances."

"No! You will not separate me from my husband."

"You can follow in your vehicle."

"I don't have one with me, and I wouldn't use it anyway. *I am staying with my husband.*"

I'm practically snarling. I'll go completely feral if they attempt to stop me. If anyone's that foolish, they'll find themselves at the tip of Alejandro's blade—blades.

"Okay. They're almost there."

I fall silent, reassuring her every couple of minutes that I'm still there until the ambulance arrives. I do my best to stay out of the way, but I bare my teeth when they suggest I find another means to get to the emergency room. It feels like forever, but it's only a ten-minute ride. Then I'm rushing alongside the gurney, my hand wrapped around Alejandro's. His grip isn't what it should be, but it's not as weak as I feared.

"Mrs.—?"

"Trevisan."

The nurse's brow furrows as she stares at me before glancing over her shoulder.

"You told the paramedics that the patient's name is Alejandro Diaz and that you're his wife. Your name doesn't match."

"Not everyone is from a Puritanical country that subjugates women and identifies them by the men who own them. I'm Italian, and my husband's Colombian. Women don't change their last names. Now tell me what the hell is going to happen to my husband."

I word vomit my annoyance. It's none of her fucking business why my name doesn't match, but my righteous indignation is a successful distraction.

"My apologies. The nature of your husband's injuries means a doctor will see him shortly. In the meantime, if you can follow me to registration, you can check him in with his insurance information."

Only in America do hospitals care more about who's paying the bill than how badly the patient needs care. There's no way Alejandro will move back to Italy with me, so that means me permanently moving to the States. This is one of those things I'm forced to accept, even if it goes against my European sensibilities. Thank God Alejandro's independently wealthy, and his family is obscenely affluent. I don't have to fear him suffering because I couldn't pay.

The nurse walks away, and I'm glad to see the back of her. Before I turn to the man at the registration desk, I muster the water works. I force tears to my eyes, letting them spill down my cheeks. I cry hard enough that my nose runs. Only then do I face the guy. I make sure my hand trembles as I pass the insurance card to him. If he asks questions I can't answer, I can play up the distraught wife role.

It takes ten minutes before I'm done. A nurse ushers me back into an ER bay where they check my vitals because I started coughing from the smoke inhalation. They bring in pre-surgery wipes, so I scrub my hands, face, and neck to remove the soot from them. I'd prefer a shower, but it's enough to make me presentable.

They offered me a hospital gown when I got to the ER bay they assigned me, but I refused. I convinced—badgered—a young nursing assistant to find me a pair of scrubs. At least only my hair reeks of smoke. Everything checks out well enough for me to demand I go back to the waiting room rather than remain hooked up to machines that won't shut the fuck up.

I'm left twiddling my thumbs for two hours before the cavalry arrives. It's fucking impressive. Like, everyone in the ER waiting area freezes as Alejandro's family arrives.

The men are—I don't have the words for the pure animal magnetism they all exude. Matáis, Enrique, Luis, *Tres J's*, and Pablo all stand well over six feet tall with sun-kissed brown skin. They're all stacked with muscles upon muscles; their custom-tailored suits barely contain their raw power.

The women are beyond sophisticated with an air of complete control anywhere they look. Elodie is only slightly fairer than the other women, but her dark hair makes her blend in. Elodie, Catalina, Luciana, and Margherita sweep into the waiting area as though they dare anyone to stand in the way of their family. I notice three younger women who must be Javier's and Pablo's wives, and Jorge's fiancée. The two blondes and one brunette aren't quite as intimidating as the older women, but they're intense.

Margherita and the woman who must be Madeline march to the nurses' station and begin an animated conversation. I catch snippets as the two midwives demand a full rundown of Alejandro's diagnosis and care. The poor guys behind the desk stare wide-eyed at them before Margherita leans across the desk until her nose is practically up one of the nurse's. The guy drops into his chair and rapidly types.

Catalina and Matáis approach me, and I struggle to rein in my emotions. I'm so fucking relieved they're here, but guilt ravages me as I remember my family's responsible. No—not my family, but one member and a clearly psycho ex-boyfriend. But any connection to me makes all of this so much worse.

"They won't let me back there, but I've gotten updates. He's sleeping right now. They gave him some powerful painkillers that knocked him out. The burns aren't as bad as we initially feared, so they won't transfer him to the burn unit. It was the heat more than the flames that caused his pain. He shielded me from the worst of it."

"What happened?" Matáis's voice is unnervingly quiet.

"My aunt."

I stare down at the floor, shame igniting goosebumps all over my body. I inhale, then swallow before looking at the couple who —for a brief moment in time—were going to be my in-laws. I can't imagine how they'd welcome me into the family now.

"What do you mean your aunt?"

Catalina's biting tone makes me want to cringe. She doesn't speak any louder than her husband, but I feel it in my marrow. I know they'd never make a scene somewhere so public, but the quieter they are, the more I fear their retribution.

"We didn't figure out much, but it was my mother's sister and an ex-boyfriend in the warehouse. It shocked my mother to discover *Zia* Cosima threatened me. Neither Alejandro nor I know if they handled the explosion or if that was someone else."

"Your ex-boyfriend?"

"Yes. We haven't been together since I was twenty-one, so nearly ten years ago. It shocked me to see him. Alejandro and I believe it was an unsanctioned attack. I don't know why *Zia* Cosima or Zorzi would set off an explosion while they were in the building. I suspect someone either wanted them gone along with us, or they didn't know my aunt and ex-boyfriend were there."

Enrique steps forward, standing on the other side of Catalina from Matáis. Her husband's arm is around her waist, and her older brother wraps his arm around her shoulders. A moment later, Luciana and Luis join us. They practically form a circle around me as they stand arm-in-arm. The four siblings bear a remarkable resemblance to one another, almost like two sets of twins. It's a unified force standing opposed to me. I want to sink into the ground.

"Vittoria, we don't blame you."

It's Luciana who speaks up. I want to believe her, but it's a struggle since I blame myself.

"Could this be a jealous ex-boyfriend and an overprotective aunt?"

I shift my focus to Enrique as he speaks. I shake my head.

"I don't think so. Zorzi and I haven't seen or spoken to each other since I graduated university. He's married and has two young children. My *zia* and I have always been super close, even if she's not an easy woman for most people to like. Zorzi's a Made Man, so he would've been there if Don Piero or my father ordered it, but I don't believe they did. My *zia* being there was far more shocking."

"What did they tell you?"

"That whoever hired me wanted me dead alongside Alejandro. *Zia* Cosima mentioned the Galicians. Alejandro was unconvinced since something went wrong with a deal. It sounded like they wronged him, not the other way around."

"He was. There's no way anyone in Spain would strike out like this. They rely on our exports too much. It was someone else."

Enrique sounds so certain that I don't question his explanation. He opens his mouth to say more, but a nurse approaches.

"Mrs. Trevisan, your husband's asking to see you."

I cringe internally before looking at Alejandro's parents. I don't know which is worse: Alejandro wanting to see me before them or hearing someone claim I'm their son's wife.

"Does Alejandro know his parents are here?"

"Yes. He asked for you, ma'am."

"But—"

"Mrs. Trevisan, your husband's very insistent. He was ready to pull his IV out and find you himself."

Catalina and Matáis chuckle while the others smirk.

What the ever-loving fuck is with this family?

They never react the way you'd expect.

"Hurry up and see our son before he drops dead trying to find you." Catalina gives me a little nudge.

"I only said—"

"We get it. You were here, and we weren't. Go see our son."

Matáis nudges his chin toward the doors through which the nurse appeared. I follow the woman past several curtained bays before I hear rapid fire Spanish followed by placating Spanglish.

Fuck.

I hurry before an irate jaguar emerges from the closed curtains. That's what Alejandro reminds me of. Sleek and elegant to look at but an apex predator to his core.

"Jandro?"

I push aside the curtain to find him sitting with his legs over the edge of the bed, glowering at a man who's probably not even a nurse. They probably walked in to take his vitals, only to wind up in his crosshairs.

"Chiquita?"

"Sí, papí."

I opt for Spanish since the term *papí* doesn't automatically have the same connotation as saying Daddy. It can be romantic or platonic slang.

"Ven aquí, chica."

"Sí, papí."

Despite his wounds and clearly medicated state, I don't miss his commanding tone. I want to submit. Even though he's the injured one, I breathe easier knowing he's in control. I could be if I had to, and I would be if I were alone. But I know he needs this as much as I do.

I approach, and he holds out his hand. The moment I lay mine on his, his fingers curl around my palm. I expected to see bandages covering them, but it's only a large pad and a single layer of gauze on each. I don't know how he wasn't more severely burned, but I'll take the small mercies.

He tugs surprisingly hard, and I stumble into him. I try to avoid slamming into him, but his arms wrap around me. He's definitely on something because both of his hands slide down to cup my ass. He'd never do that if he were in full control of his faculties. I might have to lead for a while after all.

He attempts to stand, but I press down on his shoulder. He

remains seated, but he tries to pull me onto his lap instead. I compromise and sit beside him. He shoots me a scowl before twisting with a grimace. Our mouths come together, as we cup each other's faces.

Much like his hands, his face isn't as bad as I braced myself for. There's more of a Band-Aid than bandage on it. Not even butterfly stitches. All the soot that covered us made it hard to determine the full extent of his injuries, and I feared the absolute worst. His hair still smells smoky like mine, but they cleaned him up. He's wearing a hospital gown instead of his filthy clothes.

Neither of us cares about the people moving around us or the machines beeping. We don't care about the announcements or how awkward the position is. We cling to each other.

"*Mierda santa, chiquita.*" Holy shit, little girl.

"*Lo sé, papí.*" I know, Daddy.

We kiss again as Alejandro's hands roam over me. I'm apprehensive to do the same. I don't know what injuries he might have that I didn't see. I don't want to hurt him.

"*Chica*, touch me. I crave it. It'll cure me far better and faster than anything else."

I lean in to whisper in his ear. "If my touch is so curative, then a blowjob might make you superhuman."

"Don't joke about that, *chica*. Otherwise, I'll drag you into the closest storage room and push you down on your knees. Fuck. The idea of your lips around my cock—fuck, my family won't be able to see me for at least an hour. It'll take that long for this hard-on to go down without your help."

"If your family weren't here..."

I arch my eyebrows at him, and he pounces, knocking me backward on the bed. His IV lines aren't long enough for him to crawl on top of me. If he weren't connected to the machines, I think he'd probably lift me to straddle him. I giggle as he kisses along my neck. If anyone walks in, they'll see his sculpted ass hanging out the back of his hospital gown. The man clearly doesn't care.

"Little one, in all seriousness, are you okay? Did you get checked out?"

"Yes, I'm fine."

"*Chica.*" The warning rumbles in his voice.

"Seriously, I'm okay. I have a headache, but nothing else. Neither my throat nor my chest hurts. The headache's more from worrying about you than the fire or sedative."

He brushes the backs of his fingers over my left cheekbone.

"You're so damn precious to me, Vita. I can't lose you."

"I'm not going anywhere. I already knew I wasn't, but I had more time to mull it over since the attack. I don't know how it'll work, but I want it to. I'm a constant liability to you. Anyone from my past could appear like they did today. It'll suck your family in. They won't approve."

"Yes, they will. They already do. We would've gone nowhere alone if they didn't."

"That was then, this is now. A shit ton's happened since we left your uncle's house."

"Just a day in the life."

"Stop, Jandro."

I snap at him more than I mean to. I don't appreciate his dismissiveness. I know he's attempting to downplay this, so I won't worry as much. But it feels like he's mocking my fears.

"Come closer, little one."

Short of sitting on his lap, I really can't get closer. He loops his arm around my shoulders and encourages me to rest my head against his shoulder.

"I'm sorry, *chiquita.* I didn't mean to diminish your fears, but you know this life. Any of us could be the target or the cause. My family understands that because we've gone through it before. As long as you aren't actively working against us, then you're one of us. If you still want us, then that's what's happening."

"Of course, I want us. I didn't just walk through fire for nothing."

He flashes me a grin before pulling away to resume his kisses along my neck. I lean my head away from him as his teeth graze the cords of my neck before his tongue soothes the tingles he created. How the hell can he be the singularly most erotic man I've met when he's connected to an IV and monitors in a hospital gown.

"Lie down with me."

"What? No. There isn't enough room."

"There would be if you laid on top of me." He waggles his eyebrows and shoots me a boyish grin.

"And press your back into the bed? Not a chance."

"Then lie on your side and let me curl around you. There's plenty of room. Besides, my back only has a few grazes. My clothes got holes in them, and I lost some hair on my arm and leg, but the rest of me was just extra sensitive from the heat. The smoke did the most damage, and as you can see, I'm breathing and talking just fine."

"Your parents deserve to see you. I'll consider it once they move you into your room."

"Fine."

I rise and stick my nose out of the curtained bay, asking a passing nurse if Alejandro's parents can come back here. He says yes and offers to get them. Alejandro's arms snake around my waist, and I feel just as happy as he does that we survived.

"Cover yourself up!"

I attempt to turn in his arms, but he merely gives me a squeeze before letting go.

"If you turn around, you'll only make it worse, little one."

He climbs back into bed and adjusts the sheets just in time for his parents to step through the curtains. I do my best to stand out of the way, allowing his parents each to have a side. But the warning in his gaze tells me I better not go too far.

"Fear not, Son."

Matáis gestures for me to trade places with him, moving closer to Alejandro's feet, allowing me to hold my boyfriend's hand. I like the sound of that nearly as much as husband. I can get used to either—both. It's sweet that father and son understand each other so well, even if it's embarrassing.

I still feel guilty for what happened, and knowing he'd rather have me closer than his father only amplifies it. However, his father takes it in stride. From Catalina's expression, I get the impression there was a time when Matáis was Alejandro, and Catalina was me.

"They said I need to be here for at least two days. They warned that I'm feeling far better than I will in a few hours. They put something good in through my IV, but it's tablets from now on. They'll keep me for monitoring. *Papá*, did anyone think to grab my laptop?"

Is this man really wondering about work right now?

"Pablo did. You can have it tomorrow. You need to sleep today."

"I want to look up a few things. Can I see Joaquin next? I want to run something by him."

"No, *frijolito*. You can rest. Your cousin will be there when you're better."

"*Mamá*, I'm not asking him to stop by so we can game. I want him to dig into some stuff."

My stomach knots as my gaze shifts from parents to son.

"What kind of stuff, Jandro?"

Chapter Twenty-Three

Alejandro

I need to explain my thoughts fast before my parents and Vita lose their shit. My parents definitely won't want Joaquin coming with me. We're likely to work for the next few hours, but they'll want me to nap. I can't exactly Houdini like I did when I was a kid and didn't want to sleep.

"I doubt too many people know Cosima and Zorzi are dead. Unless your mother told your father or Don Piero, only she knows what happened to her sister. It wouldn't surprise me if she told your father. We can use this time to our advantage."

"Damn it! I need to call my mother back. She probably thinks we're dead too. I can't believe I didn't think of that."

Vita's horrified expression makes me feel badly because her attention's been centered upon me. Even when she waited alone, she clearly wasn't thinking about what her mother must be going through.

"Call them."

"I will. Excuse me."

She doesn't look like she wants to leave, but she steps around *Papá*. However, she pauses before she moves aside the curtain.

"What should I tell them, Jandro?"

"As much of the truth as you think they need."

"Until we know more, the only truth they need is that I'm still breathing. I can text them that."

There's a bitterness to her tone I'm unaccustomed to. I should've done more to comfort her rather than tease her. I'd hoped to distract her from how shitty I surely look. My face still sports the bruises from Cosima's henchmen. Turns out the cut on my face wasn't as bad as I feared. The doctor said the scar will barely be noticeable. So much for improving my menacing aura.

While the injuries aren't severe, I don't want her to guess how much pain I'm actually in. It'll worry her and only compound her guilt. I blame her for nothing, but I know she's ashamed of her family. If the situation were reversed, I'd feel the same way. Except my family would *never* be so dishonorable.

Even at Juan's worst—when he could've brought down our entire empire because he went after Laura—we didn't turn against him. We banished him, but we didn't turn on him. We found out he returned to New York a couple hours before Maks and his family struck. We did our best to get to him, willing to defend him despite the shit he piled upon all of us. We didn't save him, but we retaliated. Even though we knew—we conceded—he was in the wrong, family doesn't turn against family.

"Vita, call them. Your parents must be in a panic right now. I'm surprised your mother hasn't been calling every five minutes or insisted Serafina track you down."

"She may have. I turned it off. I didn't want the tracker on."

She pulls the device from her pocket and turns it back on. The moment the phone is active, alerts go off like someone's in cardiac arrest. She winces as she swipes the screen.

"I really better call. Excuse me."

I watch her walk away, noticing she left the curtain open just enough for me to see she doesn't go very far. My *chiquita* gets me.

"If you won't let Joaquin see me, then please ask him to look up some things for me. I want to know what that building was and who owned it. I want all of Vita's *tía's* and her ex-boyfriend's financial statements for the last six months. I want a list of their known associates, all their travel records, and all their phone logs. I want to know who they're sleeping with and who they aren't. I want to know what Piero thought about them and the last time he spoke to them. I want to know what Cosima's and Zorzi's relationships were like with Vita's parents and with Piero. Hell, I want to know the last time either of them went to the dentist. This would go a lot faster if you let me work alongside Joaquin."

"No. Jorge can help him with all the financial data. Pablo and Javier will do whatever Joaquin asks."

"I know, *Mamá*, but—"

"But?"

I tuck my chin and lean back against my pillows. I know better than to say more, so I look at *Papá*. That's a lost cause, and I know it, but I had to try. If it's for my wellbeing, *Papá* won't consider disagreeing with *Mamá*.

"*Mijo*, your *mamá* is right. Let your *primos* do the work for now. You can make it up to them later. I'm certain Pablo, Jorge, and Javier would love to use your jet for getaways with their wives."

I open my mouth, then snap it shut. "*Sí, papá*."

I like it a whole lot better when I'm listening to Vita say "yes, Daddy," than me acquiescing to my parents.

I observe Vita through the opening in the curtains. She swipes a hand over her hair before she appears to brush tears from her face. I sit up farther, ignoring the searing pain in my back and shoulders. Whatever good stuff they gave is starting to wear off already. Or maybe I should be a better patient and sit my ass still. She inhales and straightens her shoulders before turning around. Our gazes lock, and I catch her moment of surprise. She didn't want me to see her like that.

"Vita?"

I push back the covers as she returns. Both of my parents reach for me, but I ignore them. Holding my gown shut in the back, I rise. My free arm reaches out to her. She hesitates, then steps close enough for me to wrap my arm around her waist and draw her against me.

"*Mamà* had to tell *Papà* and Don Piero. They called Don Salvatore. He's searching for me. I told *Mamà* to call it off, that I'm fine. It's too late. I'm certain Don Salvatore's already called your *zio*."

"And nothing catastrophic happened. Otherwise, *Tío* Enrique would've come back here. At the very least, he would've called or texted *Papá*. I'm certain he's taken care of it."

"This is my fault, Jandro."

"No, it's not. Cosima said the Galicians were after me. It's on them if that's even true."

"But she and Zorzi wouldn't have gotten involved if it weren't for me."

"That makes no sense. Think about it. If they weren't angry that the hit didn't happen, they wouldn't have gotten involved. This was about me not dying."

"I—"

"Vittoria, let us help. Alejo needs you here. His *primos, tíos*, and I will collect the information he wants. Once we have everything, we'll sort it out and strategize. Keep my son from getting too agitated."

Vita leans back far enough to see over my shoulder as my father speaks. She nods, and I kiss her forehead.

"Mr. Diaz?"

I turn toward the nurse who stepped into my bay. She appears friendly, but I'm skeptical of anyone I don't know. When all four of us stare at her, she steps back, instinctively avoiding our forceful presence.

"Your room is ready for you. We're going to take you upstairs. Could you get back into bed, please?"

"I'd prefer a wheelchair since I'm certain you won't let me walk."

"Fine. I'll bring one around. Just give me a moment."

She disappears, but she's back before we can resume our

conversation. It takes ten minutes to get me settled into my room. We stopped at the nurses' station where my parents and Vita insisted on meeting all the medical personnel on the floor. They learned when the shift changes, so Vita will return to learn the names and faces of the new group.

"We'll be back in the morning, *mijo*."

My father gives me a careful embrace as he speaks. Then my mother does the same. Vita and I are finally—blessedly—alone. There's a solid door between us and the rest of the world. There's no window in the door, so Vita and I are a little twitchy. We won't know who's entering the room until it opens.

"Lie next to me, little one."

"You're too big. There's not enough room on there for me."

"I'll turn on my good side."

While my arm and leg didn't get burned, they did get bruised. I shift around until I'm nearly against the guardrail, but there's enough room for Vita to fit if she lies on her side too. She's tentative as she eases on, but I pull her snuggly against my chest the moment she settles. I reach around her.

"What're you doing?"

"Enjoying my girlfriend's company."

I pull the scrubs pants' drawstring loose before my hand slides down the front. Someone must have given her a pair since her clothes were ruined. My hands are large like the rest of me. My long fingers slip between her legs, my middle finger rubbing her clit.

"Daddy." It's a strained whisper as she squirms.

"Shh, *chiquita*. We've been through a lot today. Let me take care of you."

"You should rest while you can. You know hospitals aren't where you stay to get better with how they won't leave you alone for more than an hour. They'll be here to check your vitals soon. Sleep before they disturb you for that."

"I can sleep when I'm ninety."

I nearly said when I'm dead. Figured that might upset her. I continue to toy with her clit as I feel her grow wetter. I'm growing hard as a steel stake. It tempts me to take her into the bathroom and fuck her from behind.

How sexy is that?

Wheeling an IV stand in with us to a bathroom that has a shower seat and handrails on both sides of the toilet.

"Daddy."

Fuck. The way she says that word.

That's it.

Sexy or not, I'm fucking my woman.

I push her pants down over her hips until I can slide my fingers into her. She rolls toward me, her hand slipping beneath my hospital gown. This gown beats my suits for easy access. I might switch to these permanently.

That's the drugs talking.

I'm the only one in the family who doesn't mind wearing suits every day. I'm just so used to them I don't think twice about it. My cousins think they're too starched and stuffy. They complain the ties are nooses. I look at them as my suit of armor. My wealth and size impress and intimidate before I say anything. They keep most people at arm's length.

Not my chiquita.

Her hand around my dick is euphoria in the making. She opens to me when I press my lips to hers. Our tongues tangle as she lets me lead. We understand each other. She's completely competent and independent. But she enjoys having that weight lifted off her shoulders sometimes. Adding it to my shoulders gives me the control I crave, not because I'm a megalomaniac, but because being out of control means people I love die.

Do I count Vita on the list of people I love?

Yes, idiota. You have since nearly the beginning.

Denial is futile.

I shift my weight to ease her onto her back, my leg settling between hers. I press my thigh against her cunt, and her hips rise and fall as she rubs against me. My mouth stifles her moan, but I still hear it. I move again, squeezing my hips between her legs.

"Jandro, we can't."

"I think we're proving we can."

"We shouldn't."

"Who says?"

"Common sense. We're in a hospital room where anyone could walk in at any moment. We're only here because you were injured in an explosion that nearly killed us only hours ago."

"Being inside you is just the treatment I need."

"Daddy, what if you get hurt?"

I see the genuine fear in her eyes, and I have a moment's doubt. But that's all it is. A moment. I pull away, and relief and hurt war in her gaze. I climb off the bed. With one hand, I grab hers and yank her onto her feet while the other grabs my IV pole. I tow both of them behind me as I make a beeline for the bathroom.

"Jandro?"

"Shh."

She bends as best she can to pull her pants up enough to make it easier for her to walk. I allow that, but I'm soon guiding her into the smaller room and shutting the door behind us.

"Strip."

"We can't."

I'm standing behind her, and we're looking at each other in the mirror. However, her refusal prompts me to step to her right. I yank the pants down before my right hand presses between her shoulder blades. My arm is too sore to do more than place light pressure, but she knows what I want. She leans forward. My left arm is unimpaired, so I bring my hand down across her ass.

"I will have what's mine, *chica*. I told you the best treatment is you. Are you going to deny me what'll cure me?"

"Daddy, don't—"

"Whatever you're about to say will only lead to more spankings."

I'm raining them down as I speak. With each one, her hips bump into the sink, but the moment my hand retreats, she pushes her ass back to chase it. She wants this, but she's denying it because of guilt. She believes she should think this is wrong, but she doesn't. Her body tells me what her mind won't.

"You know you want my cum on your thighs as we fall asleep. You want to feel me explode inside you because I can't get enough of you. That I'll never get my fill. You want to come because I'm the one touching you, filling you."

"But you're hurt."

"The injuries are inconvenient, but they aren't life threatening. I've endured far worse and come out the other side. If you truly refuse, say so now."

We stare at each other for a moment before she shakes her head.

"Does that mean you refuse or you don't refuse? You have to say it out loud, *chiquita*."

"I don't refuse. I want it too."

I kiss her neck and shoulder as my hands fondle her tits beneath her shirt and bra. Her skin is like the smoothest satin. Her nipples are tight peaks for me to toy with just like her clit. She reaches behind her to lift my gown as she spreads her legs. She turns her feet inward and angles her hips to take me. With one thrust, I'm inside her.

"Fuck, little one."

"I know, Daddy. Just be careful."

I chuckle before I kiss her temple. It's affection I've never felt before. Her fear moves me. No other woman's ever cared like she does. I want to allay those fears while making her body sing. My left hand continues to play with her breast while I lower my right one to her hip. I won't admit it, but having my arm raised hurts like a motherfucker. Enough to make me nauseous.

I thrust into her over and over, leaning my body to cover hers as her hands brace herself on each side of the sink. Our attention's riveted to the scene we make in the mirror. Her head tilts back to rest against my shoulder.

"You're so fucking hot, Daddy."

"No one's hotter than you."

She turns her head, and our kiss is far more tender than the way I'm treating her pussy as I pound into her. My right hand slides forward until I can rub her clit again. She pushes away from the sink and gasps. She screws her eyes shut as her hands curl into fists.

"Vita?"

"Don't stop. Please, may I come, Daddy? I'm so close."

"Yes, baby girl. I'm on the edge too."

It's embarrassing how fast this is going to end. But she does this to me. I have no restraint. She rides my cock as I keep rocking my hips to drive deeper into her.

"*Jandro!*"

It's a whisper-scream. It comes out softly, but from the way her mouth falls open, I know she's fighting not to let the entire hospital know how well her man fucks her.

"Come for me again, Vita."

"I'm trying. So intense."

"I know, *mi Vita.*"

"You call me that—your life—as a play on my name. But, Jandro, *eres mi vida.*" You are my life.

I don't hold back. My *huevos* contract, and I'm shooting my cum deep inside her. Both hands ground her as her ass presses against my groin.

"Take all that I have, Vita. Take what no one else ever has. *Tú también eres mi vida.*" You're my life too.

We stand together, my arms wrapped around her middle as we float back down to Earth. Our breathing's ragged as her hands stroke along my forearms.

"Jandro, I needed that. I didn't want to admit it because it felt like it should be wrong. But being with you is never wrong. At the moment, it's the only thing that's right."

"Come, little one. Let's cuddle."

I've never said those words before. So many fucking firsts with Vita. If it weren't her, I'd never say that. Only she gets this softer side of me. I'm certain it's not the drugs speaking because those have definitely worn off. I'm feeling each pain intensely. I grit my teeth because if Vita realizes how badly I hurt right now, she won't forgive herself.

She pushes my IV pole as we walk out of the bathroom. It

only takes a couple minutes for us to be arranged comfortably on the bed. Then it all fades to black despite the discomfort. My body's reached its limits for right now.

Curled around Vita is the most peaceful I've ever been. That's why it's a fucking shock to wake to my girlfriend with her hands around a woman's neck and wrist.

Chapter Twenty-Four

Vita

"What the fuck are you doing? Who are you?"

Even though I feel surprisingly rested, I'm an extremely light sleeper. Hazards of the job. I just woke to a strange woman entering the hospital room with a syringe in her hand. I don't recognize her from my introduction to the staff, and as I glance briefly at the wall clock, I know the shifts haven't changed yet.

"I said, what the fuck do you think you're doing?"

I remember Alejandro telling his parents that they aren't giving him more pain medication intravenously. Yet this woman's trying to inject something into Alejandro's IV. I push up from where I reclined to see her badge more clearly. It definitely doesn't match the other ones I've seen so far today, and there have been several. It's ringing every alarm in my head.

Get her away from Alejandro.

I spring from the bed, nearly tripping over the IV lines. I'm careful not to tug them straight out of Alejandro's arm. It surprises me that he's not awake too. I know the medication they gave him must have worn off already.

Did she already put something into his IV, and I slept through it the first time?

Anger pulses within me as I wrap my hands around her throat and wrist. I squeeze with all my might. I stare at her as she turns rose, then fuchsia, then scarlet. I memorize her features: the mole near her left ear, the scar beside her right nostril, the birthmark on her right temple. Her hair's a mousy shade of blonde, and her eyes are a bland shade of brown. She's shorter than me and probably weighs twenty pounds less. I'm using the latter to my advantage.

She fights against my hold, trying to pry my hand free from her throat. I could squeeze a fuck ton harder and choke her out. She can still breathe, even if it's a struggle. I force the haze of fury aside and formulate a rational thought. I need to know what the fuck she's doing.

"Ma'am, ma'am."

She chokes out the words as she tries to thwart me. She had her chance to explain. I loosen my hold only ever so slightly just in case she had a legitimate reason, and I startled or intimidated her too much at first.

"What are you giving him?"

"A pain medication."

"What's it called?"

"Are you his wife?"

"Yes."

"I didn't see your name on any of his charts. You're not cleared to know personal things about this patient's medical treatment."

"I'm here. I came in with him. I've been by his side. You found us in bed together. I say that tells you I'm his wife."

"Are you though?"

The way she asked that question chills my blood. She knows more about us than she'll say outright. That's my warning. I tighten my grip again, fully prepared to kill this woman right here, right now. I wrestle the syringe away from Alejandro's IV. It doesn't have the pointy tip since it was to be added to his IV. But when she shoves it against my arm, I know she's trying to pierce the skin. With no needle, it won't, but it'll bruise. Like I don't already have enough of those.

I headbutt her, sending her and the syringe flying. She had no opportunity to depress the plunger into the IV, and without breaking the skin on my arm, whatever she intended to give Alejandro hasn't entered either of our systems.

She lands hard on her back. I follow her, straddling her torso and punching her. She fights back, giving me a few well-placed jabs to my ribs. She's stronger than I expected. The gleam in her eyes as she defends herself makes my heart race more than the exertion. She's a mercenary too. After she did whatever she intended to Alejandro, I would've been next.

"Vita?"

Alejandro's raspy voice permeates the murderous fog clouding my mind. I don't dare take my eyes off this killer.

"Jandro, are you okay?"

"I am, and you are, but she won't be. What's going on?"

His tone's so casual—almost amused—as I beat the woman to a near pulp. I think the arrogant man's getting off on me protecting him.

"I didn't meet her at the nurse's station. The shift hasn't changed, and her badge isn't right. She was trying to inject something."

I punctuate my last word with my fist to her cheekbone. Immediately, she goes limp. I frisk her, finding a pocketknife in her scrubs. It's not a large blade, but it's certainly sharp. I'll use it on her in a heartbeat if I must.

"Jandro, we need your family. Didn't they leave guards here for you?"

"They did, but they must be outside the ward, rather than outside my door. That's something to be sorted out at another time."

All I do is nod. I keep a close eye on my newest nemesis, waiting for her to wake. But when there's no sign she will, I turn my full attention to Alejandro.

"You look better than I expected, but you still look like shit.

It's clear you're in significant pain, Jandro. You need a real nurse in here to administer the medicine."

"We can't do that with her lying there. And she's a mercenary, isn't she?"

"Yes. You know she won't give anything away."

Attempting to interrogate her will be futile.

"We'll call my cousins, and they'll dispose of her."

"Can you get cleaners in here, or do I need to leave no trace?"

"The latter would be better."

I can clean up the blood that's trickling from her nose and mouth, but if I have to cut up a bitch, that'll get messy fast. We'd need a team to sweep through here to remove all biohazards. It's not impossible, but it's hard to keep that inconspicuous.

I straddle the woman again, wrapping my hands around her throat, my fingers feeling around for the most sensitive parts of her neck. When I'm in position, I quickly snap it. I glance at Alejandro, concerned about what he might think of my unrelenting brutality.

All I see is pride. What a fucked-up pair we make if murdering somebody without reservation makes him proud of me. But I suppose it shows we're well-suited to each other.

I shift positions, rising to my feet so I can heft this bitch over my shoulder and carry her into the bathroom. When I come back into the main part of the room, I find Alejandro on the phone with Pablo, explaining that we need his help as fast as he can get here. I can't hear the other end of the call, but I don't doubt Pablo's reassuring him the cavalry's on the way. It reminds me of how his family appeared when they arrived in the emergency room. They definitely weren't trying for inconspicuous that time.

It feels like forever before Alejandro's cousins arrive. In reality, it's about an hour. I had a nurse come in and give him some painkillers, praying she had no reason to check the bathroom. Finding the dead assassin would've been most inconvenient.

Alejandro's resting now. Not what I would call comfortably, but it's bearable. At least, that's what he's telling me.

I do my best to move out of the way when the men enter. The five of them suck the oxygen from the room. There's barely space for me. However, Alejandro shoots me the same look he did when I attempted to move out of the way for his father. I change course and stand close to his head where I can hold his hand.

"What the hell happened?"

It's Javier who demands an answer. The man isn't what anyone would call chatty.

Alejandro looks to me.

"I woke to a strange woman walking toward Alejandro's IV stand. I didn't recognize her as any of the nurses I met when we came up here. I knew the current rotation wasn't over. When I asked her who she was and what she was doing, she was evasive. She knew I'm not Alejandro's wife, despite what I said when we arrived. Her strength surprised me as she defended herself. She was a mercenary as well. Whoever this is won't stop until *they're* dead."

I refuse to put out in the universe that Alejandro could die instead. I won't even consider that possibility anymore. It's startling to know that in less than a week, the man I'd committed to kill is the one whose life I put ahead of anyone and everyone else's.

It seems illogical, but I don't believe there's a specific time frame for knowing if someone will be a major part of your life. Not only do I know Alejandro will be, but it's in a romantic capacity, not platonic.

"Where is she now?"

Joaquin's question interrupts my rumination. I point toward the bathroom. He walks over and opens the door just enough to peer inside.

"Vittoria, did you recognize her at all?"

"No. Do you?"

"No, she's not anyone we've faced before or hired."

In the world of mercenaries, loyalty lasts only as long as the job. Your ally can become your enemy from one day to another. So, it wouldn't have shocked me if Joaquin said they knew her.

"We need to get you out of here, Alejo."

Jorge opens the backpack he carried inside and pulls out a fresh set of clothes. Alejandro curls his lip and nostril in disgust when he sees what Jorge brought him. His cousin's flippant as he drops the clothes on the bed beside Alejandro.

"Yeah, well, the last time I lent you one of my suits, it came back in three pieces, and not the three you got it in."

My brow furrows, not understanding why the clothing matters right now. It's a pair of track pants, a t-shirt, and Jorge just dropped a pair of tennis shoes on the floor next to the bed.

"I don't know, maybe because I prefer not to look like I'm six and on the way to a playdate."

My gaze shifts from Alejandro to Jorge. In no realm of reality could anyone confuse Jorge for a child, not even a teenager.

"It's better if you just smile and nod."

I glance at Pablo, who's grinning.

"Where can you take him that's safe? Can you even get him out of the hospital right now?"

"We can, and we will. This isn't our first jailbreak of this sort. Pablo and I will help Alejandro get dressed if you'll distract the people at the nurse's station. Joaquin and Jorge will scout the path out for us."

Javier's plan is reasonable, but I still glance at Alejandro first. I trust his family members to do any and everything to keep him safe, but I'll still defer to him since I don't know them as well as I do him. That thought again reminds me of how little time we've spent together.

Once this chaos is over and we can return to normal, I'll have to consider if this relationship is real or just a product of extreme circumstances. I want to believe it's real, but maybe reality will dawn on Alejandro, and he'll remember why we met. That it was because of my job.

I lean forward and buss a kiss on Alejandro's forehead. The

arm without the IV cups my cheek. He draws me close enough to kiss me before whispering in my ear.

"Soon, *chiquita*. I'll have you bent over a table before the day's over. I want that silky cunt wrapped around my cock as I hear you scream my name. You're going to take all my cum like a good girl and beg for more."

I nod; unsure my voice won't crack if I speak. It's suddenly boiling, and it's not because there are five human-sized furnaces in here. He gives me another peck before I walk around the bed and pull the door open. I step out and look around. With one more glance at the door, I make my way down the hallway. I'm certain Jorge and Joaquin slipped out behind me, but I didn't hear them.

"Hello. Can I help you?" I'm greeted by a cheery woman who glances at my guest sticker.

"Yes, I'm Alejandro Diaz's wife."

I wait a moment to see if the name registers with her. Her eyes widen in shock. It's clearly written across her face. I'll take that as a yes.

"Hello, Mrs. Diaz."

She stutters her greeting. I offer her the most reassuring expression I can muster.

"Your shifts just changed, so I'm here to get acquainted with everyone working in this ward right now. Ensuring my husband's safety is very crucial."

Her mouth remains hanging open like a beached trout, but she nods her head vigorously. It takes a few seconds before she gathers her wits, then calls the other staff over to meet me. I make a show of examining each badge and staring at their faces as though I'm memorizing every feature.

Of course I am, but I don't need as long as I draw this out. I infuse my tone with appreciation as I thank them and back away from the desk. When I get back to Alejandro's room, it's just as Pablo opens the door. Rather than surround me like the Diaz men did leaving the hotel, it's now my responsibility to guard Alejandro. Pablo shifts to be behind him while Javier and I flank him.

I see the perspiration on Alejandro's brow that wasn't even

there while we fucked in the bathroom. It was clearly a struggle to get the clothes on over what he called grazes, and it only takes a moment to realize the shirt is too snug. It would be tight on Jorge, but it's straining at the seams on Alejandro. He's not so much bigger than the other guys that they can't share clothes. It's obvious from the earlier conversation that they do, but it must be far easier for the other guys to borrow Alejandro's clothes than the other way around.

We make our way to the elevator, and I notice two women walking toward us. They aren't wearing scrubs or lab coats. I don't see visitors' stickers or hospital lanyards and badges. Immediately, my defenses go up. They're staring at Alejandro.

I quickly realize the only threat they pose is drooling on my boyfriend. Their gazes sweep over him before dashing to his cousins, then me. They look appreciatively at Pablo and Javier too, but their attention inevitably returns to my boyfriend. He's the hottest, and his cousins both wear their wedding rings.

They join us at the elevator, and I step in front of Alejandro as though I'm holding the door open to usher them inside. I glare at them, and they have the decency to appear embarrassed. I swear one guy chuckles, but I'm not sure who.

When we're all on the elevator, Alejandro wraps his good arm around my waist and kisses the top of my head. He brings his lips close to my ear.

"Fear not, little lioness."

I wait for him to say more, but nothing's forthcoming. The women get off on the third floor, and we continue down to the fourth level in the underground parking lot. As we exit the elevator, I glance up at him.

"You may as well be parading down Fifth Avenue in lingerie with how that shirt clings to you. I forbid you from wearing anything this tight, and if you own any gray sweatpants, they are for my eyes only."

Javier and Pablo laugh, thinking I'm joking, but Alejandro's gaze locks with mine, and he knows there's no humor in what I say. His arm tightens like a steel band around my waist, lifting me off my feet and bringing me eye to eye. He gives me a smacking kiss before whispering to me.

"Yes, *chiquita.*"

That sobers both of his cousins. I glance at each of them before returning my gaze to Alejandro. My brow furrows.

"I'll explain later, *chica.*"

Pablo and Javier fall into formation, suddenly back to being bodyguards rather than Alejandro's cousins and best friends. Joaquin and Jorge meet us in a vestibule outside the elevators.

"Any problems getting down here?"

Pablo shakes his head in response to Jorge's question. I'd noticed the men had earpieces earlier, so if anything had come up or there was a barrier to our escape route, the men would've communicated that way.

We're on the lowest parking level now, so when we step out, the floor's nearly empty. It means the scattered bodies stand out.

"What the fuck?"

Chapter Twenty-Five

Vita

I glance up at Alejandro, his expression fierce.

"Those are our men."

The moment the words finish falling from his lips, the sound of gunfire echoes in the concrete jungle. All of us twist toward the sound as men in black balaclavas, turtlenecks, and cargo pants emerge from the far side of a delivery van. *Tres J's* and Pablo draw their weapons, returning fire. Both Javier and Joaquin reach down to their ankles and pull out their spare handguns.

Javier gives me his while Joaquin hands the other to Alejandro. Now that we're all armed, we move together, keeping Alejandro in the center since he's the most likely target if it isn't me. He's not at his full strength, despite amazing me at how he's hanging on.

"How many do you count?"

I wonder the same thing Pablo does. I scan our surroundings as Javier answers.

"Five by the van. But there have to be more to have gotten so many of our guys."

I wish I could see through metal and concrete to know what's on the other sides of the vehicles and the floors above us. Parking all the way down here would've made getting Alejandro out of here less noticeable. However, it also means our attackers can use the emptiness as their defense. No witnesses mean they don't have to hold back.

"There are two more near the east wall."

I jut my gun in the direction I mentioned before shooting a man who thought he was out of sight. We position ourselves so our backs are away from our attackers but not open to anyone ambushing us from behind. Car windows shatter, bullets ping against metal as they hit doors and hoods and trunks. The cacophony of noise makes it difficult to tell where our targets are and how many of them lurk.

We fight our way to one of the four SUVs that have bodies surrounding them. There's burning pain along the bottom of my left ribs. I force myself to swallow the grunt as I suck my stomach in. I know it's just a graze, but it still hurts like a motherfucker. However, I remind myself that Alejandro's injuries are worse than this minor scratch. If he can muscle through this, then so can I. He hasn't complained once, and neither will I.

While bullets hit vehicles in our way as we move, we're not shooting indiscriminately, much like Alejandro and I didn't when the two SUVs attacked us on the road. We're all firing wide to hit as many as we can, but we're not shooting just for the sake of wasting bullets.

"Get in on the passenger side, Vita."

All of us sprint the last couple of feet. Pablo jumps in the front passenger seat while Jorge goes to the driver's side. Joaquin opens the trunk while Javier opens the rear passenger side door. I get in and slide across, reaching for Alejandro as his cousin helps him into the SUV. Doors slam as Jorge turns on the ignition.

I glance over my shoulder to see Javier and Joaquin shutting the back hatch with them inside. They pass rifles like Alejandro gave me in the town car. I hand two to Pablo while Alejandro insists upon getting one. Ammunition follows, and I hand that out as well. Then *Dos J's* climb from the trunk into the third-row seats. Jorge's got a lead foot as he peels out of the parking spot.

Drivers backed all four SUVs into their spaces, clearly prepared for the possibility we'd need to make a hurried escape just like this. Bullets pepper the doors and windows, but it doesn't slow Jorge. In fact, he plows into two men, sending them flying. There's no way their bodies survived the impact of this tank slamming into them at fifty miles an hour. We race through the garage and out onto the street.

I glance back periodically, watching the van follow us. When I'm not sweeping my gaze over our surroundings, I'm watching Alejandro grow paler by the moment. I fear what his wounds must look like. I don't doubt he got sweat in the ones on his back while we had sex. Now all of this jostling and running must be horrible on them, especially his leg. I know it wasn't burned, but it has to be sore as fuck. I wrap my arm around his shoulder, encouraging him to lean against me.

"Alejandro, Alejandro."

I tap his cheek when he sags against my shoulder. He's not just tired or falling asleep. He's dead weight from passing out. Pablo looks back at me as my fingers find Alejandro's pulse on his neck.

"Let him rest, Vittoria. It's the best thing for him right now. His body and mind need it, and he'll be in absolute terror if he wakes. If it's before we get to the safe house, knowing you're in danger will make him lose his shit."

"But I can defend myself. I helped all of you defend him."

Jorge glances back at me in the rearview mirror. "What about any of the men in this family makes you think Alejandro would accept any risk to your safety? Your ability to fight is neither here nor there."

I turn to look back at Javier when he concurs with his brother.

"None of our wives are shrinking violets. My Maddy has her own history with a syndicate that started well before she and I got together. That doesn't mean I don't go berserk the moment I perceive any threat to her. It's not that I believe she's incapable. I simply refuse to consider any danger to her as acceptable. Granted, she's just as protective of me."

The pride in Javier's gaze matches what I saw in Alejandro's when he realized just how I'd defended us. There's seriously something not quite right about any of us when our capacity for violence and interventions is a turn-on. But that's just how syndicate life works.

I'd rather they be with me than against me. That's for damn sure.

We're silent as we travel through the outskirts of NYC to Queens. It doesn't take long for me to recognize we're in Jackson Heights. I watch as we pull toward a gate that slides open immediately. I see none of the men press any buttons, nor did they speak to anyone. There must be guards on the lookout. We pull into another underground garage, and my heart rate spikes.

"Don't panic, *chiquita*."

I glance down at Alejandro, who is now looking up at me.

"This entire block is ours. We're safe here."

I nod, not entirely convinced, since the vehicles followed us all the way from Yonkers to here. There's no way I'm going to lower my guard until we're safely inside a building with Alejandro surrounded by guards. However, I breathe a little easier when the gate closes behind us, and we descend the ramp inside the garage. When no one joins us, I'm on slightly less alert as we exit the SUV. Joaquin and Javier help Alejandro toward an elevator.

"*Chiquita*, you know this is our neighborhood. We do business in the bodega on the other side of this building. When we need more privacy, we have offices upstairs. We'll go there now. We can rest until we decide our next moves."

"Okay, if you say so."

My head's suddenly pounding, and I don't have the energy to disagree. So, I merely nod. We arrive at the office, and it only takes one glance inside to understand this isn't where they conduct normal work. The sofa in here looks like it belongs in a jail cell. The desk chair is far more appealing. It's clear anyone sitting on that sofa is there because they majorly fucked up and they're there to face the consequences of their poor decisions.

"Jandro, you need to lie down. You can't do that in the desk chair, but that bench is going to be far too hard for you."

"*Chica*, I've slept in far worse places than this. I'll survive just fine, but I have some boo-boos you can kiss if you're really that worried about me."

"All right, lover boy."

Javier teases him as he guides his cousin to sit. When he lurches sideways, Jorge rushes forward to catch him. I cock a brow as I sweep my gaze over the men as if to say, I told you so. But none of them appear any more concerned than they did when we arrived here.

"*Chiquita*, come sit with me."

I oblige. He watches me approach, and I know the moment he spots the dark patch on my shirt.

"Vittoria, what is that?"

He punctuates each word as he lifts his good arm to point at my ribs.

"It's nothing, Alejandro. I'm fine."

"The fuck you are. That's blood. And since you went near none of our attackers and none of us bled on you, it must be yours. Let me see."

His cousins take what appears like a choreographed step back from us as Alejandro struggles to his feet. His right arm shoots out far faster than I expected. His hand fists my shirt over my chest. He might be injured and still somewhat sedated, but he's a man with unbelievable strength. I know he's reining that in, but the force leaves me unable to stand my ground. He lets go of the front of my shirt long enough to yank at the hem, lifting it high enough to see the graze over my ribs.

"Motherfucker. Why didn't you say you were injured, Vittoria?"

"Stop calling me that."

I practically want to stomp my foot in frustration, but I'm not a five-year-old having a tantrum. I'm an adult who doesn't want to be treated like a child.

"This is serious."

"I know that. You don't need to use my full name to convey the gravity of this situation, *Alejandro*."

I use a mocking tone when I state his name. We glare at each other, and it's as though we're back in the hotel room. It's incredible to believe that was two days ago. It feels like a million years. His fingers are gentle as they brush the skin beside the wound.

"If you ever get hurt again and don't tell me the moment it happens, Vita, I will bend you over my knee and spank you until my hand hurts."

I feel the heat rush through my cheeks. I don't shift my gaze from him, but I hate his cousins heard him issue that threat. The door opens behind us, and the men file out. Someone closes it with barely a click.

"I can't believe you just said that in front of all of them."

"They're giving us privacy as a couple to talk, but they didn't leave out of shock. We're no different from the other couples in my family. I'm certain of it. We may not discuss what happens behind closed doors between man and wife. But it wouldn't shock me in the least to know my cousins have the same dynamics with their wives as you and I have. They aren't out there clutching their pearls."

"I don't care. That was supposed to be private between us."

"All bets are off when it's about your safety, Vita. I've never wavered on that."

"In the grand scheme of things, a mere scratch seems completely unimportant compared to your injuries, a shootout, or the men lost to an ambush."

He grips my chin, tilting my head back farther, then holding it in place.

"Nothing—not a damn thing in this world—will ever be more important than your safety. You understand me, *chiquita?* Nothing."

I swallow before I try to nod. He won't relax his grip enough for my head to move.

He wants my answer spoken.

"I understand, Daddy. I'm sorry I worried you, but will you please sit down before you pass out?"

He wavers a little on his feet before lowering himself to the bench.

"There's a first aid kit in the bottom left drawer of the desk."

I fetch it and rummage through it. I find what I need and lay the supplies out on my lap. When Alejandro reaches out to help me, I gently brush his hand away. His fingers wrap around mine, and I know it's futile to fight him when he pushes my hand down to the sofa.

He tears open the antiseptic wipes and holds up my shirt. Air whistles through my teeth as I inhale, the sting making me wince. In front of anyone else, I'd hide the pain. I'm not compelled to do that in front of Alejandro. It doesn't feel like a weakness to admit the graze hurts.

"Sit still, little one. I don't want to hurt you more."

"I know, Daddy. Thank you."

He's efficient as he cleans the graze and the surrounding area. He applies a bandage that covers the entire wound. His gaze lingers before he looks up at me.

"I'm doing a shit job protecting you, *chiquita*."

"What? No. You're far more injured than me, and it happened because you put yourself in danger for me."

We come together in a languid kiss that restores my strength to face the world. I'm whole again as I inhale Alejandro's breath. It's life sustaining. He lifts me onto his lap despite my momentary objection. The man isn't superhuman no matter what he thinks. I still fear how all of this will catch up to him. He wraps his arms around me, and I lean against him. We hold each other, both relieved we're safe. Neither of us rushes to end the moment, but duty calls.

"Thank you for letting me take care of you, *chiquita*. I need to speak to Joaquin and see if he's learned anything."

"I'll get them to come back in."

"No, it's safer if no one sees you're here. We got you into the garage, an elevator, and this office without running into any of our men. That was a blessing in disguise. I'll text them."

He walks around the desk and pulls out what appears to be a burner. His fingers rapidly tap the screen. Then I hear the whoosh of the message sending. It's only two minutes later that the men file back into the office.

"A little, not nearly as much as I'd like. With more time, I'm certain I'll find more."

"What do you have so far?"

I snap my mouth shut, recalling in a meeting like this, normally no women would be present. Alejandro slides his hand into mine as he returns to sit beside me on the sofa. The other men stand around the office while Joaquin sits at the desk with his laptop open.

"I looked into the Galicians immediately. There's no unusual money exchanging hands with them. The emails I hacked mention you. Don't get me wrong, they're pretty fucking pissed, but nothing shows their involvement. It's not necessarily a dead end, but there's no clear connection. Right now, if I had to put money on it, they're not involved."

Disappointment fills me since we're no closer to understanding why any of this is happening. Even if we can't figure out why, I'd at least like to know who. It's frustrating as fuck.

Pablo's phone rings, and he turns the screen toward us before answering.

"*Hola, tío.*"

Enrique responds in Spanish, demanding to know what's going on. Apparently, none of Alejandro's cousins gave him any details before they took off for the hospital, and they don't know we headed back to Queens.

"What happened?"

It's Pablo who responds since Enrique called him.

"A woman attempted to drug Alejandro in his room. Vittoria

took care of it. There was an ambush in the parking garage. We lost our men, but the rest of us are at the bodega."

"Alejo, you better call your *mamá* before she skins me alive. Ellie won't come to my rescue either."

Enrique's voice carries a rueful tone. While it might be easy to think he's joking about his wife, I'm certain he's not. Elle has three adult sons, so I'm certain she understands Catalina's concerns.

How fucked-up is that he just heard Pablo mention two attacks, and he's not demanding more details?

I know he'll get them soon from one of the other guys, but I suppose the fact Alejandro isn't back in a hospital bed means it's not a cause for panic.

"I will, *Tío*."

"Joaquin, any news?"

"Nothing beyond what I shared with you earlier. Did you speak with Salvatore?"

"I did. I mean, if you can call our screaming match a conversation. I doubt he understood my Spanglish, and I didn't understand all of his Itanglese, but we know we're pissed. And for once, it's not at each other, even if it got heated."

I remain quiet despite the volley of questions bouncing back and forth in my head.

"*Tío*, if he's not pissed at us, then why were you yelling?" Javier's question is one of mine, and I'm sure the others are wondering the same thing.

"He's already aware Alejandro and Vittoria are together. He wouldn't admit how he knew. I'm certain Piero's spoken to him, but I got the feeling he knew well before today. He was livid that Vittoria was in danger and that anyone dared include her in an attack on us. He demanded the construction project in Elizabeth in exchange for staying out of this. I told him we'd hand over the project to him for information. I clarified that doesn't mean we want him involved. We just want to know what he knows. He refused, saying information would cost more, and the only way he'd agree to it is if we let him handle whoever's behind this. It makes me think that perhaps it's the Torettas and the Carosis after all."

That's a punch to the gut, if it's the *Mala del Brenta*. The Torettas I can understand. They're bonded to the *Mala del Brenta* by blood and by marriage. However, I can't hold it against them, since business is business. But the notion that Piero either sanctioned this or turned a blind eye hurts more than I want to admit.

The man's known me since the day I was born. He's my godfather, after all. As I consider it more, something feels wrong about the explanation beyond my familial connection to Piero. I shift my focus from the phone in Pablo's hand to Alejandro. He gives me a reassuring nod, encouraging me to continue.

"I know I'm biased here, and I certainly don't want to believe my own people are behind the assassination attempts on me, but I really don't think it's the *Cosa Nostra* or the *Mala del Brenta*. I think Salvatore's hedging his bets and trying to buy time to investigate on his own. I think he suspects the Camorra or *'Ndrangheta*. He doesn't want to admit those allies are getting the better of the *Cosa Nostra* and *Mala del Brenta*. He definitely doesn't want to admit anything's happening in this turf war that he doesn't know about."

"That could well be true. We won't know unless we can speak to somebody in the midst of this."

"I agree, Enrique. It's time to call Don Piero."

Chapter Twenty-Six

Alejandro

To say I'm uneasy about this call puts it mildly. I'd rather have a prostate exam while getting a root canal. But we hang up with *Tío* Enrique, and Vita takes the burner I offer her. My cousins and I cluster together as it rings on speakerphone. Pablo's going to interpret for us since he's the only one who speaks fluent Italian. The rest of us have a smattering, most of it consisting of profanity.

"Who is this?"

That much I understand. Piero certainly doesn't trust calls from unknown numbers. I can't blame him. When they come in, we always know there's a possibility it's legit, so we tend not to turn them down. However, most of us like surprises as much as a hole in the head.

"Don Piero, it's Vittoria."

In the background, I hear a man shout Vita's name. It's most certainly her father.

"Toria, where are you? What's happening? Who are you with? Are you safe?"

Pablo rapidly interprets the barrage of questions. Vita remains calm as she explains she's with me and we're safe. She offers nothing more. Instead, she asks her own questions.

"*Papà*, what was going on with *Zia* Cosima? What did she have against me?"

"That psychopath was lucky she was burned alive in that fire. Otherwise, I would've flown there and tortured her to her last breath."

"But *Papà*, why was she involved? And why take us to Yonkers? It seems so unusual."

"We don't know that yet. But I suspect I know some of why she got involved."

There's a pause, and I keep expecting Piero to pipe in. However, he remains silent. Just like *Tía* Elle is a mother and wouldn't protect *Tío* Enrique against my *mamá's* fury, Piero's also a father, so he's not interrupting his *consigliere*. The concern in Vita's father's voice reminds me of *Papá*. I'm glad to hear how protective the man is of his daughter, despite her job.

"*Papà*, Enrique spoke to Don Salvatore. From what I can tell, it may not be *Cosa Nostra*. Can you promise me it isn't?"

The silence stretches before Piero chimes in.

"Before you became a target, I thought it might be the Torettas. But I ruled them out the moment we knew you were a target. However, I can't say with certainty that it's not them. I'll speak to Don Alberto as soon as this call ends. We've been allies since his nephew and I were both underbosses. I want to believe he'd tell me the truth, given it means putting me in a position to choose them over my *consigliere*. Vittoria, there's no guarantee he will. I can't be sure I'd believe what he'd say, but I'll try. I'll put extra surveillance on the Camorra and the *'Ndrangheta*."

I wait for either man to offer another solution. To even negotiate with my family or me for Vita's sake. But the line goes quiet. My gaze meets Vita's, and she shrugs. We have nothing more to offer. And if they do, they're unwilling, so the call ends there.

"I'll call Friedrich and see what he knows."

"Who?"

Apparently, my dossier didn't extend to my cousin's soon-to-be in-laws. It's obvious Vita doesn't recognize Jorge's fiancée's brother-in-law. It came out during threats on Anneliese's family that her sister's then-boyfriend, now-husband, was a Camorra member. The man did what he could to leave syndicate life behind. However, there's never really a way to get out completely.

When Jorge's soon-to-be father-in-law was held hostage, it forced Friedrich to get involved all over again. His family offered Anneliese's protection in his hometown of Essen in Germany. As far as I last heard, he hadn't returned to an active status with them as a Made Man. However, it's not impossible that he has. At the very least, he might be aware of what's happening in this proxy war, or he can gain that information.

While Jorge speaks fluent German, the call's in English, which is good since nobody could interpret for the rest of us.

"Jorge, is everyone all right?"

"No, Friedrich, and I believe you know that already. We're getting sucked into your family's business again."

There's a pause before Friedrich responds. I'm certain he's weighing his options.

"Really?"

"Yes. Whatever's still going on with your war against the *Cosa Nostra* and *Mala del Brenta,* the *'Ndrangheta* targeted my cousin and his girlfriend. I need to know what's going on."

"Which cousin?"

"Alejandro."

"And the man has a girlfriend?"

There's mocking skepticism in his voice. Does he believe I'm incapable of having a relationship? Does he doubt it would be with a woman?

"Yes. They're a lot like Liesel and me."

Friends and family call Jorge's wife Anne. Only he calls her Liesel. It's definitely a family thing for us. We all find unique nicknames for the women we love. *Papá* calls *Mamá* Caty. No one else would ever dare. Sometimes she goes by Lina, but seldomly these days.

"So, you mean he's basically engaged?"

Jorge smirks at me. I shoot him a defiant glower, warning him of retribution if he embarrasses me in front of Vita.

"You could say that." Jorge's attention returns to the call.

"I can understand then why your cousin would be particularly sensitive to any threat toward this woman."

"And you can imagine why I'm so protective of my cousin-to-be. So, I'd like to know why your side targeted my cousin and are now after Vittoria."

"Vittoria who?"

"Vittoria Trevisan. What did Alejandro do to get on your side's radar that they'd put a hit on him?"

"What makes you think anyone in the Camorra or *'Ndrangheta* are after Alejandro?"

"We have it on good authority that it's not the *Cosa Nostra* or *Mala del Brenta*."

"That doesn't mean it's anyone in Italy. Your cousin's pissed off people all around the world. They could be a homegrown enemy for all you know."

Breathe.

Let Jorge handle this hijueputa.

"And you know how politics work in New York. No lesser branch will act against their New York leader."

"Someone might have taken it upon themselves. Perhaps you should search your own backyard."

"Perhaps you could be a little less evasive if you aren't hiding something."

I wish I could punch the guy. I just want a solid explanation to prove if his side's involved. Holding Vita's hand grounds me, keeping me from getting up and pacing. It's not something I usually do, but I'm also unaccustomed to being this ball of nervous energy. It's unsettling to feel out of control like this. Vita senses it because she wraps her free hand around my forearm and gives it a squeeze.

"Friedrich, you're making me think you're up to your eyeballs. If you or your people are striking out against my family, we won't accept that silently. Would you want Liesel or Heidi to know?"

"You wouldn't dare bring this up to either of them."

"Liesel knows something's going on with Alejandro and Vittoria. She knows someone injured Alejandro. She already has questions. It would be a shame if I let it slip, wouldn't it? How quickly do you think she can call Heidi once she finds out? And how fast do you think Heidi will find you when she does?"

"This is bullshit, Jorge, and you know it. You do everything you can to keep Anneliese out of Cartel business."

"And I will continue to. But I also won't lie to her if her family on one side is targeting her family on the other."

"You'd really destroy her relationship with her sister since Anneliese will pick your family, and Heidi will pick mine?"

"Are you so sure about that? Heidi's met Alejandro before. It's not like he's some faceless stranger to her. She knows Alejandro helped save your father-in-law's life and Liesel's. At the very least, this will make things very chilly between you and your wife. That's the last thing you need."

There's a moment of silence on Friedrich's end. Then the sound of a door shutting before a car starts, and the call switches to Bluetooth.

"Look, you know I can't tell you everything. You know where my loyalty must lie. But the last thing I want to do is hurt my wife. If something happened to Alejandro, it would upset her."

"It would upset Liesel even more."

"And that would also upset my wife. Heidi and I just found out something she planned to tell Anne today. They might even be on the phone together now. We swore not to tell anybody outside our immediate family. If this gets out, I'll know it was you or your cousins. All of you, right now, need to swear to this secret to protect Heidi."

My cousins and I exchange glances before we speak together.

"I will."

If it's a promise we can keep, we will. But if it's one we can't, then all of us will mitigate as much damage as we can. But we'll always put our family first. It's why we rarely swear promises unless we know what it is first.

"Heidi's pregnant, and it's extremely high-risk. She's on bed rest for the foreseeable future, which could mean the entire pregnancy. She's only eight weeks."

"Is there anything we can do to help? My wife's a midwife."

"And my mother's a midwife too."

Javier offers Madeline's help just as Pablo offers his mom's. Friedrich might not be my favorite person right now, but we all have a shred of decency for the women. We know wrong from right, even when we choose to ignore it. But the decent thing to do is offer help even if we're a continent apart. None of us believes Heidi will accept the offer if for no other reason than logistics. It's still the right thing to do.

"I won't say anything to Liesel, so she'll have nothing to tell Heidi. But that's on the condition you help us."

Jorge's tone is almost—*almost*—conciliatory. He'll give an inch while taking the mile, and Friedrich won't know what's happening until it's all done.

"I don't know that much, but I'll try to find out. What I know for now is that Cosima's had a longstanding affair with the *'Ndrangheta* don. When I say longstanding, I mean decades. I don't know if she's traded *Mala del Brenta* secrets. But whatever's going on right now, she's taking their side. Before she began the affair, the don had a different mistress. The woman was also *Mala del Brenta*. Her husband's still a *capo*, and so is her son, Zorzi."

Vita covers her mouth to silence her gasp. I let go of her hand and wrap my arms around her, concerned by how pale she's gone. It's clear this news stuns her. I encourage her to lean her head against my shoulder as I kiss her forehead. Then I turn my attention back to Jorge.

"That may explain how Cosima and Zorzi's connection to the *'Ndrangheta* and how they learned of Alejandro and Vittoria's involvement. That still doesn't explain why."

"Give me some time, and I'll find out."

We remained at the office for a few hours until it went dark, then we moved our meeting to *Tío* Enrique's house. We're in a heated conversation about confronting the O'Rourkes since they're funding the Camorra and *'Ndrangheta*.

"Vita, you are not coming to this meeting. I am *not* putting you in front of the O'Rourkes. Whether they know about you or not is irrelevant. Maybe you're right, and they don't, but I'm not dangling you like a steak in front of a pack of hyenas."

The heated conversation is between Vita and me. She actually thinks I'll let her come to a sit down with the O'Rourkes. The woman is out of her mind.

"And I'm telling you I know more about the four syndicates in Italy than any of you do. I might not know why they're after us, but I know more about how they operate than you'd think. I'll know faster than you do whether the information the O'Rourkes give you is legit, bullshit they made up, or bullshit fed to them that they're passing along. It could take Joaquin hours to fact-check what I can tell you in a couple of minutes."

"I still don't want you anywhere near them, and I definitely don't want you going to the strip club."

"Embarrassed of what I might see you doing?"

The men in my family remain silent as Vita and I go toe-to-toe. Her last comment makes me go rigid. I inhale deeply, pushing back my shoulders and standing to my full height, not because I'm attempting to intimidate her but because I'm shocked by what she just said. I take a moment to breathe before responding.

"You think so little of my feelings for you? That I'd—at best— just flirt with some women, or—at worst—fuck them."

"I don't think the latter, but the former is highly likely."

My relatives cringe and all lean away, knowing Mount Alejandro's about to explode. It tempts me to drag Vita from the room to unleash all my thoughts on this matter. It sorely tempts me to spank the infuriating woman.

"Let us be extremely clear about something, Vita. You and I had the same boundaries, and just like I don't think you'll betray me or our relationship, I would *never* do the same to you. The reason I don't want you there is that you're a gorgeous woman who customers might confuse for an employee. You surely haven't forgotten how we met."

It's her turn to go rigid and stand to her full height. The color rises along her neck, and she practically vibrates with anger.

"Do you plan to abandon me once we get there, so I'm alone long enough for someone to confuse me?"

"Of course not. I'm just as worried about what somebody might say to our faces if they confuse you for a dancer there for her shift. I'd have to kill the fucker."

We glare at one another.

"Don't you have security cameras and microphones throughout the club?"

"Yes." I narrow my eyes, guessing where she's going with this.

"Do you have a back door?"

"Vita, even if I can slip you inside the club and you watch everything that's happening from the locked office, it's still unsafe for you to be there."

"Do you believe now that we're together, I've suddenly forgotten how to defend myself? I've been a spy and a mercenary since I was twenty-two."

"Believe me, I'm well aware of your history and your abilities. But why tempt fate?"

"Because this is about my life as much as it is yours."

I know she's right about it all, and I know fear drives me. I even recognize how irrational that fear is. But I can't help it. I'd do anything to keep her from being exposed to additional threats. It's still against my better judgment. However, I relent with a single nod.

"Thank you. I promise I'll stay out of sight."

I turn my attention to *Tío* Enrique with his poker face. I can imagine what he's thinking, but neither his expression nor his posture gives it away. However, my cousins don't bother hiding their smugness. If my parents wouldn't string me up by my toes and leave me dangling there for a week, I'd tell them all to fuck off. But it's a family rule to never swear at one another in earnest. Once in a while, sure, we can get away with it if it's in jest. But I wouldn't be joking this time.

"Pablo, set it up."

Chapter Twenty-Seven

Alejandro

Even though Dillan and *Tío* Enrique are equivalent, Dillan and Pablo are the same age. They've known each other since they were in peewee sports. Pablo grew up in New Jersey while Dillan grew up in Queens, like most of the rest of us. He and Juan never went to school with the O'Rourkes. However, we played peewee, little league, and club sports together. As often as we were rivals, we were also teammates. Our dads took turns bringing the orange wedges and juice boxes to each game.

Within the hour, I'm shutting the door to the strip club's office and making my way to the mezzanine level. The dim lighting and private tables make this a spot where many of our shady deals happen. It's that way for all the syndicates and their strip clubs. Boardrooms are for above-board business. However, when legit businesspeople want to do illegitimate business, they meet us in places like this; a den of iniquity in the seedy underworld.

Despite Javier and Joaquin both being older than me, I sit to Pablo's right while *Tres J's* remain standing as our bodyguards. Dillan and his cousin Finn sit across the low table from us. Finn's younger twin brothers, Shane and Sean, and another set of brothers, Cormac and Seamus, stand guard for their skipper. Such stupid names for roles in the mob. They couldn't come up with anything better than titles from the ship their family came over on.

"What do you want, Pablo? I'd rather be home with my family than shooting the shite with your ugly arse."

"But the drinks are on us. How many bottles of whiskey will you make your way through?"

The digs at our families' origins are a given. It's like heckling a rival sports team. We all take it in stride, so it doesn't faze Dillan. His mocking laugh is the same one he's had since we were all kids. He and Pablo do all the talking while my gaze sweeps over the other mobsters.

Something about Cormac feels off. He's a shady fucker to begin with and always has been. But the warning bells are ringing even louder than usual. Our gazes meet, and we both reflexively cock an eyebrow before glowering at each other. While I might focus my gaze on Cormac, I still listen attentively to Pablo and Dillan.

"O'Rourke, we know about you and the Kutsenkos. We've kept our noses out of your squabbles despite what happened to Jorge's soon-to-be in-laws. Never once did you or the bratva thank us for not retaliating as harshly as we could."

"Am I supposed to be grateful that you did us some great deal?"

"Yes." Pablo's response is so deadpan it hangs in the air before Dillan cackles.

"You're crazy if you believe we owe you shite, Pablo. Jorge's in-laws were unfortunate collateral damage. We apologized. Move on."

I force my fingers not to flex into a fist because I know it wouldn't go unnoticed, especially since Cormac's still staring at me.

"We're not telling you to back off supporting the Camorra and the 'Ndrangheta—"

"Good thing because we wouldn't."

Dillan interrupts Pablo, but my cousin continues as though Dillan said nothing.

"—We are telling you to warn your minions what will happen if they insist upon persecuting Alejandro and Vittoria."

"You're making a lot of speculations here, Pablo. You have no proof to show they're involved in whatever shite Alejandro got himself and his woman involved in. I heard that a woman nearly got the better of you, Alejandro. Slippin' up. Maybe you should think with your bigger head."

It's not a direct insult to Vita, but it's still a veiled one at my expense. I grit my teeth before I say something I can't take back. The impetuousness I've allowed myself with Vita can't happen here. The stakes are far too high for everyone involved.

"What, cat got your tongue, Alejo?"

It's Cormac who takes the dig. The muscle in Dillan's jaw ticks once, but beyond that, there's no outward sign he's annoyed at his cousin for speaking.

"What's got you so pissy today, Cormac? Your brother steal your favorite toy again?"

"Funny, dipshit."

"Maybe you're the one behind all of this, Cormac, since you can't let go of how I bested you all those years ago. You've always been a petty Betty little bitch."

When we were in college, we both ran underground gambling rings through the fraternities. We didn't go to the same school— I'm a fuck ton smarter than his dumbass—but the bookies we used sometimes overlapped. One guy fucked Cormac over because he thought he could make more by pitting Cormac and me against each other. He died for his sins.

One of the few times Cormac and I agreed on anything.

But before that happened, I cost Cormac three-million-dollars in gambling wins. It's not my fault I'm better at card and dice games than he is.

"You assume I'm still hanging on to all that."

"Aren't you, though?"

"For feck's sake, Alejandro, I don't care about what happened nearly ten years ago. I just dislike you because you're a piece of shite."

"No, you still care because you peaked back in college and haven't come up with a creative idea since then. You're pissed I'm way wealthier than you will ever be."

Pablo redirects the conversation before it can fully deteriorate into a pissing match.

"Dillan, you have a choice. Get the hit called off, or we'll start supporting the bratva in this little war of yours. Not only will we funnel money to them, but we'll also make it look like you're responsible for shit going wrong for the Mancinellis. Do you really want three against one right now? Can you afford to fight a war on that many fronts?"

Dillan knows his family's limitations, just like we do. Two against one is still doable. But if three out of the Four Families are against him, then they're all fucked beyond belief. There's no way they can hold their own when all three of us are after them. He's too shrewd to allow his ego to get the better of him for this.

"We didn't cause any of this, Pablo. So if—and that's a very motherfecking big if—we can help you out, you fecking owe us."

"The only thing we'll owe you is not cleaning out every account you have in your little offshore enterprise. Get this taken care of, Dillan, and maybe we won't blow up any more of your shit."

All the O'Rourkes know we mean the labs they have in the Amazon. We allow the other three families to have three labs each. Any more than that is pushing our graciousness to the limit. If they fuck around right now, they'll find out that we'll take it *all* from them. Not a single lab will remain, and they'll never get another.

The meeting ends, and my family follows the O'Rourkes downstairs. *Tres J's* escorts them to the door. They've just walked outside when flames leap into the air and shrapnel from their SUV pummels the building. Guns are drawn before any of us know what's happening. Instinct demands all of us prepare to defend our respective families.

Call it PTSD or a trauma response from nearly being blown up twice, but I'm ready to shoot, then ask questions. The O'Rourkes, with their men who waited outside, burst back into the strip club. The shootout in the parking lot was bad enough, but this is an even more confined space. Fortunately, we're meeting here during the few hours the club is closed.

"Diaz!"

Dillan's voice is close enough to me that I pivot on my toes from where I squat behind a booth.

"You fecking trapped us. You know these sit-downs are supposed to be neutral."

"You stupid piece of shit. We didn't do this. Why would we blow up your vehicle right by our building?"

I yell my thoughts before anyone else can answer Dillan. He points his gun directly at me, but neither of us pulls the trigger. It's unfortunate for the men who work for both ruling families. They're our targets. While all's fair in a situation like this, no one in *los Diaz* or the O'Rourkes will aim for the leaders. If we get injured in the crossfire, that's on us. Dillan and I don't lower our guns but shift our attention to guards who are fair game.

The situation intensifies as more Diaz men stream into the building, boxing in the O'Rourkes. It doesn't make Dillan and his family reckless out of desperation. Just the opposite. Joaquin tries to call off our men and send them back, hoping to de-escalate the situation that's rapidly growing out of control.

Glass shattering turns my head toward the bar as one bottle after another falls from the shelves. That anyone who's targeting the booze over a man grabs everyone's attention enough to cause a ceasefire. My heart drops to my toes as I watch Vita shooting at the bottles with her right hand while her left has a handgun pointed to the crowd. She's watching where she's aiming into the crowd rather than at the bar.

"*Enough!* I saw who did it. It wasn't Diaz or O'Rourke men."

I lower my weapon as I bolt to her. She clicks the safety back on both of her weapons, pointing them at the floor. I position myself in front of her as a shield in case someone loses their fucking mind and believes she's fair game.

"Jandro, I saw it all. I tried to get to you, but your guard wouldn't let me out of the office. I tried my best, but the guy's a behemoth. He didn't flinch when I punched him in the face or the gut. It was only my foot to his *huevos* that finally got him out of my way. He wouldn't believe me when I said it was an emergency and that I knew what happened. I get he was doing his job, but I could've prevented this fuckstorm."

Men from my family and the O'Rourkes tentatively draw closer.

"Jandro, we have a big fucking problem. You need to see what I did."

The dread in her expression and voice alarms me more than the shootout itself. It's wall to wall as six O'Rourkes and five Diaz men along with Vita crowd into the office as I play back the CCTV from outside the building.

A man emerges from a vehicle parked facing the O'Rourke SUV. He takes out the three men standing guard with a gun that has a silencer. Then he opens a duffel bag and pulls out what we all recognize as an explosive device. He disappears from the camera for a moment, and we can all guess he slipped underneath the SUV. When he reappears, Vita reaches for the remote in my hand and hits the pause button.

"Jandro, I know exactly who that is."

"You do?"

"Yes. Look at him closely. Do you recognize him?"

Something tickles my memory telling me I should, but I can't place him.

"That's Patrick, my date to the O'Rourkes gala."

"What?"

None of us yell, but with eleven masculine voices in a confined space, it's easy to guess how loud that was.

"I need to speak to him. I need to know why he went from working alongside me to being my enemy. Not just my enemy, but someone who accepted the job to kill me. We've been rivals, and we've been friends. We've been more than friends, but we've never tried to kill each other before."

I loathe hearing she has a sexual past with this *carechimba*—face of a vagina—but it's not like either of us were virgins beforehand. It'll always be entirely possible for us to run into past partners. It doesn't mean I'm eager for it to happen.

"You are not going anywhere near this fucker."

"I have to. You know he won't tell me anything over the phone."

"You aren't making his job easier by standing in front of him. That's not happening, Vita."

Since we're hardly the first couple to argue over each other's safety, the other guys remain quiet.

"I'm not asking your permission, Jandro. This needs to happen."

"If you're going to meet him, then you're doing it under my conditions."

"If I go with an entourage, he won't show. And you're not coming with me so he can get a two-for-one. That *pezzo di merda* isn't getting a one-for-one."

"No. That does nothing to reassure me, Vita. You don't want to know what will come of this if you insist."

I can guarantee every guy in here, especially the married ones —so all but Joaquin and me—know precisely what I mean. If we weren't trying to destroy each other, our similarities would probably make all members of Four Families besties forever. As Vita and I stand off against each other, Dillan steps forward.

"Pablo, we'll do our part and dig to see what the hell's going on, on our end."

"You have until tomorrow night to figure this shit out. Otherwise, we'll handle it all."

"The feck you will. This is *your* personal family matter that spilled over into trying to kill *my* family. Be glad all of you are still breathing rather than your parents planning wakes. Accept my graciousness with the sincerity it's offered."

That makes everyone in my family, including Vita, snort.

"Whatever, feckers. Until tomorrow night."

Dillan and his ragtag bunch of cousins take off, leaving my cousins and me to stare at each other. No one's staring at Vita because I know none of us want her to believe we're blaming her for what happened. We don't, so we don't want her to misunderstand and confuse curiosity with blame.

"What're you going to do, Jandro? Because I still intend to meet with Patrick."

"I think you and I need to have our own meeting at our place."

"Our place?"

"Yes. We're going home to the condo."

Even though she's spent no time there, I can already think of the place as being her home too since I can't imagine being apart from her. It's not just that I'm controlling as fuck and don't want her out of my sight or my reach because I'm convinced she'll die the moment she is. I genuinely want her company when we're not trying to sort out this chaos.

There's not much more we can do here at the club. My cousins, Vita, and I agree we'll give Joaquin a few hours to investigate more. Vita compromises, accepting she needs to know as much as possible before she reaches out to Patrick.

I don't agree with her meeting him, but I also don't fight her anymore. Once we're in the town car I called for, Vita doesn't fight me when I pull her onto my lap. In silent agreement, she strips off her pants while I unfasten mine. I push down my boxer briefs enough for my dick to spring free. The moment we were alone in the car and kissed, it came to life. Now she straddles me and slides down until I'm buried inside her.

"Daddy, I don't want to argue about this. Please let me say my piece, and I'll listen to yours, and then we'll figure things out later. You don't know Patrick like I do. Even though I don't know his reasons for getting involved, I'm confident he'll talk to me before he gives anything away to you. You wouldn't be the first one to torture him. He's gotten away each time. The only way he won't is if you kill him. And if you kill him, then we can't learn anything from him. I'm not ruling out your right to torture him and kill him. I'm asking that you let me have a go first."

"I understand that, Vita. And I don't disagree with what you're saying. It's the logistics of it. There's no way in hell I'm letting you go alone. I know you're right. If he thinks you came with guards or me, he won't talk. Not only that, he's likely to finish the job on you. And I can't stomach the idea of losing you. Nothing could be worse than that. You're my everything."

"I feel the same, Daddy. All of this, since the moment we met until now, has been nonstop intensity. I'm sure it's amplified our feelings. But the only way it can make them bigger and louder is if they already existed. This whole thing is testing us. But we're not letting it break the bond we have. Just the opposite."

"*Chiquita*, I don't think I could go on without you. If something happened, I'd never force you to stay with me. You can leave whenever you want. But if things end between us, it won't be my choice."

"And you believe it would be mine, Daddy?"

"It would have to be."

"That's not happening. I'm not going anywhere. We're in this together for good."

She leans forward as I grip her hips. We needed the closeness of our bodies joined. The intimacy of being one with no end and no beginning. Now we need another layer of that connection.

As we move together, our tongues duel as our bodies move in sync. I don't remember the drive from Queens to Manhattan ever being so fast. But it feels like it's only moments later that we pull into the garage beneath my building. I work to get her off as we pull up to the elevator.

"Daddy, I'm so close."

"Me too, *chiquita*."

She grasps the headrest behind me as she grinds her clit against my pubic bone. I press my heels into the floor as I thrust into her.

"Daddy, I'm coming. I'm coming."

"Me too, little girl."

With a moan from her and a grunt from me, we both come. Couples can spend their entire relationship trying to synchronize their orgasms. It comes naturally to us. That's its own sign.

I know my driver won't interrupt us until I tap on the window. The delay in doing that surely gives away what we're up to if the vehicle's shaking didn't already. We take our time exchanging soft kisses before she lifts herself off me, and we put our clothes back on. The uncertainty and irritation that crackled between us earlier is gone as we ride up the elevator arm in arm.

"Just give me a moment in the bathroom."

"All right."

I head into the kitchen to make us something to eat since we both agreed we're starving again. Our meals have been unpredictable for the last couple days.

"Should I open a bottle of wine?"

I look over at Vita when she comes to stand beside my wine rack. "If you'd like to."

She peruses the bottles until she finds one she likes. She opens it and pours us each a glass while I finish cooking. We seem like such a normal couple as we share dinner together. We're both growing sleepy after we move to the couch to watch TV.

"Do you want the last bit of this wine, Jandro?"

"Let's split it."

She rises and heads back to the kitchen. When she returns, each of our glasses is only a quarter full. I down mine in two swallows before we head into the bedroom. I barely get through brushing my teeth before everything grows fuzzy. I head back into the bedroom already knowing what's happened. I stumble to the bed where Vittoria lies.

"You drugged me."

Chapter Twenty-Eight

Vita

The betrayal in Alejandro's eyes cuts me to the quick. It's even worse than what I hear in his voice.

"I did, Daddy. It's for your own good. You may never believe me, but I have to do this. There's no way you would ever allow it. I swear I'll be back before you wake up."

"*Chica.*"

He tries to reach for me, but I'm certain his limbs feel like stone, and his eyes grow glassy as he watches me.

"I pray you can forgive me, Alejandro, but I'll accept it if you can't. I'm doing this for you, even if you think I'm selfish for doing it my way."

It's not until his eyes are closed and his breathing deepens that I dare approach. I press a soft kiss to his forehead, but back away in a hurry, not trusting he's as sound asleep as he appears.

I look around his bedroom, then in the living room and kitchen until I find a set of keys to a Porsche. I might have overcome two obstacles, but the biggest one awaits me outside. I have to ditch the guards posted outside the condo door and in the lobby.

It was far easier snooping through Alejandro's medicine cabinet when I excused myself to go to the bathroom. I went in there with a specific intent. I breathed easier when I found the bottle of powerful muscle relaxants. It was nearly entirely full and must be left over from Alejandro's last significant injury. I crushed one on a tissue and carried it back out to the dining room with me.

It took all my restraint not to keep checking my pocket to be sure the tissue was still there while we ate. I dropped the powder into that last quarter-glass of wine. I feared he'd complain there was something gritty in the drink, but he downed the wine in two swallows, so I doubt he tasted anything.

I still have the burner from the bodega office. Alejandro gave it to me on the way to Enrique's. He's still got *Zia* Cosima's phone. I also have the gun Javier handed me during the hospital parking garage shootout. The phone goes in my front left pocket, and I tuck the gun in my waistband at my lower back. I brace myself as I open the door.

"*Hola, señorita Trevisan.*"

"*Hola.*"

The guard sizes me up as I smile. I grabbed the bag of trash from the kitchen before opening the door. I hold it up and scrunch up my nose.

"It smells."

The guy stares at me for a long moment before nodding. He clearly questions me, and I don't blame him. He should.

"I'll take it for you, *Señorita.*"

"Thank you."

I hand it off to him before closing the door enough for it to click. But then I pull it open and watch the guard stroll down the hallway. I slip out and make my way to the emergency stairs. I don't doubt security's watching my every move. I bolt down two flights before opening the door and heading to the elevator. There's no way I can make it down twenty flights of stairs without taking so long the guards catch me.

I hop on the elevator with a silent prayer of thanksgiving that I'm not alone. The family of five shifts to make room for me, and I keep my head down and hide amongst them. I get off on the first level of the parking garage and click the key fob.

Lucky guess that I'd find it on this level. I figured our driver pulled all the way into the ground floor here for the same reason we attempted at the hospital. Fewer people to notice us. However, Alejandro parked on the top level to make it easier in case he needs to leave in a hurry. I pull open the door to his Porsche and slip inside. One of the many times I'm grateful I'm European. I don't even think twice about driving a stick shift.

I pull out of the garage and get my bearings in Manhattan. I recognize enough around me to know I'm in the recently gentrified Hudson Yards area. Developers have built some of the most high-end condos in this area. Once I figure out where I am, I point myself in the direction I need. When I cross out of Manhattan and get onto a small side street, I pull over. I dial my last known number for Patrick. It rings through to voicemail. That's no surprise. A moment later, I get a text.

PATRICK

New phone, who dis?

He thinks he's far funnier than he ever has been.

ME

Lisa Jennings

I use the persona from the gala. Immediately, the phone rings.

"Lisa, Lisa, Lisa. To what do I owe the pleasure?"

"What the ever-loving fuck, Patrick?"

"A job's a job, but it's not work if you love what you do."

"You're a fucking psychopath."

"Takes one to know one."

"Patrick, meet me in two hours. We end this."

"Why should I agree?"

"Why shouldn't you? This is far more efficient than you hunting me. Whether we agree to meet or you stalk me, there's only one outcome to all of this—one of us dies. So why waste our time playing cat and mouse when we don't have to? I know you're a sick fuck and you enjoy that. But the sooner you kill me, the sooner you can move on to the next job and the next paycheck, right?"

"You make it sound so sexy, Lisa."

"Two hours, Patrick."

"Where at?"

"The gazebo, Westerleigh Park on Staten Island."

"Why the fuck would I want to go to Staten Island?"

"Because that's how everybody feels. It's the least likely place anybody's looking for either of us."

It's known as the "borough of parks," so there are plenty of places for me to pick.

"Fine but make it three hours."

"What, you in the middle of getting a mani-pedi, Patrick? You just want me to dance to your tune."

"Whatever my reason is my reason. Three hours, Lisa."

"Fine."

We hang up, and I count my blessings he's giving me more time than I thought he would. I still have somewhere else to go before I can meet him, and it'll take me an hour to get to the park. I pull back onto the street and wind my way through the outer borough until I approach a neighborhood that'll take all my skill to get into.

I park three streets over before leaving the car and scouting my surroundings. It's a massive neighborhood that's expanded to merge with an adjacent one. I take fifteen minutes before I find a spot where I can get over the community wall without landing in the wrong backyard.

It's another five minutes of sitting in a tree waiting for my chance to drop into the backyard I want, praying the fence isn't electrified. It takes every bit of cat burglar skill I have to get over the fence without triggering the alarm or catching any of the patrolling guards' eyes. I recognize the type of wall around this property. It's the kind that has sensors on the top that'll go off if anything heavier than a pigeon lands on it.

Before I got out of Alejandro's car, I checked his glove

compartment and found a lock-picking kit. Christmas came early. I stick to the shadows, moving in between the patrols until I can get to a patio door. From there, I'm inside within moments.

I wound up in the family room. I open the door, hoping to slip out and make it to the study, but a gun pointed at my chest greets me.

"Vittoria, you have twenty seconds to tell me what the fuck you're doing in my house."

"*Buonasera, madrina.*" Good evening, Godmother.

Sylvia Mancinelli isn't exaggerating when she tells me I have twenty seconds. I know her daughters are probably home, but even if they weren't, she's still one of the most capable women I've ever met. She may have gotten the title by marrying the NYC don, but the woman could run any Mafia without batting an eyelash. The title's earned as much as it was given.

"Why's your family trying to kill me?"

She tilts her head to the right as though she's considering what I asked. She's one of the most intelligent women I've ever met. She's highly educated from the most elite schools and universities. She's practiced law in France, Italy, and the States. She's also the most elegant woman I've ever seen.

While the Kutsenko brothers' mother, Galina, is the most breathtaking beauty, no one surpasses Sylvia's natural sophistication and elegance.

"Why would you think anyone in my family wishes to kill you, Vittoria? Guilty conscience? Paranoia?"

"It could be that, *Madrina.* Or it could be the kidnapping, two explosions, and two shootouts in the past two days that're making me nervous. I won't live to see my next birthday when you give such thoughtful gifts."

"Do you believe it's my father or uncles trying to kill you?"

"Either, both? I don't know for sure. That's why I came to ask you."

"Salva."

She calls out to her husband while her gun's still leveled at my heart. I've known her since I was a toddler. There's not a doubt in my mind she'll kill me if I breathe one too many times or I blink for too long.

"Sylvie?"

Don Salvatore rounds a corner, a shocked expression as he takes in the scene.

"Vittoria?"

"Good evening, Don Salvatore."

His lips twitch.

"She's been very formal this evening, Salva. She didn't ask me for my *torcetti*."

A twisted dough cookie—my favorite thing Sylvia makes.

"I want to know why your in-laws are trying to kill me."

"I take it Alejandro doesn't know you're here?"

I shrug nonchalantly, which makes Salvatore laugh.

"Oh, you will not be so smug when your boyfriend finds you. He's dead or drugged if you're here alone."

I force myself not to react since what he said hits the mark.

"You know who my neighbors are, don't you, Vittoria?"

"I'm guessing someone in Alejandro's family. Pablo?"

"Yes, on one side. One of my nephews lives directly across the street. I've never known you to be so foolish as to arrive some-where unprotected."

"You're assuming I am."

"Should I have Sylvie check you for a wire?"

"You know I wouldn't do that."

"Do I, though? You sneaked into my home, surely armed, while my children sleep upstairs."

"And if I'd wanted to do you harm, I would've. I wouldn't have been so relaxed as to be caught if my goal was to kill any of you. I just want information."

"Why're you so convinced it's my family, Vittoria? If anyone were to go after you, it would end the alliance with your family."

"I'm a gun for hire. The rules don't apply to me the way they do other women. Someone put the hit on Alejandro. And because I didn't carry it out, I'm now a target too. I'm curious why someone wants to kill Alejandro right now. But I'm more curious why they'd target me as well."

"You know about this job, and you failed yours. You switched sides. The hunter became the hunted."

"Plenty of mercenaries fail to complete jobs without being killed, so why the death sentence for me?"

"We need to move this conversation to my office. I don't want the girls to overhear if they wake."

Salvatore leads Sylvia and me to his office where he has a biometric keypad to open the door. I'm certain the numeric code that goes along with the fingerprint is more highly guarded than the Vatican's gold.

"Vittoria, despite you breaking into my home, I'm still glad to see you safe. What your aunt did…"

Sylvia's expression hardens as she trails off. She and *Zia* Cosima never got along. Sylvia never cared whether she was the most beautiful woman in the room, but *Zia* Cosima did. She couldn't stand Sylvia's effortless grace always outshone her hardened beauty. My aunt saw a competition in everything, and Sylvia didn't give a shit. That made her far more attractive to people than *Zia* Cosima's features ever did.

"I'm finding betrayal comes in many flavors right now. Apparently, my aunt not only betrayed me, but our people."

I wait for any reaction from either of them. I'll only get what they're willing to give, which is nothing.

"Ah, so you found out about Cosima's love life. She spent an awful lot of time going to Reggio. Why no one questioned her love of that shithole is beyond me."

Of course, the Sicilian thinks Reggio—the capital of the Calabria region—is a shithole. I'm Venetian and agree. But once again, there's a hierarchy within the Mafia, and Sicilians would prefer they never be lumped in with those of us from *il continente* —the continent—mainland Italy. They'd also prefer to think they're the only ones who merit a capital M, but Mafia is as Mafia does.

"It's unfortunate you don't pick your men very well, Vittoria.

First, Zorzi, the illegitimate son of the *'Ndrangheta* don. The oldest child, but never able to inherit. Then, your co-conspirator at the gala. And finally, Alejandro. Why couldn't you settle down with a nice boy from Venice?"

If Salvatore's tone weren't so fucking patronizing, his expression might be one of a kindly uncle. I half expect the next words out of his mouth to be, "you should smile more." I know he's doing it to goad me, so I won't let it work.

But it's an effort.

"If you know about *Zia* Cosima and Zorzi, and you know about Patrick, then help me understand what's really going on. Who hired me?"

I look between the couple, and neither shows any sign they'll cooperate. Fucking infuriating. I knew they likely wouldn't, but I'm risking everything with Alejandro for this. I need something. Eventually, Salvatore relents.

"Vittoria, you're looking in the wrong places."

"What?"

"The person who hired you isn't Italian. However, I suspect the person who ordered the hit on you is."

"They're separate?"

"Yes. Poor coincidence."

That leaves my mind scrambling.

"So, the person who ordered the hit on Alejandro—are they here in the U.S.?"

"That's my best guess. It could be from somewhere else. I don't know for sure, but I've at least ruled out the four Mafias for that. Who you pissed off enough to want to kill you is beyond me. I haven't found that yet."

"Have you been looking that hard?"

I should've stopped while I was ahead. The moment the words tumble from my mouth, both Sylvia and Salvatore glare at me. I sound incredibly ungrateful. I'm certainly not making friends and influencing people with this attitude.

"My apologies, Don Salvatore. I'm not exactly at my best right now."

"Understandable."

"I'm trying to determine which attacks were about Alejandro and which were about me. *Zia* Cosima said it was the Galicians who went after Alejandro, but I don't think that's right. I think she spewed lies."

"She most certainly did. Almost every other word out of that woman's mouth was a lie if she wasn't in the classroom. How somebody so wretched could be so good with children absolutely defies all reason."

Clearly, Sylvia was not a fan of my aunt, even in death. Her conscience doesn't bother her to speak ill of the dead.

"If it wasn't the *'Ndrangheta* after Alejandro, could they still be after me? And the kidnapping and explosion were just wrong time, wrong place for Alejandro?"

Salvatore cocks an eyebrow. "Possibly. My guess is those were two separate events. Somebody tried to cash in on your *zia* already having the two of you tied up."

"So, my *zia* kidnaps us to get to me. And then whoever wants to take out Alejandro blew up the warehouse."

"It wouldn't surprise me if that were the case."

"If this wasn't about punishing me for an unfinished job, what have I done to piss off somebody else enough for them to order my death?"

I speak my thoughts aloud, and Salvatore and Sylvia's expressions match. They basically silently ask me how stupid can I be when the list is a mile long? I have over one hundred and fifty confirmed kills. That leaves a lot of families and employers pissed off.

"Assuming it's not your family or my people, could it be the Camorras working with the *'Ndrangheta*?"

Salvatore shakes his head. "No. I highly doubt that. They prefer to stick closer to home right now after all that went wrong and started this petty war."

"Okay, if you're right that it isn't one of the four Mafia, then why did Zorzi and *Zia* Cosima work together?"

Revulsion flashes across Salvatore's face. "Don Pasquale

wasn't the woman's only lover."

I jerk back; my revulsion making my throat burn.

My zia really took my sloppy seconds? Or God, could it have been she was with Zorzi when we were teens? Was it some sick Mrs. Robinson fetish, and I'm the sloppy seconds?

Makes me want to vomit just thinking about it.

"Whatever her reason, do you believe she enlisted his help?"

"Most likely. He may have been an idiot, but he was a capable idiot."

"The possibility remains it could be the *'Ndranghetas'* don who's after me, but not anyone from the Carosis or Torettas or the Camorras."

"That's right, but my money's still on someone outside the Italians or Sicilians."

I stare Salvatore dead in the eye. His heterochromia's almost hypnotic.

"And it wasn't you?"

"You've been Serafina's friend since you were both in diapers. I've always considered you extended family, Vittoria. Mercenary or not, I don't murder women, and I don't murder family."

"You might not, but would you hire someone to do it for you?" I hold my breath, fully expecting Salvatore to kick me out if Sylvia lets me live long enough.

"No, I did not."

"Thank you."

I can attempt graciousness at least once in this conversation.

I run through all the confusing, circular arguments. Salvatore doesn't believe it's the *Mala del Brenta, Cosa Nostra, 'Ndrangheta,* or the Camorras. However, he's not entirely ruling out the *'Ndrangheta* since *Zia* Cosima was banging Don Pasquale, and Zorzi was the man's illegitimate son by another woman. She banged both of them.

Whoever took out the hit on Alejandro isn't the same person after me. The person who hired me is likely in the States, but my persecutor could be from anywhere. Alejandro and I are in danger because of each other and on our own.

"Where do I look here in the U.S.?"

È come cercare un fottuto ago in un fottuto pagliaio. It's looking for a fucking needle in a motherfucking haystack.

"I don't believe it's anyone in the city, but it could be Boston, New Jersey, Philadelphia, Chicago, L.A., San Francisco, Miami. The list's too long to simply guess where to begin. I don't have an answer for that, Vittoria. That's something your new family will have to figure out for your sake. And for your sake alone, I will intervene if I can, not just to keep you alive, but Alejandro as well. Has your father had anything to say about your future husband?"

I shake my head.

It's the same in all Four Families here in New York. It seems a foregone conclusion that when any of these men finally date, it's with the purpose of marrying. None do it casually or to pass the time, even to avoid loneliness. It's all or nothing with all of them.

That's why it no longer jars me to hear people speak as though Alejandro and I are already engaged. Just as it didn't take long for me to adjust to the idea of being with him, it took next to no time to adjust to other people's belief that we're together.

"I need to get going. I have somewhere else to be before I go back to Alejandro's."

Salvatore cringes.

The fucking don of New York City—of the Eastern Seaboard —of all the motherfucking United States just cringed.

Fuck my life.

"Remember, he's a big guy like Gabriele. Whatever you drugged him with is likely to wear off far faster than you expect."

I merely nod, not wanting to confess my sins aloud. It surprises me, but I appreciate the hugs Salvatore and Sylvia give me. This time, I use the front door and walk out the property gate and neighborhood gate without skulking.

I glance at the clock on the dash as I start the car. I have just enough time to make it to my meeting with Patrick. The burner rings, and I glance down.

Double fuck my life.

Chapter Twenty-Nine

Vita

I debate whether to answer it. Either way, I'll have hell to pay.

"Hello?"

"*Chiquita*, I will blister your ass when you get home, and then I will fuck you into next week. Thank God you're okay."

I suppose that's one way to express concern. Fortunately, he can't see my smile, since I'm certain he wants me to take him far more seriously. I certainly don't doubt he'll follow through on what he says, but it's nowhere near as intimidating as he probably wants.

"Look in your rearview mirror, *chiquita*."

I glance back and see the Mercedes right behind me. All the windows are tinted to the point of being barely street legal.

"Wave to me, *chiquita*."

"What—how—Fuck my life."

Shit just got as real as shit can get. Alejandro's chuckle would be sexy if I didn't truly fear for my ass now.

"Little girl, we have trackers on everything. My car, my weapons, everything. I knew where you parked. That's how I was waiting for you. I know you went to Salvatore's because of the tracker on the gun."

"You have a tracker on that?"

"Of course. We can't risk leaving evidence behind. We need to account for all our weapons."

That's an inconvenient truth.

"Alejandro, I have somewhere else I need to go before I meet you at the condo."

"*Dios mio, chica.* You are not naive, so you cannot possibly believe you're going anywhere without me now that I've tracked you down."

"Wishful thinking?"

"Delusional. Where are you meeting Patrick?"

"How'd you...? Staten Island. There's a park there. I only know it because of a job a year ago. Someone from out of town."

"I'll hang back, but my cousins are behind me. We'll all fan out and surround the park."

"Are you crazy? Are they all in cars like yours? You don't think a Porsche and your Mercedes won't stand out in that part of the borough? It's bad enough the only set of keys I could find were for your little race car."

"No. They're in subtler vehicles. They didn't leave in quite the hurry I did since you made it easy for them by strolling into their neighborhood."

Oh, hell.

Pablo was probably watching me from his front door.

"You can't lose your shit, Alejandro, if you think something's going sideways. You must let it play out."

"I won't let him kill you first, Vita. If I think he's going to take the shot, then I'll do it first."

"Maim, don't kill."

"I make no promises, little one."

"Fine."

There's a pause for a moment before I share what I learned.

"Alejandro, Salvatore thinks the hits are separate jobs, that whoever's targeted you is here in the States. Whoever's going after me could be from anywhere. He's pretty confident it's not anyone in Italy or Sicily after you. He doesn't know why *Zia* Cosima and Zorzi got involved if it turns out the *'Ndrangheta* didn't make me their mark. But it goes beyond *Zia* Cosima having an affair with Zorzi's father. Apparently, like father like son."

"Ugh, that's disgusting."

I can't imagine Matáis and Alejandro would ever share a woman—if some alternate universe swallowed us whole and made them cheaters.

"I agree. But according to Salvatore, they'd been together for quite a while."

"Could it have really been something personal with your *tía* and ex-boyfriend? You wronged them both somehow?"

"Maybe. I don't know."

We're approaching the park on Staten Island, so Alejandro lets me know he and his cousins are turning off and will surround the park. He takes a left, and behind him I see another car that's far more inconspicuous. The same is true for the two behind it.

I breathe a little easier.

I find a spot to park and go to the well-lit gazebo. Patrick might suspect—actually, he'll probably assume—I picked this place so Alejandro could spy. But this also isn't some shady back-alley deal. He knows I picked this place as a general deterrent from him killing me where anybody could witness the scene.

I'm five minutes early, but Patrick shows up exactly on time. He's certainly an attractive man, and I enjoyed the times we were together. But his commitment to killing me makes him rather unappealing these days.

"Patrick, what the fuck?"

"Don't take it personally."

"How can I not? You're trying to kill me."

"I'm trying to do a job."

Something's amiss with him. It's not like we're emotionally close, even if we've worked together and fucked. But I know him well enough to sense he's lying—that it isn't a job.

"Patrick, is this personal?"

"You think awfully highly of yourself if you believe I care enough about you to want to kill you."

"Then how much am I worth?"

"Ah, my sweet Vittoria, you are priceless."

"Bullshit. How much are you being paid to kill me?"

"It's not just about the money."

"Then what is it about, Patrick? If I'm going to die, then why be evasive? It's not like I'll be able to tell anybody after the fact. Why not just let it all out, and I'll take it to the grave?"

"Nope, don't think so."

His dismissive tone rankles.

"Then I'm going to believe this is personal, and you only said that to insult me. Are you crying into your Cheerios because I didn't fuck you the night of the gala? That I'm fucking someone else instead?"

His cheeks flush, and I realize I hit the mark.

"I never took you to be a Suzy Homemaker, Vittoria, but now you want to settle down."

"Why should that matter to you? If I did, I'd be one less competitor on the field. You could snag jobs I'd normally take. You don't have to kill me to do that."

"True. But I want to watch your boy toy beg for your life before I take it."

He draws his knife from his pocket. I don't outwardly react even if my heart rate picks up. I don't want to die, but more urgently, I don't want Alejandro to kill him prematurely.

"Patrick, were you the one who shot into the hotel room?"

"No, that definitely wasn't me. You know I would've hit the right person if it had been."

"What about my kidnapping and the explosion?"

"The explosion was a hidden blessing. It didn't kill you or Alejandro like it was supposed to. It got rid of the two people who could've stolen that satisfaction from me."

"You never once made it clear you wanted something more from me."

"If I had, would you have been with me?"

"No."

I answer the question honestly because he'd know if I lied. He glowers at me, not appreciating my bluntness. I press on.

"Patrick, you've always known there was no chance between us. Even if there were, did you really want me that badly?"

I don't believe for a moment this is about unrequited love.

"No. But I'd rather no one have you than that piece of shit."

"What do you have against Alejandro?"

"You want him."

The man is truly not right in the head. He doesn't want me enough to ever make it clear he wants more than our few one-night stands. Yet he won't let me be with anyone else. He's so committed to that he's willing to die for it.

"Patrick, what're you hoping to gain from all of this? Do you want me dead?"

"Not particularly, but I accept the inevitable now that you've chosen him."

I inch closer to him. I'm certain Alejandro's having a conniption right now. I can hear his snarly voice in my head. And my ass has phantom pains from the spanking I've earned.

"Tell me what I can do to end this, Patrick."

"Will you beg for his life?"

"If I have to."

"Will you beg for your own?"

"If you insist."

I take another two steps forward, bringing me nearly within his reach.

"Would you fuck me to save his life?"

"If that's what it would take, I'd never willingly do that."

A man would have to force me before I'd voluntarily betray Alejandro like that. What I already did was bad enough, but Patrick doesn't need to know.

"Is that what it'll take?"

I lift the hem of my shirt, and his eyes dart to the bandage over my ribs.

"Was that you? Did you orchestrate the nurse and the shootout at the hospital?"

"Yes, you weren't supposed to get hurt. The bag of shit who did that is dead." He points to the bandage.

"Thank you."

I only say it to stroke his ego. I cross my arms as though I'll lift the shirt over my head. Instead, my left hand grabs my gun. I aim and shoot him in the belly. He looks down as he instinctively covers the wound before looking up at me.

His expression—the definition of horror.

I lunge, grab his knife, and slash it from his inner left collarbone to his armpit. Then, I twist my wrist, dragging it across his chest to his nipple, and stab at his sternum. Between the gunshot and slashing, blood sprays across me, and I know I look like the movie character Carrie.

"Patrick, you know none of these wounds'll kill you quickly. I could still keep you alive if you give me what I want to know."

"You know I don't fear death."

I lift the blade to the bridge of his nose, then drag the flat side of it along his left nostril before repeating it on the right side.

"No, you don't fear death, but you fear your looks fading. You could die handsome, or I can ensure you're a grotesque remnant of what you once were. Then I'll take a photo and send it to your parents, so the last thing they remember of you is the hideous monster I made you."

I rest the tip of the blade on his lower lip. I can and will do worse if he refuses to cooperate. His body trembles, and he sinks to his knees, no longer able to support his own weight. When he topples forward, I pluck his gun from the holster at his lower back. I kick both ankles to check for a spare gun. He has none. I dig my foot underneath his shoulder and lift before forcing him onto his back.

"You wanted the man I fell in love with as collateral damage for me not wanting you. All you did was test and prove it's him and me against the world. Can you say any of this bullshit was worth it? Give me the information I need, and I'll make your death painless. Refuse me, and I'll have Alejandro fuck me right in front of you. I'll put a fucking zip tie around your balls and make you jack off but not come."

"And you want to call me a sick fuck, Vittoria?"

"I'm pissed you want to kill me, but that doesn't even come close to the pure loathing I have for you for targeting Alejandro. That is what my vengeance is for."

Chapter Thirty

Alejandro

I emerge from the bush behind which I've hidden for the last five minutes. I settled myself there when I spotted Patrick approaching the gazebo. I creep forward, ensuring I'm at an angle where neither Vita nor Patrick can see me.

Half of me is proud of Vita's interrogation tactics. The other half of me wants to haul her over my shoulder and spank her ass all the way to the car, then take us straight back to our condo where I can spank her some more.

As I listen to Patrick ramble about his bizarre obsession, it's hard to believe he could be so fucked-up. But if any woman could drive a person to distraction—to the point of believing that if they can't have her, then nobody can—it would be Vita.

I force myself to remain silent and out of the way as the conversation progresses. There are so many times I want to intervene. However, I know that would destroy the progress Vita's making. I hate the danger she's in, even if I'm aware it's nothing new to her. Just because she can handle herself in situations like this doesn't mean I want her to.

I fully recognize the hypocrisy of that, considering what I do for my family. I can't imagine her as a mercenary once this is over. But I must accept she may want to continue this occupation. I hope she won't, since what she does is a choice, as opposed to the life I have no choice but to live.

"What do you have against Alejandro?"

"You want him."

It shocks the shit out of me as Vita draws the information from Patrick, and we learn who's actually after me. I reach into my pocket and withdraw my phone, opening the group text that all the men in my family are on.

ME

Can you believe this shit?

While all the men here are wearing earpieces that are recording and transmitting to *Tío* Enrique, *Tío* Luis, and *Papá*, none of us can speak. We must rely on text to communicate.

JAVIER

Ese cabrón está realmente loco

That fucker really is crazy.

PABLO

She's good at this.

It tempts me to type back "too good," but I keep that thought to myself. Instead, I send a different message.

ME

I want to know how he found out where to be and when. Did someone tell him, or has he been hacking?

Since there's no immediate answer, I lock my phone and slide it back into my pocket.

"Patrick, you know you're breathing your last breath. Explain to me how you know so much about where we would be and what my aunt and ex-boyfriend were up to."

"Zorzi hired me to watch you."

He's practically wheezing at this point. Blood's still streaming from his gunshot wound as he presses against his belly.

"Why? What did any of this matter to them?"

"Since Pasquale only has daughters with his wife, Cosima convinced Zorzi that Pasquale would finally acknowledge him as his son and make him underboss."

I nearly snort with laughter. Vita actually does.

"There isn't any chance on God's green earth that Pasquale Borruto would ever recognize his bastard as his heir."

While I don't know him personally, I know enough about him. The guy is obsessed with his image of being the perfect gentleman Mafioso. That he's some kind of Robin Hood. It's not a well-guarded secret that he's had affairs, but they've gone unacknowledged.

"Okay, so I understand Zorzi's motivation, but what about my *zia*? What on earth did she have against me? Why target me?"

"You accepted a job that killed her illegitimate son."

"What? When the hell did my *zia* have a baby nobody knows about?"

I swear, Vita's family secrets could shock the devil.

"When she was nineteen, she claimed to study abroad. Instead, her father banished her for the semester to Marathia."

"Where the fuck is that?"

"An obscure little village of like forty people in the middle of Greece. She put the baby up for adoption. Turns out, he wound up with a syndicate family in Thessaloniki. Her father arranged it. It wasn't until seven years ago that she learned where he was and what he'd become. Ten months ago, you took that assignment in Ankara. You took out the Greek representative."

"What?"

I pinch the bridge of my nose as I listen. I'd close my eyes to picture this gnarled family tree, but I won't take my eyes off the scene lest Patrick somehow overwhelms Vita.

"That was her son. She found him because she told Zorzi to

search. When he discovered who and where her son was, she kept an eye on him."

"Do you mean she plotted my demise for months?"

"Yes."

"And instead of working with her, you were in a race to the finish?"

"Exactly."

Vita's shoulders slump as she exhales.

"Do you know what my parents might've known about my cousin?"

"I don't believe they knew much beyond he existed and lived in Greece."

I watch Vita press her shoulders back and lift her chin, her relief obvious. However, her saddened expression tugs at my heart. I can't imagine how her mother will receive this information. She already knows Cosima intended to kill Vita. But this is far more twisted than I'm certain the woman expects.

Then again, maybe not.

It would have to be a pretty fucked-up situation for a Mafia woman to go after her niece when they both are well-known members of the upper echelon's family. But it's the sort of rivalry that's made the Mafia infamous enough for movies.

"Is there anything else?"

Vita points the tip of the blade at the hollow between Patrick's collarbones. From the way he swallows, I know she is applying increased pressure.

"To find you, I dug into Alejandro further. I saw the way you watched him at the gala. I didn't like it."

"What did you learn and how?"

"I bribed—a—fuck ton of people. It—allowed me—to leapfrog until—I found the—origin."

I want the man to hurry. His halting explanation grates on my nerves. However, the typical person would've passed out a long time ago. It's clear this isn't his first gunshot wound, and he has a higher pain tolerance than most. It makes me wonder how long he's been a mercenary. My guess is he's approaching his late thirties, so a few years older than me.

"Spit it out, Patrick, and I'll put you out of your agony. I know you'll never beg for mercy, and your window to ask already shut. But you can decide how much worse it's going to get before the end."

She twists the knife against his throat as though she were drilling a hole. It doesn't break the skin, but I'm certain it feels like she's about to puncture his windpipe. Or press his Adam's apple out through the back of his neck.

"Who's after Alejandro?"

"Seems your fuckboy pissed off Sergei Andreyev."

My brow furrows.

When don't I piss off Sergei?

He's the NYC bratva's *sovietnik*—chief intelligence officer—and maternal cousin to the Kutsenko brothers. But there's no chance in hell he ordered this hit, nor did any member of his family.

"What did Alejandro do to make Sergei put a hit on him?"

Patrick tuts, then splutters.

"It wasn't Sergei who ordered the hit, but he's the reason for it. Alejandro pissed off Sergei because of some plan he came up with that enabled Joaquin to sabotage Sergei's intel on a major deal in Portugal. No one in the bratva reads, writes, or speaks fluent Portuguese, but Alejandro does. He intercepted and translated communications between a Brazilian cartel and a Portuguese importer. The Diazes swiped the deal right out from under the bratva's feet. It hurt Sergei's pride. What he believed was so thoroughly encrypted, Joaquin hacked so easily."

That's easy to imagine.

"Cool story, bro."

Patrick's face could curdle milk if he had it in him. He'd probably attempt to wrap his hands around Vita's throat, but he's fading fast.

"It's a little Boston-New York rivalry going on. The Volkovs are on Anton's shit list because they fucked up a deal that outed a

Ponzi scheme Anton has built for the past year. Now they all have the FTC breathing down their necks. Dmitri Volkov hoped to get back into the New York bratva's good graces by doing Sergei and Anton a favor. He believed offing Alejandro would be restitution for the problems he caused."

"Is he fucking stupid?"

"Yes, incredibly. He wants to mutiny against his nephew, the current *pakhan*. He's in way over his head, both the jobs his nephew entrusted him with and this rogue scheme."

"And does the Ivankov branch know what the Volkovs have done?"

The Kutsenkos may run the bratva now, but their branch's still known for Vyacheslav Ivankov, who founded it when he was sent from Russia to establish the bratva in the States. Apparently, he killed too many people there, so they exported him to the U.S.

"Your guess is as good as mine on that. Even if Joaquin successfully hacked their shit, they're far more tight-lipped than the Volkov branch."

That's something for my family and me to consider. Once I can get Vita the fuck out of here and back to the condo, I'll need to meet with my *tíos* and cousins to figure all this shit out.

It's like a fucking onion. Too many damn layers, and all of them stink.

"Any last words?"

Vita keeps the knife against Patrick's Adam's apple, but now she puts the gun's muzzle to his forehead. By now, I'm certain she senses I'm here. Patrick's too weak to react, so I approach the gazebo's steps. Vita doesn't bat an eye as she pulls the trigger, blowing a hole straight through the center of Patrick's forehead.

His body tumbles backward, blood pouring from all his wounds, his eyes entirely sightless. I slide my arms around her waist, drawing her back to my chest. She leans against me as I kiss the top of her head. As we hug, I turn off my earpiece. I don't need my family listening to our private conversation.

"Seems like such a waste."

"I know, *chiquita*, but if he hadn't gotten involved, we wouldn't know what we do now."

"True."

"You can end this, and we can begin our life together, *chica*, if that's what you want."

She turns in my arms and despite the mess, she's still the most beautiful woman I've ever seen.

"I want nothing more, Daddy."

The relief that courses through my body overwhelms me. I swallow and nod, choked up for the first time since I was a child and learned what happened to *Tío* Esteban, my cousins' dead *papá*.

"*Chica*, you know there's a reckoning coming your way."

"I never doubted that."

As we gaze at each other, I see the hesitation in her eyes.

"You knew a punishment was inevitable, but you doubt my forgiveness."

"How could I not, Jandro?"

"I'm angry at your methods, and I won't deny a sense of betrayal. However, I understand it. There'll be more times than I can count where you won't want me to go on a mission, and I'll do it anyway. You'll have no say in it. Whereas I insisted upon deciding for you, putting you in a position where you felt backed into a corner. Rather than working with you, I worked against you. That's not what I wanted, so I see my fault in all of this. Considering you wanted to kill me, my forgiveness is unconditional. Once given, we move on. A good nap seems not so bad."

She releases a strangled laugh, not appreciating my glib humor. I turn my earpiece back on and let my cousins know we're ready for the cleaners to come. They'll strip away any evidence of what happened here. Despite the gazebo's lighting, it's dark now. If they'd met any earlier in the day, we wouldn't have had the luxury of such privacy. The crew will need it to disguise their activities.

Javier agrees to follow Vita and me in my Porsche and leave it in the garage before a town car picks him up to meet Madeline when her shift at the hospital ends. Vita and I make our way to my Mercedes where I pop the trunk and open my go bag. I have wipes to remove camouflage paint and blood easily.

I shield her as she strips off her outer layers and drops them into a black trash bag. The cleaners will destroy them, so she leaves none of Patrick's bio-waste behind. She dons the sweatshirt and sweatpants I keep in the bag. Before donning the pants, she holds them up and shakes them.

"Not a fucking chance you're wearing these again in public."

I chuckle. She's genuinely opposed to me in gray sweatpants. The last time she mentioned them wasn't the first time I'd heard them referred to as male lingerie. I don't get it, but I'll take her word for it.

Our ride home is quiet. We hold hands the entire way back. Once we're in the condo, we head directly to the bathroom. I turn on the shower to let the water heat.

"Let me help you, little one."

With the worst of the mess already wiped off her hands, face, and neck, the sweatsuit can go in the laundry rather than me disposing of it. I strip it off her and put it on the counter before giving her a hand into the shower. I practically rip my clothes off before joining her.

I love my shower.

It has two showerheads, so water can beat down on my back after a hard workout or long day while I wash my hair and scrub the rest of me.

I love it even more now.

Neither Vita nor I need to freeze while waiting for a turn under the water. The grazes on my back sting, but considering how much worse my injuries could be, they're little more than an annoyance. At least, that's what I tell myself.

She lifts her face and lets the stream pour over her before running the water over her hair. I indulge and gorge myself on the view of her shapely body. I see the same things many would consider imperfections as I did in the hotel. But to me, they make her perfect.

She's real.

I run the backs of my fingers from her collarbones down to her nipples, tweaking them before sweeping my palms over her ribs, waist, and ass. I ditched the bandages on my hands while making dinner since they got in the way. I peeled the dressings off my cheek and back at the same time. As my *abuela* would say, I'll let the air get to them.

I grab her and pull her onto her toes. Our lips fuse, and I lift her to wrap her legs around my waist. My bruises ache all over, but I didn't lie when I told her before that I've been in worse shape. Nothing is keeping me from making love to my soon-to-be wife.

"God, I want you, Daddy."

"Then take me."

I slide her cunt down my cock.

"Fuck! That feels amazing, Jandro."

"I agree."

I nip at her lower lip as I press her back against the wall. Our kisses are sloppy and passionate. We cover each other's faces, necks, and shoulders—anywhere we can reach before returning to each other's mouths. Our tongues tangle, and she sucks mine just hard enough for my body to take over and thrust into her. My hands on the back of her thighs guide her to rise and fall as she rides me.

It's our simmering sexual attraction that always crackles between us when we're close, but it's also relief that we survived to be here together.

Hotel room shooting.

Highway shootout.

Kidnapping.

Explosion one.

Wannabe killer nurse.

Hospital shootout.

Explosion two.

Did I miss anything?

It's utterly insane, yet a couple days in the life of a Cartel boss and a mercenary.

We're a fine fucking pair.

"Harder, Daddy. Fuck me till I'm sore."

"You're going to feel me inside you long after I pull out. You're going to ache to have me back."

She cups my chin.

"Promise?"

Before I can answer, she swoops in for a kiss. She's as demanding as I am. I dig my fingers into her thighs and pull her tighter against me—not that our bodies can truly get any closer.

"I'm nearly there, Daddy. May I come?"

"No."

She shrieks in disapproval and tries to grind against me faster. I lift her off my cock and put her back on her feet.

"What're you—"

I cut her off mid-sentence by dropping to my knees and licking her clit. When I suck, both her hands tunnel into my hair and press my face to her pussy. I draw her left leg over my shoulder as I plunge my tongue into her. She moans as her nails graze my scalp. Her shoulders press against the wall as her hips undulate against my mouth. Her free hand claws at my back—still careful of my few nicks and cuts—as her desperation grows. When I know she's on the brink of not holding back, I lower her leg and rise.

"Daddy?!"

I press her down to the floor, then stroke myself until I come across her chest. She stares at me, bewildered, as she rises.

"Did I forget to mention your punishment already started? Orgasm denial is the first phase."

Her mouth hangs open as she works through what I just said.

"How many phases are there?"

"Not sure. I'll let you know once we're done."

I pump shampoo into my hand before working it through her hair. Her hands fist and pound the wall behind her as her head flops forward. She's pissed at me because I made her sore and achy like I promised but didn't let her come. She feels out of control. Rather than push me away out of anger or hurt, she leans into me, trusting me. She accepts this dynamic: the punishment and the reward that'll eventually come.

"Jandro, I'm sorry."

"I know you are, baby girl."

"I'll accept whatever punishment you decide."

"Good girl."

I feel her breath against my chest when she sighs. Her body visibly relaxes as she presses it flush to mine. She lifts her head to make it easier for me to wash her hair. I help her rinse the suds from it before lathering body wash on my poof and running it over her body. I drop to the floor again, this time to wash her legs and feet. While I lavish attention on her lower limbs, she washes my hair.

When we're both clean, I spin her around. Rather than lean against me, she levers her body, so her shoulders, chest, and cheek are against the wall, while her hips push back. She turns her toes inward as I spread her ass cheeks.

"Your tight little ass will be mine too. I'll fill your mouth and belly, your pussy, and your ass with my cum whenever the fuck I want, *chica*. You're mine."

"I am. I have been since we met."

I slide my left index finger through her cream before pressing against her rosebud. She tries to clench her ass at the invasion, but she relaxes immediately.

"Should I stretch you before I fuck you here?"

"No. I want you to claim it."

I didn't expect that answer. It gives me pause.

How much pain does she enjoy?

"Vita, do you want it that way because you think it should be part of your punishment?"

"No. I'd say that anytime we want to do butt stuff. I don't need plugs to prepare me. As long as you don't cram your dick in me, I can take it. With you, I'd rather not wear them as preparation. If you want me to as foreplay or punishment in their own right, then fine. But I want to take you as is."

"You want my dominance."

"Yes."

"If you refuse the plugs, then I insist on lube."

"Definitely. I want you to dominate me, not rip me apart."

I ease my finger in and out with shallow thrusts, a hint of what it'll be like when I fuck her there. When I'm finished toying with her, I wash my hands, then turn off the water. She pushes open the shower door and hands me a towel before wrapping her hair in one. She grabs another to wrap around her body. I hate seeing it covered.

Once we're dry, and we've hung up the towels, I lead us to the bedroom. I grab a pair of boxer briefs but nothing for Vita. I sit on the edge of the bed before lifting her to straddle me. If I didn't have the underwear on, I'd be inside her again. My cock was already alive and twitching before we left the bathroom. I need the material barrier, or I'll distract myself.

"I'm going to spank you, *chiquita*. It won't be gentle or quick. I'm no longer angry, even if I am still hurt. I will never spank you while angry. I won't let that emotion drive me, and I never want to underestimate my strength. I won't risk hurting you."

"Yes, Daddy."

"Why am I spanking you?"

"How far back should I recount my sins toward you?"

"Just tonight."

"Rather than discuss it with you because I didn't like your initial decision, I took it upon myself to handle things. I knew how strongly you'd object, so I drugged you."

Her face drains of color as she admits the transgression. Perspiration beads along her hairline, and goosebumps form on her arms and legs. I grow concerned as I see her physical reaction, but I'm scared when she trembles enough to shake.

"Vita?"

"I'm so, so sorry. I know you said you'd forgive me, but what if you decide you can't? What if you can't get over the betrayal? What if—"

"What if I love you, *chiquita*?"

I didn't plan those words; they just sorta tumbled out.

"Really?"

"Yes, little one. I love you."

"How?"

I chuckle, even though I know I shouldn't.

"You've worked your way into my heart. We haven't known each other nearly long enough by most people's measure. But time isn't a luxury to them. It is for us. I won't waste it wondering if I'm rushing. I'm in my thirties, and until you, I'd met no one who grabbed and held my attention like you. You're my first and last thought every day. I'd met no one outside my family who makes me want to take care of them or be protective of them. No one I'd trust to walk into battle alongside. No one who makes my heart and body ache to be near them. No one who feels like a partner. You might not feel the sa—"

"Shh."

She puts her right index finger against my lips as her left hand cups my chin, lifting it.

"I love you too."

"You do?"

She chuckles at my surprise. I mean, I've wanted her to love me back since I began putting the pieces together that I've fallen in love with her. I just didn't expect her to get to the same place as me so quickly.

"I feel like I've lived a hundred lives since graduating university. At least twenty different personas. I've mingled among high-society and dregs of society. I've been all over the world. I've met no other man who makes me excited to see him. I've met no other man who makes me feel cared for, makes me feel special and valued. I trust next to no one, but I trust you. When I realized that, I knew I was already in love with you."

She gives me a peck on the lips before sliding off my lap. She stands beside my legs and watches me expectantly.

"I'm going to use my hand, but I'm inclined to use something else too. I don't know what your threshold for pain is or what kinds of implements you're comfortable with."

"It's pretty high for most forms of pain. I'm fine with belts, crops, whips, floggers, hairbrushes, paddles. That sort of stuff."

"Which do you want tonight? Belt or hairbrush? Wooden spoon or plastic spatula are also options. I don't keep a stash of BDSM toys or implements here. I've never had a woman here before."

"Really?"

"I belong to a club and have had past arrangements, but they never came here. This is my sanctuary from the world. I also don't trust strangers in my home. There are too many risks."

"You trust me here."

"You are hardly a stranger. You are part of my sanctuary."

Despite what we've faced together, she's still a reprieve from reality. I suppose she's my safe space. I want her to be part of my family, and they're the only ones welcome here.

"You choose, Daddy."

The trust in her gaze is everything to me. I rise and cup the back of her neck as I kiss her forehead.

"Belt for tonight."

"All right."

I head to my closet and pull out one of my wider ones. I fold it in half and snap it, making her tense as I approach. I wrap the buckle and leather length around my hand several times, then slap my other palm with the tail. I chose this one over a narrower one that would deliver more sting because this won't be a quick spanking. This will diffuse the pain with a deeper impact.

Our gazes meet, and Vita nods.

"Give me your consent aloud, Vita."

"I agree to this, Daddy."

"What's your safe word? We didn't establish that the last time I spanked you."

"*Moleche.*"

"What's that?"

"Green crabs. *Moleche col pien* is fried green crabs with eggs. I was way too young when I learned how they're prepared, and it scarred me for life. I absolutely hate them. I will *never* ask for them, certainly not that dish."

"Okay, little one. Lie across my lap."

I position myself on the bed and open my legs. She steps between them and leans over my left one. I pin her thighs between mine, knowing the pain will make her squirm. I don't want to hurt her by accident. I place the belt beside me because I'll warm her up with just my hand.

"Are you ready, *chiquita?*"

"Yes, Daddy."

"Use your safe word if you need it. Don't take more than you can manage because this is a punishment. If I harm you, you'll break my trust again."

"I know, Jandro. That entirely defeats the point. I want you to see I trust you and that you can trust me. I know you'll observe me and watch for and ask about my limits. I won't hide anything from you."

I lean forward and kiss her shoulder just before I bring my hand down on her horizontal crack. She grunts and inhales, but she does nothing else. I rain down several spanks over the fleshier parts of her ass, but I keep returning to the first spot. After ten on each side, I rub my palm over her heated skin. I ease some of the burn, but only temporarily.

I wrap the belt around my hand, leaving six inches loose. I flick my wrist to deliver diagonal sharp spanks that sting. I give each cheek love, five on each. She stomps her feet and wriggles, but she never reaches back. Instead, she grips my ankle. It's halfway through this first round with the belt that I feel her shudder. I know she's crying, the sobs making her shoulders shake. It breaks my heart because I know she regrets her decision to drug me and escape. I don't want her to regret the success she had with Patrick. I can separate the parts of the event and only be upset about one.

"*Chiquita?*"

"I'm all right, Jandro. I can do this. It hurts like a mother-fucker, but keep going, please."

I unravel the belt and fold it in half. This position will focus the pain in smaller, rigid areas that'll intensify it compared to my hand and the single layer. I vary the blows from spanks—swinging my arm with a broader angle—to strokes—a longer swing for a heavier blow. I'm always mindful of my strength and to not overestimate what Vita can take. I'm careful not to leave welts. She'll have a few slight bruises, but I don't want welts as reminders.

Some might argue they'd be a deterrent, but I don't want either of us to have an ongoing reminder. I ensure I vary where the leather lands until I'm up to twenty lashes. I toss the belt aside and give Vita a chance to breathe for a moment while I caress her burgundy-colored ass. I'm certain she believes she's on fire with the way her entire lower half likely burns.

I help her sit with her ass cradled in the space between my legs. She sobs as her head rests on my shoulder.

"It's done now, *chiquita*. We're back to how things should be. You and me against the world."

"You really forgive me?"

"My love is unconditional. Of course I forgive you."

"But I—"

"Made a shitty decision that endangered both of us, but you did it with only good intentions. We've returned to the equilibrium we're finding. We both got what we needed. Now it's time to move on."

"Thank you, Jandro. My ass will hurt for hours, but my mind and heart are clearer."

"Stand up."

She rises, and my hands on her waist keep her from wobbling like a day-old lamb. I grab the belt, and she pulls away.

"Hold out your wrists."

She does as I command, but I notice her gaze jumps to the bedside table. My lips twitch as I fight not to smile.

"I'm not shackling you to the drawer handle."

"Only because it's a knob?"

"No. Though we'll have to figure out something for the headboard."

There's nothing to anchor restraints, so I stick with wrapping the leather around her wrists. I cinch it tightly and wrap the remaining length around and through the buckle, knowing she won't easily break free. I guide her arms over her head as I press between her shoulder blades, letting her know I want her to lean over the edge of the bed. I nudge her feet apart as I drape my body over hers. I'm careful not to press too hard against her ass, using my chest to pin her to the mattress.

"Do you feel how much larger my body is than yours?"

"Yes."

"Can anyone or anything get to you without coming through me first?"

"No."

Her one-word answers are breathy and fucking arousing. I slip my boxer briefs off, then my cock nestles between her ass cheeks.

"I will always be your shield, Vita. Let me stand beside you, but I will always protect you from any threat. Let me love you."

She shudders beneath me, and I watch a tear slip from beneath her closed eye.

"I will. I love you, Jandro."

"I love you, Vita."

I kiss her temple, then her cheek, and finally her shoulder. I lift my chest, but she shakes her head as best she can while pressing one cheek against the mattress. My right hand extends over my head, and I clasp both of hers in one of mine. My left hand guides my cock into her cunt. I may have told her I'd fuck her ass soon, but she's way too tender for that tonight.

"This is where I belong. Inside of you. I want to bring you pleasure, comfort, safety, and happiness. I want to do it in a way no other person has the right or privilege to. I want to give myself to you the same way. Do you accept?"

"Good God, yes!"

I draw back and thrust hard, pushing her entire body against the bed. I do it three more times.

"You are mine, Vita. I will have all of you and nothing less because I won't give you less than everything I can."

We both know my limitations are greater than hers. There's the beast in me I never want her to see. The parts of my work she can never know. She might guess, but I can never confirm. The secrets I must keep and the secrets I want to keep. Those can't be hers, but everything else is.

"Jandro, we'll always look over our shoulders because my past will never be far from us. But my present and future are with you. Just like you, there are things I'll take to the grave that I can never tell you. But I'll give you all that I can. You're mine, and I'm yours."

I withdraw from her and lift her onto the bed then climb on. I recline against the pillows as she straddles me. My hands allow her to only take the tip.

"Lean forward, hands on the headboard."

"Yes, Daddy."

I guide her shins over my thighs, catching her feet between my legs. I surge up as I press her hips down. I lodge myself deep in her, and she screams as I fill her. I wrap my hand in her tangled, damp hair and fist it.

"Ride my fucking cock, *chiquita*. Beg for more."

"Yes! Fuck me, Jandro. Hard. Fuck me sore."

I let her grind her clit against my pubic bone as she rocks her hips. I set a pace that makes the bed slam against the wall. Thank goodness for penthouses. I have no neighbors beside me because my condo takes up the entire front side of the building. Joaquin lives across the hall from me, and his condo takes up the entire backside.

"I don't hear you, *chica*."

"More, Daddy! Fuck me... Please, harder... I want to come... Please make me come... I want to make you come."

She obeys me, begging every few thrusts as her tits swing above my face. I lift my head and shoulders off the bed and latch on, alternating sides as I suck and bite.

"I'm getting close, Daddy."

I shift how she rides me, making her bounce on my dick. She shakes her head, not liking how her clit isn't getting the friction she needs.

"Third phase, *chica*."

"*NO!*"

She wails her response, clearly not in agreement with my plan. It's as much an orgasm denial for her as it is for me—except I'm doing it to keep from ending this prematurely. She's got me harder than I've ever been. That's saying something because I'm in a perpetual state of blue balls with her. I'm hard all the damn time.

My free hand wraps around her throat, and she leans into my hold.

"Real breath play or just this?"

"Real."

I gradually tighten my hold, watching her every reaction. The last thing I want is to terrify her or hurt her. I want—need—her to know her trust isn't misplaced. She rides me as I choke her. Her eyes close, but it's her choice. They don't droop shut. I don't ease up. She grows wilder as she goes back to rocking on my cock. I shift my gaze from her face to her hands over my head. Her fingers are claws before they ball into fists and press against the headboard. She throws her head back as best she can, giving me the entire expanse of her throat. Color blossoms on her cheeks and darkens by the second.

I release her, and she inhales a deep gasp. I slip my hand into her hair and push her toward me. I kiss where my palm just rested before devouring her mouth. I push her away and return my hand to her throat. We go through three rounds of choking and kissing before her expression intensifies. I know she's close to her orgasm.

"Come for me, *chiquita*."

She does her best to nod as I tighten my hold the most I've done so far.

"Five...Four...Three...Two...One. Now, *chica*."

I release her, and her back arches as she screams, and her cunt clamps around my cock.

"Daddy!"

"*Chica!*"

Fucking hell. This is the most powerful orgasm I've ever had. They keep getting better every time I'm with Vita. Every time I fall for her a little harder, the experience becomes a little more intense.

I sit up and release her hands. She caresses my shoulders, and I realize her bondage may have put me in control, but denying her touch was a punishment to myself.

How do I balance my need for control and dominance with my need to give in to her?

Chapter Thirty-One

Alejandro

I left Vita sleeping. I know how emotionally exhausted she must be since she explained the conversation with Salvatore and Sylvia just before she fell asleep. I'd give anything to spend the night alongside her, but I don't have that luxury right now. Instead, I'm sitting in *Tio* Enrique's study as his phone connects a call to Maks.

"It's never a pleasure, Enrique."

"I'm hardly calling to invite you over for tea."

"What do you want?"

"So grouchy, Maks. Not getting enough beauty sleep?"

"Don't fuck around, Enrique. The twins and Laura all have the flu. It's been a long fucking night."

Laura grew up next door to Pablo and Juan. We've known her since we were all kids. It's how Javier and Madeline met years ago, long before they got together as a couple. Before Juan fucked it all up, Laura and Madeline considered *Tio* Enrique their uncle.

The hostilities have dimmed now that Madeline's part of our family. She's as close to *Tio* Enrique as she was as a kid, and Laura's coming around. She's no longer threatening to gouge the L and the M out of *Tio* Enrique's arm.

They're two points on a cross with P and J as the other two. He has a cluster of three stars on the back of his right shoulder, each with a J in the center. On his opposite shoulder is a sun with an A in the center. All his *sobrinos* and his honorary *sobrinas* are immortalized on him, proof that nothing can separate him from family.

Despite the improvement in his relationship with Laura, Maks still can't stand him. He'll forgive none of us for the shit that's happened ever since he and his brothers and cousins became involved with their wives.

"Maks, we gave you the opportunity to clean house and unfuck yourself. When things went to shit in Germany, your lazy ass did diddly. We went from a humongous problem to a potentially insurmountable one."

"What the fuck are you going on about, Enrique? Your hyperbole is annoying."

"I'm talking about the Volkovs."

Tío says nothing more, waiting for Maks to speak. However, we all know he won't admit anything.

"They're grown-ass men, Enrique. They make their own decisions."

"And they beg for scraps from your table every morning. You're losing more and more control by the day, Maks. How much longer do you think you can last?"

Maks's laugh would terrify a lesser man. None of us flinch.

"The Volkovs are insignificant. They're like little worker bees. Each has a very short life expectancy. When one falls, there're plenty more to replace them."

"I'm glad you think that, Maks, because I'll happily wipe out all of them and leave you to deal with the Albanians taking their place."

We all know that chaps his ass, since that'll be monumentally inconvenient if the balance of power shifts that significantly in Boston.

"Whatever they've done isn't my problem, but I'm certain it's an unintentional benefit for all the shit your family's caused mine. Take it on the chin like a man, Enrique."

I clench my jaw since Maks is only digging himself deeper into this. This isn't a good time for his machismo. The only thing that can come of it is regret. I'm certain Maks is swearing up a storm in at least two languages, despite no outward sign he's pissed.

"You'll be the one taking it, Maks, and you won't enjoy where I shove it."

"Enrique, threaten me all you want, but it won't change what's already happened."

"I think you know by now that I don't make threats. I merely make promises. So, hear me very well. I promise I'll destroy everything in Boston if you don't get this shit under control right now. I've given you the benefit of the doubt not once, but twice. Third time better be the fucking charm for you."

Tío Enrique ends the call before Maks can respond. Everyone turns toward me. It's *Papá* who speaks first.

"How do you want to play this, Alejo?"

They'll defer to me since this is about my woman. They'd take my input if it was just about me, but they'd only defer to *Tío* Enrique. However, since Vita's involved, I take point on this.

I'm our family's chief strategist to begin with. I learned how to play chess when I was four and have been a master ever since. All those board games people gave me as an only child gave me plenty of time to come up with different ways to play against myself. I spent tons of time strategizing.

"We need to decide what we're taking from the bratva and how to end this shit in Italy. It's only going to drag on if we don't. Retribution on one front, peacekeeper on the other."

Pablo nods along with what I'm saying. "I agree. Shit's getting far too out of control in Italy. They're going to bring way too much attention to all the syndicates if they keep going the way they are. That means international law enforcement scrutinizing everything. The more pressure applied on the leading families, the more it's going to cost all of us. The infighting'll embolden smaller factions to think they can step in. They can't, but it'll cost us time, effort, and money to get rid of them too. None of this is good for our economies."

"That's what I'm thinking too, Pablo. We have the means to pay off all four Mafias. It'll piss off Salvatore, Dillan, and Maks, which is the cherry on top."

But what it really does is show the ultimate flex. We have the power to end a war and make four syndicates bow to us. If we position it correctly, then we'll have the other three families indebted to us.

"Pissed off as they may be, none of them comes out the winner. Only we do. You know that means a trip to Italy, right?" *Tío* Enrique raises his eyebrows as he stares at me.

It's moments like this where it's almost eerie to see myself nearly thirty years in the future. I glance at *Papá*. He and I sit exactly the same. Our left ankle crossed over just above our right knee. Our hands rest on the seats beside us in exactly the same position. While I may be the spitting image of *Tío* Enrique, there's no doubt I am my father's son.

"Pablo, can you come with me as my interpreter?"

"Of course."

"We are coming too." *Tres J's* speak in unison.

If only we were still all bachelors and ten years younger, the trouble we could get in together. Some might think I mean drunken debauchery. I'm thinking gambling and extortion.

We spend the next hour planning the trip, deciding we'll work our way from north to south, starting with Vita's family. I'm exhausted by the time I make it home and slip into bed beside a very naked Vita.

"Daddy?"

Her groggy voice is husky and alluring. She's warm and soft in all the right places. I slide closer to spoon her, but she rolls toward me, drawing her top leg over my hip. Fuck if I don't feel the heat from her cunt.

It's an invitation I'd be rude to refuse.

"I didn't mean to wake you, *chica*."

"I'm glad you did. This is far better than sleeping alone."

I sit up and reach for the bag at the end of the bed. I may have made a pit stop on the way to my *tío's* earlier. I rummage in it and pull a few items out.

"What's all that, Jandro?"

"Presents."

"It's not Christmas or my birthday."

"Presents for both of us."

She sits up and reaches for the bag, studying what I've already pulled out as she does. There's a clear spark of interest as she assesses the blindfold, crop, and *Ben Wa* balls I laid out. She peers inside the bag and finds a bevy of implements.

Flogger.

Paddle with holes.

Paddle without holes.

Bullet vibrator.

Vibrator with a clit stimulator.

Butt plug.

Handcuffs.

Wartenberg pinwheel.

Under-the-mattress restraint set.

Nipple and clit clamps.

Shibari rope.

Candle wax.

Ball gag.

Lip spreader gag.

Vaginal spreader.

Lube.

I may have had a field day in the sex shop. I may have been ten minutes late to the meeting at my *tío's*. I may have had the most fun shopping *ever*.

"Did you buy out the store?"

"I left a few things for us to browse together."

I rip open the packaging of the items I pulled out. I wish I didn't need to charge the vibrators. I'll be sure to plug them in when we're done.

"Don't threaten me with a good time, Daddy."

She grins before leaning over to kiss me on the cheek. I turn my head and snag a kiss on the lips. It tempts me to draw it out and make it a proper kiss. But I want us to begin.

"Lie back, little one."

She obeys me immediately as I rise from the bed. She scoots closer. I help her adjust the pillows, so she's comfortable but can still see everything I'm doing until I put the blindfold on. I considered the handcuffs, but I want her to touch me this time. I pick up the crop and hand it to her. She swishes it through the air before landing it across her left breast.

"I know your ass is sore, *chiquita*. I'll be careful."

"I don't mind you giving me a hot ass."

I slip my hand beneath her and squeeze her ass cheek. "You already have the hottest ass I've ever seen."

Her skeptical expression has me snatching the crop from her and pulling her right leg wider. I flick her clit, and she yelps.

"If I say it's the hottest ass I've ever seen, then you better damn well believe it's the hottest ass I've ever seen. I'll never lie to you about my feelings for you. I have no interest in hiding my attraction to you. You will not argue, and you will not convince me otherwise. Speak poorly of yourself or doubt my feelings, and I'll punish you. You might not believe me or agree with me, but you won't change my mind about how much I crave every inch of you."

"Yes, Daddy."

I grab the velvety bag that contains the *Ben Wa* balls and drop the small objects into my hand. I roll them on my palm before easing them into her pussy.

"No matter what, keep them inside you until I say you can let them go."

"Yes, Daddy."

I slide the blindfold over her head and adjust it until I'm certain she can see nothing but darkness if she opens her eyes. I latch onto her right nipple and suck as hard as I dare. Her back arches as she moans. My left hand lifts and squeezes the mound while my right hand flicks the crop against her right inner thigh. She sucks in a breath, and her belly caves and flexes. Her legs spread farther apart. My lips release her nipple.

"*Chica*, this is entirely for your pleasure. This has nothing to do with your earlier punishment."

"Okay."

I chuckle at her distracted response.

"That laugh does things to me, Jandro."

"Oh, really?"

I deepen my voice to the one I've used as a Dom in the past. She moans as she presses her heels into the mattress to raise her hips in her quest for her clit to get some attention.

"Yes, really. All dark and broody like your expressions. It makes me want to run my hands all over you and sit on your cock."

I wrap my fingers around her right wrist and lift her hand to my abs. They flex as she spreads her fingers. I draw her hand down over each peak and valley, then along the V-shaped groove I know she loves. She needs no guidance when she reaches my dick. She wraps her hand around it and strokes.

I groan.

Fuck. I want her so damn much.

Take your time.

Don't end this because you can't control yourself.

My head falls back as I close my eyes, my turn to be deprived of one of my senses. My keen sense of smell registers a mix of shampoo and her natural scent. I hear our soft pants. I feel her soft palm surrounding my hard-on.

I want to taste her.

I want to be tasted.

I climb onto the bed and shift over her until I'm partially reclined. I lift her and turn her until she's kneeling with her cunt in my face, her mouth inches from my cock. She reaches out and finds me again. With no prompting, we dive in. She practically swallows me whole as I lap at her pussy.

She must have Kegeled to keep from dropping the balls while I moved her.

That makes me think again about how tight her cunt gets when she's about to come. My cock twitches, and she hums. I flick her clit before licking it with the flat of my tongue. I thrust my tongue inside her as her head bobs.

The head of my cock brushes the back of her throat, and I wish she could relax enough to swallow me. Instead, she strokes the part of me that's too much for her. Perhaps in time…

I lick the full length of her cunt, my tongue stopping as it passes over her rosebud. Her ass clenches at the unexpected intrusion, but she quickly relaxes. I spread her ass cheeks as I play with her clit again. I picture thrusting into her ass while teasing her with a vibrator. I know I'd feel it through the thin wall. I'd experience what she was. It would add another layer of intimacy.

"May I come, Jandro?"

"Yes."

I rub my stubble against her inner thigh before sliding my hand around the front of her to rub circles over her clit. I thrust three fingers into her as my tongue dips into her cunt beside them. She sucks harder and faster. It takes all my resolve not to come yet.

"I'm coming!"

I let her ride out the euphoria before repositioning her to ride me reverse cowgirl. She braces herself against my thighs until she's following the rhythm I set. Then she leans back, her hands searching for my abs. Her fingernails graze over them, making them flex of their own accord. She arches her back, trusting I'll support her as she slides her hands up to my chest. My left hand slides down from her waist until I reach her clit.

"Fuck, Daddy."

"I am, *chiquita*."

I feel the *Ben Wa* balls as I press them against her G-spot. It's an unfamiliar sensation because I honestly forgot they were still inside her. I like it, and from the way she's shifting restlessly as I thrust into her, I know it's affecting her too. I lift her hands from me and move her arms forward as I sit up. I wrap mine around her, my hands coming up to cup her tits while I kiss her shoulder.

She moves her hair over her opposite one. I nip with my lips and teeth until I get to her earlobe.

"Mine, Vita."

"Yes."

I wrap my right hand around her throat, and like earlier, she leans into it. This time, I keep the pressure light. It's more symbolic than controlling. Her left hand reaches back over my shoulder to cup my head.

"Mine, Daddy."

"Completely. Forever."

"Am I truly your girlfriend?"

"Absolutely. You'll be my wife as soon as you're ready."

"In the morning?"

"Maybe evening. Give your parents a chance to get here."

There's a jeweler in the Diamond District who's made a killing off the Four Families since we give him a revolving door of business. Or at least we have for nearly eight years. That's coming to end soon, but I don't doubt business will pick up again in about twenty years when the youngest generation shops for their rings there. I'll happily contribute to the man's retirement fund in the morning.

I force my ever-strategizing mind back to the present. She twists toward me as though she's looking over her shoulder, but the blindfold keeps her from seeing me. Even with her eyes covered, I can read her expression. It's not surprise. It's deter-mination.

"Don't suggest something you can't promise, Jandro."

"It might not be tomorrow night, but it will be soon, Vita. Nothing will keep me from claiming you, keeping you, and loving you."

My arms encircle her waist, preventing her from doing more than breathing. Even then, I steal her breath with my kiss. It's enough for us to both come. I fill her cunt until it's dripping down my cock. I gather her hair in one hand and end the kiss. My lips find a spot at the top of her back where a shirt will cover. I suck hard enough to bruise, marking her in a place only we'll know about. I give her four more, forming a circle. A symbol for the rings I'll put on her finger. No end and no beginning.

A mission of this proportion can't be rushed if we want all the moving parts to work together. It's been a month since Patrick died. It's been a month since the last attack on Vita and me. We've been lying low in the condo most of that time. I haven't proposed, and we haven't eloped. We agreed to wait until everything's settled before getting engaged. We don't want to begin the next phase of our life with upcoming battles looming over our heads.

So much togetherness could wear on people's nerves. But we're doing well together. I have a gym in one of the spare bedrooms, so we work out together and alone. Both of us favor two workouts a day when we get the chance. We've stuck to running on the treadmill rather than exposing ourselves while running outdoors.

It's not as though we haven't seen daylight or breathed fresh air. We go to the grocery store together and run other errands as needed. We have an entourage with us now. We sense when the other needs space. And if we don't, we communicate well, so we're not trampling on each other's toes.

"Jandro, what do you want for dinner tonight?"

She names two Venetian dishes, while I suggest two Colombian ones. The two she suggests, sarde in saor and bigoli in salsa, are sardine dishes. My revulsion is immediate. She laughs and admits my reaction is the same as when she hears about the little green crabs she hates.

We've been learning more about each other's upbringing and cultures. I'm not quite an honorary Italian yet, but I can do more than just swear in the language. She's definitely an honorary Colombian since she's learned our accent and many colloquialisms to add to her already fluent Spanish.

"Jandro, I love our time together, but won't your family expect you to get back to work soon? Won't you have some trips to Colombia coming up?"

She's deduced much of what I do when I travel there. I'm my *tío's* fixer and chief negotiator in our homeland, the land of cocaine and honey. Fuck the milk; you can get that anywhere. It's ground zero for our largest enterprises. I don't need to explain what I'll do when I'm there.

I haven't divulged all that's planned for our retribution. My family agreed Vita should know what's happening with hers. She's aware we intend to buy their support. When the time comes, she'll put in a good word for us. We hope once the *Mala del Brenta* fall to us—I mean ally with us—the others will take the cue and accept our help. For now, the price of peace for them is keeping any future squabbles away from my family, which now includes Vita.

"No, *chiquita*, there's nothing pressing. You know I've been working from home a lot. Nothing emails and phone calls can't handle."

South America's been shockingly quiet lately. Ever since we eliminated *Tío* Humberto—my *mamá, tíos,* and *tía's tío*—nothing's boiled over. It was a reminder that anyone we don't consider family will meet a violent end. He committed fratricide and murdered my *abuelo* along with having a hand in *Tío* Esteban's murder. *Tío* Luis has reminded a few people of their place within the prisons, but beyond that, there's been no need for me to handle anything in person.

She assesses me skeptically, and I know she believes I'm downplaying things, but I'm not. All things considered, there haven't been any other fires to put out lately. It's actually making the men in my family twitch. This much calm usually comes right before a storm. But so far, so good.

"Will you hand me the eggs, please?"

I pass the carton to her before chopping plantains.

"I admit, Jandro, you're far more domestic than I expected. Domestic and domesticated."

I playfully growl at her and snap my teeth.

"Yes, I don't think it'll take much to housebreak you."

I chuckle. "I can cook and clean, *chica*, especially if you agree to wear that French maid's outfit I got you. That feather duster has your name on it."

She giggles, and the sound goes straight to my cock. Last night's roleplaying was among the best so far. I'll gladly scrub the toilets from now until eternity if she lets me use feathers on her again.

We're seated at the table when my phone buzzes. I pull it from my pocket and read the text.

"I tempted fate, didn't I, Daddy?"

She's taken to calling me that more often since we've had privacy here. I love it every time she does. It has nothing to do with age play or a DDLG relationship. That's not our thing. It reminds me of the trust she's placed in me and how far we've come.

"It's time, *chica*. I don't know how long I'll be gone for, but I'll call and text when I can."

"I appreciate that. I know radio silence is actually a good thing."

In our world, no news is good news.

"We can finish dinner, then I'll take you to my parents."

It didn't thrill her at first when I proposed she stay with my parents while I'm gone. However, she listened to my reasons and agreed that with no family here and her only friends being the Mancinellis, she didn't have the resources in place if something were to go wrong. She'll have men I trust guarding her, but it's not the same as my cousins being there for her. Plus, I don't want her to get lonely.

I've spoken to Carmine, and between his grunts, I got him to agree to look out for her in the case of an emergency and for some reason she couldn't get to my family. He's also agreed to make it easy for Vita to visit Serafina at either of her bakeries. I survived dinner with them here two weeks ago. The women had an animated conversation after being apart for so long. Carmine and I managed not to stab each other with our butter knives.

Once we've loaded the dishwasher, we grab the bags we packed a few days ago and head to my parents'. Everyone's meeting up there, so Vita and I said our private goodbyes earlier today. We've been doing that every morning, noon, and night in case that was the day I had to leave. I force myself not to picture what we did earlier when I handcuffed her to our bed. We got a new headboard and footboard set just for that.

If I do, I'll wind up with a raging hard-on in front of my parents and my *tíos* and *tías*. Just the thought of Vita does that to me. When I see or hear her, or catch a whiff of her perfume, I'm practically baying at the moon. I'll never get enough of her.

It doesn't take long for my cousins and I to say our goodbyes and take off.

Chapter Thirty-Two

Vita

I'm struggling with Alejandro leaving me behind when he and his cousins depart for Italy. My fears stem from being left behind as a mercenary *and* as a Mafia daughter. As though one isn't enough, I have both. He's headed to see my family and adding incalculable danger to his already tenuous hold on life. I know his cousins are the best people to be with him as a team, but I can't help feeling I've left him vulnerable.

The Diaz family may work with and against Italian Mafias, but they aren't Mafia.

I am.

They may know plenty, but I know more.

I've trusted Alejandro to protect me from our previously unknown assailants, and I've trusted him to take care of me emotionally and physically when we're having kinky sex. I've gotten the better end of the deal in this relationship. All I've done is endanger him, while he's done all he can to make me happy.

It's not that I owe him or am obligated. I want to be there with him to help, to make the mission easier, to be an extra set of eyes, ears, and hands. But I also know I could just as easily make it worse. I'm not a Made Woman. I'm not supposed to know a sliver of what I do about the inner workings of the *Mala del Brenta* or any other Mafia, but I was a far too inquisitive kid and teen. It's why becoming a spy, then a mercenary, wasn't a stretch for my moral boundaries. I had none by the time I graduated university.

"Vittoria?"

I turn toward Catalina as she approaches me in her living room. I sense her sadness from saying goodbye to Alejandro. He travels so much that she must feel this weight far too often. I wonder if he fully understands what it means for her to always be left behind.

Matáis doesn't go on many missions because he's the forward face of most of the Diaz family's legit businesses. They need him out of danger and with the least questionable trail of dubious activities.

But I know there were several years during Alejandro's training when Catalina's son and husband left together for the unknown. Now her husband might be by her side, but her only child is gone. Her instinct to protect him practically radiated from her as she hugged him one last time before he gave me a sizzling kiss, then left.

"Please call me Toria."

"Thank you. Would you like some tea or coffee? A snack?"

"I'm all right, thank you."

Everyone convened here, and we shared a meal as a family. I discovered it's tradition. If a mission's planned far enough in advance, then the family gathers before the men leave. It was the most normal family meal I've ever had—like non-syndicate level normal. It was just a bunch of parents teasing their children, and husbands and wives joking about household chores and grocery shopping. It was playful competitiveness among cousins and childhood friends.

Truthfully, it was utterly extraordinary by any standard but unbelievable when you remember who these people are. Some of the wealthiest and deadliest men and women in the world.

"It's different, isn't it?" Catalina offers a maternal smile that makes my shoulders slump.

Back home, nuclear families gather when they can, but it's never the extended family too. I remember when it was *Mamà*, *Papà*, my brothers, and me. When I was little, it was just *Papà* leaving, but eventually my brothers joined him. It was always at least *Mamà* and me left behind. I thought I was prepared for Alejandro to leave because I've waved goodbye before. However, it's an entirely different sensation when it's your partner, the person you love most in this world who's walking into the unknown.

"It is. This is worse than anything before. I don't know how you do it when it's your son."

If this is excruciating, then how will I survive if Alejandro and I have sons?

"Is there a choice?"

Her question's so simple yet so complex.

"No."

"Then you learn to live with it. When you look at any of this as a choice, you fool yourself into thinking it can be something different. For us, it never will be. This is who we are. Leaving and surviving isn't an option. Ignoring a threat to this family leaves us vulnerable. Vulnerability isn't an option when so many people depend upon us for their safety and livelihood. Grief is an inevitable lifelong companion, but who wants to willingly add to it by not protecting our own, our family?"

She's right.

"Sit with me." She gestures toward a loveseat.

"I know it doesn't get easier, so I won't ask if it does. But what do you do?"

"I focused on Alejandro and keeping him distracted when Matáis would leave. Luciana and *Tres J's* would come over once they moved here. Now that it's the *niños* leaving, I have Matáis and Luciana. We distract each other."

I look toward Luciana who's sitting on a sofa between Madeline and Anneliese. I shift my gaze to where Luis and Margherita sandwich Florencia on their own sofa. Elle and Enrique share another loveseat.

Their living rooms are all enormous. I've never seen homes that can fit so much seating in one room.

It's an odd observation, but I noticed it at Enrique and Elle's, and it's the same here. Both homes have enough bedrooms for everyone to stay comfortably. It's a huge house for a family of three. I realized quickly that it wasn't their affluence that prompted them to buy the mansion. It was to have room for the family to gather.

Luciana's house is the same—we drove past it—and only she lives there now. But apparently each of her sons still spends the night there at least once a week. Two of the three now have wives and one has a fiancée who join them. It's not because she can't live on her own. The men, and now their wives or fiancée, enjoy her company.

"I feel so badly for Luciana."

"She definitely has it the hardest, but my little sister is the bravest person I know."

Alejandro explained how rivals with a longstanding grudge murdered Luciana's husband, Esteban, in front of *Tres J's* while the men were still young boys. They remained in Bogotá for several years after Esteban's death. However, the situation became untenable. Street gangs targeted the brothers, and men kept attempting to force Luciana into marriage. They moved to the States as the brothers became tweens. Now, when *Tres J's* leaves, Luciana is alone. She stands to lose all the men she loves most.

Could I wind up in the situation?

There's only one answer to that.

Yes.

"I admire your sister's dedication and fortitude."

In the month we've spent waiting, Alejandro and I have talked about what a future might look like for us. We talked about marriage and children, even though both still feel so foreign to me. I accepted I would have neither when I became a mercenary. They still seem like such hypotheticals rather than certainties.

Alejandro admitted he hopes we only have daughters. His cousins feel the same. They'd love nothing more than for the Cartel to end with their generation. That the women in the family be untouchable to whichever family takes over and that no more Diaz men have to serve the Cartel. The genetic lottery makes that unlikely, but, apparently, it's in all of their daily prayers.

"Faith helps." She offers me another kind smile that has a wistful note.

Turns out Catalina, Luciana, and Margherita are devout Catholics. Elodie and the men are lapsed like I am. Picking which commandments to follow makes our relationship with God complex. But they say there're no atheists in foxholes. In the Four Families—three Catholic and one Eastern Orthodox—that's true. It's the same for mine. We're all more than C and E—Christmas and Easter—Catholics, but the hypocrisy and duplicity aren't lost on us.

"I—"

The burner phone buzzes in my pocket. I pull it out, not recognizing the number. I set up my regular phone number to forward calls to this one. I've used Alejandro's secure line at our condo—I've gotten used to thinking of it that way—to speak to my parents a few times. They've just been quick check-ins, a silent agreement among us not to discuss anything that puts me in the middle.

Everyone looks at me as I rise. I walk over to Enrique and show him the screen. He frowns and shakes his head while shrugging.

"Do I answer it?"

"If you want."

Well, that doesn't help much.

"Hello." I answer with the call on speakerphone.

"*Señora* Diaz-to-be."

That's a fucking odd greeting.

"Who is this?"

"A neighbor to the north."

An Eastern European sounding neighbor.

I watch Enrique's face, and I know he recognizes it. So does Elle.

A knot forms in the pit of my stomach. It's bad enough that Enrique knows who this is. That Elle does too makes me want to vomit. That's not a good sign.

Elle stands next to me and whispers in my ear.

"Yuri Volkov."

My eyes widen.

The man's supposed to be dead.

He's the Boston bratva's former *pakhan*. His nephew inherited about five years ago.

Is he calling me from the grave?

Wouldn't surprise me if he's a bona fide demon.

"How's the weather in Boston?"

"You know who I am, *Señora*."

"I do. Your reputation precedes you."

"But was it Enrique or Elodie who told you who I am?"

"Like I said, your reputation precedes you."

"But I died before you became a mercenary."

I don't like that he knows anything about me when I know so little about him.

"Infamy lives on."

What the fuck does he want?

He's toying with me, and I can't show my impatience.

He cackles before coughing.

Not dead—yet, but ill enough he stepped down.

"What do you want, Mr. Volkov?"

"Your boyfriend needs to stay away from Boston."

"He likes chowder."

I have no idea if Alejandro does or doesn't.

"Be that as it may, he's not welcome here."

"Then you should've left him alone."

Does he think Alejandro's in Boston?

Is that where he really went and not Italy?

I stare at Enrique, trying to determine if Alejandro lied to me about his destination. It wouldn't surprise me if he did, but I'm assessing the realistic danger Alejandro's in right now when he's supposed to be somewhere over the Atlantic.

"What's done is done. Put the past behind you, *Señora*."

The word sounds so strange with his Russian accent. He keeps on insisting upon using the honorific for married and older women. He's making a point that I'm a Cartel woman, not a Mafia one. He's not the one who gets to sever my ties to my family.

"Calling me doesn't do that. What do you want, Yuri?"

I can be patronizing too. Any false respect I used before is gone now.

"Tell Alejandro and his family to stay out of Boston, and we'll leave you both alone."

"You believe I, as a woman, can convince the Cartel's ruling family to do anything."

"I think your golden cunt could convince Alejandro of anything. You have him pussy whipped."

I want to sink through the floor.

Mortified.

That's what I am.

Mortified.

It's not like I believe anyone in his family doesn't know Alejandro and I have sex. They've surely figured out we have tons of it. We're not unlike any of the other couples who can't keep their hands off each other, but I don't need that rubbed in his parents' faces.

"If you're going to insult me, then this conversation ends."

"My apologies."

Coglione. Fucker.

"I'll pass the message along. Goodbye."

"Uh-uh-uh. We're not done. He won't survive putting a foot in Boston. He won't come alone, so that means his cousins will die too."

"Why risk annihilation?"

Yuri cackles again. It's like nails on a chalkboard. He's aware we've learned of the Volkovs' involvement, so he anticipates retaliation. The last we heard, it was Dimitri—Yuri's nephew—behind this because of the shit he fucked up for Anton. Yuri comes as an even greater surprise.

"My family's going nowhere. Pissed off as the Kutsenkos are, they need us. If you kill us, then you'll not only piss off the New York bratva, you'll wind up with a far worse family in charge here."

"You believe that gives you carte blanche to murder any Diaz man."

"It does. It's not in your in-laws favor to seek retribution."

The man's truly senile.

"You risk more than you can gain, Yuri. Why is Alejandro worth so much to you? It can't just be you thought you were doing Sergei a favor."

"I have my reasons."

"Who'd he reject?"

"My niece."

That stuns me.

I expected him not to name anyone, but if he did, it would be some guy Alejandro wouldn't do business with. I look at Catalina and Matáis, who appear as bewildered as I am.

"Why would Alejandro be involved with your niece?"

"Grad school sweethearts. He refuses to step up as a father to his son. I'm tired of waiting."

Can my heart stop while my mind runs a mile a minute?

My gaze sweeps the room. Madeline, Florencia, and Anneliese appear horrified but not because they believe him. Catalina, Matáis, Luciana, Luis, Margherita, Enrique, and Elle appear disgusted and enraged.

Catalina joins me, standing on the opposite side of Elle. She leans in to whisper directly in my ear.

"That is absolute bullshit. If my son had a child, there's no way in hell he'd ever deny the child. He'd abandon this family before abandoning a son."

"Did you come up with that lie on your own, Yuri? Or is your niece that good at manipulating you? Alejandro has no children."

"Look at the image I sent you."

My phone buzzes with a text message. I look at the screen and tap the text icon. I pull it up and tap on the image to enlarge it. It's a paternity result saying Alejandro's ninety-nine-point-nine percent likely to be the child's father.

"All this proves is you have a computer and a printer."

"Give up Alejandro, *Señora*. He has a family, and there's no room for you."

"This is the most poorly concocted lie. Why are you making things so much worse for yourself? Does Rurik know what you're doing? Does he know what you're claiming about his sister?"

Yuri's other nephew, Rurik, is now *pakhan*. He's close to his twin sister, and he'd have beaten down Alejandro's door years ago if this were true.

"Who do you think got the DNA test done?"

"How did you get any of Alejandro's DNA to test it?"

"You assumed the fire eliminated all traces of you being in that warehouse."

I've watched Enrique since my gaze landed on him right after Catalina denied Yuri's claim. He rolls his eyes. I'm certain this isn't true. The Diaz family wouldn't be that careless. They had their men drive up there as soon as they learned where we were. The team swept the place and got Zorzi's and my *zia's* remains out before the authorities could inspect the scene. There's no way they left anything on the metal that cut Alejandro—assuming it hadn't melted.

"*Señora*, pass along the message. Alejandro stays away from Boston and pays all the child support he owes my daughter."

The line goes dead.

"*¡Esto es ridículo! ¡Mi hijo jamás lo haría!*" This is ridiculous! My son would never.

Catalina's tone strikes a chord of fear in me. Her expression drives it home. The woman is ready to go on a rampage. I'm not far behind her. She turns to me and clenches her jaw before she takes a breath and speaks.

"Toria, those are lies. Alejandro would never do something so irresponsible. And if he had been careless, he would've taken responsibility."

"I know, Catalina. Alejandro would *never* ignore his child regardless of how the child came about. I never believed any of it."

Catalina turns toward Matáis, and his expression matches his wife's. Enrique steps forward and puts a staying hand on his sister's arm.

"*Hermanita*, we'll handle it." Little sister.

He gestures toward Luis. The woman's at least eight inches shorter than her brothers, but in that moment, she's more intimidating than either of them could ever be. She ignores Enrique and keeps her attention on her husband. He slides his arms around her waist, and Enrique steps back.

"*Mi amor, confía en nosotros. Lo solucionaremos.*" My love, trust us. We'll make it right.

Alejandro's mother narrows her eyes at her husband before she glances at Luciana. My gaze shifts to my future aunt-in-law. What I see passing between the women makes me want to run and take cover. There's a storm brewing, and I'm about to be in the eye. I shift my focus to Madeline, Florencia, and Anneliese. They look as wary as I feel.

"Yuri is not only trying to destroy Alejandro, he's trying to take our daughter with him. I want him gone."

Daughter?

She's accepted me into the family, and Alejandro and I aren't even engaged.

I mean, we pretty much are.

I force myself not to look down at my ring finger. It's feeling naked right now. Alejandro hinted he'd change that when he returns.

"*Mi amor*, he won't sleep another night."

"It's not just him. His family and Maks's need to understand."

Enrique steps forward again with Elle beside him this time.

"*Hermanita*, we'll go up there and sort it out. Luis, call the pilot."

"I'm going, Enrique."

"Catalina—"

"*Hermano*, you won't convince me. Not if it involves *mi hijo*." My son.

The irate woman stresses the last two words in Spanish. She could jab her finger into her chest and not convey stronger emotions than her tone already does. I know they're mostly speaking English for the other women's—except Florencia—sake. But Catalina's accent's gotten so strong I'm not sure the non-Spanish speakers can understand her.

I'm unsure why this is the hill she's willing to die on. I can't imagine she's gone on other missions, but she won't back down. As though she reads my thoughts, she turns toward me.

"We have history with this family. Yuri tried to kidnap Alejandro when he was five. He thought I wouldn't notice because Luciana, Margherita, and I were chatting while the boys played in the park. Luciana and *Tres J's* came to visit while Esteban was away with Enrique. He banked on the cousins being just as excited to see each other as I was to see my sister. The *cabrón* still has three bullets inside him. One from each of us. No one touches our *niños*. Now *Señor Sin Huevos*—that's where I shot him—thinks he can get revenge. *Ni de puta casualidad.*" Mr. No Balls. Not a fucking chance.

"Caty—"

"Come with me or not, Mati, but I'm going."

"You can't kill them all."

"Watch me."

Husband and wife stare at each other. I believe Matáis isn't exaggerating. I think he genuinely fears his wife will annihilate the Volkovs if she goes to Boston.

"We're going too."

I swing my head toward Luciana and Margherita as they join the men. Only Luis hangs back, shaking his head. The man clearly knows when he and the other men are outnumbered.

"Kiko." Elle rests her hand on her husband's arm much like Enrique did to Catalina.

"Not you too, Ellie."

"The ladies and I are your best bet. I know Boston better than any of you, and I know Yuri as well as you, Luis, and Matáis. I know where he hides. They won't expect us. They don't know who I am because my family still guards that secret. I can get us in and out faster and with no one noticing far better than you can."

"Ellie, no."

If this weren't so dire, it would be astonishing to watch the *jefe de jefes* face off with one of the world's most infamous and elusive mercenaries.

"I'm going too."

Catalina turns her head toward me. "I never thought you wouldn't."

Chapter Thirty-Three

Alejandro

"Piero, thank you for meeting with us."

"Alejandro, it's good to see you in one piece."

Not good to see me, just good to see I'm alive.

Better than him being disappointed I'm alive.

"We've tried to stay out of your war, yet you and your enemies and allies draw my family in. We should've ended this after what happened to Anneliese's family. Instead, we gave everyone in Italy and Sicily the benefit of the doubt and focused on the O'Rourkes and Kutsenkos. Our graciousness is over. Accept our offer, Piero."

I haven't told him yet what we're willing to offer. It's irrelevant. We could offer the moon or a pile of shit. He will bend to my will.

"You come to my home. You—"

"You're a don, not Marlon Brando. We're here to help. No one in Sicily or the Continent will lose, so you all win."

"That's not a win. That's a stalemate."

"Call it a truce."

"Not good enough, Alejandro. The war didn't start to keep things the same."

"It won't remain the same. Each family will come out richer for it. You'll get money and territory beyond your borders."

"You think you can play God."

"No, but I'll be an avenging angel if anyone comes near Vittoria ever again."

I shift my focus to Vita's father who's remained quiet after our initial greeting. He defers to his don, but I know he has thoughts he wishes he could share. Our gazes lock, and I know he agrees with me. He'll support anything that protects his daughter.

"Don Piero, we stand to gain as much as we could lose."

Nicolò states the obvious, so it's almost patronizing, but it's also common sense. It's the gentlest nudge he can give in front of us. Piero stares at me, ignoring my cousins. Pablo sits to my right while *Tres J's* stand behind our chairs in Piero's study, much like they did during our meeting with the O'Rourkes.

"What're you offering?"

"Each faction gets ten million to divide amongst themselves. Each family gets two of our trade routes into the Netherlands, Belgium, or the UK."

Those are among the largest narcotics markets in Europe. The Netherlands and Belgium are the gateways to Europe, and the UK has a high consumption. We're also among the leaders in weapons trading in the Western Balkans and Turkey. Our dominance in the region means we have money to spare.

"We have those already."

Hijueputa desagradecido. Ungrateful son of a bitch.

"You can accept our offer, or we can take it all from you. If you wish to live by 'it's better to give than to receive,' we're happy to accommodate your generosity."

I keep my tone casual and my body language relaxed, but they know a jaguar does the same while it observes its prey.

"You expect us to be happy with your handout while you give the same to our enemies."

"We're giving you first pick."

"And that makes it better?"

"It does when we've put no restrictions on which we'll give away. I never said I'd be so accommodating to anyone else."

"You'd give away your best access?"

"Only to you and only for Vittoria's sake. But the offer isn't open-ended. It has an expiration date."

Piero's disdainful expression turns into a glower. I shrug.

"Piero, my family won't strike yours, but our offer to help won't last forever. If you turn your back on us now, we'll do the same when you need us. And with the way things currently stand, you will need us. You and the Torettas are in a better position than the Camorra and *'Ndrangheta*, but when we lend them our support, you'll lose your advantage."

Nicolò assesses me, knowing I'm not bluffing. He's determining how significant their losses will be if they reject us. He glances at Pablo and knows switching to Italian won't do them any good because my cousin'll just tell me everything.

I observe the don and his *consigliere's* silent communication as they look at each other. From what I learned on the plane, they've been best friends since they were in kindergarten. They bullied all the other kids, then they extorted them in high school. Their family names made them untouchable. They trained back-to-back, becoming Made Men together. It was a foregone conclusion Nicolò would rise to *consigliere* when Piero ascended to his throne.

I've seen the same thing among *Papá*, *Tío* Enrique, and *Tío* Luis. I have a vague memory of *Tío* Esteban being no different. My cousins and I are like this too. Reading one another's minds—the synchronicity—comes from a lifetime of trust and loyalty. Family by blood and by choice.

I allow the silence to stretch, knowing filling it won't convince them. It's their turn to come to me. After all, I flew a quarter of the way around the world to meet them. That I'm uninvited is semantics.

"We want a route in the Netherlands and in Belgium."

Of course, they do.

"We'll give you the second most profitable routes through Antwerp and Amsterdam."

"Second?"

"Don't bite the hand that feeds you, Piero."

"We'll think about it."

I rise, and so does Pablo, signaling the meeting's end. I extend my hand, and Piero shakes before I reach out to Nicolò. Pablo does the same.

"Piero, I told you we won't strike you for Vittoria's sake. But fuck us over, and I'll see it as an affront to my future wife. I won't forgive."

His left eye twitches, but he nods. From the corner of my eye, I watch Vita's father. His expression's not friendly, but it's not as aloof as it was when we arrived. I think I've earned his approval. I pray I have.

Once we're in our vehicle on the way to the airport, my cousins and I discuss the meeting.

"How long until he thinks he can slide by?" Javier truly trusts no one outside the family.

"After the wedding. Probably before the reception's over." Jorge has little faith in any of the Italians.

"We planned to work our way south, but perhaps we should go to Sicily next. See the Carosis' ally before their enemies, that way they don't feel left out." I genuinely want my cousins' opinions even though this is my mission to lead.

"No. I say we see the Camorra next. We have an in with them through Friedrich, even if he's in Germany. We already told him we'd visit, so I'm certain he called the don to let him know. If we're delayed or they find out we chose another Mafia over them, then they won't be as receptive. We use whatever reaction we get from the Camorra and 'Ndrangheta to wrap things up with the Torettas." Jorge's argument is valid.

"All right, we continue as we planned. The Camorra in Naples, then the 'Ndrangheta in Calabria."

We chat about the most recent soccer matches we've watched, who's gotten gains when we work out, and what we want to eat when we land. Basically, the same shit we always talk about when we're killing time.

"That went about as well as seeing the Camorra. *Carachimbas de mierda.*" Fucking faces of vaginas.

It loses something in the translation, but I'm pissed. While Piero wasn't excited to see us, he saw the merits of our argument. The Camorra and 'Ndrangheta weren't as amenable. Not that we assumed they would be, but they dug their heels in, bragging that the Carosis and Torettas couldn't hide behind us forever. They can't and won't, but they didn't put themselves in our crosshairs.

"I'll wire the money to their offshore accounts." Jorge has his laptop open while we ride to the airport.

"And I'll let our *regios* know what's coming."

Pablo mentions our *regionales*; they're the ones who oversee trade routes and commerce in specific regions. It has nothing to do with being royal or regal.

"And I'll let *Tío* Enrique know we're implementing our fallback."

We always have contingencies for our contingencies. If they hadn't cooperated, we'd have blown shit up left and right until they begged us to accept their apologies. We won't blow up every-thing, but we'll punish them.

"*Hola, sobrino.*"

"*Hola, tío.*"

My cousins echo me as we greet *Tío* Enrique.

"*Niños*—"

"What happened?"

Five voices ask the same question. Our *tío* only calls us that when he's about to break bad news.

"Where are you?"

"In the van on the way to the airport."

Europe still doesn't have enough large SUVs to carry so many men our size. We're in a passenger van with one leading and one following, both filled with our men.

This is going from bad to worse if *Tío* Enrique's ensuring we're truly alone.

"Alejo, Vittoria got a call from Yuri."

"That *cabrón?* I thought he was dead. What'd he want?"

There's a protracted pause.

"He claimed you impregnated his niece and are a deadbeat dad."

"He motherfucking what?!"

I see red. The allegation alone is enough to turn me into a blaze of fury, but he said that to Vita.

"Alejo, no one believes him. Vittoria basically told him he's full of shit."

"That means jack shit to me. He told her. I'll fucking kill him."

"About that..."

I sweep my gaze across my cousins, and our expressions surely match to the point of being uncanny. The Diaz family genes are stronger than our non-Diaz genes. We're five peas in a pod. But none of my cousins feel the overwhelming rage I do.

"What did our *mamás* do?"

It's Joaquin who voices what we all want to know. It's one thing to attack us in business. Our mothers stay out of that. But when the attacks get personal, there's no holding them back. Take every stereotype of Latinas ever created and multiply them by infinity. That's our *mamás*.

"Fucking hell, *Tío*. There won't be a brick left standing in Boston. Please tell me they haven't left yet."

Jorge's voice trembles, and there isn't a damn thing unmanly about it because we'd all be the same. We're surely all a shade of green as our stomachs flip.

"We're on the way to the airport."

"*Mamá?*"

Once again five voices fill the air.

"Only Ellie is with me in the town car. Your *mamás* and their men are in the SUV behind me."

"*Tía* Elle, you have to stop them." I'm flat-out begging.

"I'm the one who told your *tío* he can come or get out of the way."

I run a hand over my face as I look at my cousins.

"Maks is going to shit a brick."

"Maks understands his place." *Tía* Elle's voice could freeze a volcano.

"*Tío?*"

He knows what I'm asking, and I know the answer. But I need to hear him.

"Vittoria's in the SUV with them."

I'm going to be sick. I'm ready to hyperventilate. Of course, I fear for all their lives. They're on a mission, but knowing both my parents and the woman I love could die together makes my ears ring and the blood pound in my temples. My gaze hops from Jorge to Joaquin to Javier. They only have one parent left. I look at Pablo, who's already lost a brother and could lose both of his parents.

This is a fucking disaster of epic proportions.

"Where's my wife?" Jorge, Javier, and Pablo ask together.

"Luis and I are staying behind with them. They're at my house."

Tío Enrique's comment does nothing to reassure me. Only Anneliese isn't a sharpshooter, but Jorge's been teaching her. She's fucking close. Madeline and Florencia have killed before. None of them would flinch before pulling the trigger. It's only a tiny mercy that they aren't on the way to the airport too.

"I need to talk to *Papá*."

"Alejo, that isn't wise. There's no way *Tía* Catalina won't listen too." Pablo warns me, but I don't care.

"I'll take my chances."

"*Sobrino—*"

"No! I'm not losing everyone I love. I've almost lost Vita too many times since meeting her. *Papá's* come close to dying more times than I can count. You know *Mamá's* the most ruthless of all your siblings."

My mother is the kindest, funniest woman you'll ever meet, but cross her... Or worse, cross our family—her husband and child...

"We need to go home."

"Alejo, you need to finish things with the Torettas. How'd things go in Calabria?"

"*Tío*, changing the subject doesn't change any of our minds."

"You will finish the job."

I grit my teeth, and my nostrils flare. Once again, my expression matches my cousins'.

"*Sí, jefe.*"

All of us respond the same way. That wasn't our *tío* making a request. That was our boss giving a command.

"How did things go?"

"The same as in Naples. They agreed eventually."

"Give them the reminder, then go to Palermo."

"But that'll delay our return by at least two days."

"Then so be it."

My cousins close their eyes, and I do the same. We count to ten before we open them. The habit ingrained in us as children when we learned to contain our frustration when things didn't go our way. At three, none of us knew we were already in training.

"*Sí, jefe.*" I answer on everyone's behalf.

"I'll be in touch when we land, Alejo. I'll keep you posted."

Tía Elle's tone is as unbendable as *Tío's*, but it's quieter. I believe and trust her, but I'm still panicking.

"*Gracias, tía.*"

The call ends, and the five of us sit in silence, digesting what we just heard. Syndicate business isn't supposed to touch the women in our families. They're to be revered, placed on a pedestal and protected. They're to keep their hands clean. They're untouchable.

Those are the fucking lies told to young men. Or rather half-truths. We do all those things because we want to and because they're the right thing to do.

What nobody says is that we keep them out of syndicate business because they're far more ruthless than the worst of us. While women are more likely to bring world peace than a bunch of men, they're also the ones who could burn it all down with a single match. Their collective patience and memories exceed men. No one will convince me otherwise.

What we're all thinking is the world peace they could bring isn't what the UN envisions. It's the women of the Four Families banding together, bringing along our septs and branches. If the other three families learn the women in mine marched into battle because of this personal attack on me—the absolute worst slight to my honor—they'll show the world why their men are as powerful as they are. It's the women who stand beside them; the silent force that truly keeps the balance of power. There'll be peace because there's nothing left.

"We need to get our shit done fast."

"We know, Javier." I close my eyes again and swallow. "*Lo siento.*" Sorry.

He doesn't deserve me snapping at him. He takes it in stride, understanding that as much stress as he and the others are under, it's even worse for me because Vita's in the middle of this.

"We'll send half the men back up to Naples. We'll take care of this shit in Calabria tonight. We leave for Palermo in the morning."

I force myself to think clearly.

We head back to the airport and explain to the men the new assignments. We don't explain why. None of them need to know, and they're all wise enough not to ask. The men who remain go to the hotel with us.

It's the middle of the night when my cousins and I, all dressed in black with tactical gear, approach the port city of Reggio Calabria. It's not only where the 'Ndrangheta are based, it's also the largest port in the area. It's at one end of the shipping lanes across the Strait of Messina, the route to Sicily.

"We're in and out in less than ten."

My cousins and I each partner with one of our men, fanning out to the warehouses and docks we know the *'Ndrangheta* control. We don't give a shit who's waiting at home for the *'Ndrangheta* men running the shipyard. It's like a movie as we pick off anyone in sight. It's not shoot first, ask questions later. There are no questions we care to ask. We're carrying explosives that'll light up the night like it's New Year's.

My partner—José—and I scout our dock and quickly realize there're people on the nearby boats who'll see us working and would most certainly notice a pile of explosives sitting between their vessels.

"I have to go in."

José takes the backpack I hand him and opens it along with the one he carries while I strip off my shoes, shirt, and pants. I'm never excited to get into the water in a marina. Too much oil in the water, but necessity dictates I do. As I shove my clothes into the backpack I carried, I glance at the next dock over and notice Pablo doing the same thing. He must sense me because he glances over. We nod.

While I undressed, José prepped the explosives to make it easier for me once I'm in the water. Our backpacks are water-proof, so I lift mine and strap it to my front. I ease into the water like some spec ops guy in a movie. All of us have the camo paint on to disguise us. We've been told with our dark eyes, we often appear like soulless demons when our lighter skin's covered.

Good.

Motherfucker.

This water is fucking freezing.

My huevos just sought shelter inside me.

I glide under the dock and snap on my headlamp. I keep it tilted down enough for me to see but not to be a beacon to anyone else. Pablo—our highly trained biologist and chemist—is our explosives expert. He works alongside Javier, whose undergrad was in engineering, even though he became an attorney. I trust them to ensure I don't blow myself up.

I work efficiently while I attach the bombs to the farthest part of the dock I can safely reach and the part closest to shore. We want nothing left. I swim back to the shore and hoist myself out just as Pablo does the same. There's no time for us to dry off, so we use our shirts to shake off enough water for us to struggle into our pants. Then we're stuffing the shirts back in the bag and taking off.

"Everything set?" Pablo glances over his shoulder.

"Yeah. You?"

"Yeah. The one at the end didn't attach well, so we need to get this done."

I tap my earpiece, and I hear *Tres J's* responses. They, along with their men, sprint out of the warehouses and join us at the SUVs. We pile into the vehicles, and Jorge and the other drivers reverse out of the marina. They could turn around, but we want to watch the show. Pablo has Joaquin's laptop, and he's tapping away like an evil genius bent on global destruction.

Okay.

Maybe that's a little exaggerated, but he's concentrating extra fucking hard.

"*Tres, dos, uno.*"

The night sky resembles ancient Pompeii with flames leaping and debris dropping like blobs of lava. The docks explode into shards of concrete and wood, rising then falling. The buildings' glass, drywall, and steel burst outward like one of those decorative boxes strippers supposedly pop out of.

Alarms and sirens go off as screams fill the air. We're now outside the marina's gates and pulled off onto the side of the road in the shadows. Jorge and the other drivers turned off our headlights a quarter mile before we got here and have kept them off. We're well hidden as we wait. It's ten minutes before emergency services arrive with enough crew and tools to put out anything. Firefighters work to control the dock fires, protecting yachts and commercial vessels, to stop the spread of sparks to nearby structures.

It's nearly an hour before Don Pasquale and his underboss arrive. Both men gesture animatedly as we use our parabolic sonic listening devices, and Pablo translates. They're swearing up a storm as they argue over who's the likely culprit. Even from a distance, it's easy to recognize which man is the don since the firefighters keep their heads lowered whenever they address him. Everyone else stays away while the underboss directs their men to investigate.

"It's Dante." Joaquin hands me his phone.

"How'd it go?" He's leading our team of *sicarios*—hitmen—in Naples.

"A booming success. There's nothing left, *Capitán*."

"Good work. Any of the Camorra show up?"

"Yes. The don and *consigliere*, but they left just as angry and confused as they arrived. We used the parabolic listening devices and the translation app to know what they were saying. They suspect the *Mala del Brenta* and *Cosa Nostra*."

"All right. Thank you. Get to the airport and get down here fast."

"*Sí, capitán.*"

My cousins listened to the conversation, so they're up to speed on what's happening in Naples. We slip out of our parking spots and head to the airport. While we're on the road, I call the *'Ndrangheta* don, knowing he'll be extra pissed to learn we were so nearby, and they had no clue.

"*Chi diavolo è questo?*" Who the fuck is this?

Pablo whispers the translation.

"Don Pasquale, this is Alejandro Diaz. We met indirectly this evening."

The man switches to English for my benefit, and I can tell he's unimpressed when he answers.

"What does the Cartel want now? What do you mean we met indirectly? I've been at my office all night."

"Until you arrived at the marina."

"You?"

"Me. Hold on a moment while I add someone to the call."

"Don't tell me to hold on. What the fuck do you want?"

I ignore him as I make it a three-way call with the Camorra don, Gennaro Ricciardi.

"Gentlemen, you've both witnessed the consequences of being uncooperative. Would you like to reconsider how you return our generosity?"

"*Figlio di puttana.*" Motherfucker.

"*Pezzo di merda.*" Piece of shit.

I'm uncertain who calls me what, but I don't care.

"The *Mala del Brenta* took my offer, and I expect the *Cosa Nostra* to do the same. It's the beginning of a beautiful friendship with them. You, on the other hand, are not making good choices. Tonight was a taste of what I'll do if you drag your feet again. Take the money and the trade routes, be more cooperative the first time I tell you to, or I'll keep blowing up warehouses. I'll move on to factories, and I'll shut down your imports *and* exports. You will lose far more than you stand to gain. When you do, it'll strengthen the *Mala del Brenta* and *Cosa Nostra*. They will sweep in and sweep you out. This agreement not only brings peace but also prosperity."

I give my speech, then fall silent. I'm certain they're texting each other like teens hiding their phones in class. They want no one knowing they're consulting each other. I feel like playing the music from *Jeopardy*.

While they're hemming and hawing, we arrive at the airport. We'll have a while to wait before the jet arrives with the guys from Naples. Once the calls end, we'll all catch a nap. I just need this shored up before I can rest.

"Fine, Diaz. You have a deal."

It's Gennaro who relents first.

"You can expect your first installment tomorrow morning."

"Installment? Wait—"

"You think I'm giving you that much money and access without a sign of good faith on your part? How have you lived this long?"

Pasquale intervenes before this deteriorates, and I go ham on their asses. We have time to blow up more shit down here while we wait for our men to arrive.

"We'll accept what you send and look forward to doing business with you. We'll keep our end of the agreement and not contest the boundaries between our territories and the *Mala del Brenta* and *Cosa Nostra*. We'll cooperate the next time you make us an offer we can't refuse. Thank you, Alejandro."

I didn't expect the 'Ndrangheta to be the reasonable ones, but I'm happy it only took them losing about six million each in property damage and lost goods. I don't want to be here any longer than we have to. I've barely hung up with the two leaders when my phone rings with a number I don't recognize.

"Hello."

"*Signore* Diaz, this is Don Alberto Toretta. You've had a busy night."

"I have, but you already knew I would. Have you spoken to Piero?"

"Yes, and Salvatore. Save yourself the trip. We'll agree."

My brow furrows as I look at my cousins. That's *way* too easy.

"Are you accepting because Piero made a sound argument, because Salvatore's insisting, because you don't want your properties blown up, or because my girlfriend is best friends with your granddaughter?"

"Yes. All of the above, *Signore* Diaz. It wouldn't be good for business or my family to refuse."

He attempts to muffle a hacking cough. It's one of a man who doesn't just have a cold or the flu. It's a man who smoked way too much in his life. His voice is reedy compared to what I've heard on phone taps and recordings. I suspect his nephew, Francesco, will be don before the end of the year. I almost feel badly for Sylvia and Serafina. Sylvia will lose her father, and Serafina her grandfather.

I don't, but almost.

"Tying up loose ends?"

There's a pause before the older man answers. "You could say that."

"Should Vittoria call you or go for a visit with Serafina?"

I learned during our dinner with Serafina and Carmine that Vittoria used to go to Sicily on vacation with Serafina, Serafina's parents and sister, so she knows Alberto. She was as close to the older man as she could be without being family. She'd been fond of him as a child, so I won't deny her the chance to say her goodbyes.

"Not yet, but soon...Thank you."

He tacks on his gratitude at the end, and I barely hear him. This time, it isn't because his voice's weak. He just doesn't want to admit his appreciation.

"The first installment will be available tomorrow."

"And you won't interfere any further as long as Vittoria is safe. *Capisce.*" You understand.

"*Capisco.*" I understand.

I guess I do know some Italian that isn't profanity. I've heard Salvatore bark the word to his nephews many times, and I've heard their response.

I'm happy to stay out of all of the European Italians' business for the rest of my life, but that won't stop me from being a meddlesome fuck for the Italian Americans. Salvatore isn't off the hook for life just because he helped negotiate this truce among his family.

Alberto says his goodbyes just as I do, and the call ends. By the time we're done, the jet's landing. It's only a thirty- or forty-minute flight from Naples to Reggio Calabria.

"*Primos, vamos a casa a ver a nuestras mamás.*" Cousins, let's go home and see our mamas.

God only knows what our women have blown up by now.

Chapter Thirty-Four

Vita

It's been ages since I've been in Boston. I love the city. There's plenty to do and plenty to see. The people might be "Massholes" when they drive, but for the most part, they're nice enough. I've never been here for pleasure, but I've seen various parts of the city —some better, some worse.

I've been to Lynn before.

Lynn, Lynn, city of sin.

You never come out the way you came in.

A fun little ditty I learned the first time I came here. It's a North Shore town and hosts a fairly large Russian community. It's not where Yuri Volkov lives—now that it turns out he isn't dead. Oh, no. He moved his ass over to Chestnut Hill in Brookline to rub elbows with the proper parts of society—but he spends plenty of time here. Loan sharking, fencing, and extortion don't go over as well in Chestnut Hill where the average household income is six figures.

Instead, he takes advantage of Lynn once having the third-largest Russian community in the States. The *testa di cazzo*—dickhead—has a predictable routine which includes coming to Lynn to relive his nineteen-nineties glory days as an enforcer. He may as well strut around in an Adidas track suit and gold chain to complete the stereotype. Maybe a few ruby and emerald rings to boot.

"Is that him?" Luciana points toward the *stronzo*.

"Yeah. The one on the right."

Elle, Luciana, Catalina, Margherita, Matáis, and I are in a commercial van that looks like it belongs to a high-speed internet provider. There's a camera with a mic in what appears to be the keyhole on the front passenger door. We're watching Yuri and three men sitting outside at a coffeeshop. They act as though they don't have a care in the world as Yuri pours vodka into one guy's glass. Definitely not on the menu for most people.

"Yuri, aren't you worried about sitting out here? Diaz family won't ignore your claims."

A guy in a blue pinstriped suit with a heavy Russian accent, sitting to Yuri's left, sounds nervous. When I say heavy, I mean "strong like bull." No a, an, or the in English because those definite articles don't exist in Russian.

"No more than I've ever been, Boris. Look at me. I sit outside because no one dares approach me. Those who do, haven't survived."

I can practically hear Catalina grinding her teeth. I glance at Matáis, and his fists are balled on his lap. I return my attention to the screen as the men continue to chat. Nothing useful comes of it until the end, when the quietest man finally joins the conversation.

"Yuri, what about our shipment from Montreal?"

I assume they mean weapons, but it could be something else.

"What about it, Mikhail? They're just after-market car parts. You're making it sound like bigger deal than it is."

By after-market, he means black-market, stripped-down parts. Montreal is one of the most notorious places for unrecovered car theft. The vehicles get jacked and are almost immediately on ships to Europe. They're often gone before the owners can report them missing. I don't readily see why car parts are coming to Boston from Canada. It doesn't seem profitable for anyone.

"You know it's not air filling those tires."

As one, all of us in the van grin.

Jackpot.

"I know, I know. Rurik thinks I'm headed to Cape for weekend, but I'll be in Brighton South. Don't worry."

"Where's Rurik going to be?"

Mikhail presses a little too hard, and Yuri turns a steely gaze on him, assessing his colleague. If the guy doesn't back off, he'll die before the deal happens. I observe Yuri's drinking buddies more closely. I assess their body language and where they're looking as their gazes wander from the conversation.

"They're agents."

"What?" Luciana turns her attention away from the screen to look at me.

"I don't know which agency or even which nation, but they're undercover."

"How can you tell?"

Matáis sounds genuinely curious, when I feared he might be dismissive. I should've given him more credit.

"It's their subtle mannerisms. I don't believe they're Russian, even though their accents are accurate. The way they survey their surroundings. They're not looking for who's going to kill them, or at the very least rob them. They're looking for who sticks out as a potential criminal they can arrest or flip. It's too speculative. They aren't spies. They're law enforcement."

"And you believe Yuri hasn't keyed in on that?" Catalina tilts her head as she puts the men's body language under a microscope.

"I think he has, and he's toying with them. I don't know if he's got at least one of them on his payroll, or he's just biding his time. Maybe he intends to bait them into giving away their investigation. Maybe he's manipulating them to take out a rival. There are too many variables for a hypothesis, but these men'll get in our way if we aren't careful."

"These men knew what they were getting into when they took

their jobs. If they fear for their lives when they face us, then they should've picked another line of work. I'll sleep just fine when they're dead."

Catalina plans homicides as casually as she would order coffee. I shift my focus to Matáis, and I know he won't disagree.

"What do we know about Rurik?" Luciana changes the subject by asking a question I don't know the answer to.

It's Matáis who does. "Shrewd businessman. Before he took over as *pakhan*, he was a lot like me. The forward face of their legit enterprises. He gained many people's trust and earned his family millions through his aboveboard connections. Even now, many question just how dirty he can be when he maintains what appears to be a pristine corporate reputation. He's a shark, but an ethical one."

Matáis can't say the last bit with a straight face, and the rest of us laugh.

"Yuri, where will Rurik be?"

Our attention returns to the screen as Yuri's staring match ends when Boris echoes Mikhail's. The guy in the middle, sitting across from Yuri, has fallen silent. He was the chatty one earlier, which makes this sus. What made his attitude change?

Yuri flicks a hand by his right thigh, and I doubt the other men notice. His attack dogs—bodyguards—materialize and stand behind the men. He dips his chin toward the man in the middle, and two guards grab the guy's shoulders.

"Don't you want to know where Rurik is too, Vlad? Five minutes ago, you couldn't shut fuck up. Now you're so quiet. Why, huh?"

Despite his decades speaking English, he—like his companions—still drop the definite articles. It tells me he learned the language later in life. Probably after he moved here.

Why're they speaking English?

I expected we'd need a translation app for the others to understand, or I'd be interpreting.

This hasn't felt right since the beginning.

I wondered about them speaking English when the four men sat down together, but I let it go. Now I'm certain Yuri's doing it because he assumes at least one of them's wearing a wire. He doesn't want any confusion when he skirts around the questions he doesn't want to answer.

Fuck.

The last thing we need is to take out three agents if they're in the wrong place at the wrong time tonight.

But I'll do it if it means Yuri understands he reached way too far when he targeted Alejandro.

"I'm quiet because I'm waiting for your answer." The man's defiance borders on the suicidal.

"Rurik is with his mother."

That's anticlimactic. I didn't expect that. I shift my focus to Catalina, hoping someone can explain why Yuri wouldn't just say that earlier.

"His mother's terminally ill. She's in hospice."

Elle's the one who explains. If anyone would know, it's her because she's from Boston and from her past. In a normal situation, it would sadden me to hear this. But if Rurik allowed Yuri—turned a blind eye or is so ill-informed about what's going on—to target Alejandro, then I have no sympathy for him.

The men rise and part ways. It's time for us to end this fucking shit.

Matáis maneuvers the van into a street parking spot on the backside of the salvage yard. We followed Yuri here after waiting for him for most of the day and into the evening. He disappeared into a restaurant and didn't come out until after dusk. We kept our distance as we tailed him to ensure he didn't notice us. This isn't the same van as earlier. That was far nicer. This is a sixteen-passenger van that looks like it's on its last legs. It blends in far better here.

"Mati, you good?"

Catalina looks over at her husband as she checks her rifle. Matáis didn't bother putting up an argument when Catalina—who's leading this mission—told him he'd remain with the vehicle. In fairness, it's pretty much the most important job on the mission. No vehicle means no escape. It doesn't matter if you hit the mark if you can't get away.

"In and out, Caty." There's warning in his tone.

"I won't waste time, Mati, but you know I'll have my pound of flesh. We all will."

I remain quiet and so do Elle and Luciana, but we're all thinking the same thing. Yuri and anyone unfortunate enough to be with him will suffer.

Matáis sighs and nods. It's not like he's pussy whipped or anything, but he and Catalina have been married for nearly forty years. He knows which battles to pick. They exchange a kiss that makes me look away.

Oh, God.

They're practically my parents!

Could Alejandro wind up with a little brother or sister the same age as our kids?

From the way they kiss...

I don't know why he's an only child, but it's definitely not from lack of passion.

Luciana elbows me and grins. "Welcome to the family. It's a wonder I only had three since my Este and I were the same. Pablo and Juan were difficult deliveries for Margherita, even though she's a midwife, so she and Luis only had two. They—" She smirks in her sister and brother-in-law's direction. "—only had one because Alejandro used to scare the shit out of them with the way he could disappear. They said their hearts couldn't take the risk of having more than one. The *niño* could disappear while you were looking at him, I swear. Luckily, he was usually looking for food or playing outside on his swings. However, losing him in the Bogotá airport and finding him chatting with the pilot and co-pilot sealed his fate as an only child."

I picture a miniature Alejandro wandering through the congested airport, impatient for his flight. I'm surprised Luciana didn't say he was charming the flight attendants. I bet he was cute as sin when he was a child because he certainly is handsome as sin now.

I drop additional ammunition into my cargo pocket before pulling on my beanie. All four of us women have bulky hoodies on to disguise our shape and beanies to cover our long hair. We have camo paint on to keep our skin from glowing in the dark. Gloves hide our skin and leave no traces.

Matáis sprayed the sliding passenger door earlier, so it's silent as it opens. Elle pulls it nearly closed but not all the way. While Elle and I were trained for missions like this, Catalina and Luciana weren't. At least, that's what I assumed until I watch them fall into position like well-trained Cartel soldiers. Catalina leads with Luciana behind her right shoulder and me behind her left. Elle brings up the rear, pivoting frequently to ensure no one follows us.

Margherita's on her own mission right now. We'll meet up with her after we're done with Yuri. Hopefully, she's as successful as the rest of us intend to be. Matáis has a drone buzzing overhead, so he'll direct us as our eyes and ears around the entire salvage yard.

"*Osa uno, claro avanzando.*" Bear One, clear moving forward.

Catalina is Bear One, Luciana is Bear Two, and Elle is Bear Three—as in Mama Bear. I'm *Cachorra*—Cub. I think it's rather sweet.

We advance to the fence, where I step around Catalina and cut the wires until I can pull it back wide enough for all of us to pass through. I resume my position in our formation until Matáis guides us to a vantage point where we can see and hear the meeting.

"Yuri, your nephew won't like this."

It's the man from the café today. The one who told Yuri that the shipment's more than just ordinary car parts.

"I give no fucks what he thinks, Mikhail. He's little boy who's not ready for job like this. He should stay with his mama and let me run things again."

Elle gave me an abridged history lesson on the way up to Boston. The Elite Group—a bratva branch's senior council—ousted Yuri. They brought Rurik to power instead of waiting for him to inherit after his uncle's death. They allowed Yuri to retire.

"Canadians should be here in ten minutes. They texted me when they got off highway."

According to Elle, they forced Yuri out for botching several major deals that cost their branch millions. It landed four high-ranking *bratok*—soldiers—in prison with life sentences. They took the fall for Yuri—of course. He was their *pakhan* at the time, so they'd never narc on him.

On the way here tonight, Elle also shared that Yuri refused to allow Rurik's mom to get treatment while Rurik was away at university. Rurik didn't know the severity of his mother's condition until he moved back to Boston after studying at Stanford. Apparently, the woman's been holding on for the past six years with inoperable cancer. Rurik stepped in to get her proper care; however, she's exhausted all treatment, so now they're waiting.

"If they're not here in fifteen, I'm leaving. You deal with them."

If Yuri weren't going to die tonight, I'm certain Rurik would do it the day his mother passes. She's Yuri's younger sister. If he weren't Rurik's uncle, he wouldn't be alive. According to Elle, as long as his mother's alive, Rurik can't bring himself to kill his uncle. He'd be too ashamed in front of his mother. All bets would've been off once she died. I almost feel guilty that we're robbing him of that. Almost, but not really.

"Yes, Yuri."

Mikhail sounds deferential, but the four of us watch him roll his eyes as Yuri turns away.

"Tractor trailer approaching from the west end of the lot." Matáis gives us an update.

We hear the truck rattle toward us before we see it. When it comes into view, there are six vehicles that have seen far better days. I suspect they were fine when they crossed the border. Then someone bashed them up, shattering the windows to make them look ready for the junkyard.

We observe as the driver pulls around to the spot in front of Yuri, Mikhail, and eight of their *bratoks*. Neither of the other guys from this morning are in sight. It makes me wonder if they're staked out somewhere nearby.

"Mr. Volkov, thank you for letting us dispose of these here. They don't look in good shape, but there are plenty of serviceable parts left."

Yuri shakes the driver's hand before prowling over to the trailer. He climbs onto a tire then onto the truck. He's more agile than I expected. He moves along it, inspecting the vehicles. He arrives at an SUV with a spare tire on the back hatch. He pulls a knife and slices into it, pulling back the rubber. White powder pours out of the slit. He presses the rubber back into place before swiping his index finger through the tiny mound at his feet.

He rubs his finger along his gums.

Disgusting.

So unhygienic.

"Good stuff. Pay him."

Yuri gestures between Mikhail and the driver. The money exchanges hands. Once the driver inspects the cash and accepts it, the bratva soldiers hurry forward to unload the truck. Once they've parked the six vehicles side-by-side, it's time for us to move.

Elle fires the first shot—a bullet between the driver's eyes. There's no time to marvel at her expertise. The moment blood squirts from his forehead, the men reach for their weapons. Matáis assured me Catalina and Luciana were sharpshooters, but I had my reservations—until now.

I watch the women pick off two men with speed that rivals mine and Elle's. The eight soldiers are down within seconds. Elle disables Mikhail with a bullet in each shoulder. Catalina shoots Yuri in both feet, knocking him to the ground as he howls. We step out of the shadows.

"Who fuck are you?" Yuri bellows, his fractured English taking some of the power from the phrase.

"The last person you're going to see alive."

Catalina marches over to him and draws back her left foot. She drives it into the guy's *coglioni*—balls. Alejandro told me Catalina and Luciana both played D1 soccer in university. Apparently, that means the highest level of collegiate sports in the States. Both played forward and were top scorers. With the force I watch her put into that kick, I'm certain her team was victorious at most matches.

Elle and Luciana drag Mikhail away and interrogate him. Catalina and I remain focused on Yuri.

"*Suka!*" Bitch!

"Swear at me all you want, little man. It'll make cutting off your *huevos* all the more enjoyable before I shove them down your throat. You'll swallow them because they're too small to choke you."

I don't know if she understood the word or just guessed it was profane. She nails him again, this time aiming higher to get his dick. He writhes in pain as he grabs his crotch.

"Do you know who I am, *Señor* Volkov?"

"Some crazy Latina whore."

"Mmm-mmm. Watch it, *Señor*. My husband can hear you. He's very protective. I'm Catalina De Santos Diaz."

She lets her name hang in the air, and I watch the moment Yuri realizes who he's gawking at. The color drains from his face.

"I see you recognize my name."

She squats, but not within arm's or leg's reach for Yuri—not that he's doing much with bullets in each foot and his hand still cupping his groin.

"Can you guess why I'm here, *Señor?*"

She exaggerates the honorific, and it's condescending as fuck. She's my heroine.

"Did little Alejandro need his mommy to save him?" Yuri aims for patronizing, but he's gasping too much.

"My son doesn't need me to rescue him. He has his future

wife for that." She gestures toward me. "This isn't about saving him. This is about punishing you. You looked in my son and future daughter's direction. You put targets on them. Those two things are a given in this life. It comes with the territory. I hate it, but I accepted it long before my son was born. However—"

She rises and drives her right foot into his belly, making him double over again. She spits in his face. It's an impressive amount.

"You sealed your fate by accusing my son of being a deadbeat dad. Your lies attack his honor as a Diaz. That—that I will not forgive. The Diaz men are many things, but nothing—*nada*—comes before family. To claim he fathered a child he's ignored—that he even fathered a child without being married to the woman—after all, we're still Catholic—means you claim he has no integrity. You will discover what it means to cross a Cartel mother, *Señor* Volkov. Strip him."

The men who remained in the shadows outside the junkyard stream into the area. Three of them rush forward and grab Yuri. The other seven head to the vehicles to unload the real shipment.

I glance over at Luciana and Elle and notice Mikhail isn't doing too well. Luciana's brass knuckles plow into his face. She and Elle are standing off to the side, so when the inevitable blood sprays from the man's mouth, it doesn't hit either of them. Elle has a thin wire wrapped around his throat. I can see where it's already cut into his skin. She has the ends overlapping, and she pulls tighter when the man doesn't respond to whatever Luciana just said.

I shift my focus back to a naked Yuri, who's trying to squirm away. Dirt covers his ass and the backs of his legs. He looks pathetic.

"Since you claimed my son couldn't keep it in his pants, I figured I'll make the same claim about you." She pretends to lean forward and peer down. "I think my foot shoved your *pequeña polla* y *huevos* inside you. I can't find them." Little cock and balls.

I step forward, standing across from Catalina. "Let's see if I can find them."

I use the muzzle of my rifle to poke around between his thighs.

He tries to kick his legs at me, but I step all of my weight onto his left shin.

"If Alejandro had a child, I would love them like my own. I'd accept them and their mother. That isn't the part that bothers me. What I can't forgive is the slight against his honor. You tried to disgrace him with your lies. You wanted to make him look small in front of the other syndicates because everyone knows what family means to *los Diaz*. You underestimated just how far we'll go to avenge that name."

It's not mine yet, but I'll defend it like it is.

I jam the muzzle toward his ass crack, and he howls as he tries even harder to evade Catalina and me. She slams the butt of her rifle into his diaphragm. I pull my knife from my pocket and position myself above his head. I trail the tip of the blade along his cheek, pressing just enough to nick without cutting the skin. His gaze meets mine as he stares up at me, my face hovering halfway over his—always mindful that he might spit at me.

I have a serious aversion to that.

Gross.

"There's more to this than your bogus claim. Why did you really target Alejandro? Are you trying to burrow that far up the Ivankov branch's asses that you thought this would score you major points? Or did they order you to do it?"

"No, no. They definitely didn't order me to do anything. When you started shooting, I thought it was them. They aren't— uh—pleased with me right now."

How the mighty have fallen.

A little pain, and he's spilling his secrets.

"Whose puppet are you?"

He glances between Catalina and me, obviously weighing how much more pain and humiliation he can bear before he dies. It's clear the moment he decides to tell us everything, hoping we'll kill him the moment he's done. Fat fucking chance.

"Podolskaya are pissed at Maksim and his brothers again. They made peace few years ago, but it fell apart when Kutsenkos refused to renew industrial machinery deal with

Polish corporation. Kutsenkos don't approve of corporation's business practices. Allowing Podolskaya to be heavy investors was their biggest complaint. Without Kutsenkos' backing, business is going under. Podolskaya are losing millions and want revenge."

Yuri's accent has thickened so much that it's difficult to understand him. It's more than just dropping the definite articles. He's slurring his words, and his voice is raspy too. We don't have much more time before he passes out.

"And since they don't dare attack the Kutsenkos directly, they ordered you to kill Alejandro and make it look like the Kutsenkos were involved."

It's not challenging for me to surmise the simplified version of the plan.

"*Da*." Yes.

"Why were you involved?"

"Podolskaya helped put my family in power here. We owe them for that, but I was one who told them to invest in Polish business. They blame me, so this is my punishment."

Catalina chuckles, and it sends chills down my spine.

"You've been doomed to die since the first time you heard Alejandro's name. If it isn't us, then it'll be the Podolskaya for failing or the Kutsenkos for making them the scapegoat. What else do you know?"

She places her booted heel on top of his right foot, prepared to apply pressure if he doesn't answer quickly or thoroughly enough.

"Maks and his brothers warned me you'd retaliate. They're focused on Moscow and dealing with their enemy there. They left me to defend myself."

"Is there even a child or did you completely fabricate that?"

"My niece has child and refuses to name father."

Catalina steps on his injured foot. "You're a sicker fuck than I already thought to bring an innocent child into this. It would've been far better if you'd made that up like you did the paternity results. Rather than kill you and dump you, we're going to make sure every Russian neighborhood in Boston understands your fuck-up. We'll remind them that *los Diaz* are *the* Cartel in the States."

She pulls her own knife from her belt and squats beside Yuri again. This time, she grabs his right hand and severs his thumb.

"I should shove this up your ass. *Hombres.*"

She calls out to the men who're not done collecting the hidden products from the tires and chassis. They've stripped out radios and catalytic converters along with siphoning gasoline.

"*Sí, señora.*" Rafael, the leader, steps forward.

"*Córtalo en pedazos. Deja una rama en cada barrio. Entrégale la cabeza a Rurik. Deja su pene y sus huevos con su esposa.*" Cut him up. Drop a limb in each neighborhood. Deliver his head to Rurik. Leave his cock and balls with his wife.

"*Sí, señora.*"

A laugh comes through our earpieces. I'd forgotten Matáis listened to all of this.

"Caty, we have a shipment going out to St. Petersburg in two days. Send his heart and entrails to Moscow."

It'll be a detour for their men, but it'll be worth it to warn away the Podolskaya. Catalina and I walk away from Yuri and head to Luciana and Elle. We're about to ask them what they learned from Mikhail, who's bleeding out from a slashed throat, when Matáis patches through a call from Margherita. We can all hear it through our earpieces.

"I got into the hospital without a problem, but it wasn't so easy to get into the pharmacy. It took forever to rewire the alarm to make it look like it was still on even though Marco turned it off. I got what I needed and with my badge turned around, I made it to Igor. No problem injecting the narcotics. It'll definitely look like a delayed overdose."

Igor's Yuri's son. Apparently, he's a good enforcer but dumb as shit. Their Elite Group would never let him become the *pakhan.* Our men tracked him down and roughed him up. They dropped him off outside the ER. We didn't have what we needed on hand, so Margherita used her NYC hospital badge to disguise herself. She shot Yuri's son up with enough narcotics to prompt an investigation. It'll tie up the Volkovs for weeks with at least the DEA. If Yuri's death turns out to be a blessing in disguise for them, the investigation won't be.

"*Buen trabajo, hermana mía.*" Good job, my sister.

"Learn anything from this one?" I point to Mikhail.

"Not much. He's definitely an agent—ATF—but too new to understand everything he heard and saw." Elle shoots the dead man an annoyed expression.

"New to the case?"

"New to law enforcement. He could only relay events and conversations. He didn't understand half the subtext. Dumbass was going to get himself killed one way or another."

"Did he admit he was an agent?"

"Not in so many words, but Luciana did a good job getting him to confess."

"Oh?" I shift my focus away from Elle.

"I stabbed him in his *micro pene* a few times. He didn't like that." Micro dick.

"Are you done?" Matáis's voice once again comes through the earpieces.

"*Sí, mi amor. Es hora de volver a casa con nuestro hijo.*" Yes, my love. Time to go home to our son.

The four of us walk through the main gate as the Cartel men take care of what's left of the man who fucked up royally and the idiot agent.

"*Mamá!*"

"*Mamá!* Vita!"

I wince at the irate bellows from the other side of the barely open front door. There's a chorus of five voices calling for their mother and one calling me. Alejandro and his cousins rush into Enrique and Elle's house. Five enraged faces that are all far too similar glower at their mothers. Alejandro's gaze darts between Catalina and me. He's unsure who to rip into first.

It's Pablo who leads. "*Mamá*, I can't believe you. You could've gotten yourself arrested, sneaking into that hospital."

"So?"

Pablo throws his hands up in exasperation.

"*Mamá?*" Alejandro sounds as exasperated as Pablo looks.

"You thought I'd ignore this?"

"I'd hoped."

Alejandro sighs as he regards his mother. She, Luciana, and Margherita wear unrepentant expressions, and Elle merely looks smug as she smiles. Before anyone can say more, Florencia, Madeline, and Anneliese come downstairs. It cuts the conversation short as husbands greet their wives. All but Joaquin lift their women off their feet and practically devour their wife or fiancée. Luis and Enrique greeted their wives just inside the door, so they'd already had their reunions.

"Is it done?" Florencia sweeps her gaze over the men and women.

"It is."

Alejandro and Catalina respond together. The relief on the men's faces is sweet. It's clear how much they care for their wives and mothers. I believe it upset them more to know we got involved than it did the women when the men took off for Italy. We're accustomed to them leaving, not knowing when they'll return and often not knowing where they're going.

It's a taste of their own medicine in the worst way. They're not equipped—not conditioned—for this kind of fear.

"Jandro, did things go well with Piero?"

"The best of all the meetings, but we'd expected that. They and the Torettas agreed with little negotiation."

He arches an eyebrow at me. I know that means the other two syndicates likely lost a few hundred thousand euros, maybe even a few million. Serves them right for not acquiescing to my boyfriend. We won't discuss more in front of Florencia, Madeline, and Anneliese.

It makes me feel guilty that they're excluded, but they reassured me when we returned before the guys that they don't want to know more. Ignorance is bliss. They feel badly that I know as much as I do.

Perhaps Alejandro will tell me everything—or maybe a fraction, but I won't press to know. I won't put him in the position of refusing me or feeling guilty over divulging too much to me. This is syndicate life homeostasis. The men return; the women greet them, and whatever happened while the family was apart ceases to exist. We all trust that whatever separated us is resolved.

For Catalina, Margherita, Elle, Luciana, and me, it is. Yuri's dead. He can't spread any more lies about Alejandro. The Volkovs understand they're on notice—with everyone. Rurik called Enrique before we got on the plane. Matáis explained Rurik made some sort of restitution, and Enrique's satisfied. How things stand with Maks isn't my problem, but I know it's not good.

That's putting it mildly.

Alejandro hugs his father, and it appears that Matáis passes something to Alejandro, but I can't tell what it is. All of us move into the living room, and the couples take seats while Joaquin sits with Luciana. He drapes his arm over the back of the loveseat casually, but it's clear he's hovering over his *mamà*.

Before I can sit, Alejandro shifts his hand in mine and lowers himself to one knee. I gulp, a lump forming in my throat.

Is he?

Oh, shit, he is!

"*Mi amor*, I knew when we met you changed my life. You impressed me and intrigued me when you came to New York. I fell for you in the club, and I fell in love with you in the hotel. I didn't realize how deeply until we fought alongside each other for the future we're destined for. You're my soulmate and the one person I want to create a life with. Will you marry me?"

"*Sì, amore mio*." Yes, my love.

I'm too emotional to speak English or Spanish, reverting to Italian. Alejandro rises after slipping the ring on my finger, and I nearly knock him over as I dive into his arms. The kiss we share would have parents covering their sons' eyes if they could reach. We keep it short, but it's intense.

"*Chiquita,* I love you more than life." Alejandro whispers this to me, keeping his pet name private, even though I'm certain the other men call their women that too.

"I love you too, Daddy." I whisper just as quietly, a secret I'm sure I share with the other women.

Never did I imagine the man I set out to kill would be the one man who makes me feel alive.

Epilogue

Alejandro

I roll onto my side to gaze at my wife as we lie on a double beach lounger. I can't believe today's our fifth wedding anniversary. We're back in the Seychelles where we honeymooned. We've been here for a week, and we'll spend another one here.

"What're you thinking about, Daddy?"

"How'd I get so lucky?"

"You've asked me that nearly every day for five years. How do you not know the answer yet? You're mostly perfect most of the time."

"That doesn't mean I'm lucky."

We've had this talk over and over because I'm still in disbelief that my soulmate is this intelligent, resilient, fearless, and kind person. She grins at me as she rolls onto her side to face me.

"You hit the genetic jackpot, and you're fucking sexy as fuck. That's your luck. How could I not fall for you?"

She teases me with the same answer she often gives. She reaches out and trails her fingertips from my temple to my jaw before she leans in to brush a kiss across my lips.

"Did you know you're even luckier than you realize?"

"Oh?"

"You get to be a *papà*."

My eyes widen so much they hurt. My heart races as I replay her words over and over. I reach for her and pull her on top of me as I roll onto my back. She straddles me, and I harden immediately.

"Really?"

"Yes, Daddy."

"How?"

I babble the stupidest question. I've known how babies are made since I was at least eleven, and from how her cunt rubs against my cock, I can guess how we conceived. This position or at least one of ten others.

"Should I remind you?"

We're on a private beach under a cabana that blocks us from anyone's prying eyes unless they're out to sea. We've sunbathed naked every day since we arrived. It's not that either of us cares about tan lines. We're enjoying sex on the beach every chance we get. Vita rocks her hips as she coats my cock.

I sit up, one hand fisting her hair while the other rests at the base of her throat. I reject the idea of tightening my hold, now I know she's pregnant. Instead, it rests heavily—possessively. She lowers herself onto my dick, and we both groan. That moment when our bodies join never gets old. That first sensation of her taking me into her, no end and no beginning.

She shifts from resting her hands on my shoulders as she sank onto me to crossing her wrists behind her back. We'll have to rethink how we enjoy kinky sex. I never want to hurt her, and now that there's a little life growing inside her, I won't risk her or our baby.

"How long have you known, *chiquita*?"

I know she hasn't seen a doctor since we arrived, but maybe she brought a test with her.

"The morning we left."

"You've kept this to yourself for a week? How long did you suspect you were?"

I know she hears the hurt in my voice. She wraps a lock of my hair around her index finger as her nails skim over the top of my spine.

"I threw up two mornings in a row, and the *fette biscottate* I baked the other day made me want to gag. It's never done that before. I took a test the morning we left. I waited because I wanted us to be completely alone."

I twist to peer around the cabana shade and realize none of my cousins are nearby. There wasn't a chance in hell we were traveling anywhere without a retinue of guards, and the other men in my family are the only ones I trust for this. It's that way when any couple travels. I've left Vita at home to guard my cousins and their wives. It's just how things work.

During other trips out to the cabana or beach, the guys have given us space but were within yelling distance. Right now, I can see them much farther in the distance and back at the house. I don't know how Vita convinced them not to be closer because I'm certain she wouldn't tell them our news before telling me.

"Are you excited, *chiquita?*"

We started talking about trying a month ago, so Vita went off her birth control. Apparently, she and I are pretty fucking fertile.

"I am, Jandro. I can't believe we're going to have a baby."

"I hope they look like you, little one."

"And if I want them to look like you?"

"Definitely more like you."

I press her head forward and capture her mouth in a kiss no one should witness. I spank her playfully, and she rides me as she throws her head back. The creamy expanse of her neck calls to me. I lick from her shoulder up to her jaw before nipping at the bone. I bite her earlobe before blowing lightly into it. She moans just like I knew she would. I kiss behind her ear.

"Fuck, *chica.* You're going to squeeze the cum from me before I'm ready for this to end."

"I can't help it. I want you so fucking deep inside me, and I don't want to let go."

"Who decides?"

"You do."

I lift her off me and place her on her hands and knees as we face the water. I snag her flowing cover up and twist it until I drape it over her shoulders, crisscrossing it between her tits, then drawing it under and lifting them before tying a knot behind her back. I made an improvised harness. Our Shibari rope is in our room. If only I'd known to bring it with us. I wish I'd brought several implements out here.

I snatch her towel from her side of the lounger and twist it before pressing her to lower herself to her shoulders. She places her right cheek on the cushion while I draw her arm back and use the towel to bind her wrist to her thigh. I wriggle my towel out from beneath us and repeat my handiwork on the other side. She does her best to watch me, but I know her view's limited.

Positioning her the way I want, I bring my right hand down on her ass. As I lift it away from her right ass cheek, my left hand lands across her left ass cheek. I spank her like I'm playing the bongos. I twist my left wrist, so I can smack her horizontal crack. That makes her lurch forward as I grab the knot at her mid-back. I pull her back toward me before my free hand contacts her upper thigh. I know that smarts the most since she was unprepared.

"Daddy!"

She practically wails the word before she thrusts her hips back for more. I grab both and impale her. I nearly lose control as I think about the child growing within. We made it together, but it makes Vita mine in a way that takes my normal protectiveness and possessiveness and amplifies it a thousandfold at warp speed. I already have no limits to what I'll do to protect her but knowing we're having a child together unleashes something in me—a depravity she can never know about, and I pray I never use.

"Mine, *chica*."

"Yes!"

Even after all these years, I never tire of reminding her. She's sworn she'll never tire of hearing it. She understands my possessiveness is never about limiting her freedom and choices. It's ensuring no one can get away with stealing them from her. She's told me she's never felt more independent than she has since we got together. She's no longer beholden to an intelligence agency or an employer.

She's taken a couple odd jobs, only allowing the other three families to know they hired her after her mission's complete. I follow up by reminding them they owe us a favor now. That's a sweet satisfaction I never envisioned.

I pull out, and her hands twist against her restraints as she reaches for me. I thrust three fingers into her and work her G-spot. She pants between moans. I work her pussy, sliding my pinky in as well. She grows wetter with each stroke of her inner wall. She coats my fingers enough that I ease farther into her until I'm up to my wrist.

"Jandro, I'm so fucking full, but it's still not enough. Only your cock will be enough."

I swipe my fingers inside her, looking for her cervix. When I find it—easy to do since I've fingered her most days for the last five years—I slide my index finger over until I know I've landed on her A-spot. I angle my fingers, so I can massage that along with her G-spot.

She trembles as the sensations overwhelm her. I reach around her until I can tweak her nipple. Hard. She cries out again, the blend of pleasure and pain bringing her close to orgasm.

"Please may I come, Daddy?"

She already knows the answer, but I give it with an extra tight pinch while I stop moving the hand drilling her cunt.

"You shouldn't have kept that secret for so long, little one. Now I'll keep you from coming."

"Dear God, you aren't going to edge me for a week are you?"

There's genuine trepidation in her tone. I've never gone that long, but we've played games where I've made her wait a couple days. When we do, I edge her throughout the day, having complete free use of her.

"Fear not, *chiquita*. You're going to keep coming until you're so spent you beg me to stop. Only then will I fuck your ass until I blow my load there."

I stop tugging her nipple and move to rubbing her clit. I know my wife's body better than I know anything else. I feel her on the cusp of coming, so I freeze. I waited for the frustrated pants to lessen before continuing my assault on her patience. I taunt her, using her need against her as we go round and round in circles. Orgasm denial drives us both wild. During the infrequent times I let her take charge, she tortures me ruthlessly.

"Jandro, please! Everything's more sensitive than usual. I can't control myself like I usually can."

Beside her telling me she threw up twice, it's the first sign her body's changing. I kiss the back of her shoulder as I gentle my hand inside her and return my other to her clit. I rub slow and firm circles over the bundle of nerves. She lifts her hips as high as she can, seeking my cock. I rest it in the division between her ass cheeks.

"May I?"

"*Sí, mi amore.*"

Her body clenches as her arms strain along her sides. When she comes down from her high, I ease my hand out of her pussy and replace it with my dick. I fist her hair with one hand while the other grips her shoulder. I nearly lose control again as I pound her pussy; however, I'm careful not to harm her. She loves it when it hurts, but I never want to take it too far. I'm ever mindful of my greater size and strength.

I pull the towels loose, freeing her hands. I bring her body up to kneel before me. Conscious that her tits are likely more sensitive than I realized, I cup them, enjoying how the harness lifts them even higher. I consider whether they're any fuller than usual. I think they might be.

My thumbs roll over the tightened peaks while our hips rock in unison. I'm creeping too close to my orgasm, so I shift our position again. I lower her until her chest's against the cushion. I hover over her back, most of my upper body weight on my forearms as my chest brushes against her back. She pulls her arms up and rests them between her body and my arms. Our fingers entwine as we both grip the end of the lounger.

"*Te amo, mamacita.*" I love you, little mama.

For the first time, that word has its true double meaning. She's a sexy as fuck woman, and she's a mother. I'm certain I'll call her that as much as I do *chiquita* and *chica.*

"*Ti amo.* I love how that sounds, Jandro." I love you.

I speak fluent Italian now, so we often switch interchangeably among Spanish, Italian, and English. Half the time we don't even notice.

"Come for me in five—four—three—two—one. Now."

My command triggers her orgasm. She loves it when I count down, my voice enough to control her body. We're not in a D/s relationship, but we love the power exchange during sex. I pull out and ease myself into her ass just like I said I would. The vise-like grip forces my release before I'm all the way inside.

"Fuck, Daddy. So big."

"So fucking tight, *mamacita.*"

She giggles, and I groan, nearly in pain from how her body swallows mine. We lie together, enjoying the peace after the frenzy.

"I love how loved and safe you make me feel, Daddy. You always have."

"I'll protect and love you until my last breath, *chiquita.*"

It's just who I am. I've spent my life protecting the Cartel. Now I protect my wife and the family we created together.

Join Alejandro and Vita at their wedding rehearsal dinner where Joaquin meets a woman he can't ignore. Follow Alejandro and Vita home for an extra steamy scene the night before their wedding. Subscribe and download.

One night of passion was all they meant to have when Joaquin and Patricia slip away from Alejandro and Vita's wedding reception. Except that one night left a lasting impression. Now people are after Tre, she's harboring more secrets than she can count, and Joaquin's ready to unleash the full power of the Diaz Cartel in *Cartel Devil*.

Bonus Epilogue

Vita

"Ready for tomorrow, *chiquita?*"

One moment, it feels like years since Alejandro proposed. Another moment, it feels like a day ago. But really, it's been three months. Things wound down with the war among the Mafias once they accepted the Diazes' intervention. It hasn't been dull among the Four Families, and that's what's kept us from having the wedding.

The Four Families have been at one another's throats, stirring up shit worse than it has been in ages. The O'Rourkes and Kutsenkos are still vying for supremacy in Eastern Europe with the Kutsenkos finally taking a hardline against the O'Rourkes. They've both tried to blame the Diazes for various things they've done to the Mancinellis. They fooled no one, so the Diazes and Mancinellis have struck back. But that only increases the rivalries since neither family wants to be out done with the trouble they cause and their retaliation.

"So ready, Daddy. Can you believe we're finally at our rehearsal dinner?"

We just came from the church where the wedding will take

place tomorrow, and now we're going to a family favorite restaurant in Queens. Ironically, it's at the opposite end of the block from Salvatore's favorite place.

"Time's dragged waiting for this, but on the other hand, it's flown by."

"I was just thinking that. You've had to be in Bogotá a few times, and that's when it's dragged. But when we're together, there never seems to be enough time. It goes so fast."

"I know, little one. But we have a month in the Seychelles coming up."

"I feel badly that the other wives will be without their husbands for a few weeks."

Alejandro's cousins will rotate guard duty while we're away. They'll use Alejandro's jet to come and go, since none can be away for the entire month. Not between work and not wanting to leave their wives behind. I know Alejandro wishes they could all be with us, but he understands and accepts that would be unreasonable.

"You know I'll do the same for them. They'd rather their husbands be away to protect us than have to live with something going wrong without them there."

He told me what happened to Maria Mancinelli before she married Matteo, but he was her only family member guard on a trip to Miami. He also told me what happened to Niko and Anastasia Kutsenko and their cousins Pasha and Sumiko when each couple went on a trip. Pasha and Sumiko even had more family with them than the other couple, and they still faced an attack.

"I do, but I still can wish it didn't have to be this way."

"Because you value family just as much as I do."

Alejandro guides me to face him before he gives me a kiss just inside the restaurant's doorway.

"We haven't even tapped our glasses yet, and you're already showing off."

I pull away to look at my friend, Patricia, who I met through Serafina while they were in university together. She's beaming at us as she waggles her eyebrows. She sweeps her gaze over

Alejandro then gives me a conspiratorial wink. I know she's not checking him but exaggerating her attention to make me laugh. I think most women understand I'll claw their eyes out and shove them down their throats if they look at my fiancé the wrong way.

"Alejo was a greedy kid. Not much has changed. He has OCD—only child disorder."

Joaquin joins us, and I observe Patricia assessing him just like he does her. Subtle as they are, there's definitely attraction between them. My cousin-to-be has been away for nearly six weeks. No one's said where, but I suspect Asia. He and Patricia met an hour ago at the church. Their paired together in the wedding party. She's a bridesmaid along with Florencia, Madeline, and Anneliese. Serafina's my matron of honor. Carmine's not stopped twitching since they arrived at the church. He's not a fan of being in the jaguars' den.

"I had to be with you and your brothers around. There wouldn't have been anything left to eat if I didn't hoard it."

Alejandro teasingly bumps into Joaquin's shoulder. A smaller man would've been knocked off balance. Joaquin doesn't even sway. Patricia definitely notices that.

"I just stopped to let you know I confirmed all suites at the Waldorf for tomorrow night. You and your bridal party have early check-in, so you can ready there whenever you want."

"Thank you."

Alejandro and I respond at the same time. We smile at each other, and he tightens his hold around my waist. He leans to bring his lips to my ear.

"The things I'm going to do to you tomorrow night in our suite."

I feel the heat rising in my neck.

"We better find our seats. I'm sure everyone's starving."

I don't want my friend and soon-to-be relative seeing me flush. Not that it would take much for them to guess what Alejandro whispered about, but I don't need to confirm it. The four of us walk to the table, where Alejandro and I have the center seats. I notice Joaquin pulls out Patricia's chair and helps slide it back in.

Then he heads to the opposite end of the table to do the same for Luciana. He sits next to her. I glance up at Alejandro.

"He can be charming, but he'll never not be shy around strangers."

"I thought maybe—"

"Oh, he is. But he's more likely to miss his chance to shoot his shot than score a date."

I watch Joaquin as Alejandro speaks before shifting my focus to Patricia. Her cheeks are pinker than usual, and our gazes meet. But I'm certain she meant to look past me to Joaquin. For both their sakes, I hope neither makes a mistake.

"I can't wait to escape upstairs with you, *chiquita*."

We agreed to spend the night at the hotel to begin our private celebration early. Alejandro's hand slides up my leg beneath the table, pulling my gown along with it. Then it settles against bare skin and burns where it rests. A shiver tries to escape, but I stifle it and the moan caught in my throat from how my pussy aches from his palm resting so close to it. I don't notice Matáis blessing the meal as I stare at my husband.

My husband.

God, I love the sound of that even if it isn't official until tomorrow.

The meal continues in a blur as we pause between courses when people clink their knives against their glasses, prompting us to kiss. We don't need any encouragement. We just need the excuse. It's the rehearsal dinner, and it seems like people want to practice just as much as we do. Alejandro's sworn he has the good sense not to shove any cake in my face. He knows his mother would likely catch him before I could. If tomorrow night is anything like the dessert we're sharing now, it'll erotic as fuck as we feed a shared slice with each other.

The restaurant is closed to anyone outside our family, so they cleared space for a dance floor. I discovered all of them took ballroom dancing as children, so there isn't a single person with two left feet. Our first dance reminds me of that night in the club. It's far more appropriate for the crowd, but we move together with the same synchronicity we've always had, even from the very beginning. It's not long before others join us, and I spy Joaquin and Patricia looking at each other but not partnering. I glance up at Alejandro as we dance near his cousins and their wives. Pablo, Javier, and Jorge grin.

The evening passes faster than I imagined with rounds of toasts, dancing, and laughing. However, the moment I've craved all night can't come soon enough.

"Let's go, *chica.*"

Alejandro wraps his arm around my waist and escorts me off the dance floor. No one says anything as we make our escape, but I'm certain every Diaz knows we took off. Their situational awareness wouldn't allow them to lose track of one, let alone two, members of their family. Guards escort us to the town car, following us to the hotel. Then they're with us in the elevator, and as much as I want to complain, they accompany us up to our floor and to our door.

Then we're alone.

Fina-fucking-lly.

"Jandro, what's that?"

I point toward the bedroom, aghast at what greets me.

"Don't worry. No one else knows it's here. I arrived before the others and checked in. I got everything set up and went to another suite to get ready."

"That explains how. It doesn't explain what."

I step away from him, a hypnotic-like pull to investigate the sex dungeon he made out of our hotel room. I wander in and look around.

"That didn't explain how after all. How could you get all of this up here with no one noticing?"

"So, I might have skipped past several hours in my explanation. While you were getting a massage yesterday, I checked in here. Everything was in unmarked boxes, so the bellmen helped me get everything up here. I assembled it all before going to the rehearsal. It's why I was nearly late."

"It must have taken you hours."

"About three."

I walk around the room, examining the miniature BDSM dungeon he created. There's a Saint Andrew's Cross, a spanking bench, a swing with a stand—rather than ceiling mounted, and under-the-mattress restraints. On top of the dresser is a paddle, a whip, a flogger, a riding crop, handcuffs, *Ben Wa* balls, a spreader bar and a vaginal spreader, a feather duster, and nipple and clit clamps. I stroll along the piece of furniture to examine every implement before walking around the room to draw my hand over the new editions to the room's furnishings.

"Daddy, are we going to use all of this?"

"If you want, *chiquita*. If there's anything you don't want, then it goes home for another day. If there's something you want to spend most of the night with or go back to, then just tell me. Whatever you want is what I want tonight."

"You're letting me lead."

His chuckle is sinful delight. "I didn't say that, little one."

He steps behind me and unzips my white cocktail. If I didn't love it so much, I'd tell him to cut it off me. I know he has his knives with him. Today of all days, he wouldn't go weaponless. Neither would I. Neither of us will be tomorrow. He already discovered the garters with knife sheaths.

There won't be a garter toss. A few people outside the family suggested it, and I thought Alejandro might murder them. He might have spent most of the meal with his hand up my gown, but no one could see that. He wouldn't even consider doing something like that where others could see—at least, not outside a BDSM club.

"No one has ever been more gorgeous than you, Vita. The moment I saw you at the end of the aisle, I glimpsed heaven. Nothing could be more beautiful than the sight of you walking toward me."

"You have always been the handsomest man I've ever met, but the sight of you wearing the ring we chose together surpasses anything I imagined."

I draw his hand up my belly and over my breast before

guiding it to rest over my heart. I gaze down at it, loving the symbol of our commitment. Neither of us underestimates the power of our mutual possessiveness. Not when he entwines our fingers, so our rings rest next to each other. We both love the symbol that declares we belong to one another.

He pushes my dress down my body, allowing it to pool around my ankles until I step out of it. He gathers it from the floor and drapes it over a chair before coming to stand in front of me. He kneels on one knee to unfasten my shoes and slip them off before rising.

"If I'd known you wore nothing but your knives, I would've mauled you before we finished our vows."

I decided to forgo lingerie and go for the shock value.

From his expression, I'd say it worked. He tugs at his tie with one hand while the other undoes his vest's buttons. He shrugs out of his coat and vest, not caring where they land. He drops the tie as he works his belt. I try to help, but my hands only get in the way of the speed at which he moves. It's only when he reaches down to pull off his socks that my hands get close enough to do anything. I unfasten his trousers before hooking my fingers into the waistband of his boxer briefs. I pull the last two pieces of clothing off, and he's finally naked too.

I reach to slip off the garters, but he stays my hands.

"It's kinda hot."

He quirks a brow and shoots me a boyish grin. I close my eyes to keep from rolling them. When I open them, I wrap my hand around his cock.

"May I stroke you, Daddy?"

"Yes, little girl."

"May I suck you off, Daddy?"

"Later, *chica*."

I playfully pout as I slide my hand up and down his dick.

Fuck if he doesn't have the most mouthwatering cock I've ever seen.

"Can we start with the spanking bench?"

"If that's what you want, *chiquita*."

I release him before he guides me to what looks a bit like a gymnastics vault. There's a step to bring me high enough to drape my body over it. There are also vertical handles for me to grip.

"What do you want to begin with?"

"Flogger, please. Oh, and a blindfold if there is one."

"Of course."

He grabs one I hadn't seen from the dresser and covers my eyes. He steps away to fetch the flogger and whatever else he has in store for me. He trails the thongs down my back and over my ass, swishing them across my upper thighs. I feel tiny barbs that will add an intensity to the sting.

I can't wait.

The first lash lands lightly across my ass. I'm not fooled into thinking it'll stay this way. This is a preview. A tease.

His left hand rubs my shoulder before his fingers trail along each side of my spine. It distracts me, so I lurch forward when the flogger lands sharply across my lower back and ass. It rubs my clit against the leather covering. Alejandro creates a figure-eight pattern, but he varies the rhythm. I can't predict that, so my ass clenches each time I think he's about to strike. In turn, he waits until I relax before landing the leather tails over my mid and lower back, my ass, and my upper thighs. I cling to the handles and stomp my feet.

He allows me to catch my breath.

"Are you all right, *chica?*"

"Yes, Daddy."

Just when I think he might be ready to move onto something else, the flogger lands across my ass while a crop swats my cunt.

"Jandro! Holy fuck!"

When I try to bring my thighs together, he's quicker than me. He slaps the inside of my right thigh. When I obey the silent command, he nails my clit with the crop.

"Daddy!"

"Yes?" His tone's exaggerated casualness.

"Fuck me."

"Fuck you? As in literally?"

"Please!"

I sense him step away then move in the opposite direction from where I want him. His hand cups my chin, and the tip of his cock skims my lips. I open immediately.

"Shh, *chica*. No talking."

He presses forward, and I take his cock into my mouth. My tongue sweeps over it as it glides toward the back of my throat then retreats. He does this four times before he presses it in and doesn't move—at least not his cock. His bare hand lands on my right ass cheek. It's enough force to press me forward, forcing me to take him practically down my throat.

"Snap if it's too much, little one."

I hum my agreement. He alternates cheeks as I suck on him. When I taste his precum, he pulls out.

"Not yet, baby girl."

He helps me stand and guides me toward the dresser. He turns me away from it before lifting off the blindfold.

"Look."

I twist to see over my shoulder. My ass is apple red. There are no hints of bruising, but it'll sure as fuck be sore for the next couple days.

"Thank you, Daddy."

I'm panting from the exertion of withstanding the spanking as well as my desperate need to feel him buried inside my pussy. He assesses me, and I'm uncertain what he decides. Whatever it is has him reaching past me for the nipple clamps. He leans forward and sucks my left nipple so hard it feels like he might rip it off me. Then it's a rhythmic draw as his tongue flicks the puckered flesh. He attaches the clamp and screws it tight before repeating the process on the other side.

"Saint Andrew's Cross, please."

He leads me over to it with the blindfold still in his hand. He helps me, guiding me to face the wood. I fear I'm in for more spankings. I don't know if my ass can handle that. He fastens me to the X shaped restraint. He slips the blindfold back on and steps back.

I wait.

For what feels like hours.

Then his tongue slides into my pussy.

I didn't sense him approach or lower himself to kneel. That's the only way he could reach. His hands grip just above the ankle restraints, holding my legs tightly as he glides them upward. It's almost a massage. It makes me squirm when his thumbs sweep up the inside of my thighs, forcing a shiver from me that I can't avoid.

He chuckles like earlier.

I think I just flooded his mouth.

He sucks on my clit before nibbling. Then he flicks his tongue before sucking again. He brings me to the edge over and over until I'm pleading for dear life.

"Daddy, I need you...Please...I feel so fucking empty...I need you...Please fuck me...Daddy!"

The last comes out as a scream as he once again disappears. He whips the blindfold from my head and moves so I can see him.

"Vita?"

He sounds in a panic, and I realize that last scream of frustration frightened him. He fears he went too far.

"I'm all right. I'm just so aroused it hurts. My entire body feels like it's burning me alive. My cunt aches more than it ever has."

"Shh, *chiquita*. I was already about to make it better. Let me get you down."

He's quick to unfasten the cuffs from my ankles and wrists. Then he lifts me off, his one arm strong enough to hold me as he steps away. He shifts me to carry me bridal style to the swing.

Seems rather fitting since I'm a bride and all.

He sets me on my feet before checking the swing's straps and the frame's sturdiness. Once he's satisfied, he turns to me.

"Do you want to straddle and ride me? Or do you want to recline? I know your ass is tender. Which would be better?"

"I want my body pressed up against yours, Jandro. I need you to—"

A lump rises in my throat, and I suddenly feel close to tears. I refuse to ruin this because I suddenly have a hormone drop—or is it a hormone surge. I don't know, but I'm getting emotional.

"Baby girl, come here. Shh. Let me hold you. You did so well on that bench. So strong and brave. Nothing tastes better than your sweet pussy. I love having my *chiquita* for dessert."

He draws me against his chest, wrapping his arms around me. He's so careful when he lifts me, and I wrap my legs around his waist. He's gentle as I slide down his cock. I shudder with relief, and he groans.

"*Chica.*"

"Daddy."

We speak at the same time. We rest our foreheads together as he steps back and lowers us onto the swing. He helps me slip my feet into loops like stirrups and to find the ones I can hold onto. Then he pushes off, and we sway a few times before experimenting with moving together.

"Can we install one of these at home?"

"I already ordered it."

It's that boyish grin again that sends a surge of affection through me. I dive in for a kiss, letting go of the loops to burrow my hand into his hair and cup his jaw. It's my turn to devour him. My kiss is aggressive—demanding—unsatisfied until his hands on my waist lift and lower me. I use the stirrups to help me push off, to make riding him easier. I don't break the kiss as my hands find their place on the straps again.

I don't know how long we swing, but I love every second of it. I grind my clit against his pubic bone, and I feel the stirring deep in my pussy.

"May I come, Daddy?"

"Yes."

It's a ragged whisper, and I know he's close too. His arms tighten around me, and I've never felt safer than I do when I'm in my husband's arms.

"I love you, Jandro."

"I love you, Vita."

"Always and only you."

I don't remember how we came up with saying that last bit together, but now we always do. He's spent his adult life as a protector and provider. First for his family and cartel, and now for me. I'll never take for granted the faith he's always had in me.

God help anyone who forces me to protect him again. I won't even leave ash in my wake.

Don't miss the next installment

Meet Joaquin and Patricia in *Cartel Devil*, coming 2026.

One night with Joaquin Diaz left me with more than a memory.
He was supposed to be a mistake.
A beautiful lapse in judgment.
A secret I could bury with the wedding and the sunrise.
But some nights leave a mark that doesn't fade.
Joaquin is the last bachelor standing in a family built on power, loyalty, and bloodshed.
Cold.
Controlled.
Lethal.
The kind of man a woman survives... not forgets.
And no matter how far I run, that night still binds me to him.
He knows I work for his rival's wife.
He knows she's one of my closest friends.
He knows I'm close to his cousin's wife too.
What he doesn't know is why I really left Boston.
Then I'm attacked.
And suddenly, the safest place is with the most dangerous man I know.

Joaquin was already lethal.
With me, he turns relentless.
Watchful.
Possessive.
Merciless about tearing down every wall I built.
The closer he gets, the harder it is to keep my secrets buried.
The harder it is to ignore what one reckless night left behind.
Now someone is coming for us.
Maybe from New York.
Maybe from Boston.
Maybe because of the past I thought I escaped.
I should have left Joaquin Diaz in the past.
Instead, the cartel devil is closing in.
And this time, he won't let me go.

Meet Joaquin and Patricia in *Cartel Devil*, coming 2026.

Thank you for reading
Cartel Protector

Sabine Barclay, a nom de plume also writing Historical Romance as Celeste Barclay, lives near the Southern California coast with her husband and sons. She loves her days at the beach soaking up way too much sun, a good Netflix binge, and a strong hot chai. Her heroines are independent women who can defend themselves but love their Alpha heroes who want nothing more than to protect their soulmates in her Mafia Romances. She's Gen Y/Oregon Trail and loves creating engrossing contemporary romances that will make your toes curl and your granny blush.

Subscribe to Sabine's bimonthly newsletter to receive exclusive insider perks.
www.sabinebarclay.com

Join the fun and get exclusive insider giveaways, sneak peeks, and new release announcements in
Sabine Barclay's Facebook Dubious Dames Group

Do you also enjoy steamy Historical Romance? Discover Sabine's books written as Celeste Barclay.

The Cartel Brotherhood

Cartel King
BOOK ONE SNEAK PEEK

ENRIQUE

She's going to fall off that fucking ladder.

I slow my pace to a jog as I approach a house with a woman far too high on her ladder, leaning far too much to the right as she tries to fish something out of her gutters. She's got to be about five-five to my six-three.

I could reach whatever she's fishing around for. She's more likely to fall off and break something. I should mind my own business and keep going with my run, but there's no way I'm doing that. I wouldn't if it were a woman of any age, and I wouldn't if it were an elderly person, either.

If it were a guy my age, maybe I'd let him deal with it, but for her —there's something in how she's reaching. Some frustration I can feel even from here. I approach slowly as I walk up the driveway. I'm only halfway to her when a humongous dog comes bounding toward me.

No wonder there's a baby gate across the entrance to her open garage. The massive beast doesn't bark, but he growls. It's a

Mastiff, much like the one Laura Kutsenko has, except this one is a different color and easily weighs about fifty pounds more than her giant companion. I wonder if this one is as much of a love bug as Laura's. At least, that's what she's always claimed.

The woman on the ladder speaks to her dog, giving him a command.

"Hush, Constantine. Lie down."

The dog immediately obeys, but he inches closer to the baby gate, still growling at me. It's only then that the woman notices me. She grips the ladder as she jerks away. I hurry over and grab the ladder, tempted to demand she come down from there.

"Who are you?"

If anybody's going to do the demanding, apparently it's her. Not that I can blame the woman, since I'm a complete stranger.

"I'm Enrique. I saw you as I was running. You looked a little wobbly up there."

"Well, I was okay until I was startled—but thank you."

Dismissive is the only way to describe her now. I don't blame her for that either. She's a woman in a precarious position with a strange man looking up at her. Now that I'm certain the ladder won't fall over, I step away. I don't need to look like a perv staring up her shorts.

"Would you like some help? I can easily reach whatever you're going for."

Cartel Viper
Cartel Prince
Cartel Rose
Cartel Protector
Cartel Devil

Do you also enjoy steamy Historical Romance? Discover Sabine's books written as Celeste Barclay.

The Ivankov Brotherhood

Bratva Darling
BOOK ONE SNEAK PEEK

LAURA

As I sit across from the four Kutsenko brothers, I press my lips together to keep from drooling. No four men should be so strikingly handsome. Not all from the same family, anyway. I fight a valiant battle against letting my gaze drift toward the eldest, Maksim, whose ice-blue eyes bore into me. After years of negotiating billion-dollar investment contracts while facing countless ruthless businessmen, I've learned to keep my expression studiously blank. But it's a true struggle today. Instead, I focus my attention on the squirrelly lawyer sitting across the conference table. While he's disingenuous with each comment, he's a good negotiator. But I'm better. How cliché am I?

While I feel Maksim watching me, I focus on Dmitry Yakovitch as he continues to argue the merits of the venture capitalist company I represent, RK Capital Group, merging with Kutsenko Partners. What he means is the merits of Kutsenko Partners acquiring RK Capital Group, then stripping it and making it another money-laundering shell corporation. While most people in New York have little awareness of the Russian mafia, I do. The Kutsenko brothers' names appear on no titles or deeds anywhere in New York City, but it wasn't difficult to determine which shell companies likely belong to them. Their assumption that I'm unfamiliar with them is proving beneficial to me as they continue to whisper amongst themselves in Russian. I think they may even believe they're convincing me that they don't speak much English.

The senior partners of RK Capital Group know who I'm negotiating with, though they may not know I'm aware of these Russians' more nefarious operations. They've given me the go-ahead to agree to a merger with an eventual acquisition, but only for the right price. A price to the tune of twenty billion dollars. Considering an investment firm like Goldman Sachs is worth nearly one-hundred-and-twenty billion dollars, my clients' asking price appears reasonable.

"Mr. Yakovitch, I shall stop you now." I raise my left hand, pen caught between my index and middle fingers. When I have his attention, I lean back in my chair and casually twirl the pen over my index finger and thumb. "Fifty billion is my clients' asking price. You know that. Your clients know that. RK doesn't oppose the merger. What they oppose is the insulting offer you've made. It's nearly noon, and I'm hungry, Mr. Yakovitch. I have a delicious ham sandwich waiting for me. I even have three chocolate chip cookies waiting for me. If we aren't going to make any progress, I shall let you go, so I can move onto my eagerly anticipated lunch." I cant my head just enough for me to appear as though my gaze rests solely on the opposing attorney's face, but I can see each Kutsenko brothers' reaction. My face battles yet again against showing my emotions as I fight not to smirk. Their muted but surprised expressions confirm what I already know.

"Please tell your clients to make a reasonable counteroffer, or I will conclude this meeting and enjoy my ham sandwich and cookies."

Dmitry glares at me before turning to Maksim and his three brothers. In rapid Russian, he doesn't interpret my suggestion. Oh no. There's no need for that. I can't catch every word because his voice is too low. But I catch something along the lines of "The bitch refuses to budge. What now? A fucking ham sandwich. More like a stick up her ass."

Maksim swivels his chair to look at his brothers. In Russian, he says, "Fifty billion is ridiculous. She's not so stupid or naïve not to know that. My guess is they'll settle for twenty billion. We offer fifteen."

"That's barely better than what we already offered," Aleksei, the second-oldest brother, argues. "She'll be eating the fucking sandwich and dipping her cookies in milk before we walk out the door. We need the buildings."

"We offer twenty, Maks," Bogdan, the youngest, insists.

As I watch the brothers discuss, their voices barely lowered, I pull my lunch sack from the black leather satchel by my feet and set it beside my laptop. It's a ridiculously pink floral bag with an embroidered monogram, the L and D overlapping. It's an empty prop, but they don't know that. I watch as five sets of eyes narrow. I offer a smile that would appear innocent in any setting other than this meeting. It's patronizing, and I know it.

Bratva Sweetheart
Bratva Treasure
Bratva Beauty
Bratva Angel
Bratva Jewel

Do you also enjoy steamy Historical Romance? Discover Sabine's books written as Celeste Barclay.

The Mancinelli Brotherhood

LUCA

This asshole is pissing me off. We've been going around in circles for five minutes, and the longer we stand out here, the greater the likelihood someone will spot us. I have a sixth sense about these things. It's why I'm still alive at the ripe old age of thirty-one.

"Espinoza, enough already. Either sell to us or don't, but we set the price. Your tequila is good, but it isn't nectar from the gods."

I'm watching Carlos Espinoza, some lackey for the Mexican Culiacán Cartel, try to maneuver me into paying more than the agreed upon price. I know it's so he can skim off the top.

"It's as close as you're going to get. You've upped the order, so the price per case goes up."

My uncle, Salvatore Mancinelli, is the New York don. He negotiated this deal, and I warned him it was a bad idea. But what do I know as his underboss and heir? I'm not backing down.

"Haven't you ever heard of a bulk discount? The more I order the better the price should be. No one else around here is buying from you. You know we're your only choice in three out of five boroughs. You aren't going to the Bronx because you won't get more than pennies there. You aren't going to Queens because you don't want to run into the Colombians. You aren't going to Manhattan because then you face the bratva along with us. And what are you going to do in Staten Island? Sell to us anyway? We control Staten Island and Brooklyn when it comes to liquor stores, so take the money and go."

"Luca, there are plenty of liquor stores in Brooklyn that aren't owned by Italians. I'll go there."

We aren't friends. He's patronizing me by using my first name. Fuck him and the horse he rode in on. I have other solutions for this shit.

"And I'll just take what I want from them for free. That's not a half bad idea. The deal's over. Take your shit with the worm in it and go."

"Motherfucking racist. Not all tequila has a worm in it."

"You're selling Mezcal. It's known for the fucking worm. I wouldn't start calling me names, you *penche hijo de puta.*"

Fucking son of a bitch.

He has twenty-five crates of stolen tequila that he's trying to offload because he knows he can't sell it at his own liquor store.

"What did you call me?"

Carlos takes what he thinks is a menacing step forward, and his two bodyguards do the same. Not smart. Neither of my two bodyguards nor I react, but the three men in each of my cars open their doors. They won't do more than that. It's just a reminder that the Culiacán can try, but the *Cosa Nostra* still run New York City.

"This is the third and final time I say this. Sell or leave."

Every head turns toward the liquor store's back door as it opens. A gorgeous blonde steps out, and I wish I had the time to appreciate her beauty, but she's about to die. Carlos and his men draw their guns and pivot toward her. My men pull their weapons too, but we keep them pointed at the Mexicans. The woman stands like a deer in the headlights for a second before ducking behind the industrial garbage dumpster like a frightened rabbit. Three shots hit the metal almost at the same moment. That's all it takes for my men and me. The two bodyguards standing with me aim for a guard each, and I set my sights on Carlos. We squeeze our triggers, and the men fall. Screeching tires tell me Carlos's driver takes off. I hear more gunshots as at least one soldier in my cars tries to shoot the escaping vehicle. Glass shatters, but the sedan keeps going. I hear more tires squeal as one of my SUVs takes off and chases the guy. I holster my gun and wave my men to do the same.

I inch forward toward the trash can, but I see the shadow shift. The woman bolts from the other side. She's still the frightened rabbit, but I'm the fox pursuing her. She's fast, I'll give her that. But she has to be at least a foot shorter than me. My legs are a lot longer and cover a lot more ground with each stride.

She weaves among the cars, most likely believing it's harder to hit a moving object. She isn't wrong, but I have no intention of shooting her. I push myself harder and pounce as she darts out and tries to cross the last stretch of parking lot to reach a better lit area near a bus stop. I lunge.

"Stop running, *piccolina*. I won't hurt you."

I wrap my arms around her and pull her back against my chest, but I'm quick to spin her around and put space between us as I grasp her arms. Of course, she fights me.

"If I wanted you dead, I would have shot at you, too."

"It doesn't mean you won't kill me after."

She's breathless as she continues to struggle. I almost let go to take a step back, insulted at what she implied. But I can't blame her. If I were a woman, I'd be terrified of the same thing.

"I'm not going to rape you. I'm going to talk to you."

"Talk? You are not a man who talks if you just killed a guy."

"To keep him and his men from killing you. I told you, if I wanted you dead, I would have shot at you too. And I wouldn't have missed."

She stops struggling against me, but her eyes continue to dart from one place to another, trying to find somewhere to flee. I know I can keep her in place with only one hand, so I release her left arm.

I still have a firm hold on her right one, but I haven't held it nearly as tightly as I could.

"I'm Luca. I know you figured out you interrupted something you shouldn't have. Did that man know who you are?"

"Yes."

"What about his driver? Would he know you?"

"Yes."

"Do you have a name?"

"Yes."

"*Piccolina*, we won't get very far if yes is all you can say. Are you willing to answer me with more than one word?"

"No."

I knew that was coming, and I grin. I can't help it. I wasn't wrong about her being gorgeous, but I doubt she wants to know that's what I think. At least, not if I want her to know I won't assault her.

"Fine. I have more than twenty questions I can ask that you can answer with one word. Do you work at the store?"

"Sometimes."

Ah, an improvement.

"Did Carlos know you were still working?"

"No."

"Do you have a car, or do you take the subway or bus?"

She raises her chin and remains silent. Smart but counterproductive.

"The subway or the bus will get you killed. You're too easy to find and follow. Do you have a car?"

"Yes."

"Can you stay with someone instead of going home?"

She refuses to answer.

"If that man knew you and you sometimes work in the store, then he knew where you live. If he found that out, so will someone in his cartel."

"I know. Let me go. The longer I stand here, the more likely someone is to come back for me."

"No one will touch you while I'm here."

"Arrogant. If he shot at me, he would have shot at you."

"And he would have died, anyway. What's your name?"

"Jane."

"Look, I know you won't get in one of my cars and let me drive you somewhere. In most cases, I would say that's a smart move. But you did nothing wrong tonight except for leave work at the wrong time. I know that, and you know that. But the Culiacán won't see it that way, *piccolina*."

She freezes for no more than five seconds before she trembles so much that I can see it. I don't know what drives me next, but it's the same instinct that's made me call her little girl three times. I pull her to my chest and tuck her head against it. I stroke her hair down to her shoulders, rubbing my hand up and down her back. This is the most inopportune moment to notice she isn't wearing a bra. I will my body not to react.

"What does that mean?"

Her voice is barely more than a whisper, but I know what she's asking.

"It means little girl."

"I should be insulted, but the way you say it..."

"It has nothing to do with your height. I know you're not a child." God, do I know she's not. She feels amazing. Her tits are soft as they press against me, and I can see she has the most delectable ass. I'd love nothing more than to cup it and squeeze until she goes up on her toes and begs for me to wrap her legs around my waist and fuck her. For fuck's sake. Stop, you disgusting asshole. That is not what you need to be thinking about.

"Why didn't you shoot me? Whatever you were talking about, if it was with a Cartel member, then it wasn't completely legal. Carlos didn't want me alive to talk about seeing you together. Why are you letting me live?"

"I told you. You did nothing wrong but try to leave work. He should have checked the building before starting the meeting. That was on him. The only thing I take issue with is you leaving by yourself and walking into a dimly lit parking lot. I suspect you do that often, and that's too dangerous. Jane Doe, I don't hurt women."

Sabine Barclay

Mafia Sinner
Mafia Beauty
Mafia Angel
Mafia Redeemer
Mafia Star

Do you also enjoy steamy Historical Romance? Discover Sabine's books written as Celeste Barclay.

The O'Rourke Brotherhood

DILLAN

I hate meetings like this. I don't need to wear pants from some shitty off-the-rack suit that are too tight to *try* to make my dick look bigger. I'm secure in my cock size, and I don't need to show how big my balls are for people to know I run this part of the city. I loathe strip clubs too. I'm past the point where naked women make my jimmy do jumping jacks. I can appreciate a hot bod and gymnast level strength, but it does nothing for me. These douchebags? They're practically ready to come in those cheap arse pants. Why am I here? I keep asking myself that.

Seamus and Shane are doing just fine with these negotiations. I'm just here to look good. I'm the muscle today. Or rather my name and my position. Who the fuck thought— way, way back in the day —that giving the mob hierarchy nautical names was a good idea? Fucking Skipper. This isn't motherfucking Gilligan's Island. None of these numb nuts are the Professor, even if they think they're fucking Mr. Howell.

But who is that? If this is *Gilligan's Island*, then she's Mary Ann.

I glance at Seamus, but he's focused on the Albanian he's trying
not to lose his shite at. Shane smirks at me when I dart my gaze to
him. I cock an eyebrow as the waitress walks over. She's definitely
not a dancer. She has too many clothes on. But you can barely call
the pieces of thread she's wearing clothes. She's got on a bikini top
that's barely more than pasties, and the skirt she's wearing would
make my Catholic grandmother do somersaults in her grave.
It's the standard uniform for this place, but somehow it doesn't
look right on her. Not because she doesn't have a banging body
because she does. Not because she's a butter face— but-her-face —
as in great bod, not so great face. She's beautiful in a super under-
stated way. That's part of what makes her look out of place. She
has next to no makeup on. I think those are even her real
eyelashes. The natural beauty is drawing way too much attention.
"'Scuse me."
She tries to step around Zef Hoxha, the *kyre* of the Albanian mafia
here in New York. When he reaches out to grab her wrist, I'm out
of my seat with my hand around his. He never gets a chance to
touch her because my hold is so tight he can't bend his fingers. I
keep squeezing until it must feel like I'll snap the bones.
"No touching."
Zef drops his arm as much as my hold allows. I let go and stare at
him before I tilt my head toward the waitress. I narrow my eyes,
and he knows what I expect.
"I apologize, miss."
"That's all right, sir. Here's your drink."
She's polite as she hands him his glass. Unfortunately, to put
down the rest, she has to bend forward, giving everyone a view of
her glorious cleavage. Tits and arse are what sell here, and she has
them in spades. I'm certain it's why my cousin hired her. If I sit
down, everyone will know I'm just as guilty as these fuck nuts
because she's made my dick do something that hasn't happened in
a strip club since I was like twenty-three. I'm now thirty-three.

Mob Boss
Mob Star

Cartel Protector

Mob Princess
Mob Saint
Mob Bride
Mob Knight

Do you also enjoy steamy Historical Romance? Discover Sabine's books written as Celeste Barclay.

A small press bound by the belief that every voice matters.

Sign up for our newsletter to learn about new releases and more.
https://oliver-heberbooks.com/subscribe/

Follow us on social media:

facebook.com/oliverheberbooks

instagram.com/oliverheberbooks

amazon.com/oliverheberbooks

youtube.com/@OliverHeberBooksPublisher